Praise for the novels of

DIANE CHAMBERLAIN

DIANE CHAMBERLAIN

BREAKING THE SILENCE

MIRA

ISBN 1-55166-484-4

BREAKING THE SILENCE

Printed in U.S.A.

To David,
my Tex-Mex and Amana guy.

I'm grateful to Jane Drewry, Liz Hain and Joan Winslow
for nurturing this story and for being gentle with me
when my plotting went astray.

Thanks to Ann Allman, Barbara Bradford, Alana Glaves,
Pat McLaughlin, Priscilla McPherson, Joann Scanlon
and Brittany Walls for their caring and careful critiques
of outlines and early drafts, and to hot air balloon
fanatic Dan Heagy and reference librarian Henry Zoller
for helping me bring a dose of reality to my
fictitious world.

And a special thank-you to my agent, Ginger Barber,
and to Amy Moore-Benson and Dianne Moggy at
MIRA Books.

AUTHOR'S NOTE

Although Saint Margaret's Hospital and its staff are imaginary, the experiments described in *Breaking the Silence* were actually performed at psychiatric facilities and universities during the 1950s, with governmental sanctions. On the cusp of the millennium, it's difficult to appreciate the fear and paranoia the Cold War era generated in American citizens and politicians. When the extent of the experimentation became known in the late seventies, a congressional committee investigated the impact of that research on unwitting subjects. The need for informed patient consent and the federal approval of new drugs—two protections we take for granted today—resulted in part from this investigation.

1

The phone rang a few minutes after eleven on Christmas night. Laura was at her computer in the study, as usual, but she quickly reached for the receiver. She knew who was calling.

"He's asking for you," the nurse said. "I think you'd better hurry."

"I'll be right there."

She ran through the living room, past the darkened Christmas tree and up the stairs to the second floor of the town house. Although she tried to be quiet, the bedroom door squeaked as she opened it, and Ray lifted his head from the pillow. He was never an easy sleeper.

"The hospital called," she said, slipping off her robe and pulling a pair of jeans from her dresser drawer. "I have to go."

Ray sat up and switched on his bedside light. "Is he…?" He didn't finish the sentence as he reached for his glasses on the night table. He looked dazed, blinking against the intrusion of light in the room.

"He's still alive," she said. "But I think this is it." She heard the lack of emotion in her voice as the calm and collected scientist in her took over.

"I'll come with you," Ray said, throwing off the covers. "I'll get Emma up and she and I can wait in—"

"No." She pulled her sweater over her head, then leaned

over to kiss him. "You and Emma stay here. No sense waking her up. Besides, I need to get there quickly."

"All right." Ray smoothed his hands over his thinning brown hair. "But call if you change your mind and want us to come."

He looked like an oversized little boy, sitting on the edge of the bed in his striped pajamas, and Laura felt a quick surge of love for him. "I will," she said, giving him a hug. "Thanks."

Outside, the air was still and cold. She drove quickly through the neighborhood, the houses and trees ablaze with colored lights. On the main road through Leesburg, she hit red light after red light, and even though the streets were nearly empty, she stopped dutifully at each of them.

Her father had wanted no heroic measures, and he'd received none. Although Laura agreed philosophically with his decision, her emotions were another matter, and these past few days she'd been hoping for a miracle. She wasn't ready to lose him. Carl Brandon had been the one consistent person in her life, always there for her. Her relationship with him had not been perfect, but who had a perfect relationship with their father? He'd turned eighty a few months ago, right after the cancer came back. She'd given him a party after hours in the Smithsonian's Air and Space Museum, turning on the planetarium lights for him. It would be his last party, and she knew there was nothing he would love better than to gaze at the sea of stars above him. He'd nearly ignored the guests in favor of the mechanically created sky.

Only a few cars were parked in the visitors' lot, and she found a spot close to the hospital entrance. Inside, the lobby was eerily empty and dimly lit. Shivering as she walked through it, she tried to prepare herself for what lay ahead. She would find her father at peace. He was not afraid of dying, and that comforted her. He had an astronomer's appreciation of his own irrelevance. When your passion was the sky and the stars and the planets, the insignificance of your life was a given.

So, she would hold his hand as he drifted away from her. She would be very strong. Then she would drive home and Ray would comfort her. In the morning, she would tell Emma that Poppa had died. She had already tried to explain to her five-year-old daughter about Poppa's illness, trying to equate what was happening to him to what had happened to Emma's guinea pig the year before. But Emma, despite asking dozens of questions, seemed unable to grasp the concept of *forever*. And Laura, who had always scoffed at the notion of heaven, found herself using the idea to comfort Emma. And at times, herself.

She knew the instant she entered her father's room that he was not at peace. He was clearly worse than when she'd seen him that afternoon. His breathing was raspier, his skin grayer, and he was agitated. As he reached for her, his long arms trembling in the air, he wore a look of desperation on his once-handsome face.

She took his hand and sat on the edge of his bed.

"I'm here, Dad." She guessed he had not wanted to die without her at his side and wished she'd ignored those red lights to get to the hospital sooner.

He held both her hands in his weak grasp, but even with her there, the desperate look did not leave his eyes. He tried to speak, the words coming out between his gasps for air. "Should...have...told..." he said.

She leaned close to hear him. From that angle, she could see the stars of Aries through the hospital window. "Don't try to speak, Dad." She smoothed a tuft of white hair away from his temple.

"A woman," he said. "You need..." Her father's face,

gaunt and gray, tightened with frustration as he struggled to get the words out.

"I need to what, Dad?" she asked gently.

"Look..." His lips trembled from the strain of speaking. "Look after her," he said.

Laura drew away to study his face. Could he be delusional? "Okay," she said. "I will. Please don't try to talk anymore."

He let go of her hand to reach toward the night table, his arm jerking with the motion. Laura saw the scrap of paper he was aiming for and picked it up herself. Her father had written a name on the paper in a nearly illegible scrawl that threatened to break her heart.

"Sarah Tolley," Laura read. "Who is that?"

"Friend," he said. "Important...has no...family." He swallowed with effort, his Adam's apple a sharp blade beneath the skin of his throat. "Promise."

He wanted her to look after a woman named Sarah Tolley?

"But...who is she?" Laura asked. "*Where* is she?"

His eyes were closed. "Meadow...Wood..."

"Meadow Wood Village?" Laura pictured the attractive, Victorian-style retirement home on the outskirts of Leesburg.

He nodded. At least she thought he did.

"Can you tell me what you want me to do for her?" she asked.

"Take care..."

"Take care of her?" Laura asked. "But I don't know her, Dad. I've never even heard you talk about her before."

Her father's paper-thin eyelids fluttered open, and she saw panic in his eyes. "Promise!" he said. In a nearly spasmodic movement, he reached toward her as if trying to grasp her shoulders, but he caught his fingers in the chain of her necklace instead. She felt the chain snap, and the pendant fell into her lap.

Unsettled by his panic, she caught his hands. "It's all right, Daddy," she said. "I promise. I'll take care of her."

"Swear…"

"I'll do it, Dad." She leaned back to slip the scrap of paper into her jeans pocket. "You don't need to worry."

He sank back against the pillow, pointing one trembling finger toward her neck. "I broke…"

"It's all right." She lifted the necklace from her lap and slipped it, too, into her jeans pocket. "It can be fixed." She took his hand again and held it on her thigh. "You rest now," she said.

Obediently, he closed his eyes, their small battle over. Small battles were nothing new between them. Her mother had died when Laura was seven, and her father had been a difficult parent, demanding and controlling, but always attentive. She had been his top priority, and she knew it. He'd instilled in her his love of astronomy, although for him it had been a cherished avocation rather than a profession, and he was responsible for the person she'd become. His methodical shaping of her had at times been painful and contentious, but she was grateful for it.

She sat there for hours, holding her father's hand as it grew slacker and cooler in her own. Taped to the wall was a picture Emma had drawn for him a few days earlier. It was one of those typical five-year-old's drawings. Vivid blue sky. Yellow sun. Green tree. A child dressed in blue and purple, wearing a broad smile, the sort of smile Emma herself wore more often than not. Laura studied the drawing, saddened by the incongruity of that happy child with the scene in this room.

She looked out the window again. Aries was gone, but she could see Jupiter near the center of Aquarius. She closed her eyes, and it was a minute before she realized that her father's breathing had stopped. Sitting very still, she held his lifeless hand in hers, as the room filled with a silence as deep as the sky.

2

The eastern sky was purple with the approaching dawn when she arrived home from the hospital. Ray was brewing coffee, wearing his blue terry-cloth robe, a splash of color in the white, uncluttered kitchen. He walked toward her once she was in the door, his arms outstretched, and she could tell he hadn't slept well. Dark circles marred the skin beneath his eyes, and the stubble of his beard was white. For a moment, she felt the fear of losing him, too. He was sixty-one, twenty-one years older than she, and these last few years had taken a toll on him. When she buried her head against his shoulder, she wasn't sure if her tears were for her father or her husband.

"He died about an hour ago," she said, drawing away from him. She wiped her eyes with a tissue, then took the mug of coffee he handed her and sat down at the table.

"I'm glad you got to be there with him," he said.

"It was upsetting." She held the mug between her cold hands. "I thought I'd just sit with him while he...slipped away. But he was very anxious. Really wired. He asked me to take care of some woman I've never even heard him talk about before, and he made me promise I'd do it. It was as if he couldn't let himself die until I swore I'd take care of her."

Ray frowned. "Who's the woman? And what did he mean by 'take care of'?"

Laura reached into her jeans pocket for the scrap of paper, which she flattened on the table. "Sarah Tolley," she said. "She lives in Meadow Wood Village. You know, that retirement home?"

Ray turned away from her to pour himself more coffee. He was quiet, and she imagined that he, too, was trying to puzzle out her father's request. His body looked thick and shapeless beneath the robe. Too heavy. It wasn't healthy to carry around so much weight. She wished he'd take better care of himself.

"And you don't know her connection to Carl?" he asked finally, his back still to her.

"I have no idea. He said she's a special friend. Or important. I don't remember his exact words. He could barely speak." The conversation with her father now seemed vague, as if she'd dreamed it. "He said, or at least implied, that she has no one else to take care of her. No family."

"Sweetheart." Ray sat down at the ancient oak table and rested his hand on top of hers. "I think this was the ranting of a dying man," he said. "You know he's suffered from dementia on and off this past week. The medication—"

"I know, but he seemed clearheaded about this. You should have seen him, Ray. It was so important to him. And where would he get this name from?" She pulled her hand from his to touch the scrap of paper. "She must mean something to him. Maybe he had another life we knew nothing about. I'm going to call Meadow Wood Village later today to see if this woman actually lives there."

Ray's expression was the one he wore when he lobbied politicians on Capitol Hill. She saw the calculated patience in his face, the tightness in his lips, and knew he was choosing his words with care.

"It's probably not a good time to discuss this," he said, his tone even, his hand on hers again, "because you're understandably upset and feeling pretty emotional about Carl. But I really want you to think about the fact that he ran your life when he was alive and now he's trying to control it from the grave.''

She knew what he was talking about. Sometimes her father's love had seemed tied to her achievements, and, no matter what she accomplished, it was never quite enough. But it seemed harsh, almost cruel, for Ray to imply that her father's deathbed wish was a final act of manipulation.

She leaned toward her husband, feeling tears fill her eyes. "This is the last thing my father will ever ask of me," she said. "I promised him I'd do as he requested, Ray, and I will. I don't know what this—" she looked at the piece of paper "—Sarah Tolley was to him, but there is no way I can simply turn my back on her."

"Damn it!" Ray slammed his mug on the table so hard she jumped, and coffee splashed onto the white place mat. He stood up. "Here you go again, throwing yourself off the deep end headfirst. Don't you have enough to do? Aren't Emma and I ever enough to satisfy you?"

Startled by his outburst, she could not find her voice. She stared at her husband while he plowed ahead.

"Why do you always need to have a million projects going at once?" he asked. "Have you looked at your life lately? You just got back from a month of research in Brazil, you drive to Baltimore to teach at Hopkins one day a week, you're overextended at the Smithsonian, and last week you told me you're going back to Brazil next summer. What happened to your promise to *us*, huh?" He leaned on the table, his hands balled into fists. His knuckles were white.

Laura reached out to touch his hand, confused by his sudden, dramatic change of heart. "But you said it was fine for me to—"

"You said we could spend next summer at the lake house, just the three of us," he interrupted her. "Like a normal family, instead of one where the wife and mother drags her kid all over the place, chasing comets and traveling around the world giving speeches and accepting awards and who knows what other crap, while her husband sits home and gets rejection letter after fucking rejection letter." He stood up and wiped the back of his hand across his chin. The white bristles of his beard stood out against the red of his face.

Laura pressed her fist to her mouth, stunned by his uncharacteristic fury. He'd never spoken to her this way before, never uttered a word of complaint about her career. She'd had no idea his unhappiness with her ran so deep.

"Mommy?"

She turned to see Emma standing in the doorway of the kitchen. Her fine, nearly black hair was a mass of tangles, her blue eyes wide above cheeks lined with indentations from her blanket. The ragged old bunny she'd slept with for years was clutched in her arms, its place secure despite the two new stuffed toys Emma had received for Christmas. Standing there in her red flannel pajamas, she looked tiny and delicate.

Laura got to her feet. "Good morning, honey," she said. "Did we wake you?"

"What's wrong?" Emma looked from Laura to Ray and back again.

"Go back to bed, punkin,'" Ray said, the anger out of his voice, though not his face.

"Nothing's wrong," Laura said. "Daddy and I were just having a very loud discussion. We didn't mean to wake you up." She would tell her about Poppa later. She couldn't get into that now.

Emma's eyes were on Ray, who had turned away to rinse his mug in the sink.

"Why are you up when it's still dark out?" Emma asked.

"Come on." Laura guided her with a hand on her shoulder. "You're right. It's too early to be up. Let's get you back to bed. Maybe we should all go back to bed for an hour or two."

Emma held Laura's hand on the stairs, nearly stumbling in her sleepiness. Laura tucked her back into bed, the sheets still warm from Emma's body.

"Is Daddy mad at me?" Emma asked.

"At you? Of course not." Laura smoothed her daughter's satiny hair. Emma *did* have a way of getting on Ray's nerves, and he sometimes complained about her disturbing him when he was working on his book. Occasionally he would even yell at her. "He's not mad at you at all," Laura reassured her. "He's just a little frustrated right now. We can talk about it more later, if you like, when it's time to get up for real."

"'Kay," Emma said, shutting her eyes.

Laura leaned over to kiss her, pulling the covers up to her daughter's chin. She stood up, coming face-to-face with the shelf of Barbie dolls above Emma's bed. Even in the darkness, she could see that Emma had arranged the dolls in contorted positions, probably pretending they were gymnasts. It put a smile on Laura's face. The first in a while.

She needed some time to herself before returning to the kitchen and her angry husband. She walked down the hall to her bedroom, where she pulled the broken necklace from her jeans pocket and opened the jewelry box on her dresser. The box held only a few pairs of earrings, a couple of bracelets. She was not much on jewelry. It didn't fit her life-style. Her running-off-to-Brazil-and-traveling-around-the-world-giving-speeches life-style. She winced, still stinging from the hostility behind Ray's words. Where on earth had that come from? Had he been carrying that resentment around inside him all this time?

She studied the necklace in her hand. It was rare for her to see it lying loose, because she wore it all the time. Her father had first fastened it around her neck when she was eight years old. It had belonged to his mother, he'd told her, after whom she'd been named. The pendant was a large gold charm that always made Laura think of a woman wearing a broad-brimmed hat, although different people seemed to see different things in the intricate shape of the gold. Holding the necklace up to her bare throat, she studied her reflection in the dresser mirror, her gaze falling immediately to her gray roots. She hadn't realized they were so noticeable. The silver lay in neat lines on either side of the part in her hair. She'd gone gray early, and had been masking that fact with her natural golden brown shade ever since her late twenties. Her hair was still long, past her shoulders. It was very good hair, thick and strong, her only concession to vanity, and even that was limited. She was vain enough to dye her hair, but not vain enough to rush to the hairdresser's when the roots began to show. Or to powder her nose when it began to shine, or to remember to put on lipstick before a speaking engagement. She was a naturally attractive woman, and that was fortunate, since she would always choose peering into a telescope over a makeup mirror.

She should go downstairs to Ray, but instead she sat on the edge of the bed. As long as she'd known Ray, he'd suffered from depression and dark moods, but this anger, this near rage she'd just witnessed in him, was new. The rejections were getting to him. A retired sociology professor and one of the most compassionate human beings Laura had ever known, Ray had been working on a book about the homeless for many years. It was a labor of love for him, about a cause to which he'd devoted much of his life. The book was heart-wrenching, disturbing and beautifully written. A year ago he'd started submitting it to publishers. Since then, the pile of rejection letters on the desk in his home office had grown.

He'd never before criticized her for putting her career before her marriage and her child. She was stretched thin, that was true. She usually took Emma with her when she traveled, though, and she thought Ray liked having the time alone to focus on his book. Perhaps he *had* liked it, in the past. But a few months ago, while studying the sky from their lake house in the country, Laura discovered the tenth comet of her career. Except for the fifth, which had been a lovely thing with a long, full tail, the comets she'd found had been small and of interest primarily to other astronomers, but this tenth one promised to be spectacular. Although it was currently little more than a fuzzy speck in a good telescope and would not be visible to the naked eye for a year and a half, she'd been immediately deluged with awards, speaking engagements, media attention and offers to fund any research she chose. Meanwhile, Ray was collecting his rejections. Her success, she now feared, was a knife in his side.

She heard Ray climbing the stairs in his slow, measured pace. In a moment, he was in the room and he sat next to her, his arm around her shoulders.

"I'm very sorry," he said. "Forgive me, Laura."

"No," she said. "*I'm* sorry. You're right. I've been caught up in my own life too much lately. I haven't given enough of my time to you and Emma."

"No, no," he protested. "I didn't mean any of that. I was just—"

"I think you *did* mean it, Ray. You were angry and your

true feelings finally came out. I won't go to Brazil during the summer.''

"Oh, Laurie, I really didn't mean for you to make that sort of change in your—"

"I don't want to go," she insisted, and she meant it. Ray had compromised his needs for her over the years. It was her turn now. "I'll take a break after this coming semester. We'll go to the lake house and just play, all summer, the three of us. All right?"

Ray hesitated. "And you won't bother with that woman in the retirement home?" he asked finally.

"She won't take much time," she said. "I just need to check on her. Make sure she's all right, like Dad asked me to do."

His arm fell from her shoulders. "Please don't." His dark eyes pleaded with her.

"Ray, I won't let it interfere with us," she said. His distress seemed so out of proportion to what she was suggesting. "I know Dad was demanding of me, but he was also my inspiration and my greatest champion, and now he's gone." Her voice cracked. "I can't let him down. I can't have promised him something, something so *simple,* and then not follow through on it. You understand that, don't you?"

He sighed and stood up. "I'm going down to my office," he said, and she knew he was through with the conversation.

She watched him pad out of the room in his terry-cloth slippers and thought of following him, but exhaustion stopped her. Better to wait awhile, anyway. Maybe later they would both be more rational.

She undressed quietly and got into her side of the bed. It was cold between the sheets, the sort of cold that no amount of covers could relieve, and she felt alone. Her father was gone. She had no family left, except for Emma and Ray. And at that moment, the Ray she had known and loved seemed lost to her as well.

smoothest course could follow," and she felt it now. Her father was gone. She'd been raised, late career had not. So Ray. And in that moment, the Ray she had known and loved seemed lost to her in ways.

3

Emma was sitting on the floor of her room, absorbed in her new tropical fish puzzle, a gift from her teenage baby-sitter, Shelley. Laura hunched down next to her. It had been two weeks since Christmas, yet this was the first time she'd seen Emma play with the puzzle. It was taking her some time to get over Poppa's death.

"I'm going out for a little while," Laura said, tucking a strand of Emma's hair behind the little girl's ear. "Daddy's downstairs in his office." It was good that Emma was so wrapped up in the puzzle. She would be little bother to Ray.

Emma held up a piece of the puzzle. "I know what *this* is," she crowed. "Do you, Mom?"

"Fish scales?" Laura asked as if she weren't quite sure.

"Right! And it goes right here!" Emma dropped the scales into the picture. "Are you going to work?" she asked, reaching for another piece of the puzzle.

"No. First I'm going to drop off my broken necklace at the jeweler's. Then I'm going to visit someone." She stood up. "I won't be long."

"This one's an eye," Emma said. "I can't wait till when I have it all done. Can we put paste on it and hang it up like we did with the other one?"

"Sure, if you like. But then you won't be able to play with it again."

"That's okay." She looked up at Laura. Her eyes were the same color as her pale blue sweater. "Mom?" she asked.

"Honey, I really have to get going."

"I know, but do you want to look at one of my books with me?"

"Tonight. Before bed." She bent over to kiss the top of Emma's head. "I'll see you in a little while," she said.

"'Kay," Emma said, returning her attention easily to her puzzle.

She was an independent child, far more independent than other five-year-olds Laura had encountered. People had been surprised to see her at Poppa's funeral, but Laura had prepared Emma well for what she would see and hear, and she was certain she'd made the right decision in taking her. Emma finally seemed to understand the permanence of Poppa's death after attending the service. Her daughter hadn't cried during the funeral, but she'd put her little arm around her mother in comfort each time Laura began to tear up.

Downstairs, Laura found Ray in his office, his manuscript on the desk in front of him, but his attention focused on something out the window. She put her hands on his shoulders, the gray plaid flannel of his shirt warm beneath her palms.

"I won't be long," she said. She looked out the window herself, trying to determine what had caught his eye, but saw nothing other than the row of town houses across the street. Each of them was identical to the house in which they lived, each of their slanted roofs was covered with a thin layer of snow.

"Please don't go," Ray said, his gaze still riveted outside, and she knew he was slipping into one of his dark moods. She'd known Ray for ten years and had been married to him for nearly six. During that time, he'd seen several psychiatrists and taken a myriad of antidepressants, but nothing could hold off the darkness for long.

In the two weeks since her father's death, Ray had apologized repeatedly for his outburst, assuring her he was not upset about her career. Still, the words he'd said that morning echoed in her ears, and she didn't believe his retraction of them. In his moment of anger, he'd finally spoken the truth. Wanting to honor his feelings, Laura had tried to set her father's request aside, and she was able to do so with reasonable success until the call from her father's attorney.

"Who's this Tolley woman?" the attorney had asked her. He told her that her father had paid the entrance fee for Sarah Tolley to move into Meadow Wood Village five years earlier. Not only had he continued to pay her monthly rent, he'd also left a large sum of money in trust for her so that she would still be taken care of after his death.

"I don't have a clue," Laura had told him, but her father's arrangements left her even more certain that Sarah Tolley had somehow played a significant role in his life. She had to see her. When she told Ray her plans, he grew sullen.

"I'm leaving," Laura said now, bending over, pressing her cheek to Ray's temple. "I'll be back in an hour. I promise I won't stay longer than that. Emma's completely absorbed in her fish puzzle, so you should be able to work undisturbed."

He said nothing, and she removed her hands from his shoulders. He was giving her no support on this. Even in Ray's blackest moods, it was out of character for him to treat her so coolly. It was almost as though her desire to carry out her father's last wish had come to symbolize her inattention to him. She wondered if it was all right to leave Emma with him today.

"I'll be back before you know I've gone," she said, and she turned to leave the room before he had another chance to change her mind.

She dropped her broken necklace off at the jeweler's, then drove across town to the retirement home.

Meadow Wood Village was a charming place, a large, three-story building that managed to look well-aged and homey despite its relative newness and size. Its siding was a pale blue, the shutters white. An inviting porch ran across the entire front of the building. A place like this could take the fear out of growing old, Laura thought as she walked to the front door.

The building was as warm and inviting inside as it was out, and it smelled like cinnamon and vanilla. The carpets and upholstery were all a soft mauve-and-aqua print. Laura stopped at the front desk, where the receptionist looked up from a stack of paperwork.

"I'm looking for one of your residents," Laura said. "Sarah Tolley."

"I'll call her attendant for you." The woman motioned toward the lobby. "Have a seat."

Laura sat on the edge of one of the wing chairs, and in a few minutes, a young, heavyset woman wearing a long floral jacket came into the lobby.

"You're here to see Sarah?" the woman asked. She looked frankly incredulous.

"Yes," Laura said. "My name's Laura Brandon. I don't actually know her…know Sarah," she said. "She was a friend of my father's, and he died recently. He'd asked me to look in on her."

The woman lowered herself into the chair closest to Laura's. Everything about her was round: her body, her face, her wire-rimmed glasses, her button nose.

"I'm Carolyn, Sarah's attendant," she said, "and I have to say, I'm a little surprised by this. No one ever comes to visit Sarah."

"My father must have," Laura said. "Carl Brandon. He was about six feet tall, very slender, eightiesh, and—"

Carolyn interrupted her with a shake of her head. "*No one* has ever come to see her. I would know."

"That just doesn't make sense." Laura saw her own puzzled reflection in the attendant's glasses. "Well, can you tell me about her?" she asked. "How old is she?"

"She's seventy-five. And she's in the early stages of Alzheimer's. Did you know that?"

Laura sank lower in her chair. "No. I don't know a thing about her."

"She's in excellent shape, physically," Carolyn said. "She takes the exercise classes in our pool. And the Alzheimer's is barely apparent, so far." She sat forward in her chair. "We have three living areas here at Meadow Wood," she explained. "Independent-living apartments, assisted-living apartments, and then a separate wing for those patients who need round-the-clock care. Until just last week, Sarah was able to live in the independent-living wing, but we had to move her over to assisted-living so she could receive more supervision. You know, no stove, no lock on the door. She got lost a couple of times when she went out for a walk, so we felt it was time to move her. We can't let her go out by herself any longer."

Laura nodded. What was she getting herself into?

Carolyn leaned even farther forward in her chair. "You know what would be fantastic?" she asked. "If you could take her out for a walk some time. When the weather's warmer, of course. Sarah would love that."

Laura pictured Ray in the study, stewing in his disappointment that she'd gone to Meadow Wood even this once. "I don't know," she said. "I mean, I haven't even met her."

"The other thing you could do to help her," Carolyn continued as if Laura hadn't spoken, "would be to simply listen to her. Let her talk about her old memories. At this point, her primary symptoms are confusion and short-term memory loss. Her mind is still sharp in the past, though, and she loves to talk. But like I said, there's no one to listen to her, except me, and I have other patients to take care of."

"I really just wanted to—"

"Even though she's always up for the bingo games, and she *loves* movie night," Carolyn surged ahead, "she still spends too much time in her apartment watching TV. It shouldn't be like that. I mean, with some patients, that's okay. That's enough stimulation. But someone like Sarah needs more."

"Well—" Laura held up a hand to stop the woman "—as I said, I've never even met her. And I have a family of my own as well as a job to attend to. I only wanted to find out how my father knew her. That's all." That was not all her father had been asking of her, though, and she knew it.

"All right," Carolyn stood up, clearly disappointed. "Come with me, then."

She followed the attendant down a long corridor lined with pale aqua doors, each of them decorated with something different. Some of the doors had photographs taped to them. One had a stuffed teddy bear attached to the knocker. Another, a pair of ballet slippers.

Carolyn stopped at the door bearing a black cutout of a movie projector.

"This is Sarah's apartment," she said. "She loves old movies. We put the pictures or whatever on their doors so they know which door is theirs. Sarah's not that bad yet, though," she added quickly as she rang the buzzer.

It was a minute before the door was pulled open by an elderly woman, who smiled warmly when she saw Carolyn. "Come in, dear," she said.

Laura followed the attendant into the small living room, which was furnished in attractive contemporary furniture. Nubby, oatmeal-colored upholstery and oak tables.

"Sarah, this is Laura Brandon," Carolyn said. "She's come to visit you."

"How nice." Sarah smiled at Laura. She was tall, an inch or two taller than Laura's five-six. Her silver hair was neatly coiffed, and she bore a slight but unmistakable resemblance to Eleanor Roosevelt. She was impeccably dressed: beige skirt, stockings, beige pumps. The only give-away that she was not entirely lucid was the incorrect buttoning of her beige-and-white-striped blouse. The fabric gapped slightly above the waistband of her skirt. For some reason, that slip in the otherwise noble carriage of the woman put a lump in Laura's throat.

Carolyn glanced at her watch. "I'll leave you two to get to know each other," she said. "Enjoy your visit."

Sarah led Laura to the couch after Carolyn left. "Won't you sit down, dear?" she said.

"Thank you."

"Would you like some coffee? Or lemonade? I think I have some in the refrigerator." She started walking toward the small kitchenette, but Laura stopped her.

"No, I'm fine," she said. She looked awkwardly into her lap. "I'd like to explain why I'm here."

Sarah sat down at the other end of the couch and looked at her attentively, hands folded in her lap.

"I believe you knew my father," Laura said. "Carl Brandon."

Sarah's expression did not change.

"He died a few weeks ago and he'd asked me to...visit you. He wanted to be sure you were all right."

A small cloud of confusion slipped over Sarah's face. "That was nice of him," she said. "I can't remember who he is, though. I don't remember things too well anymore." She looked apologetic. "What did you say his name was?"

"Carl Brandon."

"And where do I know him from?"

Laura smiled. "I don't know. I was hoping you could tell me. He didn't say. I figured maybe you were old friends. He pays for your apartment. And he still will, of course," she added hastily, not wanting to worry her. "He set up a trust for you in his will."

"My!" Sarah said. "I thought my social security paid for it." She pressed her fingers to her temples. "I truly must be losing my mind. I just can't remember him. Where did you say I know him from?"

"I don't know, Mrs. Tolley. He was born in New York City in 1918. He grew up in Brooklyn. I think he moved there when he was about twelve and lived there until he was in his early twenties. Did you ever live in New York?"

"New Jersey," Sarah said. "I grew up in Bayonne."

"Well, maybe you didn't meet him in New York, then. How about Philadelphia? He moved there when he was twenty-four or so, and he worked as a physicist at Allen Technologies. He had a passion for astronomy—*everyone* who knew him knew about that. He married my mother when he was around forty. My mother died when I was a child, and my father never remarried. I don't know if he ever dated anyone or not. But maybe he knew you during that time? Could you have gone out with him at some time?"

"No, I don't know how I knew him, but I'm sure that

wasn't it. I only went out with one man in my whole life."
Sarah's gaze drifted to a photograph on one of the end
tables. It was an old, sepia-toned picture of a good-looking
young man.

"Was that the man you...went out with?" Laura asked.

Sarah nodded. "Joe Tolley. He was my husband. The
love of my life."

Laura sensed something in the tone of her voice. There
was a long story behind that photograph, and she didn't
have the time to get into it.

"So, you didn't date my dad, then," she said. "Could
you have worked together?"

"I was a nurse," Sarah said. "And I never lived in Philadelphia. I lived in Maryland and Virginia most of my
life."

"Well, this is a challenge." Laura smiled, trying not to
let her frustration show. "If you were a nurse, could he
have been your patient? He was sick for quite a while before he died. He had cancer, and was in and out of hospitals." She realized how ridiculous it was to think that
Sarah, in her seventies, could have been her father's nurse.
"I guess that doesn't make sense," she said.

"I grew up in Bayonne," Sarah said again, and Laura
guessed she was seeing the Alzheimer's at work.

"Yes," she said.

"I was a nurse on cruise ships." She stood up and
handed Laura another framed photograph. This one showed
Sarah, in her fifties, perhaps, standing beneath a palm tree,
a cruise ship looming behind her in the distance.

"That was in St.Thomas," Sarah said. "Or maybe St.
Lucia. My favorite was Alaska, though."

"Well, what a wonderful job," Laura said. "You got to
see the world."

"They have an Alaska show on the TV sometimes."

Sarah picked up the *TV Guide* from the end table and began flipping through it, and Laura felt antsy. She thought of Ray at home, staring gloomily out the window of his study, and Emma playing with the puzzle in her room. Looking at her watch, she realized she'd been gone well over an hour already.

She stood up. "I have to go, Mrs. Tolley," she said.

Sarah looked at her in surprise. "Oh, you do?"

"I'm sorry we couldn't solve the mystery of how you knew my father."

"Did you say he was a doctor?"

"No. A physicist. And an amateur astronomer."

Sarah looked as though she didn't quite understand what Laura was saying, but she nodded. "Well, you come see me again, dear," she said, walking toward her apartment door.

Laura only smiled, unwilling to make that promise. She had no more idea of why her father wanted her to take on the responsibility for Sarah Tolley than she did before her visit.

4

Something was wrong. Laura knew it the moment she stepped out of her car in the town house garage, although she couldn't have said what triggered her sense of dread. As she neared the door, she could hear a child crying inside the house. Was it Emma or some other child? The sound was unfamiliar. A wail. A *keening*.

Panicked, Laura struggled to fit her key in the lock, finally managing to push the door open. Stepping into the foyer, she found Emma sitting on the bottom step of the stairs, hunched over as though her stomach hurt. Her wailing turned to screams, and she leapt from the step into Laura's arms.

"Sweetheart!" Laura tried to keep her own voice calm. "What is it? What's wrong?" Maybe Emma had bugged Ray to read to her and, in his sour mood, he'd yelled at her, but this seemed an extreme reaction. Emma was usually more resilient than this.

Emma didn't answer her. She clung to Laura, standing now, but pressing her head against Laura's hip.

Laura looked through the living room toward Ray's office, a patch of cold forming at the base of her neck. Emma's screams could not mask the stillness in the rest of the house. "Where's Daddy?" she asked as she walked toward the office, Emma clinging to her more tightly with each step. "Ray?"

The office was empty, the pages of Ray's manuscript still piled on his desk. "Ray?" she called as she walked back toward the foyer and the stairs.

"Stay here," she told Emma, gently pulling the little girl's arms from around her hips. "I'll be right back."

She climbed the stairs, the cold patch at the back of her neck spreading down her spine. She walked through the doorway of the bedroom she shared with Ray. It was empty. Ray must have gone out. He'd left Emma alone. That's why she was so upset.

That would not be enough to undo Emma, though, and Laura remembered seeing Ray's car in the garage. She was about to leave the bedroom when she noticed a stain on the wallpaper on the other side of the bed—a red stain in the shape of a butterfly. Biting her lip, she walked slowly around the foot of the bed. Ray lay on the floor next to the window, his head in a pool of blood, a gun in his hand.

Staggering backward, Laura crashed into the dresser, knocking her jewelry box to the floor. She scattered the jewelry with her feet as she fled from the room and down the stairs.

Emma's wails had turned to a whimper, and she sat huddled on the floor of the foyer, her eyes on Laura. Laura grabbed her by the arm and led her into the kitchen, where she used the phone to call 911.

"Is this an emergency?" the dispatcher asked.

Laura's brain felt foggy. Ray was dead. There was nothing anyone could do to change that fact, no matter how quickly they got to the house.

"Is this an emergency?" the dispatcher repeated.

"My husband shot himself," Laura said. "He's dead." She had a sudden, desperate need to get out of the house. Ignoring the dispatcher's questions, she dropped the receiver to the kitchen floor, grabbed Emma once again and ran with her outside to the small front porch.

Sitting down on the old wooden bench Ray'd picked up at a garage sale, she pulled Emma onto her lap. *I'm in shock.* The thought was clinical and detached. She was nauseated and a little dizzy, and although she knew the air was cold, she couldn't actually feel it. *This is what shock feels like.* Her eyes couldn't focus, even as the police cars, the ambulance and the fire truck pulled in front of her town house, sirens blaring. Neighbors came out to their yards or peered through their windows to see what was happening, but Laura simply stared at the snow covering the front lawn. All she could see, though, was the butterfly-shaped stain on the wallpaper in the bedroom.

"He's upstairs," she said to the first police officer who approached her. She pressed her chin to the top of Emma's head as the army of EMTs marched past them and into the house, and she closed her eyes against the image of what they would find in the upstairs bedroom.

Emma had stopped crying, but her head remained buried in the crook of Laura's shoulder. She was really too big to sit on anyone's lap, but she had made herself fit, and Laura did not want to let go of her. The little girl shivered in her light sweater, and Laura rubbed her arms. What had Emma seen? Had she heard the gunshot and gone into the bedroom to investigate? Might she have actually been in the room when Ray did it? Laura should not have left her with him. She should not have been gone more than an hour.

It seemed like a long time before one of the police officers returned to the porch, carrying jackets for her and Emma. He'd brought Ray's down jacket for Laura, and she put it on, pressing the collar close to her nose to breathe in her husband's scent.

"Who was in the house when it happened?" the officer

asked, pulling a notepad from his pocket. He stood on the walkway, one foot resting on the step.

"Emma." Laura nodded toward her daughter, who had once again folded herself to fit in Laura's lap.

The police officer studied Emma for a moment and seemed to decide against questioning her.

"And you were out?" he asked.

"Yes."

"Do you know why the jewelry box and its contents were on the floor?"

"I knocked into it after I found him," she said. The image of the jewelry spilled across the floor seemed like something she'd seen days ago, not mere minutes.

"There was a note in the bedroom," the officer said. "Did you see it?"

"A note?"

"Yes. Taped to the dresser mirror. It read, 'I asked you not to go.' Does that mean anything to you?"

Laura squeezed her eyes shut. "I had to visit someone this morning and he didn't want me to go."

"Ah," he said, as though he'd found the missing piece to the puzzle. "There was a big age difference between you and your husband, huh?"

The question seemed rude, but she didn't have the strength to protest. "Yes," she said.

"So, was this 'someone' you had to visit another man?"

Laura looked at the policeman in confusion. "Another...? No. No. It was a woman. An old woman. But he asked me not to go, and I went, anyway. I was always leaving him. Always working. I left him alone too much. It's my fault."

"Now, don't jump to conclusions, ma'am. Did your husband suffer from depression?"

She nodded. "Terribly. I should have realized how bad it had gotten, but—"

"He has an old scar obviously made from a bullet in his left shoulder," the officer said. "Was that from some previous botched suicide attempt?"

"No. He got that fighting in Korea." He had survived Korea. He had not survived his marriage to her. Guilt rested like a boulder in her chest.

The police officer nodded at Emma. "Do you think I could ask her a couple of questions?"

Laura leaned back to shift Emma's head from her shoulder. "Honey," she said, can you tell the policeman what happened? Can you tell *me?*"

Emma looked at them both in silence, her eyes glazed. And that's when Laura realized that her daughter had not spoken a single word since she'd gotten home.

5

Laura sat next to Stuart, Ray's younger brother and only sibling, during the memorial service at Georgetown University. Ray had taught at Georgetown for many years, and the chapel was completely full. People stood in the rear of the building, some of them forced into the foyer by the crowd. Many were his former sociology students and fellow professors. Ray had left his mark at the university.

He'd left his mark in the streets, as well. A busload of homeless people and the staff from several shelters were already sitting in the chapel by the time Laura arrived. The news of Ray's death had brought an outpouring of sympathy from the entire metropolitan D.C. area. Ray had been loved and respected. She hoped he had known that. He'd been so wrapped up in his inability to get his book published these last few years that he'd lost sight of all the good he'd accomplished. Seeing the somber crowd in the chapel made her heart ache. She wasn't sure how she would get through this service.

She glanced at her brother-in-law. Stuart gazed straight ahead, and she could see the tight line of his jaw as he struggled to maintain control. She wrapped her hand around his arm. The hardest call for her to make after Ray's death had been to Stuart. He lived in Connecticut, and as a marketing representative for a textbook company, he traveled frequently. She'd worried he might be on the road, but

she'd found him at home. Stuart had cried when she told
him. Big gulping sobs that frightened her, they were so out
of character for him. He'd adored and admired his older
brother. Ray was all the blood family Stuart had.

Stuart was staying in the town house while he was in
Leesburg, but he was staying there alone. Laura had barely
been able to set foot in the house since finding Ray's body.
All evidence of his death had been scrubbed away by some
people the police had recommended, but still, it was impossible to be there, to *sleep* there, without feeling Ray's
presence. Stuart, though, had no negative images attached
to the town house. Besides, he told her, he would feel closest to Ray there.

Laura and Emma had been staying in the vacant, above-
garage apartment of some friends. As soon as Laura could
get things organized, she planned to move Emma and herself out to the lake house. She'd told the Smithsonian and
Johns Hopkins she would be taking some time off, sending
them scrambling to find replacements for her. She would
probably sell the town house. She could not imagine ever
living there again.

Nancy Charles, one of the geologists from the Smithsonian, stopped at Laura's pew, leaning over to take her hand.

"I'm so sorry," Nancy said. "How are you doing?"

"I'm okay." Laura tried to smile.

"You just lost your father, and now dear Ray. It's not
fair."

"No," Laura agreed.

"How's Emma?" Nancy asked. "She's not here, is
she?"

"She's with a sitter."

"Do you need any help with her?"

"No. Thanks, though," Laura said. "It's been rough on
her, but she's hanging in there."

John Robbins, a minister who'd worked with Ray in creating programs for the homeless, stepped into the pulpit, and Nancy whispered goodbye. John began to talk, and although Laura struggled to listen, her mind was still on Emma, who had refused to come to the service. All the energy Laura had put into doing everything "right" with Emma after Poppa's death had drained her, and she had no reserves left to help her daughter cope with this new tragedy. She was angry at Ray for piling a second loss on Emma in such a short time. And, of course, she felt guilty for her anger.

Emma had not uttered a single word in the four days since Ray's death. A policewoman had spoken to her the day after it happened, her questioning gentle and sensitive. Emma had sucked her thumb, something she had not done in more than a year, as she stared blankly into the woman's eyes. She'll come around, the policewoman assured Laura. Laura should talk to her, she said. Draw Emma's feelings about the trauma out in the open. But Laura could not get Emma to speak. Not through gentle coaxing, or sharing her own feelings, or even trickery. Emma had lost her voice.

It was Emma she thought of now, through speaker after speaker, until Stuart finally stood to deliver his eulogy. She found it difficult to look at her brother-in-law as he took his place in the pulpit; his resemblance to Ray was striking. He had Ray's bulky body, his large, soft chin, straight nose and wire-rimmed glasses. Nearly the only difference was that Stuart still had a full head of dark hair, while Ray had lost much of his.

"Ray Darrow was a caring brother, a loving husband and father, a dedicated teacher, a volunteer committed to the homeless, and a writer of uncommon talent," Stuart said. "He was my only brother, my only family, and he was also my best friend. He was the sort of person you could tell anything to, and he wouldn't judge you or criticize you. As most of you know, his primary concern was the welfare of others. He was a good man, and the good are often those that suffer the most. Depression had been his enemy all of his life, and he bore frustration poorly. He bore failure poorly. He bore his inability to help others poorly. He wrote a book, *No Room at the Inn,* a beautiful work of art and compassion he hoped would draw attention to the plight of the homeless and the poor, but no one would publish it. It was decidedly unglamorous. And finally he could take it no more.''

Stuart bowed his head, and Laura could see that he was struggling for composure. She willed him to find it, even though she was losing it herself. Behind her, she heard sniffling.

Stuart continued. ''Those of you here who are committed to the same causes that so moved my brother, please continue them in his name,'' he said. ''That is what he would have wanted.''

Later that night, Laura and Stuart sat together in the tiny living room of the above-garage apartment. Emma was already in bed, but the door to her bedroom was open to let in some light, and Laura spoke quietly in case she could hear them.

''I don't think it was so much the book that made him kill himself,'' she said. She was sitting next to Stuart on the love seat, facing the blue-curtained windows that looked out on her friends' house. ''I think it was me.''

''You?'' Stuart said. ''He thought the sun rose and set on you, Laurie. Don't be crazy.''

''There was a lot going on you don't know about.'' She brushed a thread from the sleeve of her sweater. ''I think that after I found the last comet, he began to feel like a failure. He kept getting rejection letters while I was getting funding for research and my picture in *Newsweek* and *Time*. I stayed at the observatory in Brazil for too long. I was very wrapped up in myself. Laura Brandon and her career. I left him alone too much."

"I think he understood that was part of your job. He was very proud of you."

"I don't know, Stu. Right after my dad died, Ray and I had a big...well, he blew up at me."

"Ray?"

"He sounded very resentful, of my job and my success. I think he must have been upset for a long time, but he'd hidden those feelings from me till then."

"Well, if he was hiding them from you, he was hiding them from me, too. I never heard him say anything like that."

The lights went on in an upstairs bedroom of her friends' house. A family of five lived there, leading their nice, quiet, normal lives. Laura envied them.

"Even when I was home," she said, "I'd be up with the telescope at night. He'd tell me how he woke up at 2:00 a.m. to find me gone, and that he missed me." She blinked back tears. "I was selfish."

"I don't know," Stuart said. "I can't imagine Ray getting upset over your work. And definitely not over your success. He wasn't the jealous type."

"Maybe not when he was feeling well, but he'd been down for a while. I don't think I recognized it. I should have picked up on it."

"You're being awfully hard on yourself, Laurie."

"I didn't tell you about the note he left."

"You didn't say there was a note."

"I just didn't want to tell you about it on the phone."

She didn't want to tell him about it now, either, but knew she had to.

"What did it say?" Stuart shifted position on the love seat to see her better.

"It read, 'I asked you not to go.'"

"What did he mean by that?"

"Well, it's complicated." Laura rubbed her eyes with her palms. "You see, there's an elderly woman living near here in a retirement home, and—"

"The one your father asked you to take care of?"

"How did you know that?"

"Ray told me about her the last time I spoke with him on the phone. He said you were all gung ho about taking care of her, and he was very upset about it."

"I think his being upset was way out of proportion to the situation, probably because he was so depressed. He wasn't thinking clearly."

Stuart hesitated. "It did seem an extreme reaction, I guess," he said. "So, that's what he was referring to in the note? That he'd asked you not to see her?"

"That's right. But I had to, Stuart." She turned to face him. "My father asked me to, and—"

"But..." Stuart interrupted her. "Your father was dead and never would have known the difference." He spoke gently, as though he had no idea how those words would cut her. "Ray was alive. For whatever reason, he needed to know that what he thought and what he wanted mattered to you."

She didn't know what to say. She'd thought Stuart would understand.

"So you saw this woman?" he asked.

"Yes. I still don't know why my father wanted me to, though. She has Alzheimer's and doesn't remember him at all."

"Alzheimer's, huh?" Stuart actually chuckled.

"I don't see what's so funny."

"You're right. It isn't funny." Stuart sobered, but it looked as if it took some effort. "Do you plan to see her again?" he asked.

"I don't think so." Laura shivered at the thought. Her last visit to Sarah Tolley was linked in her mind to Ray's death.

"Good," Stuart said. "Is she getting good care there?"

"I think so."

"Then forget about her. You made sure she's all right. You've done all you need to do. You found no meaningful link between her and your father. Leave it alone."

Stuart was right. Her father's money was still in trust for Sarah, and the attorney would handle any bills that came in. There was nothing more for Laura to do. She remembered the attendant, Carolyn, telling her how much Sarah would love to be able to go for walks again and have someone to talk to, but she quickly blocked that thought from her mind.

Stuart stood up with that same getting-to-his-feet groan Ray had always emitted when rising from a chair. "I'm going to head back to the town house," he said, stretching. "It's been a long day."

Laura stood up herself and walked him to the door, where Stuart pulled her into a brotherly embrace.

"Ray made a lot of sacrifices for you, you know," Stuart said.

She nodded, her head resting on his shoulder.

Stuart kissed her cheek, then walked out the door. Laura sat down again on the love seat.

Ray made a lot of sacrifices for you.

It hurt to think about all Ray had done for her. He'd given her the financial and emotional support she'd needed to further her career. He'd loved her through her successes despite his own failures.

And he'd even taken responsibility for the child she had never meant to conceive.

6

Laura watched through the two-way mirror as Emma's new therapist, Heather Davison, drew pictures on a large sheet of paper.

"Show me a really, really angry face," Heather said to Emma, who sat next to her at a table in the well-stocked playroom.

Emma obeyed, screwing up her nose and baring her teeth. Laura laughed quietly on her side of the mirror.

"Excellent!" Heather said. She drew a reasonable facsimile of the expression on the sheet of paper. At least that's what it looked like from where Laura was sitting.

"Now show me a very sad face," Heather said.

It was now July. It had been more than six months since Ray's death, more than six months since Emma had uttered a word. It seemed impossible. The child whose preschool teacher had called Laura to complain about her disruptive talking. The child who would follow Laura or Ray around the house with nonstop questions and pervasive chatter. It was as though she'd used up all her allotted words and suddenly could find no more.

She had regressed in other ways, as well. She was wildly afraid of the dark, needing both a night-light and an open bedroom door to be able to fall asleep. A few nights a week, she would wet the bed, and the thumb-sucking was back in full force.

Last month, Laura was finally able to move Emma and herself into the lake house for good. Or at least until she figured out what she should do next. She'd put her career on indefinite hold in order to devote her time to her daughter after taking Emma out of preschool. The house still needed a lot of work to be truly livable as a year-round residence, but Laura planned to do the painting and repairs while she and Emma lived there.

The house was on Lake Ashton, a small lake near the tiny hamlet of Paris, Virginia, half an hour from Leesburg. Ray and Laura had bought the house several years ago. Ray had balked at the idea of owning two homes when many people had none, but he knew Laura needed a place in the country, where the sky was untouched by city lights, for her observations.

There were only seven other houses on the lake, and none of them were visible from their house. The forest surrounding the lake was thick, and even from the screened porch, all that could be seen was a hint of water beyond the trees. A paved path, perfect for riding bikes or walking, circled the lake. There were a playground and a small beach, and on the opposite side of the lake from the house, a rickety fishing pier.

Laura had hoped the move to the lake would make a difference for Emma, that maybe it had been living in the tiny apartment, too close to the town house, that had left her tongue-tied and fearful. The lake house was full of happy memories for Emma. She had a friend, Cory, nearby, a little girl with whom she'd played every summer since she was a toddler. Last summer she and Cory had learned to swim, and it had been hard to drag Emma from the lake at the end of each day. But being at the lake house seemed to make no difference in Emma's condition. In a way it was worse, because now she would not go near the water

she'd enjoyed so much the year before. She was afraid of
it, giving the water's edge a wide berth when she walked
along the shore.

"Show me your happiest face," Heather said to Emma.

Emma tried. She really did, Laura thought, but the weak
smile wouldn't fool anyone. Still, Heather attempted to
translate the expression to the paper.

When Laura had registered with the receptionist in
Heather Davison's office, the woman could not seem to
take her eyes from Emma's face. "What a beautiful child,"
she'd said. Now, though, as Laura watched her daughter
through the two-way mirror, she thought that even Emma's
beauty had taken a blow during the past six months. Her
skin had grown pale, made even more noticeable by her
nearly black hair, and there were dark circles under her
light blue eyes.

"Okay," Heather said to Emma. "Now we have all our
faces. Can you point to the face that describes how you
feel today?"

Emma studied the faces for a moment and pointed to one
of them. Laura couldn't tell which one from where she was
sitting.

"Can you show me which face reminds you of your
Mommy's face?"

Emma pointed, and Laura craned her neck in vain, longing to see which face she'd selected.

Heather was Emma's third counselor. Laura had walked
out on the last one after the woman told her that she should
have taken Emma to Ray's memorial service to "help her
connect with reality," that she should have had Emma
make a gift to tuck into Ray's casket with him, and that
she should have moved immediately back into the town
house to show Emma it was in no way haunted by Ray's
death.

"Thanks." Laura had not been able to mask the sarcasm in her voice as she stood to leave midway through the session. "That was very helpful. I'll be sure to remember to do all of that when my next husband dies."

She'd listened to the advice of friends, hearing every suggestion from punishing Emma, to hospitalizing her, to buying her a puppy. Someone finally referred her to Heather Davison, a child therapist who'd had some success dealing with mute children. Heather felt like her last hope, but she'd been disappointed when she met her. The therapist didn't look more than thirty, and her style of speech was more like that of a teenager than a therapist. She wore jeans and a T-shirt, and her long blond hair was tied up in a ponytail. Emma took to her instantly, though, and that was what counted. And Laura liked what Heather had said to Emma at the start of this session.

"Your daddy's death was nobody's fault," she'd said. "A sickness in his mind caused him to kill himself. *You* don't have that sickness, though. Your mom doesn't have it, either. Most people don't have it."

Now Heather looked at her watch and stood up. Obviously the session was over, and the miracle Laura had hoped for had not occurred. Emma had not made a sound during the half hour with the therapist.

Laura met Heather and Emma in the hall outside the play therapy room, and Emma immediately wrapped her arms around Laura's legs. To say that Emma had grown clingy over the last couple of months would be an understatement.

"Hi, sweetie!" Laura said to her. "Did you have fun?"

Emma nodded.

Heather led them back to the reception area. "Emma," she said, "I want to talk to your Mom for a little while in the other room. You can play here." She pointed to a colorful play area that had attracted Emma the minute they'd walked into the waiting room forty minutes earlier. "Mrs. Quinn will keep an eye on you from her desk."

Emma whimpered her protest and clung more tightly to Laura.

Laura leaned over. "I'll just be in the next room, and we'll only be a few minutes." She walked Emma over to the toys and spent a few minutes getting her involved with the crayons and a coloring book.

"I'll be back in a minute," she said. "You stay here and play." She heard the firmness in her voice, employed more for Heather's sake than for her daughter's. What she really wanted to do was hold Emma on her lap and rock her, telling her everything would be all right. Her separation anxiety was nearly as strong as Emma's.

Heather guided Laura into her office, which was next to the play therapy room. The office had comfortable, adult-size chairs, and Laura sank into one of them.

"I'm afraid she's never going to speak again," she said.

"Oh, I think she will," Heather said. "Her lack of communication makes it harder to know what's bugging her, of course, but the truth is, children her age need to play it out—*act* it out—rather than talk it out. So, I'll work with her in play therapy and we'll see where it goes."

"I just don't know how she *feels* about anything anymore," Laura said.

"I know," Heather said. "Loss is so hard for little kids. *You* have friends in your world, but she just had you and her dad. She's lost fifty percent of her support system. And if Dad can die, so can Mom. Already, I can tell she's feeling terribly abandoned."

"Abandoned? By Ray—her father?"

"I think abandoned in general," Heather said slowly. "I think it might predate her dad's death."

"But I almost always had her with me when I traveled,"

Laura protested. "I'd have to leave her with sitters during the day, of course...." And during many nights as well. She shut her eyes. "She always seemed happy and well-adjusted. She'd love to stay with the sitters. In Brazil, her sitter had a daughter Emma's age. They had a great time together. Emma was outgoing and talkative. I know that must be hard to believe—"

"No, it's not hard," Heather said. "And it's very encouraging. If she was a strong, well-adjusted little girl once, then she has resources inside her to help her through this time. The prognosis is very good."

Laura nodded, trying hard to believe what Heather was saying.

"But I have to say that it's unusual for a selectively mute child to be mute with everyone," Heather continued. "Ordinarily, they'll be mute at school or out in the world in general, but not at home with family. Emma's case is distinctive in that she doesn't talk to anyone, not even you."

Laura looked down at her lap, where her hands were knotted together. She must have failed Emma somehow that she didn't even feel safe talking to her own mother.

"You told me she was home when your husband killed himself," Heather said quickly, obviously aware that Laura was sinking into guilt. "That alone's enough of a trauma to bring about this sort of regression, so don't go laying the blame on yourself."

Laura pursed her lips. "If you say so," she said.

"The other thing I picked up on is her negative feelings toward men."

"Really?"

"Did you see when I asked her which face looked most like a man's face? She picked the angry face."

"Well, I know she's always favored women. But I didn't think she had...negative feelings about men."

Heather shifted in her seat, ponytail bouncing, and Laura thought she knew why Emma liked the therapist: Heather probably reminded her of her Barbie dolls.

"You haven't told me much about Emma's relationship with her dad," Heather said. "With Ray."

Laura wondered where to begin. "Emma was not Ray's natural child," she said.

"Oh." Heather jotted something down on her notepad.

"No. I had a brief relationship with another man and Emma was conceived. It was a shock to me, the pregnancy. I wasn't—" she tried to find the words "—I wasn't the brief relationship type. Or even the long-and-enduring relationship type." She smiled at Heather. "I'm an astronomer. That is—was—my life. I never felt I had the time for relationships. And I was thirty-four. Old enough to know better. But anyway, I was pregnant." She had the feeling she was giving Heather far more information than had been requested. "Ray and I were close friends, but nothing more than that. Yet he was always a very caring person. He was much older than me, and he was sort of part father, part brother, part friend. I was very upset about the pregnancy. I'd never thought I'd have children, but I knew I didn't want an abortion. Still, I wasn't married. So Ray offered to marry me. I accepted. I loved him very much. But we never had what you'd think of as a typical marriage. We were more friends than lovers." She and Ray had made love perhaps twenty times in the six years of their marriage. She had wanted more, but Ray's antidepressant medication killed any libido he might have possessed, and she was careful never to press him or make him feel inadequate. He was a good husband and he treated Emma as though she were his own, and Laura could usually make herself be satisfied with that.

"What was his relationship like with Emma?" Heather

asked, and Laura remembered that was the original question.

"Well, there was never any doubt that he was her father. He was a wonderful father to her."

"Give me some examples."

"Well, he'd read her stories at night. He'd...he liked to drive her around the streets of Washington to educate her on the problems of the homeless."

Heather's eyes were wide and disbelieving, and Laura laughed. "He was one of a kind," she said.

"Yeah, I can see that," Heather said. "So what else did he do with her?"

"Well..." Laura searched her memory, finally shaking her head in defeat. "I can't think of other specific examples. But he loved her. I don't think he would have treated her any differently if she'd been his own flesh and blood."

"Did he take her places—other than the streets of D.C.? Play games with her? Teach her to ride a big wheeler?"

"No. Not those things, specifically. But he..." She gave up in frustration. "Sorry. My mind is a blank."

"You know..." Heather's voice was gentle. "We all have a tendency to idealize our loved ones who've died."

"He married me," Laura said. "He took Emma on and gave her a father. He didn't have to do that." She had to admit that Ray had never given Emma much of his attention, and when he did, it was with his own agenda in mind. He would occasionally read to her, but the books he'd select were about little homeless children. She couldn't bring herself to share that fact with Heather, though.

"Any chance there might have been some molestation going on?" Heather asked.

"No!"

"I need to ask," Heather said with a hint of apology. "I didn't pick up on anything, but we need to rule that out."

"No. Ray was not a very...sexual person. He was wrapped up in social issues, as you can tell. On every committee for social change you can imagine. He worked with the homeless. He was as driven in that as I am in astronomy. And he suffered from depression, obviously. That's what led him to kill himself."

"What was he like when he was depressed?"

Laura did not have to think hard to remember. "Sometimes he'd simply sink into a black hole and withdraw from the rest of the world. Other times, he'd be impatient and irritable. He could be short with Emma when he felt that way." She didn't like acknowledging that fact. "He'd yell at her. She could get on his nerves. But that wasn't too often." It had been more often in the period before his death, though. She couldn't deny that.

"How do you think you're doing as a mom?" Heather asked, and Laura was surprised by the sudden change in her focus.

"To be honest," she said, "I don't think I've handled motherhood very well. Or marriage, for that matter." A professor had once told her that as women moved into male-dominated fields, such as the sciences, they tended to lose their "people skills," their innate ability to nurture, to intuit and meet the needs of others. She was afraid that's what had happened to her. "Can I be brilliant in one realm of my life and a complete idiot in another?" she asked.

Heather laughed. "Most of us are, I think."

"I had one parent most of my life. I knew he loved me, and he was always very attentive to me, but he taught me more about the planets than he did about people. So what do I do? I get pregnant by some guy I barely know. I marry someone more for security and companionship than for love. I turn out just as nerdy and head-in-the-clouds as my father was. And that's what Emma's stuck with. She has no one else. No brothers or sisters or grandparents or aunts or uncles or cousins. And now no father. Just me. And I don't quite know how to do it. I'm worried I'm ruining her.''

Heather smiled. ''She's not ruined, Laura. You've described her as happy, inquisitive, strong-willed, outgoing and personable. You obviously have done something very right with her. Now she's experienced a trauma. We have to help her get through that, and then you should have your happy daughter back. The daughter you've raised better than you think.''

Laura let out a sigh.

''You're carrying a lot around with you, aren't you?'' Heather said. ''I mean guilt. A sense of responsibility. Fear.''

''I'm feeling overwhelmed these days, yes. So much going on in my life this past year. Losing Ray, and before that, my dad was sick, and...'' She thought back to the news segment she'd seen on TV the week before. Loneliness in the elderly. It had been troubling her for days.

''And...?'' Heather prompted.

''It doesn't have anything to do with Emma.''

''That's all right.''

''My father made me promise I'd take care of an elderly woman.'' She explained the situation to Heather, and how her visit to Sarah Tolley had triggered Ray's suicide.

''It was unfair of Ray to ask you not to go,'' Heather said sternly.

''Well, maybe, but he—''

''Are you going to make a hobby out of defending him?'' Heather asked. ''It was unfair of him to put you in that position. Period. So, do you want to see her again?''

Laura was unsettled by Heather's bluntness. Still, she remembered the pleading, desperate look in her father's eyes when he'd asked her to take care of Sarah. That memory had tortured her for the past six months.

"Yes," she admitted.

"Then go," Heather said. "That's your assignment for next week."

and when Laura had gone her Barbie dolls away. "I'll buy you a..." but retraced-her? I'm still so usually.

"Yes?" she replied.

"I was a..." Really? said "Here's your assignment before..."

7

The path circling the lake was so heavily forested that walking on it was like walking through a tunnel, and Laura slowed her pace to enjoy the effect. Emma, though, did not seem to notice. She trotted ahead of Laura, carrying her blue plastic case filled with her Barbie dolls and their requisite paraphernalia, eager to get to the Beckers' house.

Five-year-old Cory was in the Beckers' front yard, and she ran to meet Emma, her wild red curls bouncing around her face.

"I got a Dentist Barbie!" Cory shrieked. She grabbed Emma's arm, and Emma ran with her up the porch steps, past Cory's mother, Alison, who held the screen door open for them.

"Sorry about that," Alison said to Laura with a smile. Her own short red hair framed her face, and freckles dotted her nose. "Now you'll have to get Emma Paleontologist Barbie or something so she can keep up with the neighbors."

Laura laughed. She stood in the yard, shading her eyes against the rays of sun shooting through the trees. "Thanks for watching her," she said. "I should be back by four."

"Take your time." Alison folded her arms across her chest. "If I can tear them away from the dolls, I'll take them to the playground for a while."

Laura walked back to her own house, feeling fortunate

that the Beckers were at the lake again this summer. Cory amazed her. She'd accepted Laura's explanation that Emma wasn't talking this summer with a simple "oh," and she did Emma's talking for her when they played. Cory's father worked in D.C. and came to the lake only on the weekends, so Laura and Alison had found a resource for child care in each other.

The drive to Meadow Wood Village took her a little over thirty minutes. Thirty anxious minutes, as Laura tried unsuccessfully to forget the toll her last visit to Sarah Tolley had taken on Ray, and on Emma.

Once in the retirement home, she found Sarah's apartment by hunting for the door bearing the silhouette of the projector. Sarah answered the door and smiled at Laura. "Yes?" she asked. She was dressed in a pale blue plaid cotton jumper over a white blouse. Her silver hair looked newly styled.

"Hello, Mrs. Tolley." She could see the lack of recognition in the older woman's face. "I'm Laura Brandon. I came to visit you here last January."

Although her smile remained, Sarah looked puzzled as she let Laura into the living room.

"My father had asked me to see you," Laura said. "Do you remember?"

"Your father? He was deceased, is that right?"

"Yes!" Laura was excited that Sarah remembered that much. "And you couldn't recall who he was. But I brought a picture with me today to help you remember. And I was also wondering if you might like to go for a walk."

"A walk? Outside?" Sarah looked as though she didn't quite trust the invitation.

"Yes."

"Oh, I'd certainly love that." Sarah clapped her hands

together in a small show of joy. "They don't let me outside anymore. Keep me locked up in jail here." She chuckled.

"It's quite warm out today," Laura said. "Will that be okay for you?"

"Warm, cold or in between, just get me outside." Sarah was already walking toward the door.

"Do you have some shoes that would be better for walking?" Laura asked.

Sarah looked down at her beige pumps. "Good idea," she said. "Don't go away."

She disappeared into the bedroom. Laura's eyes fell on the picture of Sarah's husband. Joe. Was that his name? A nice-looking young man. She pulled the picture of her father from her purse.

After a few minutes, Sarah reappeared in sturdy-looking walking shoes, and Laura wondered if her father might have been responsible for Sarah's wardrobe.

"You have such nice clothes," she said. "How do you get out to buy them? Does someone take you shopping for them?"

"I love nice clothes," Sarah said as she headed for the door again.

"And how do you go shopping for them?" Laura asked.

Sarah stopped walking, apparently confused, but only for a moment. "Oh, they take us," she said. "Once a month, we can go on the bus to…the place with all the stores."

"The mall."

"Right."

"Here's a picture of my father." Laura handed the photograph to Sarah before she could start for the door again. "Do you remember him?"

Sarah carried the picture over to the end table lamp and studied it carefully.

"His name was Carl Brandon," Laura said.

"I don't think I know him," Sarah said with a shrug as she handed the picture back to Laura. "Can we go for a walk now?"

As she and Laura walked down the long hallway to the lobby, Sarah said hello to everyone, staff and residents alike. She had an "I'm gettin' out, so there" attitude about her, and she walked fast, an expectant smile on her face. It hurt Laura to see that simply getting out of the building for a half hour could give Sarah such joy. She should have come sooner, she thought, grateful that Heather had encouraged her to make this visit.

Outside, Sarah took in an exaggerated deep breath of air. "Which way do we go?" she asked.

"Whichever way you'd like."

That seemed to be the wrong answer, because Sarah's smile faded and that look of confusion came into her face again. "I don't know where anything is," she said.

"Well, let's just walk," Laura said, turning left onto the sidewalk. "It doesn't matter where we're going, really."

"That's right," Sarah said, the smile back, and she set out next to Laura at a strong, quick pace. Laura hustled to keep up with her. Whatever was wrong with Sarah Tolley was clearly confined to her mind and not her body.

A silence fell between them as they walked. It was not uncomfortable, and although Laura longed to break it with more sleuthing about Sarah's relationship to her father, she hesitated to confuse the woman any more. Laura remembered what Carolyn, Sarah's attendant, had said: Sarah loved to talk, but had no one to listen to her.

"What was it like working on cruise ships?" Laura asked.

"Nice," Sarah said.

"How long did you do it?"

"I don't know. A year. Maybe three or four."

"Carolyn said you like movies," Laura said.

"Oh, yes!" Sarah clapped her hands together again, a gleam in her eyes.

"What have you seen lately?"

"I like the movies from the old days."

"Do you have a favorite?"

"Oh, yes. It's…" Lines creased Sarah's brow, and she pouted like an annoyed child. "I can't remember what it's called," she said.

This conversation wasn't exactly taking off. "Well, I told you all about where my father grew up and where he lived," Laura said. "Why don't you tell me about yourself? You said you grew up in Bayonne?" Maybe getting Sarah to talk about herself would give Laura the clues she needed to link the elderly woman to her father.

So, Sarah began to talk, and it was as though Laura had tapped into a deep well, a well that was far richer than she could have imagined.

Sarah, 1931-1945

The third-grade class was planning a production of the play *Cinderella* for the entire school to watch. Sarah loved plays. She longed to act the part of Cinderella herself, but even though she gave it her all when she tried out, that coveted role went to the prettiest and most popular girl in the class.

So Sarah tried out for the part of one of the stepsisters, a malevolent expression on her face as she attempted to make her voice sound sinister and mean, but she didn't get that role, either.

"Who'd like to try out for the part of the evil step-mother?" the teacher asked, once the other roles had been assigned.

"Sarah Wilding should get it," one of the boys said.

Sarah smiled. Her perseverance had paid off. She hoped the teacher would simply hand her the role, since she'd already tried out more than anyone else in the class.

"And why should Sarah get it?" the teacher asked.

"Because she's the only one ugly enough to play the stepmother," the boy said.

The other children laughed. Even the teacher bowed her head in an attempt to hide her smile, but Sarah saw it, and her cheeks and neck grew blotchy with color.

The teacher raised her head again. "That's a cruel thing to say," she scolded the boy, her face very serious now. "How would you feel if someone said something like that about you? I think you need to apologize to Sarah."

The boy sheepishly turned around in his seat to look at Sarah. "Sorry," he said.

Sarah looked away from him, swallowing hard to keep her tears in check.

"Sarah, would you like the part of the stepmother?" the teacher asked. "That part requires a very good actress. I think you'd be good in it."

She didn't know what to say. Of course she wanted the part, but not that way. Not because she was ugly.

"No, thank you, ma'am," she said, her cheeks still burning.

When the play had been fully cast, the class was released for recess. Escape, finally. Instead of joining the other children on the playground, Sarah ran home.

She knew the house would be empty except for her aunt, and that was fine. Both her parents were at work in the family's clothing store, but Aunt Jane didn't work. She never went anywhere. She was always there for Sarah, and that's what Sarah was counting on.

She knew she would find her aunt in her room on the

top floor of the house, working on a quilt, as usual. Her quilts graced every bed in the house and many of the neighbors' houses, as well. The colorful squares of material covered nearly every surface in Aunt Jane's bedroom, and Sarah always found the sight of them comforting.

Aunt Jane looked up in surprise when Sarah walked into her room.

"You startled me," she said, one hand on her enormous chest. "What on earth are you doing home so early? Are you ill? Are you crying?" Aunt Jane was up and walking toward her. "What's wrong, precious?"

Sarah hugged her aunt, drinking in the familiar scent of the flowery soap she used. Aunt Jane was rooted like a tree, a solid, big-boned woman.

"Sit down on my bed and tell me all about it," Aunt Jane said, moving some of her squares to make room for her niece.

Sarah sat down, but she was hesitant to relive the humiliation. Still, this was Aunt Jane, and she knew she was safe with her. If she'd told her mother, her mother would have said she deserved the taunting because she was sloppy about her appearance. It irked her parents no end that they owned Wilding's, the most exclusive children's clothing store in town, yet their own daughter looked like a tall, homely beanpole, no matter how carefully they dressed her. "She's a poor advertisement for the store," she'd once overheard her father saying. "Nearly as bad as your sister. Good thing Jane never goes out."

She told Jane what had happened in her classroom and saw the sympathy in her aunt's eyes.

"My poor darling," Aunt Jane said, moving closer so she could put her arm around Sarah's shoulders. "But you know what?" She waited for Sarah to look up at her.

"Something good—something *wonderful*—will come out of this experience. Did you know that?"

Sarah was mystified. "What?" she asked.

"You are going to grow up to have a very thick skin," she said, "and that is an important thing to have."

Sarah looked down at her pale, bony wrist. "Thick skin?" she asked.

Aunt Jane smiled. "It's an expression. It means that no one will ever be able to hurt you. You won't be overly sensitive. What you're going through now is hard, precious, but it's good training for your future."

Aunt Jane called the school then, and Sarah listened as she told the principal what had happened and that Sarah had left early and was staying home for the rest of the day. As she imagined what the principal was saying on the other end of the line, Sarah took comfort in her aunt's theory that something good would come from this experience, and the image of her taunting classmates gradually grew hazy and indistinct in her mind.

When Jane got off the phone, she set aside her quilting and played canasta with her niece all afternoon. By dinnertime, Sarah was laughing again.

It wasn't until Sarah was a teenager that she realized Aunt Jane was not like other women her age. Other women were married and had children. They went to the market. They shopped for clothes. They liked to go out to dinner or the theater. Not Aunt Jane, who would not even set foot in the backyard. She didn't care about being married, she said, and what did she need her own children for when she had Sarah? But the truth was, ever since Aunt Jane had been a teenager herself, she had flown into a panic each time she ventured outside the house. It would certainly be hard to meet a man, and harder still to date, when you couldn't go out your own front door.

Sarah liked that her aunt was always stuck at home, even though she knew she was selfish for feeling that way. Aunt Jane had been the one constant, loving person in her life. Always home, always ready with a hug and a loving word. But as Sarah grew older, she began to feel sorry for her aunt. People called her crazy, but Sarah knew that, like herself, Aunt Jane had a very thick skin.

Aunt Jane had wanted to be a nurse, but mental illness struck while she was in nursing school and she never got to complete the program. She took pleasure, though, in passing on all she'd learned to her niece. She taught Sarah to make beds with hospital corners, take a pulse and temperature, and give sponge baths. Sarah loved her lessons, and she grew to love the idea of being a nurse herself. She'd have to study hard in high school, Aunt Jane warned her, to be able to go to nursing school.

It was good that Sarah had her studies to attend to because she had little in the way of a social life. She had plenty of girlfriends, but the boys were studious in their avoidance of her. She'd be walking down the street, and a boy walking toward her would seem interested in her, but as he'd get nearer, he would quickly avert his eyes. And if there were *two* boys, she'd see them talking and snickering about her. It wasn't that she was disfigured in any way. She was simply, unequivocally, homely, with a long, pointed nose and too little chin. New hairstyles, new makeup—nothing seemed to make much of a difference.

"You don't need a man in your life to be happy," Aunt Jane told her once. "But you do need work, and it should be work that involves you with people. Why, I'd go mad without you and your parents to look after."

That was the first time Sarah realized her aunt didn't know that most people considered her quite mad already. But those people didn't know her the way Sarah did. If

Aunt Jane was crazy, then all the world should be crazy. Everyone would be much better off.

So, Sarah decided she would be a nurse. She felt half trained as one, anyway, by her senior year of high school. Just before graduation, she learned that she'd earned the highest grades of anyone in her class and would be making the speech at the commencement ceremony.

She begged Aunt Jane to come to her graduation. "You've helped me so much to get where I am," she told her aunt one night when she was helping her iron the squares of fabric. "I want you to be there," she said. "It would mean so much to me."

Aunt Jane put the iron down and studied her niece. "You're closer to me than anyone in the world," she said softly, "and yet even you don't understand. I can't do it, Sarah. I simply can't."

"Please," Sarah pleaded. "Please try, for me?"

In the end, Aunt Jane agreed to try, but her effort turned out to be a terrible mistake. She, Sarah and Sarah's parents had to take the trolley to a street a few blocks from the school. From there, they would walk the rest of the way. But by the time the four of them stepped off the streetcar, Aunt Jane was crying. She sat down on a bench and said, "Take me home, take me home," over and over again. Her body trembled. There was no way to comfort her and no way to cajole her into continuing. Her panic frightened Sarah. She had never seen it before, because as long as she'd known her, Aunt Jane had stayed within the safe confines of the house.

"I knew this was a mistake," Sarah's father muttered.

Sarah finally gave up trying to persuade her aunt to walk the rest of the way to the school. She felt cruel that she had begged her to come to the ceremony at all. As Aunt

Jane herself had said, Sarah had not understood the depth of her fear. But she understood it now.

"We'll take the next trolley home again," Sarah said, sitting down on the bench, as close to her aunt as she could get.

"No," her mother said. "You go on to school, Sarah, or you'll be late. Your father and I will take Jane home."

Sarah looked at her aunt's pale face. She couldn't leave her here, shivering and terrified, on the bench. "I'll wait till you're all safely on the trolley," she said. "There should be another one in a few minutes." She put her arm around her aunt's shoulders. "You'll have to go across the street to catch it, though."

Aunt Jane looked across the street, and it was as if her eyes registered a vast, deep ocean instead of a few yards of asphalt. She shook her head. "I can't do it," she said.

"Jane," Sarah's father said, "act like a thirty-nine-year-old woman for once, will you?"

Sarah shot her father an angry look. On an impulse, she ran into the street and waved down a passing car. "My aunt isn't feeling well," she told the driver, a man in a business suit. "Could you possibly give her and my parents a ride home? It's over on Garrison Street."

The driver was agreeable, and somehow they managed to bodily lift Aunt Jane into the back seat. Sarah watched as the car containing her family disappeared around the corner before walking the few blocks to her school. By the time she took the stage for her commencement address, she was nearly too upset to speak. But she managed. Somehow, she managed.

No one knew much about phobias in those days. And they knew less about depression. Two weeks after Sarah left home to attend nursing school in Trenton, Aunt Jane swallowed one hundred of her prescription nerve pills and died in her sleep at the age of forty. Sarah knew why she had done it. With her away at school, there was little holding her aunt to that cold house, and yet she was trapped there by her own tortured mind. Aunt Jane had held on long enough to help Sarah survive a difficult childhood, but now Sarah was on her own, a successful adult. And Jane was no longer needed.

Sarah, deeply affected by her aunt's death, decided to become a psychiatric nurse. She read all she could in psychology, trying to understand Aunt Jane, and in the process learning a great deal about other psychiatric illnesses as her interest in the subject grew.

After getting her degree, she took a job in a psychiatric hospital in Haddonfield, New Jersey. At first, she was afraid that she would become too attached to the patients, that each of them would seem like Aunt Jane to her, and she would not be objective enough to help them. But she found she was able to separate her aunt from the others. Each patient was an individual. Each required a different sort of help from her. And each of them needed the sort of respect and compassion Sarah had learned from the aunt who would forever be a part of her life.

8

Laura sat propped against the headboard of Emma's bed, reading one of the little girl's oldest books to her. In the past, Emma would have been able to recognize some of the words in the familiar story. She'd point to them proudly, saying them out loud. But if she knew them now, she was not letting on. Her body was curled against Laura's, her thumb in her mouth, and she was nearly asleep. Good. Every night it was a battle getting Emma to sleep. There were the nightmares, the wet bed, the fear of the dark, and the general wakefulness that had plagued her since Ray's death. But she must have worn herself out playing with Cory that afternoon, because her eyes were closed by the time Laura turned the last page.

When Laura had arrived home from visiting Sarah Tolley in Leesburg, she'd found Alison Becker and Emma sitting on the front porch of the lake house, the blue plastic Barbie doll case between them on the step. After Laura let Emma into the locked house, Alison explained that her husband had arrived for the weekend. When Jim walked into the Beckers' house, Emma dropped the doll she was playing with and ran outside. Alison had to go after her. She'd been unable to persuade Emma to return to the house, and so she'd gathered up Emma's Barbies and walked her home.

"Her therapist says she's having a problem with men," Laura said, acknowledging to herself for the first time that

Heather might be right. Jim was an unusual man, though. A kindhearted soul, but large and gruff. His voice vibrated in your toes.

Laura set the book she'd been reading to Emma on the nightstand, then carefully extracted herself from beneath her daughter, tucking her and the ragged bunny under the covers.

After making sure the small, fairy-shaped night-light was plugged into the wall near Emma's bed, she turned out the light to the room, then walked down the hall to the spare bedroom. She'd been looking forward to this evening ever since her visit with Sarah Tolley that afternoon.

In the closet of the spare bedroom was a large cardboard box filled with Carl Brandon's old papers and memorabilia. Laura had filled the box while cleaning out his apartment after he died, keeping those papers that looked important and discarding many others. Somewhere in that box there had to be a clue to his relationship with Sarah Tolley.

She'd been surprised by the wealth of details Sarah could remember. After her visit, Laura had tracked down Carolyn, Sarah's attendant.

"She can remember so much," Laura told her. "Are you sure about her diagnosis?"

"She remembered things from way back when, right?" Carolyn asked.

"Yes."

"That's where her mind is still alive," Carolyn said. "We showed *The Philadelphia Story* last Friday night, and she knew all the lines. She drove everyone else crazy reciting them. But the next day, she couldn't even tell me what movie we'd seen."

Carolyn was right. After all, Sarah had not even remembered meeting Laura before.

There was a handsomeness about Sarah Tolley. She was

not beautiful, but her face radiated warmth and there was an undeniable grace in her demeanor. Laura could see the homely child behind the dignified woman, though, and knew that Sarah had not imagined those childhood taunts.

Spreading her father's papers out on the queen-size bed, she sorted through them, hunting for some reference to a Sarah Tolley or a Sarah Wilding. She found a copy of the contract he'd signed to move Sarah into Meadow Wood Village. His relationship to Sarah was listed merely as "friend." There were mortgage papers for the house he'd owned before moving to the apartment, and maintenance records for the car he'd sold years ago. There were a few pictures of her father as a younger man, and she set them on the night table. She'd take them with her the next time she visited Sarah. If Sarah had known her father from some time in the distant past, the pictures might help her remember.

There was a picture of her mother and father on their wedding day, but there were no pictures of anyone else, and Laura ruefully recalled having thrown out many photographs of strangers when she'd cleaned out her father's apartment.

She sat on the guest room bed for hours, and it was nearly midnight when she finally lay down on top of the papers and closed her eyes.

"Why, Dad?" she said out loud. "I just don't get it."

The phone awakened her early the next morning, when she was still lying fully dressed on the paper-strewn bed. Slowly, she got to her feet and stumbled toward her bedroom and the portable phone.

It was Madeline Shires, Ray's literary agent.

"I have some wonderful news," Madeline said. "We have an offer for *No Room at the Inn* from Lukens Press!"

What was Lukens Press? Laura's head was foggy from waking up so suddenly. Down the hall, she could hear Emma beginning to stir in her own bedroom. "You mean...an offer to publish it?"

"Granted, they're not one of the big players," Madeline said, "but they're behind Ray's book one hundred and ten percent. And they're ready and willing to back up their purchase with excellent promotion."

"I didn't realize Ray's book was still making the rounds," Laura said.

"Oh, sure. I never stopped submitting it. And are you sitting down?" Madeline didn't wait for Laura's reply. "The advance is fifty thousand dollars."

Laura had not been sitting down, but she did so now, perching on the edge of her bed. "But," she said, feeling dense, "Ray's dead."

"His work will live on, Laura. Isn't that thrilling? Aren't you thrilled?"

"I don't know what I am," she said. Her primary emotion was anger. Why the hell couldn't this have happened when Ray was alive?

"Something we didn't realize is that important legislation regarding the homeless is about to be introduced in Congress," Madeline said, "so that makes Ray's book timely. Lukens plans to push it into publication quickly to time its release to the legislation."

Laura could hardly speak. "It's just not fair," she said.

"I know it's not," Madeline said, real sympathy in her voice. "But Ray would have wanted this. All his work won't be in vain."

Laura's stomach was churning by the time she got off the phone, and tears burned her eyes. She could see Ray at the desk in his office, working on his beloved book until late into the night, revising and revising, trying to find the right combination of words to make a publisher see the value in his work. She could see the crestfallen look each time Madeline sent him a new letter of rejection.

She called Stuart.

"They're going to publish Ray's book," she said, explaining the situation to him. His reaction was the same as hers: joy tempered by anger that this had not happened sooner.

"I can barely tolerate the injustice of it," Laura said.

"I know." Stuart sighed. "But you know what, Laurie? Ray's gone. Nothing will bring him back. And life goes on. So, would we rather have Ray dead and his work dead along with him? Or would we rather have his work live on?"

Laura smiled and lay back on the bed. "That's a no-brainer," she said.

"Okay," Stuart said. "Then let's break out the champagne tonight, you there and me here, and we'll drink a toast to Ray."

"Okay." She shut her eyes, still tired, and still nettled by the situation.

"How's my little niece?" Stuart changed the subject. "I hope she's found her voice by now."

"I'm afraid not." Laura rolled onto her side. She could fall asleep in an instant. "Although I have her with a new therapist now who's given me some hope that she'll one day be a chatterbox again."

"I sure hope so. I miss hearing that cute voice on the phone." Stuart paused. "And how are you doing, Laurie?"

"Oh, I'm hanging in there." She heard the sigh in her voice.

"You sound tired."

She laughed. "Working two part-time jobs and doing

round-the-clock research was a snap compared to full-time motherhood," she said.

"Did you ever see that Sarah woman again?"

Laura had only spoken to Stuart a few times since Ray's death, but he'd asked this question each time.

"I saw her yesterday, actually."

"How come, hon?" Stuart asked. "Why are you bothering with her?"

"You know why. Because of my father, although I still don't know what the connection is."

"But do you really need that extra burden in your life right now?"

"You sound like Ray." He did, actually. Not only did Stuart look like Ray, but his voice had that same deep intonation.

"Well, maybe Ray was trying to protect you from overextending yourself. You have a way of doing that, you know. You just said you're tired."

"Not tired, really," she said. "Just stretched a bit. But I can afford one afternoon a week to go to Leesburg and check on Sarah. Talk to her and take her for a walk. Poor thing never gets out."

"Does she still have Alzheimer's?"

"Of course." Stuart was beginning to irk her. "That doesn't go away," she said. "It only gets worse."

"Must not be much you can talk to her about, then."

"She still remembers a lot from the past."

"Well, I hate to see you putting your limited time and energy into visiting her just because your dad laid a guilt trip on you."

Laura rolled onto her back, truly irritated now. "It's my life, Stu," she said, an edge to her voice. "I know you're upset about me seeing Sarah because it bothered Ray. But remember what you said. Ray's gone. And life goes on."

Stuart was quiet, and she regretted how harshly she'd spoken. She did not even completely believe her own words. Her guilt about Ray's death was still very much alive.

"All right," he said finally. "Sorry to hound you, Laurie. It's your choice how you spend your time."

Laura stared at the paneled ceiling. "Stuart...do you blame me for Ray's death?" Was Ray's suicide note still etched on Stuart's mind?

"Oh, no, hon," he said quickly. "Don't ever think that. I'm just worried about you, that's all."

"Well, I'm okay," she said. "So you can stop worrying."

They spoke a few minutes longer, the conversation filled with niceties to ease the tension. When Laura hung up, she remained on the bed, listening to Emma's footsteps in the hall. In a moment, Emma came into the room, bunny in her arms. She climbed onto the bed and snuggled next to Laura, and Laura put her arm around her, still frustrated by the conversation with Stuart. At least Emma wouldn't question her choices. She peered down at her daughter's face, at the unconditional love softening the little girl's features. Emma was watching her, the whites of her eyes as milky as pearls.

"What are you thinking, sweetie?" Laura asked her.

There was no answer, of course, and Laura settled for pulling her mystery child closer.

9

"I'm scared," Laura said as she took a seat in Heather's office after participating in a play session with the therapist and Emma. "It seems like the longer she goes without speaking, the easier it is for her to stay mute. I've wondered if I should pretend not to understand what she wants when she communicates with gestures. Should I make her speak before she gets what she wants?"

"That may be the way to go sometime in the future," Heather said, "but what she needs right now is support and reassurance that you'll be there for her, no matter what. You'll accept her and love her whether she speaks or not."

Heather wore her blond hair down today, and it rested, thick and silky, on her shoulders. She had on a sundress and sandals. Compared to her usual outfits, this looked like formal wear.

"They won't take her in kindergarten in the fall if she's not talking," Laura said. "I spoke with the principal."

"If she's not ready to start kindergarten, it won't be the end of the earth. Lots of kids don't start school right away. We can always find an appropriate school placement for her."

"I just..." Laura shut her eyes with a sigh. "She's always been so bright."

"She still is, Laura." Heather kicked off her sandals and lifted her legs onto the chair, covering them with the skirt of her sundress. "It was interesting having you in the session with us today," she said. "I wondered if you noticed how different Emma was with you there. She's very protective of you. Doesn't want you to know how bad she feels."

Laura reached for the box of tissues on Heather's desk. "I don't want her to have that burden," she said, blotting her eyes. "She's just a little girl."

"You've raised her to be sensitive and empathetic. That's not so bad."

Laura blew her nose. "Ray raised her to be that way, really," she said. "Remember, I told you how he taught her about the homeless."

"You and Ray raised her together," Heather said.

It seemed that Heather would not allow her to say anything positive about Ray without correcting her, but Laura opted to ignore her comment. "If she can't talk openly with me there, would it be better for me to stay out of your sessions with her?" she asked.

"For a while, anyway," Heather agreed. "You can watch from behind the mirror."

"Okay."

"The thing that still worries me more than anything is all the negative stuff about men," Heather said. "She makes this hostile face every time she plays with any of the male dolls."

"I noticed that," Laura said. Emma's disdain toward men had been impossible to ignore during the session.

"And I'm concerned those feelings have been there for a long time. From before Ray killed himself. They could have a powerful impact on the woman Emma grows up to be."

"She was playing at my neighbor's house the other day when her friend's father came home," Laura said. "He's a nice guy, but gruff, and Emma ran out of the house when he walked in.''

Heather didn't look surprised by that information. "One thing that's really obvious to me, although I know you may not be ready to admit to it, is that your husband and Emma did not have a good relationship. When I asked Emma to use the face drawings to describe her dad, she pointed to the yelling face and the angry face.'' Heather leaned toward Laura, her brown eyes earnest. "In Emma's mind, men yell,'' she said. "And men kill themselves.''

"So what can we do?'' Laura felt helpless.

"Well, play therapy can go only so far.'' Heather sat back in her seat again. "I have a question for you,'' she said. "Something I've been wondering about.''

"Yes?''

"Emma's birth father. What can you tell me about him?''

Laura laughed. "Essentially nothing. I met him one time, at a party, and that was it. Believe me, I'd never done anything like that before. I was upset that night, and—''

"That doesn't matter.'' Heather dismissed her excuses with a wave of her hand. "But I wonder if there's a chance he might like to know he has a daughter.''

"Oh, no.'' It was Laura's turn to interrupt. The idea of tracking down Dylan Geer and announcing to him that he had a daughter was unthinkable. "I'm telling you, he probably wouldn't even remember me. And I don't know where he lives. Or even what he does for a living. And—'' she laughed again "—I don't want Emma to have a father who'd sleep with someone the first night he meets them. She's already stuck with a mother depraved enough to do that.''

Heather laughed herself. "All right,'' she said. "But I'd still like you to think about it. I wouldn't want him involved, either, unless he's good father material and willing to commit to her. But he just might be someone who could correct her notion that all men are snarly beasts. You never know. It might be worth a shot.''

Laura had designed the skylight room at the lake house herself. It was a medium-size, square room on the second story, its ceiling formed by large, Plexiglas panels. The floor was completely covered in huge pillows, except for one corner where she had her desk and computer. Lying on the pillows, looking up, a person could almost pretend they were outside. Laura's telescope stood in one corner of the room, ready to be wheeled onto the wide deck that ran around all four sides of the second story, giving Laura the ability to search nearly any part of the sky.

She had fallen asleep in this room on many nights, and tonight would probably be one of them. She was dressed in her summer pajamas and nestled on top of one of the soft pillows, staring up at the constellation Hercules. And thinking. She'd been doing a great deal of thinking since her appointment with Heather Davison that afternoon.

Dylan Geer. The thought of him embarrassed and enticed her at the same time. Embarrassed her because of the way she'd behaved that night long ago. Enticed her because, well, Dylan Geer had been one irresistible man. Sleeping with him had been crazy and completely out of character for her. She had never been the sort of woman who melted at the sight of a good-looking guy. She'd grown up with a father whose idea of a great time was an afternoon in the science section of the library, and that had become *her* great time, as well. In high school, other girls thought she was strange. She *was* strange. She was the president of the astronomy club, the only girl in the science and chess clubs, and while she had plenty of male friends, few of them saw her as anything other than that—a friend.

Even in high school, career plans had been her primary focus. Her father would spend evenings looking through college catalogs with her, having her make lists of her strengths and skills. Back then, she'd doubted she would ever get married. There would not be enough room in her life for a husband and children as well as the sort of career she wanted. That had been an accurate assessment; she had not given enough of herself to Ray and Emma.

She had sex for the first time in college, with a male friend who wanted to show her what she was missing. She enjoyed the experience, especially the sense of closeness to someone she cared for, but she rarely had those feelings other girls talked about that left them unable to say "no" when an attractive guy came onto them.

That was, until six years ago when she literally stumbled into Dylan Geer at a party.

The party had been given by Rhonda Giddings, a woman who had then worked with Laura at the Smithsonian's Air and Space Museum. Rhonda was little more than an acquaintance, but she'd invited the museum staff to the housewarming for her new mansion in Potomac.

It was beginning to snow when Laura arrived at Rhonda's spectacular home, and she was in a rotten mood. Just that day, she'd been turned down for a research grant she'd worked hard to obtain. Angry and frustrated, she drank. An infrequent drinker, she was tipsy almost instantly, and as she walked from the living room to the kitchen, she wove directly into the arms of a man who took her breath away. She knew in that instant what other women were talking about. She knew, too, that she would sleep with him.

Staring up at the stars from the oversize pillow in the

skylight room, Laura allowed herself to remember him. The penetrating blue eyes. The dark hair. The amused smile. They must have talked before they ended up in one of the upstairs bedrooms, but she couldn't remember a word that passed between them. She couldn't recall what he did for a living, or where he lived, or how he knew Rhonda. What she did remember was her excitement—the visceral thrill of kissing him, of lying naked with him in the four-poster bed, while snow fell furiously outside the bedroom window. She remembered every touch, every movement of his body. It was possible, though, that she had embellished those memories over the years, because each time she and Ray made love, she drew upon them to become aroused. What she'd had with Dylan had only been sex, though. What she'd had with Ray was a love rooted in friendship.

After that night, she'd wondered if she'd always had that desire but had kept it tightly under wraps to avoid stealing energy from her work. It had taken the alcohol to free her. Maybe she'd only been fooling herself into thinking she did not have those feelings, just as she'd fooled herself into thinking she didn't care about having children. When she learned she'd gotten pregnant that night, she felt sudden, pure, unadulterated joy—tempered by the awareness that her career and motherhood would not be an easy mix. Her father was quick to point that out to her, suggesting she strongly consider an abortion. It was the only time in her entire life she defied him.

Her thoughts were interrupted by crying from Emma's room down the hall. She looked at her watch as she rose from the pillow. Eleven-fifteen. Poor baby.

Emma was standing in the hallway outside her room, barefoot in her shorty pajamas and shivering despite the warmth of the night.

"What is it, honey?" Laura asked her.

Emma sucked harder on her thumb in response to the question. Her cheeks were red and tear-streaked.

Laura crouched next to her. "Tell me what it is, sweetheart. Did something frighten you?"

Emma put her head on her mother's shoulder, her small body sighing with the aftermath of her tears. It broke Laura's heart that Emma could not give words to whatever had frightened her.

She looked over Emma's head to the child's dark bedroom. "Your night-light went out. Is that it? You woke up and it was dark?"

Emma nodded against her shoulder.

Laura stood up. "I'll put another bulb in the fairy light and then you can go back to bed."

In Emma's room, Laura discovered that her daughter's bed was wet, again. She changed the sheets and gave her dry pajamas to put on, then gave up on the idea of getting her back to sleep in her room.

"Do you want to watch the stars with me in the skylight room?" she asked.

Emma nodded.

Laura held her hand as they walked down the hall. After Ray's death, Emma had tried to climb into Laura's bed on a nearly nightly basis. It had been hard to turn her away; Laura would have loved the human touch as much as Emma. But she knew it would only hurt Emma more in the long run. The skylight room, however, was a different story.

They snuggled together among the pillows.

"Can you find Hercules?" Laura asked.

Emma pointed toward the constellation.

"And how about Cygnus?"

Emma pointed.

"And what was Cygnus?" Laura waited for an answer

82 *Diane Chamberlain*

she didn't expect to come. "Cygnus was a swan," she said, answering the question herself. "Do you remember that?"

Emma did not even bother to nod. She closed her eyes and rested her head on Laura's shoulder, and Laura was suddenly reminded of all the nights she'd watched the sky with her father. He would quiz her on what she saw. Where was Andromeda? Triangulum? What was the brightest star in Perseus? She'd felt tension during those nighttime quizzes, as though her father's love for her was linked to her correct answers. She wasn't doing that to Emma, was she? She ran her hand over Emma's satiny hair. Her daughter was every bit as alone in the world as she had been, with only one nerdy, head-in-the-clouds parent. And on top of that, she'd had a poor relationship with the man she'd thought of as her father.

Men yell. Men kill themselves.

Heather was right. Laura owed it to Emma to see if Dylan Geer might be worthy of playing a part in her life.

10

Dylan triggered the blast valve to maintain the balloon's altitude. They were off course. Not terribly so, but enough that his usual landing sites were out of the question.

"I've never seen such a beautiful sunset," the woman said to her husband. The couple was flying with him to celebrate their twenty-fifth wedding anniversary, and the woman had lost her nervousness sometime during the last hour and was no longer clinging to the leather rim of the wicker basket. Soon, though, Dylan would have to ask her to hang on again.

"Look over there," the husband said. He pointed toward the Blue Ridge Mountains, where the pink of the sunset gave way to blue-violet as darkness approached.

They're oblivious to the problem, Dylan thought, even though they'd heard him radio the crew that the wind had picked up and the balloon was flying north of the landing site. Just as well. Let them enjoy the end of their trip.

He was running out of daylight, and they needed to land soon. There was a cornfield not far ahead of them, but landing there would be messy. The crew would have to get permission from the farmer, the process of landing would destroy some of the corn, and his passengers would have to fight their way through the cornstalks to reach the crew's vehicles. He remembered the woman saying something about arthritis in her knees. No, the cornfield wouldn't do.

He spoke into the aircraft radio. "Come in, Alex."

"Yo, balloon." Alex's voice was clear, the only sound other than the occasional roar of the flame above their heads.

"I'm going to have to aim for the median strip again," Dylan said. He saw the couple turn away from the sunset to look at him, then at each other. He smiled at them and winked, but he wasn't sure they could see his expression of reassurance in the fading light.

"Cool," Alex said. "About the same spot as last time?" He'd had to land on the median strip a month or so ago.

"Right. Think you guys can get there in time to assist?"

"If we fly, man. Don't worry, we'll be there."

"Okay, then," Dylan said. "See you on the ground."

He slipped the radio onto his belt and checked the altimeter.

"Is there a problem?" the man asked.

"Very minor," Dylan said. "Remember before we boarded I explained that an unexpected gust of wind might blow us off course?"

They nodded. He had their complete attention, the sunset forgotten.

"That's what happened. So, we missed our usual landing site. I'm going to land on the median strip of one of the main roads." He intentionally avoided saying *try* to land. They didn't need to hear uncertainty in his voice.

"You're *what?*" the woman said. "What about the traffic?"

"It won't be a problem," Dylan said. "You'll see." His voice was so calm that they seemed to relax a bit. "Here's what we're going to do," he continued. "See that line of trees up ahead?"

The tops of the trees glowed a surreal pink from the sunset. The couple nodded.

"I'm going to brush over the tops of them with the basket," Dylan said. "That'll slow us down a bit. On the other side of the trees is the highway and the median strip. Do you remember what I told you about a high-wind landing?"

"Face the direction we're landing in," said the man.

"Right," Dylan said. "And bend your knees and hold on to the rope handles. And we're going to be fine."

The woman looked at him with doubt in her eyes.

"Honest," he said.

He let some air out of the balloon as they approached the trees, enough to allow the basket to coast across the treetops. Twigs snapped and leaves brushed against the wicker. He loved the sound, but the woman gripped the rope handle tighter.

"You doing okay?" he asked the couple.

"Doesn't matter how we're doing," the man said. "You're the one we're worried about."

Dylan laughed. He lowered the balloon on the other side of the trees, flying above the two lanes of traffic. They were close enough to the cars that, had it been lighter, the surprised looks on the faces of the drivers would have been visible.

The crew had not made it in time, but he hadn't expected them to.

"Bend your knees," he said to his passengers. "And hold on."

Down they went, the balloon touching the ground and being carried only a few feet across the grass by the wind before stopping. Good landing, given the circumstances. His jelly-kneed passengers hugged each other, laughing in apparent relief.

A few cars stopped along the median strip, their drivers and passengers getting out for a closer look. Dylan spotted

Alex's truck as it pulled in behind the line of cars. Brian's van was right behind him.

"Here come our rescuers," he said to the couple.

Once on the median strip, Brian grabbed the drop line, and Alex produced the stepladder to allow the couple to disembark.

"Don't know what you need us for," Brian said, acknowledging Dylan's safe solo landing.

"I wonder about that myself sometimes," Dylan joked as he helped his passengers from the basket.

Once safely out of the basket, they celebrated the successful flight with the requisite champagne toast. The passers-by kept a respectful distance from them, and Dylan knew that some of them would call him for their own balloon rides over the next few days.

The couple got into Brian's van for the ride back to Dylan's barn, where their own car was parked.

Dylan and Alex dismantled the balloon in the near darkness, Dylan glancing at his watch from time to time. He had a date tonight. It was not with Bethany, he was sure of that, but damned if he could remember exactly who it *was* with.

No big deal, he thought as he helped Alex load the basket into the truck. He would know when she showed up at his door.

11

Even though Rhonda Giddings no longer worked at the Air and Space Museum, Laura was able to track her down at her new job.

"How nice to hear from you," Rhonda said. "How've you been?"

"Fine," Laura lied, not wanting to get into all that had changed in her life since she'd last seen Rhonda. "I was wondering if—"

"When does the best viewing start for the latest Comet Brandon?" Rhonda asked. "I hear it's going to be a good one."

"I hope so," Laura said. "It should peak next summer."

"Fantastic."

"I'm calling for a favor, Rhonda," Laura said. "I'm trying to get in touch with someone I met at a party at your house quite a while ago. Six years ago, actually."

"Wow," Rhonda laughed. "I have to warn you, my memory isn't what it once was. Who are we talking about?"

"Dylan Geer." Laura cringed as she said the name. She wondered how many people had been aware that she and Dylan had disappeared upstairs together the night of the party.

"Dylan Geer! Why would you...oh, you must want a balloon ride, huh?"

"A balloon ride?"

"That's not it?"

"No, it's something else. Something personal. Sorry."

"No problem. I don't think I have a private number for him, but I do have his balloon business number. Hang on. Let me get my address book out of my purse."

Laura could hear her rummaging through her purse, then flipping through the pages of the book.

"I took my husband up for his birthday last year," Rhonda said.

"So, he operates a hot air balloon business?" Laura asked. Not exactly what she'd imagined for Emma's father, but interesting nonetheless.

"Yes. He totally changed after he left the airlines, you know."

Laura was getting frustrated trying to sort the pieces of the puzzle together. "I don't know much about him," she said. "I didn't know he worked for the airlines."

"I don't know what happened, but he quit quite a while ago, moved out to the wine country, started the balloon thing, and became something of a playboy, from what I've heard."

Great. This did not sound promising.

"Here's his number," Rhonda said.

Laura wrote down the number, then quickly got off the phone.

"Hot Air Unlimited." It was a male voice, pleasant and businesslike, and if she hadn't been so nervous, she would have laughed at the company's name.

"I'm trying to reach Dylan Geer," she said.

"Speaking."

"Dylan, my name is Laura Brandon. We met at a party at Rhonda Giddings's house about six years ago."

There was silence on Dylan's end of the line. "Sorry," he said after a minute. "I don't remember."

This wasn't going to be easy. "Well, this is a bit awkward, and I'm sorry to dump it on you out of the blue." She spoke rapidly, her nerves propelling her. "It was when Rhonda moved into that new house in Potomac. There was a terrific snowstorm. I met you there and we...well, we slept together that night. And the reason I'm calling is to let you know that I had a daughter...I conceived a child that night. Emma. That's her name. And I didn't ever plan to get in touch with you about it, because I got married shortly after that night, but my husband died recently, and Emma was traumatized by his death and now doesn't speak, and her therapist suggested I see if—"

"Whoa, whoa, whoa," Dylan interrupted her. "Slow down. Start at the beginning. You're saying we...slept together at Rhonda's?"

"Yes. Six years ago. There was a snowstorm. We nearly got snowed in there."

"I'm sorry. I don't remember this at all. What's your name again?"

"Laura Brandon." She realized as she said her name that she might not have told it to him that night. "I'm about five-six. Light brown hair. Long."

"Are you sure you have the right guy?"

"Yes. I'm sure."

"So, you think your daughter's mine?"

"I'm sure she's yours. There were no other possibilities."

"Couldn't she have been your husband's?"

"I wasn't married then." It bothered her that he would think she'd sleep with him when she was married. Of course, what she'd done hadn't been all that honorable, either. "I wasn't seeing anyone."

"But you said you had a husband—"

"I got married *after* that night. A friend married me when I learned I was pregnant. But he died a few months ago, and—"

"So now you need a new father for your daughter, and I'm the likely candidate?"

She didn't like his tone. She felt like hanging up on him, but forged ahead. "Emma's therapist suggested I see if her father—if *you*—might want to be involved with her. She thought it would help Emma to have a caring male figure in her life."

"You know, this is crazy." He laughed. "I don't know who you are. You're calling me out of the blue. You want me to be a caring male figure for a kid I know nothing about."

"She's yours."

"I don't think so. I have no recollection of even meeting you, much less sleeping with you."

"Could we at least meet somewhere? Could we talk in person?"

She heard him sigh. "I don't see the point," he said. "I'm sorry if you're having trouble with your daughter, but I don't see how I can help. And I have a bunch of calls I need to return, so—"

"Maybe you can't help," she said, "but I'd at least like to—"

"There's my other line," Dylan said. "I'm sorry... Laura, is it? Good luck."

With that he was gone. Laura held the receiver to her ear for a few more seconds before hanging up. She shouldn't have done this by phone. If she'd gone to see him in person he might have recognized her. He wouldn't have been able to escape from her and the truth quite so easily. But he sounded like a bit of a jerk. Maybe Emma was better off without him.

She and Emma went grocery shopping after dinner that evening. Before Ray's death, Laura had to keep a constant eye on her daughter in the store because Emma would wander off, pick up unneeded products, talk to strangers. Now Emma clung to Laura or the shopping cart. She tried to climb into the basket, although she was far too big and Laura would not allow it. Strangers would still try to talk to her, but Emma would stick her thumb in her mouth and avert her eyes.

"Let's get some peaches, honey," Laura said, pushing the cart toward the produce section.

Well, how would she feel in Dylan's shoes? she wondered as she watched Emma select the peaches. How would she feel if she were a guy and some stranger called her up, out of the blue, six years after the fact, to tell her she'd fathered a baby? She'd be worried about a paternity suit, that's what. She'd guess the woman had fallen on hard times and needed financial support for her child.

She paid careful attention to Emma's behavior in the store, watching how the little girl avoided the few male shoppers, slipping into the space between Laura and the shelves each time a man walked toward them. Had she always done that? The move was subtle enough that Laura was not really sure.

Men yell. Men kill themselves.

When she got home from the grocery store, Laura looked up the number to Dylan's balloon business again. Without stopping to think through what she was doing, she dialed the number and was relieved to reach a recording. Raising her voice an octave, she gave her name as Susan Lane, the first name that flew into her mind, and said she wanted to schedule a balloon ride to celebrate her fortieth birthday. When she hung up, she looked at herself in her bedroom mirror, wondering how Laura Brandon could have done such a wacky thing.

12

It was still dark when Laura reached the wine country. Dylan had told her to be at his house by 5:00 a.m. so she'd have a good view of the sunrise from the air.

"At your house?" she'd asked, surprised.

"I keep the equipment in a barn on my property," he'd explained. "I have a field I can use for takeoff when the wind is right."

The drive was about half an hour from Lake Ashton, through country that would be beautiful in daylight. Leaving Emma practically in the middle of the night had posed a problem. Laura solved it by bringing Shelley, Emma's teen-age baby-sitter from their old Leesburg neighborhood, out to the lake to stay over the night before. Shelley would be there to take care of Emma when she woke up this morning.

Pulling to the side of the road, she turned on the car's overhead light to look at the printed directions Dylan had sent her. His street was just around the next bend. She turned onto it and drove through woods so thick and deep that they would have been dark even in the daytime. Then she saw the mailbox described in the directions. It was an ordinary wooden mailbox, but sailing from the top of it, lit up by a small, hidden spotlight, was a wooden replica of a colorful hot air balloon.

The driveway curved through the woods for another half

mile before a house slipped into view from the darkness. Lighting along the ground illuminated this part of the driveway, and the windows of the house were aglow. She parked next to a van in front of the garage and got out. From somewhere to her right, she heard voices, and in the dusky light, she could make out a barn at the edge of a field. A couple of people stood in the center of the field, setting up the balloon, she supposed. She felt the first twinge of anticipation about the balloon ride itself. Until now, she'd had far bigger things than the ride on her mind.

The house was actually a log cabin, she saw as she approached. Small and relatively new. She climbed the porch steps, and Dylan came out the front door before she had a chance to knock.

"Susan?" he asked.

Laura nearly lost her voice. In the porch light, his resemblance to Emma was remarkable. Those blue eyes and the dark hair. Even his quick smile was Emma's. At least, it was the smile Emma used to have.

"Yes." She held out her hand, waiting for him to remember her, but he shook her hand without a hint of recognition. She must have made quite an impact on him that night. Or perhaps she'd changed a great deal in the last six years. In the light from the house, she could see that Dylan now had a little gray at his temples and his hairline was beginning to recede. He was wearing a short-sleeved jumpsuit, either blue or gray, with a hot air balloon design above the breast pocket.

"The crew's setting up the balloon in the field out back," he said. "Come watch."

They walked together toward the field. "Do you fly only in the morning and evening?" Laura asked, making conversation in an attempt to calm her nerves.

"Uh-huh. Weather conditions are best then."

"What if it's raining?"

"Rain's a problem. Wind is even worse. I end up canceling about forty percent of the scheduled flights."

"Guess I lucked out." The morning was balmy, the sky clear. "What do you do during the rest of the day?"

"Sleep." He laughed. "I'm up at four nearly every morning."

They'd reached the center of the field, where a huge fan blew air into the mouth of the balloon. The balloon lay on its side, and she could see the billowing of the fabric, although she could not quite make out its colors. A truck stood nearby, and two men worked near its rear bumper.

"Hey, Alex. Brian," Dylan said. "This is Susan."

The men looked up from their work. They seemed very young, at least in the dim light. One of them had long hair tied back in a ponytail. The other wore a heavy beard. Both wore gloves.

"How's it going, Susan?" one of them asked.

"Okay," she answered. "Hope you guys know what you're doing."

"Me, too," Dylan said. "Today's their first day working for me."

Laura cringed.

"Just joking," Dylan said, touching her arm. "They've been working with me a couple of years."

"Oh. Good."

He was suddenly all business as he told her where she should stand in the balloon, what sort of emergencies might arise and what she should do in each case. She tried to listen carefully, nodding in the appropriate places, but she was having a great deal of trouble concentrating. At any moment, she expected him to recognize her.

"Ready," one of the men said.

"Excuse me," Dylan said, leaving her side to walk toward the balloon. He lit the burners at the top of the basket, sending a roaring blue-and-red flame into the mouth of the balloon. Slowly, the fabric of the balloon swayed and billowed, rising into the air, like a huge animal coming to life. She could see now that the balloon had a swirling striped pattern, and it was immense.

Once the balloon had inflated above him, Dylan hoisted himself into the basket.

Laura listened as the three men ran through a preflight checklist, then the man with the beard set a stepladder next to the basket.

"Here you go," he said, reaching an arm toward her. "Hop in."

He held her hand as she climbed the stepladder, and Dylan took her other hand from inside the basket as she stepped over the rim.

"Step on the propane tank," he said. "That's it."

She stepped onto the tank, then onto the floor of the basket, moving to one of the corners as he'd instructed her to do. At least she remembered that much of what he'd told her.

"All set?" Dylan asked.

She nodded.

"Let her go!" he called to his crew.

The bearded member of the crew untied a line from the axle of the truck, then helped Dylan store it on the bottom of the basket. Dylan sent two short blasts of flame into the balloon, the sound nearly deafening. The man with the ponytail, who'd been holding on to the rim of the basket, let go, and the balloon began to rise.

The ascent was slower, gentler than she had anticipated, taking her breath away in small increments. In the east, the sky was beginning to color.

"This is beautiful," she said, thinking that he must hear that word dozens of times in a day's work.

They began to drift above the treetops, but there was no sense of motion whatsoever inside the basket. And, except for the occasional roar of the flame, the world was silent.

"Couldn't find anyone gutsy enough to come with you for your birthday, huh?" Dylan asked.

"Actually, I wanted to do this alone."

"I can appreciate that," he said. "There's nothing like being up here alone. I'm afraid you're stuck with me, though. I'll try not to intrude."

Tearing herself away from the sunrise, she faced him. The golden light made the blue of his eyes translucent. She'd seen the same phenomenon in her daughter's face and remembered why she was here. She took a deep breath. "Dylan," she said, "I've lied to you."

He raised his eyebrows. "About?"

"My name's not Susan..." She couldn't even remember the last name she'd given him. "I'm Laura Brandon."

He didn't seem to register the name.

"I called you last week," she said. "About my daughter."

His smile was gone in an instant, his eyes narrowed to slits. "I don't believe this," he said. "What the hell is your game?"

This had been a terrible idea. How else could she have expected him to react except with anger?

"I knew you didn't believe me on the phone the other day," she said, "but if you'll just take a look at Emma's picture, you'll know I'm telling the truth." She extracted the picture from her shirt pocket, her hand trembling, and tried to hand it to him. He wouldn't take it. "You'll know she's yours if you'd just look at her for two seconds," she pleaded.

"You're crazy," he said. "They should lock you up."

"I know." She was still holding the picture toward him. "This is the most bizarre thing I've ever done. But I'm sane, I swear it, and—"

"I've never seen you before in my life," he said. "And frankly, I hope never to see you again." He took the radio from his belt.

"Come in, Alex." He spoke into the radio, then to her he said, "You thought you'd have me captive up here and I'd have to listen to you, huh? Well, sorry, but you're wrong."

"Yo, balloon." Alex's voice crackled on the radio.

"We're coming down," Dylan said.

"Mechanical problem?" Alex asked.

"Nothing that simple," Dylan answered, his voice tight. "I can make Del Russo's orchard in a few minutes."

"We'll be there," Alex said.

"I'm sorry," she said when he'd hung the radio on his belt again. "This was a mistake."

"Don't talk to me, all right? I'm working."

She decided it was best to say no more as they descended. Facing the direction the balloon was drifting, she kept her eyes riveted on the trees below. They floated over them, the bottom of the basket brushing the leaves. Suddenly, the trees fell away and an orchard appeared below them, grapevines stretching into the distance in neat rows.

Two men were running toward the spot where the balloon appeared to be headed, and it was a minute before she realized they were Alex and Brian. The balloon was aimed directly at a row of grapevines, and she braced herself for the impact. But Dylan tugged on a line at the side of the basket, and the balloon instantly dropped to the ground, landing with a barely perceptible thump, neatly, tightly, between two rows of vines. Within seconds, the balloon was transformed into a pile of colorful rags strewn over the orchard.

"Help her out," Dylan said to the men, his voice gruff.

The man with the ponytail produced the stepladder again, and she climbed out of the basket, her legs like jelly.

"Take her back to the house for her car, Brian," Dylan ordered without looking at any of them.

Laura caught the glance that passed between Alex and Brian as they tried to figure out what had caused their boss's sudden sour mood.

"Yessir." The young man with the beard turned to her. "Let's go."

She followed him through the orchard, the sunrise coloring the vines a creamy yellow.

"Didn't feel too good up there?" Brian asked as they neared his van.

She nodded. It was not a lie.

He opened the van door for her, and she got in and fastened the seat belt.

"Don't feel bad," he said as he drove away from the orchard. "It happens sometimes. My girlfriend got *really* sick. I'll never get her up again."

"Thanks," she said, then fell quiet again. She would let him think her silence was due to illness rather than embarrassment and regret.

He drove her back to Dylan's log cabin, and she thanked him and got into her car. She drove down the driveway a short distance, far enough so that Brian would not see her, and stopped the car. Leaning her head against the seat back, she shut her eyes and tried to still the shivering in her legs. What an imbecile she'd been! He'd been quite a jerk himself, but she could hardly blame him. He must have thought he was trapped up there with a loon.

After a few minutes, she put the car in gear again and

started slowly down the driveway. When she reached the mailbox topped with the wooden hot air balloon, she stopped again. She pulled Emma's photograph from her shirt pocket, turned it over and jotted her number on the back. Then she got out of the car, walked over to the mailbox and slipped the picture inside.

13

Dylan was turning the salmon steaks in the marinade when he heard the front door open. He peered from his kitchen into the living room.

"Hey!" He smiled at Bethany. "Good to see you, Beth."

"Good to see you, too." Bethany walked into the galley kitchen, her arms wrapped around a paper grocery bag, and gave him a kiss.

"Can't hug you," Dylan said. "Got marinade on my hands."

"Well, I brought dessert." She pulled the cartons of Ben & Jerry's from the grocery bag, and Dylan smiled. Bethany knew his weakness.

"I also picked up your mail for you, since you obviously haven't made it to the end of your driveway today." She put the stack of envelopes and junk mail on his counter.

"Thanks." He washed his hands at the sink, then gave her a proper kiss.

"So, what's this?" Bethany picked up the photograph lying on the pile of mail.

Dylan looked at the picture just long enough to feel the return of his anger from that morning.

"Where was that?" he asked. "In the mailbox?"

"Uh-huh. Just lying loose. Who is she?"

"I don't have a clue." He tossed the picture upside down

on the stack of mail, noticing that Laura Brandon had written a phone number on the back.

Bethany looked as though she didn't believe him, but she didn't press him. He could count on her for that.

Of the women he'd gone out with over the past few years, Bethany was his favorite. She was beautiful. Besides running her own photography business, she modeled part-time, and he loved finding her face and body in the pages of *Washingtonian* magazine. Her shiny, short hair was as black as a raven's wing and she wore a perpetual tan. More important than her looks, though, was the fact that she understood him better than anyone else he'd dated. She understood that he didn't want to be tied down; he was always honest with her about that. She understood that he needed to see other women, and she dated other men. Still, Dylan feared that Bethany's carefree facade masked her real yearnings. She was only thirty-one. He knew she wanted marriage and a family, while he wanted neither. She wanted to be loved, while he knew his feelings for her would never move beyond affection. He was brutal in his honesty about that, and while she accepted his words on the surface, he worried that she expected him to change. He'd told her many times that if marriage and commitment were what she was after, she had the wrong guy.

One concession he'd made to her was that she be his only lover. She could not have a physical relationship with more than one man at a time, she'd said, and she needed to know the same was true for him. It *was* true, not because of the emotional complications more than one lover could engender, but because of the physical risk. He was enigmatic that way. He wanted to live from day to day, without a care for the future, but damned if he was going to get AIDS or something else in the process. He and Bethany had been tested. They were monogamous—sexually, anyway—and he took comfort in that.

Bethany made the salad and microwaved the potatoes while he grilled the fish on the deck. They ate at his picnic table under the thick canopy of trees, burning citronella candles to keep the bugs away.

It had been two weeks since Dylan had seen Bethany, and she looked great. He could barely take his eyes off her while they ate, and when dinner was over, he left the dishes in the sink and ushered her into his bedroom. They made love, but he sensed something was wrong. She'd been quiet at dinner, quieter still now that they'd made love. And although he was sorely tempted to simply fall asleep, he thought he'd better ask.

He propped his head up with his pillow so he could see the aquarium on the wall opposite his bed. He'd built the huge tank into the wall between the bedroom and the living room so he could see the fish from either room. Right now, the tank diffused the light from the living room, sending shimmering blue waves across the ceiling of the bedroom.

He put his arm around Bethany. "Is something bothering you?" he asked.

She nestled closer to him. "No. Not really."

"Don't believe you."

She drew in a long breath, and he braced himself for whatever was coming.

"Well," she said, "I feel a little spooked by that picture in your mailbox."

"Spooked? Why?"

"I just don't understand why it was there. Who put it there?"

He sighed. One of the angelfish darted toward the surface of the tank, then down to the bottom, where it swam in and out of the ceramic castle. "This woman made an appointment to go up in the balloon today," he said. "Alone. When she got me up there with no place to hide, she told me I'm her daughter's father. I didn't even recognize her—the woman. Not her face or her name. And I was royally pissed off. Took her back down after only ten minutes in the air. She must have stuck the picture in my mailbox on her way out."

"So..." Bethany said.

"So?"

"Could it be true?"

"I don't know what her scheme is. Her daughter's five, so it would have been six years ago. You'd think I'd at least remember something about her, wouldn't you? And you know how obsessive I am about birth control."

Bethany was quiet for a minute. "That was your bad time, though."

He hadn't wanted to think about it, but she was right. It was possible he might have fathered a child back then. He might have fathered any number of children. And although he liked to think of himself as cautious, he'd been drinking a lot in those days. Anything was possible.

"Yes," he admitted. "That was my bad time."

"So, maybe she's yours."

"And what am I supposed to do about it even if she is? The woman says she's not after money, which is good since I have none to give her. But I have even less to offer on the fatherhood level."

Bethany stroked his chest. "You *think* you have nothing to offer, but that's not true. Sometimes I wish..." Her voice trailed off.

"Wish what?"

"You'd make a good father, Dylan. You're fun. You're a kind and caring and honest person."

He remembered Laura Brandon's use of the word *caring*. Her daughter needed a caring male figure in her life.

"I'm not terrific at commitment," he said, "in case you haven't noticed."

"Maybe someday you will be."

"Bethany...I worry you've got plans for me that will never materialize."

"Yeah. I worry I do, too."

He touched her cheek. "I've been as honest as I can be with you."

"I know." Her voice was thick.

He wrapped both arms around her and held her close, knowing the gesture would have to suffice. There was nothing more he could offer her.

14

A corner of the black movie projector cutout was coming loose from Sarah Tolley's apartment door, and Laura pressed it back into place before ringing the bell. She could hear the television set blaring, and it was a moment before Sarah opened the door.

"Hi." Laura smiled.

Sarah smiled as well, although Laura knew from the blank look in her eyes that on this, Laura's third visit, Sarah was still not certain who she was.

"Is today the walk day?" Sarah asked.

"Yes," Laura said, pleased Sarah was able to make that connection. "I'm Laura, do you remember? I took you for a walk last week, and thought I'd see if you wanted to go for another one." Maybe she should try to come on the same day each week so Sarah would have something to look forward to.

"Yes, very much." Sarah stepped back to let Laura into the living room. "I remember you," she said. "You had a picture of a man."

"My father. Right. And I have some very old pictures of him with me, in case you might be able to recognize him from long ago."

Sarah walked over to the sofa to turn off the TV with the remote, then returned to Laura's side. She took the pictures from Laura's hand, holding them in the light, squinting and frowning and shaking her head. Her frustration at not being able to place the man in the photographs was obvious, and Laura wished she hadn't brought them.

"It doesn't matter," she said, slipping the pictures back into her purse. She noticed that Sarah's skirt was on inside out. "Let's fix your skirt," she said, "and then we can go for our walk."

"My skirt?" Sarah looked down at the pale fabric. "Oh, is it wrong side out?"

"Yes. Can I help you with it?"

Sarah struggled with the zipper, and Laura lowered it for her, wondering how Sarah had ever gotten the skirt on this way in the first place. She slipped the skirt down over Sarah's narrow hips and lacy white slip, and up again, right side out this time.

"There," she said, "and I see you've got good walking shoes on today, so we're all set."

"I've been putting these shoes on every day in case the girl comes…you come to take me out," Sarah said, and Laura's heart tightened in her chest. Sarah had been waiting for her. She should have come sooner.

Outside the retirement home, they began strolling down the sidewalk.

"Where is your family?" Sarah asked, surprising Laura with a question about herself.

"Well, my husband died," Laura said.

"Oh. Mine did, too."

"The man in the photograph in your apartment?"

"Yes. At least I *think* he died."

Laura was jarred by Sarah's inability to remember such a crucial fact.

"I have a little daughter, though," Laura said. "Her name is Emma."

"Emma. How old is she?"

"She's five."

"She must miss her daddy."

"Yes, actually, she does." There was a moment of silence while Laura pondered the lucidity of Sarah's comment. "My husband, who died, was not her real father," she said, wondering if Sarah would be able to follow her. "Her real father doesn't know he's her father. I've been trying to talk to him to see if he might want to be involved with her." She shook her head with a laugh. "It's pretty complicated." The explanation made little sense even to her. She imagined she'd lost Sarah sometime during the first sentence.

"So, what does he say?" Sarah asked. "The real father?"

"Well, I spoke to him on the phone and he wasn't interested in meeting her. So then, yesterday, I went up in a hot air balloon with...this is confusing."

"You went up in one of those balloons?" Sarah looked at the sky as though she might see a hot air balloon floating above them.

"Yes. He owns...he gives people rides in a hot air balloon. So, since he didn't want to talk to me, I pretended to be someone else and made a reservation to go up in his balloon with him. When I was up in the air with him, I told him who I was and tried to show him a picture of his daughter—Emma—but he was angry and landed the balloon and that was the end of that."

"Shame on you," Sarah said.

"Shame on me?" Laura asked, surprised.

"Yes. You tricked him. You weren't honest with him. About something as important as his child."

Laura actually flinched at the reprimand. "I didn't know what else to do. Believe me, I wish I could take back that balloon ride."

"Well, now you'll apologize to him, won't you?"

"I figure I'd better just forget about him." She was beginning to think Sarah was more lucid than she was herself. But then the older woman stopped walking and looked around her.

"Are we on a ship or land?" she asked. "Sometimes I just can't remember."

"We're on land," Laura said, putting her hand gently on the older woman's back. "See? See the trees?"

"Oh, yes." Sarah looked at the sky again. "The first time I ever saw one of those hot air balloons, I was on a train," she said.

"On a train?"

"Yes," she said. "I was a stranger on a train."

Sarah, 1955

"Look!" The little boy pressed his face against the train window, pointing toward something in the distance. The blond woman sitting with him followed his gaze.

"Oh, yes!" she said. "A hot air balloon. Why, there are two of them!"

Sarah sat across the aisle from the little boy and the woman she supposed was his mother, and could not help but overhear their excited conversation. Leaning forward in her own seat, she looked past them out the window. In the distance, she could see the two balloons, one yellow, the other blue, floating against the sunset. The sight nearly took her breath away.

"There are three, actually," said a man sitting a few rows behind the woman and boy.

Sarah couldn't resist changing seats now, moving across the aisle to give herself a better view. She took the empty seat in front of the man.

There were only the four of them in this car: the woman and boy, the gentleman who had spotted the third balloon, and herself. The gentleman had walked past her when he boarded the train in Philadelphia, and she couldn't help but notice him because he bore a striking resemblance to Jimmy Stewart. He was in his mid-twenties, tall and lanky, kind-faced, and just shy of handsome. Sarah was on her way home to Washington after visiting family in Bayonne, where she and her cousins had seen *Rear Window*. She'd wondered if the Jimmy Stewart man's voice would be like the actor's. It was not. Instead, this man's voice was deep and sure.

"See there?" The man leaned over the back of her seat and pointed a little to the north.

"Oh, yes!" she said as she spotted the third balloon. This one was purple and white, the colors of the sunset, and it nearly blended in with the sky. "It must be wonderful to be up in one of them."

"Yes, I think it would be," the man said, taking his seat again. She heard him open his newspaper, and she went back to reading her book, glancing out the window at the balloons until they disappeared from sight.

The sky had grown quite dark and Sarah was lost in her book when the car in which they were riding suddenly lurched wildly to the left. The little boy let out a yelp.

"What the...?" the Jimmy Stewart man said, but before he could even finish his sentence, the car lurched again, this time to the right, with an ear-splitting screech of brakes. Sarah felt the unmistakable jolt of the train jumping the tracks, and in an instant she and her fellow passengers were tumbling through the car, banging into seats and being pummeled by falling luggage. Sarah fell headfirst into the seat across the aisle. The man's newspaper flew past her face, followed by the little boy's toy truck. She tried to scream, but the sound caught in her throat. The lights in the car flickered several times before shutting off altogether, plunging them into darkness.

It was over in mere seconds. There was just enough light coming from outside the train window for Sarah to know they had landed upside down. She was sprawled on the ceiling of the car—now the floor—her skirt hiked up above her garters and her shoes missing.

"Is everyone all right?" the man asked. His voice came from somewhere behind her.

Sarah tugged her skirt down and tried to sit up, slowly, testing her limbs for breaks and sprains. "I think so," she said.

"Donny?" the woman, crumpled in one corner of the car, called out.

"I can't get out." The little boy's voice came from someplace near Sarah.

"Are you all right, ma'am?" The man started toward the woman.

"Yes." The woman stood upright, balancing carefully on the ceiling of the car. "But the boy. Donny, where are you?"

"He's here." Sarah got to her knees. In the dim light, she could see that the little boy was trapped between the luggage rack and the crushed ceiling of the car. "Are you all right, sweetheart?" she asked.

The woman and man awkwardly made their way toward Sarah and the boy.

"Oh, Donny," the woman said. "Are you hurt, dear? Can you get out of there?"

The boy was crying. It was too dark to see if he was injured.

"I can't get out," Donny whimpered. "I want to get out!"

"We'll get you out, son," said the man. He tugged on the luggage rack, but it was immovable.

The boy let out a wail. "I'm scared!" he cried.

"You'll be fine, darling," soothed the woman.

"We need something to prop under here," the man said.

Sarah remembered seeing her suitcase fly across the car. On her hands and knees, she clambered across the ceiling until she found it and dragged it back to the man.

"Perfect," he said.

With her help, he began the slow process of lifting the luggage rack, wedging the suitcase between it and the ceiling, and moving it closer and closer to the boy to widen the space in which he was trapped.

"Was it the b-bomb?" Donny asked.

"No, dear," the blond woman said. Under her breath, she spoke to Sarah and the man. "Someone told him the Communists are going to drop a bomb on us," she said. "He's always afraid."

He's not the only one, Sarah thought. Three families in her neighborhood had built bomb shelters in their backyards.

"Donny," the woman said, holding the little boy's hand. "Remember those beautiful hot air balloons? Let's imagine we're up in one of them right now. Okay?"

What a brilliant idea, Sarah thought in admiration.

"But we're *not*," Donny said, tears in his voice.

"You're good at pretending, though, aren't you?" the woman said. "Let's pretend we're up there instead of down here. We're floating on air. The sun is setting around us and the colors are magnificent. What can you see from up there?" The woman's voice was so soothing that Sarah actually felt a sense of calm surround her as she and the man worked to free the little boy.

"I see my new h-house," the boy said.

"Yes!" said the woman. "And do you see your new family? What do they look like?"

"Little, from way up here."

The woman laughed at that, and there was relief in the sound. The boy could still make a joke.

"There," said the man, finally getting the suitcase in as far as it would go.

"Can you get out, Donny?" Sarah asked. "Move very slowly." If he had any injuries, she did not want them to be made worse.

It took a minute for him to slide from the confining space into the woman's arms. From her comments about the little boy's "new family," Sarah figured she was not his mother, after all. But she certainly was relieved to have the child safe in her embrace. She wept, holding on to him, and Sarah put her arm around her.

"I'm a nurse," Sarah said. "Let's make sure he's all right, shall we?"

"Oh, yes, thank you."

The faint light made examining him difficult, but Donny appeared to have come through the ordeal unscathed, at least physically. As Sarah examined the boy, the man tried the doors at either end of the car.

"They're jammed shut, both of them," he called to the women.

In the distance, Sarah heard the wail of sirens. Moments later, the world outside the train filled with light from ambulances and police cars. The four passengers in the overturned car could now see the rest of the train. Most of the cars were lying on their sides; a few had landed upside down as theirs had. A couple of cars looked as though they had been crushed, and one was split in two. The scene was horrific, and the woman tucked the little boy's head into her shoulder so he would not have to see.

"What a disaster!" the man said. He pulled a pen and pad from his pocket and began to write something down.

Outside one of the windows, a man in fire-fighting gear suddenly appeared, knocking on the splintered glass. "Any serious injuries in there?" he asked.

"No," said the Jimmy Stewart look-alike. "We're all right."

"Can you wait there for a bit, then?" the rescuer asked. "We have some very serious injuries to deal with in a few of the other cars. We'll get back to you as soon as we can."

"That's all right," said the man. As the rescuer walked away, he turned to the women, now illuminated by the headlights from one of the ambulances. "I hope you don't mind. He said there are severe injuries up ahead, and we're all right, for the most part."

"We're safe." The blond woman sat on top of the luggage rack with the little boy curled in her arms. "We can wait it out."

Sarah sat down next to the woman, looking the boy over more carefully now that they had more light. He appeared to be fine, his face tear-streaked and sleepy.

"Well." The man lowered himself to the luggage rack opposite them. "My name is Joe Tolley. I'm a reporter for the *Washington Post.*" That explained the notepad that was now balanced on his knee, his pen poised above it. "And where are you ladies traveling to?"

"To Washington," Sarah said. "I've been visiting family in New Jersey, but I live in the District."

"With your husband?" he asked, one eyebrow raised.

"No," Sarah laughed. "Not that it's any of your business. I work at Mercy Hospital. I'm a nurse. My name's Sarah."

"And my name's Ann, and I'm a social worker," the woman with the boy said. She pressed her lips to the sleeping child's forehead. "I'm taking this little fellow to his new adoptive parents in Virginia. He's been through so much, and now this."

Tears rested in the woman's eyes, and Sarah touched her arm. She was impressed by Ann's caring nature.

"How do you do the sort of work you do when you care so deeply?" she asked. "You're more upset than he is over what just happened to him."

Ann smiled. "It's a problem for me," she said. "I've only been at it a few months, and my supervisor says I'm not cut out for this sort of work. I get over-involved with all the children."

"If you ask me, you're the type who *should* be doing that work," Joe Tolley said. "The people who work with children damn well better care about them."

"But it makes it too hard for Ann," Sarah said. "It's too hard for the caretakers if they feel every little ounce of pain the children feel."

Ann nodded. "You're right. You're a nurse, you said? You must understand, then."

Outside, men's voices filled the air. One of the ambulances took off, sirens blaring.

"I'm a psychiatric nurse," Sarah said. "And you're right. It's terribly easy to get pulled into every patient you see. You have to be careful to maintain some objectivity or else you'll be of no help to them."

"You sound like my supervisor," Ann said.

"I don't know." Joe's gaze was on the child. "I think little Donny here is mighty lucky he has Ann making this trip with him instead of some cold old prune who doesn't really care what happens to him."

"Well, my supervisor says my problem is that I have no children of my own and I try to make up for it through these little guys." Ann nodded toward Donny, asleep in her lap.

"Are you married?" Sarah asked her.

"No. And I'm already *thirty-four*." She whispered the age as though telling a dirty little secret. She was only two years older than Sarah. The difference between Ann and Sarah was that Ann thought she would get married one day. Sarah had no such illusions.

"What is it like, working with mentally ill patients?" Joe asked Sarah.

"Difficult. Rewarding. Challenging. Wonderful."

Joe laughed. "All of the above, huh? Are any of them dangerous?"

"Some."

"Aren't you frightened?" he asked. "Repulsed at times?"

"No. I think about why they are the way they are. How they were raised. How they may have been unfortunate in their lives. I try to figure out what happened to them that left them so scarred and unable to cope. Then it's easy to feel compassion for them."

He was smiling at her, a smile that softened his eyes and made her feel suddenly shy.

"So you work at the *Post*?" she asked, anxious to get the attention off herself.

"Yes, I got lucky," he said. "I worked for a few smaller papers but landed this job last year."

"What sort of things do you write?" Ann asked.

"Some editorial columns. Some news stories. An occasional theater critique. That's my favorite thing to write, actually."

"Oh, have you seen *Cat on a Hot Tin Roof*?" Sarah asked, sitting forward on the luggage rack. "I'm dying to see it."

"Yes, I've seen it, and you really mustn't miss it," he said.

"I saw *Inherit the Wind* last year," Sarah said. "It was so powerful."

"I can tell you like the same sort of play I do," Joe said. There was that smile again, bringing heat to her cheeks.

"Do you have an article you consider your best?" she asked. "A favorite?"

"I don't think I actually have a favorite," he said. "What I like to do, though, is take an unusual angle. I like to write about the human side of a story. I'm not as keen on the facts. That's why I like editorials. It's hard for me to keep my opinion out of what I write."

The three adults continued talking while Donny slept. It was odd how close you could come to feel to other people in the space of a couple of hours, Sarah thought. She felt as though she'd known Ann and Joe most of her life, and she liked them both. She actually felt as though she loved them, although that was ludicrous. Still, their warmth and their humanity touched her, and when the rescuers finally broke into their car and freed them, she felt an odd sense of loss at the realization that she and her companions would now be going their separate ways.

Before they parted, they used pages from Joe's notepad to write down their names and addresses for one another, and they exchanged heartfelt embraces as they walked toward separate ambulances.

Sarah was still thinking of her fellow travelers two days later, when she read Joe Tolley's editorial about the accident in the *Washington Post*. He wrote about strangers becoming friends through adversity, about three adults and a child drawn together by accident, touching one another with concern and respect, and leaving the scene with "genuine affection for strangers on a train."

"Would that all our contacts with one another were marked by such a sense of urgency, such a safe and necessary intimacy," he'd written. "It would be a better world."

Laura drove home to Lake Ashton from Meadow Wood Village, her mind still in the upside-down car of the ill-fated train. Sarah was a natural storyteller. She'd described the wreck so vividly that Laura had been able to visualize the scene with ease.

At the edge of the forest surrounding the lake, Laura stopped by the row of mailboxes to pick up her mail. There wasn't much, and she sat in her car and opened the only piece of mail that didn't look like a bill. It was a long white envelope, her name typed on the front. Inside was a sheet of white paper bearing one short typewritten line: *Leave Sarah Tolley alone.*

Laura turned the paper over, but it was blank on the other side, and the envelope bore no return address other than a Philadelphia postmark. A chill ran up her spine. Who would send this to her? And why?

She stared at the note, brow furrowed, for more than a minute. This was crazy. Annoyed, she tossed the piece of paper onto the passenger seat and drove through the forest toward her house. Whoever had sent the note was out of luck. They were too late. She already felt genuine affection for this particular stranger, and she wasn't about to let her be lonely again.

15

He should have thrown the picture in the trash the moment Bethany brought it into the house. Instead, he ignored it. Each time Dylan walked through the kitchen, he caught a glimpse of it on the counter, and he'd turn his gaze away. He didn't throw it away, but he didn't look at it, either. It was as though he knew that once he looked at it, everything in his devil-may-care life-style would change. He was afraid of what he'd see in that photograph.

He was making himself a turkey sandwich one afternoon, when he suddenly set down the knife and picked up the picture, his hands moving on automatic pilot. It was a studio photograph of a pretty child—a *beautiful* child. And she was his. He studied the picture, although he didn't need to do so to know that he was indeed her father. She looked very much like his sister had at that age. The same dark hair. The little arch to her left eyebrow. The bow lips. The light blue eyes that ran in his family. The same blue eyes he would see if he looked in a mirror.

He left the sandwich half-made on the counter, slipped the picture in his shirt pocket and went outside to his deck, where he lay down in the hammock. The branches above him swayed gently in the warm breeze.

Okay. He'd done it. He'd looked. He knew. So now what?

He had not lied to Laura Brandon when he told her he

didn't remember her, but he did remember the party and the snowstorm. The party had been to celebrate Rhonda's moving into her new house, a house that could easily contain five or six of his log cabins. The enormity of the mansion remained in his mind, but not much more from that night. It was, as Bethany had said, his bad time.

Never much of a drinker, he'd made up for it during those few months after the crash that had taken the lives of so many of his friends, including Katy, the woman he'd lived with. He'd spent those months in a stupor of alcohol and cigarettes and sex. Anything to help him wipe out the pain.

Pulling the picture from his pocket, he looked at it again. There was that Geer smile. Unmistakable. So, she was his child. That didn't mean he had to do anything about it. It sounded like Laura had enough money for her. He'd never wanted children—at least not since Katy died. He didn't want the responsibility of them, the possibility of pain and loss. Yet this child was already here, gazing at him from the photograph, her eyes telling him all he needed to know.

Over the next few days, he tried to lose himself in work. No matter what he was doing, though, he found himself taking the picture from his pocket from time to time, to remind himself that she was his.

One humid afternoon, he walked from the barn to the cabin to refill his water bottle, and some part of him must have known he was going to make the call. He didn't even stop at the sink before pulling the picture from his pocket, turning it over to read the number and picking up the phone.

He recognized Laura Brandon's voice as soon as she answered, and he felt an immediate jolt of dislike for her, still reeling from the way she'd manipulated him.

"This is Dylan Geer," he said.

"Dylan!" she said. "I'm really very sorry. I was an idiot."

He laughed. "No argument there. But I suppose I wasn't much better."

"I should have written it to you in a letter, maybe, instead of dumping it on you hundreds of feet in the air."

"Well, it doesn't matter now," he said, turning the photograph over to look at the little girl's face. "What matters is that I finally got around to looking at the picture, and I know you must have been telling me the truth. She's got...I don't know, the eyes, the eyebrows, everything. I've been trying my best to ignore that fact, but I don't seem to be able to. I don't know what you want from me, or what my obligation is, but I guess we need to talk about it." A shiver of dread ran through his body as those words left his mouth.

She let out her breath. "I'm relieved to hear you say that," she said. "And as I told you, I don't need financial help. I just needed to see if you might want to be in her life. Which is pretty complicated right now." She laughed.

She sounded nervous, and he felt a trace of unexpected sympathy for her.

"I'll understand if you don't want to be, though," she said. "And I hope you'll understand if I wind up not thinking it's right for her to meet you. But yes, let's at least talk about it."

"Fine. Do you want to come over here again? Or meet someplace?"

"I think the best idea would be for us to meet with her therapist. She could help us figure out how to handle this."

"She's...what's your daughter's name?"

"Emma."

"Emma's in therapy?"

"Yes. I told you that, but I don't think you were listening.'' There was no recrimination in her voice. ''Her father...her adoptive father, my husband, died in January—''

''I remember you saying that,'' he interrupted her. He'd grown up without a father himself. No doubt that was driving him.

''She was traumatized by losing him and hasn't spoken since then,'' Laura said.

''What do you mean, she hasn't spoken?''

''I mean, she doesn't speak. Doesn't say anything. She'll communicate sometimes with gestures or by nodding her head, but that's it.''

''For *months* this has been going on?''

''Yes.''

''Was she...normal before he died?''

Laura laughed. ''If you call being an outrageous chatterbox normal.''

''Poor kid,'' he said. ''She's really changed, huh?''

''It's been hard on her.''

''Well, when can we get an appointment with this therapist?''

''I have one scheduled for one o'clock Friday afternoon. Can you make it then?''

Friday was a busy day, with both morning and evening flights. He would have to miss his nap. Big deal. ''Yes,'' he said. ''Just tell me where.''

16

Laura was about to knock on Sarah Tolley's apartment door when Carolyn, the attendant, spotted her from down the hall.

"Oh, Mrs. Brandon," she said, rushing up to her. "I'm glad I bumped into you."

Laura was instantly worried. "Is everything all right?" she asked.

"Oh, yes." Carolyn was a bit winded. "I just wanted to thank you for your visits to Sarah. They've made such a difference."

"Have they?" Laura asked, surprised.

"She's always telling people about her walks. 'Well, when I was on my walk, I saw this and that,' she'll say."

"Really? We've only been out twice."

"It means a lot to her."

"She barely seems to know who I am, though."

"Well, that's typical of someone in her condition. But believe me, getting out of here once a week means the world to her."

Laura hesitated, then pulled the cryptic letter from her purse. She'd thought of showing it to Sarah, but decided against it on the drive to the retirement home, not wanting to upset her. She handed the letter to Carolyn.

"I got this in the mail the other day," she said. "Do you have any idea who might have sent it?"

Carolyn studied the one line with a frown. "God, no," she said with a shiver. "This is creepy."

"I couldn't imagine who sent it, either," Laura said, "but now that you've mentioned the fact that Sarah's talking about our walks…" She looked at the other doors. Well-worn pink ballet slippers were attached to one of them, a picture of a St. Bernard on another. "Do you think some other resident here might be envious and want to put an end to Sarah's outings?"

Carolyn studied the ceiling as though sorting through the residents in her mind. "I can't imagine who it would be. It's true that there are some women here who envy Sarah, because she dresses so nicely and is…well, a cut above some of them. But I can't see any of them having the wherewithal to type this up and mail it to you."

"Besides," Laura remembered, "it was sent from Philadelphia."

Carolyn shook her head. "I don't think it's from one of ours," she said, handing the sheet of paper to her. "But listen, please don't let it scare you off from seeing her."

"You really care about her, don't you?"

"I care about *all* my patients," Carolyn said quickly, then added, "but yes, there's something special about Sarah."

They spoke a few more minutes, then Carolyn continued down the hall, and Laura rang the buzzer next to the apartment door.

Sarah opened the door, and her eyes lit up. "I'm ready!" she said, and Laura noticed that, once again, she had her walking shoes on.

"Sarah," she said, "let's sit down for a minute first."

Sarah looked surprised and a bit disappointed. "All right." She walked across the small living room and took a seat on the couch. Laura sat in one of the chairs.

"I was wondering if it would help you to know exactly when I'm coming," Laura said. "That way you'd know when you're going for a walk. It wouldn't be a surprise. And you wouldn't be disappointed if you think I might show up one day but I don't."

"That would be good." Sarah nodded.

"Today's Wednesday. What if I come every Wednesday? Unless it's raining?"

"Wednesday is Bingo."

"Oh. So, Wednesday is a bad day for you?"

"Bingo is at night."

"Is Wednesday okay, then?"

"Yes." Sarah still didn't look too certain. "Isn't today Saturday?" she asked.

"Oh. No, dear." She surprised herself with the word *dear*. She didn't think she'd ever used it before in her life. "No, today is Wednesday. Do you have a calendar?"

"I don't think so."

"I'll get you one, and we can circle the Wednesdays. Then you'll know when I'm coming." She hoped Alison would be able to watch Emma every Wednesday afternoon.

"Good. Can we go now?" Sarah sounded like a child, and Laura smiled.

"Absolutely."

On their way to the door, Laura noticed a calendar on the kitchenette wall, the pages turned to the previous month. She said nothing.

Once outside the retirement home, Sarah began her springy step.

"Do you remember last time we talked, I told you about my little girl's birth father, Dylan?" Laura asked after they'd walked a short distance.

There was a crease between Sarah's eyebrows. "Dylan?" she asked.

Sarah had no idea who she was talking about, Laura realized. "He flies hot air balloons," she said. "Remember, you told me about the train crash?"

"Ah, the train crash," Sarah said. "I was a stranger on a train."

"That's right." She felt disturbed by Sarah's confusion but knew how to turn it around to hear the older woman sound lucid and in control. And maybe that's why Sarah loved her walks, it gave her a chance to go back to a time when she was exactly that—lucid. In control.

"I've been wondering about the train crash," Laura said. "What happened afterward?"

Sarah, 1955-1956

Sarah had finished dispensing medications to the patients in her ward when the receptionist arrived at the nurses' station, carrying a vase filled with red roses.

"Sarah Wilding," she said. "These are for you."

For a moment, Sarah wondered if it might be a joke of some sort. She had never, not once in her life, received flowers from a delivery service, and today was not even a special occasion. Her parents had given her a beautiful arrangement of poppies and baby's breath when she graduated from nursing school—to make up for the fact that they had not been with her in person, she figured.

"For me?" she said, accepting the vase. She carried it behind the desk of the glass-enclosed nurses' station, and a few of her co-workers gathered around her. Even a couple of patients peered through the glass to see who had received the flowers.

"Who are they from?" Pauline, one of the other nurses, asked.

Sarah plucked the envelope from among the flowers.

There was no card inside, merely a ticket to *Cat on a Hot Tin Roof* for Saturday night. Seat 32, row F. She showed the ticket to her friends wordlessly.

"Who on earth sent it?" Pauline asked.

Sarah shook her head. "I have no idea," she said. But actually, she did. She was afraid she might be wrong, though, and she didn't dare hope.

"Sarah has a secret admirer!" Pauline said, giving her a hug.

"There are only eleven roses," said one of the nurse's aides.

"That's strange," Pauline said, counting the roses herself.

Sarah stared at the ticket. She'd wanted to see this play for so long, and there were only two people to whom she'd recently confided that fact.

She had thought about Joe Tolley ever since that night on the train. After reading his article about the crash, she'd kept her eyes open for other articles he had written, checking the *Post* from front to back every day. She'd thought of calling the paper and asking for him, just to hear his voice again. It was silly. She had a crush on someone who was clearly out of her reach. He had to be at least several years younger than she to begin with, and he was attractive. She was popular, spirited, smart and capable, but beauty was not one of her attributes. The lighting, though, had certainly been poor in that overturned train. Still, it was ridiculous to think that the ticket and flowers might be from Joe Tolley. Perhaps they were simply a show of kindness from that dear social worker, Ann. Or maybe they *were* from Joe, and she was reading too much into the gift. Maybe it was simply a greeting from him, and she would go to the theater and sit alone as *Cat on a Hot Tin Roof* played out before her. After all, he'd already seen it. And he had carefully sent only eleven roses rather than the romantic dozen. Yet they were red. Oh, she was driving herself mad trying to think through all the possibilities! She would go to the theater Saturday night, and she would look her very best, just in case.

He was already in the seat next to hers when she arrived at the theater. The twelfth rose was in his hand, and he held it out to her with a smile. Her heart beat wildly as she took her seat.

"What a lovely surprise," she said, smoothing the skirt of her borrowed black chiffon dress over her legs.

"Didn't you know who had sent the ticket?" he asked.

"I was hoping it was you," she said, unable to believe her bravery in making that statement.

He lightly touched the back of her hand. "I was hoping you were hoping," he said.

The play began, but Sarah could barely concentrate on it, so aware was she of the man sitting next to her. He smelled wonderful; the sleeve of his jacket rested against her bare arm. *This is a miracle,* she thought.

At intermission, they strolled around the halls of the theater, chatting about the play and describing what each of them had been doing since the train crash. They wondered how Ann was doing, and the little boy, Donny. Sarah felt perfectly comfortable walking next to him, but when they stopped, when he turned to face her and she knew he could see her in the clear light from the lobby, she was consumed with discomfort.

Still, Joe looked at her with warmth in his face. His smile was ever-present and it lit up his eyes. He was looking at her, directly at her, and he seemed to be *captivated* with her looks. She began to feel lovely. By the end of the play, she'd been transformed.

After the play, he took her to a little café for coffee and

dessert. They talked about movies and plays they'd seen. He was the first person Sarah had ever met who had seen every single one of her favorites. She told him she'd read his articles and offered her opinion about each one. He was clearly taken by her thoughtful critiques, jotting down her words from time to time on his notepad. "You are even more interesting than I thought you'd be," he said at one point.

The café closed rather late, although Sarah could not have said what time it was. All she knew was that she and Joe were not finished talking. She had so much more she wanted to say to him, as though she'd been saving it up all her life for this evening. And the amazing thing was, he seemed to feel the same way. By the time she told him she was thirty-two, she had no fear that news would put him off, even though he'd already told her that he was only twenty-five.

They left the café. The spring night air was warm, and they walked across the street to a park, where they sat on a bench under the stars and talked until early morning. They stopped only for Sarah to call the woman with whom she shared her apartment to tell her she was fine, not to worry, and for Joe to call his mother to do the same. His mother was not at all happy with the call, he said. But he'd told her he was working on an important story. "Maybe the most important story in my life," he'd said.

She learned that Joe's father had died a few years ago and that he lived with his mother and older sister, both of whom sounded quite dependent on him. "They are wretchedly conservative," he said. He had been raised Catholic, and his mother and sister were devout, although Joe himself rarely attended church anymore. Organized religion was not important to him, he said. It was more important how people behaved in their daily lives than what they did on Sunday. She had been raised Methodist, Sarah told him, and although she did go to church most weeks, she agreed with him wholeheartedly.

She told him about her own family. Her father had died a decade ago; her mother shortly after. Except for a few cousins, she had no family.

He pulled a pipe from his jacket pocket and lit it, and she knew then why he emanated that rich, dusky scent. He let her try it. She loved setting her lips where his had been only a few seconds before, but she accidentally inhaled before he'd warned her not to. She choked, laughing, and relished the feeling of his hand on her back as he tried to help her.

He wanted to travel all over the world, he said. Africa enticed him more than anywhere else because it sounded so exciting and primitive, and Sarah immediately pictured herself there with him, floating on a river, like Hepburn and Bogart in *The African Queen*. Joe had a wild streak. She liked that about him.

He drove her home to her apartment. She had trouble leaving the car, leaving *him*. She wondered if he would kiss her, and to her own amazement, she leaned toward him without waiting for him to make the overture. There was no need for games here. No need for cat and mouse. She wanted him. She wanted every part of him.

He kissed her lightly, then pulled back to smile at her. "So, do you want to skip church tomorrow?" he asked. "We can go for a hike in the mountains."

That was the beginning. They spent every weekend together, except for a few hours each night when they gave in to propriety and returned to their respective homes. They saw each other frequently during the week, as well, and spoke on the telephone every day. Together, they visited the theater and the museums, saw nearly every movie that opened, hiked in the mountains and rode a tandem bicycle around the city. Joe was a risk-taker, hiking away from the well-marked trails, dodging traffic on the bike, yet she felt completely safe with him. Their relationship developed into the sort of intimate, passionate and loving union Sarah had never hoped to experience.

There was only one snag. Two, really. Joe's mother and sister. They probably would not have approved of any woman Joe chose, their own emotional needs for him were so great, but Sarah was a particular affront to them because of her age and because she was not Catholic. Sarah also feared that they found her too unattractive for their good-looking son and brother. She felt beautiful in Joe's eyes, yet she knew most of the outside world did not see that beauty in her.

She had not spent any real length of time with his mother and sister, Sarah said to Joe one day, having only spoken with them briefly on a few occasions. Determined to win them over, she suggested they all go out to dinner together.

Joe took charge of planning the outing. They would meet his mother and sister at Seville's, he told Sarah. It was a cozy little restaurant, he said. Perfect for quiet conversation.

Once seated in the restaurant with Mrs. Tolley and Joe's sister, Mary Louise, Sarah began to look around her. The dining room was indeed quiet and cozy, as Joe had promised. The lights were dim, and there was an understated elegance about the place. But as she looked further, she noticed that all of the paintings on the dark walls were of nudes. Every single piece. She looked at Joe, knowing instantly that he had brought his family here for the shock value. He was wicked. Yet she found herself stifling a laugh.

His mother and sister had not yet noticed the art on the

walls. Mrs. Tolley was too busy complaining about the table they had been given.

"It's too near the kitchen," she said, although they were several tables from the swinging kitchen door. "And there's a spot on my water glass."

"And lucky us," Mary Louise said, under her breath. "We get the colored waiter."

Sarah cringed as the waiter approached their table, hoping he had not heard the comment.

Joe smiled at her across the table as his mother gave the waiter her exacting order, and Sarah wondered how such a warm, fun-loving, tolerant man could belong to this unlikable family.

"Oh, my God." Mary Louise lowered her head after the waiter had gone. Her cheeks were crimson, and Sarah knew she'd finally noticed the walls. "Mother, don't dare look at the paintings."

Mrs. Tolley immediately raised her head to look at the wall to her left and let out a sound of disgust.

"Did you know these paintings were here?" she asked her son, anger in her voice.

"Well, of course," he said. "I think they're exceptional. I wrote about them when I reviewed this place last year."

Mrs. Tolley glared at him, then shifted her angry eyes to her daughter. "We should leave," she said.

Mary Louise leaned across the table to touch her mother's hand. "We've already ordered, Mother. We'll simply have to stay."

Mrs. Tolley closed her eyes as if gathering strength. When she opened them again, she turned to Sarah, and, with strained politeness, inquired as to how she was enjoying her job "treating the insane."

"It's fine," Sarah said. "I love the work I do at Mercy."

"Could you get a job as a regular nurse?" Mary Louise asked, a touch of hope in her voice.

"I *am* a regular nurse," Sarah said.

"I mean, taking care of people with, you know, *real* illnesses instead of...you know."

"The people I take care of definitely have real illnesses," Sarah said, keeping her voice as even as possible. "You'd only have to spend a day with them to know they can't help the way they are."

"Oh, do you really believe that?" Mrs. Tolley asked. "I think anyone who's been raised properly and who eats well and keeps company among good people will rarely have any sort of mental problem."

"Mother, that's ridiculous," Joe said. "What about your old friend, Mrs. Jackson? What did she do to deserve her transformation into a lunatic?" He turned to Sarah, a look of apology on his face. "Pardon my language," he said.

"She's a special case," Mrs. Tolley said. "If she hadn't married that lazy drunkard she would have been fine."

"Did you see her last week at church?" Mary Louise asked. "She had a *handkerchief* on her head instead of a hat."

"Oh, I know," Mrs. Tolley said. She turned to Sarah. "You don't need to wear hats in *your* church, do you?" she asked.

"Well, it's not necessary," Sarah said.

Mrs. Tolley nodded. "I didn't think so. Not the same sort of respect there, I guess."

"Mother," Joe said. "Mind your manners."

"You mind *yours*," Mrs. Tolley snapped at him. She turned to Sarah again. "He can be so insolent! He'll probably be *your* age by the time he grows out of it. Hope I live that long."

"Mother!" Joe was really angry now. Sarah had never seen that flame in his eyes before.

"It's all right, Joe," Sarah said. "I'm not that sensitive." But she was. Inside she ached from the insults, and she longed for dinner to be over. She maintained a polite and friendly demeanor as Joe's mother and sister asked her patronizing and ignorant questions about the mentally ill, but her mind was no longer on her dining companions. Instead, it was on the artwork, a powerful escape from the reality of the evening.

Directly above Joe's left shoulder was one of the most beautiful paintings she'd ever seen. The light in the restaurant was dim, but the images in the painting grew clearer to Sarah as the evening wore on. A man stood behind a woman, embracing her, and both of them were nude. Only one of the man's legs was visible, and his thigh was thick and muscled. Sarah could barely steal her eyes away from the seductive hollow of his hip. One of his hands was on the woman's rib cage, the length of one finger lying beneath the swell of her breast. His other hand rested on the curve of her hip. The woman was beautiful, her hair long and red. Her nipples were dark and erect. The dark triangle of hair at the base of her belly was just within reach of the man's fingertips.

Sarah's own nipples tightened as she studied the painting. The conversation drifted around her until, suddenly, she glanced at Joe and knew he had been watching her. Surely he knew what she was seeing above his shoulder. He smiled at her, raising his eyebrows provocatively, and the gesture felt like an invitation to her. They had not yet made love. Right now, though, she wanted his idiotic sister and mother and the rest of the diners to disappear so that she could strip off her clothes and have her way with Joe right there on the table.

After their meal, she and Joe said good-night to his family and left the restaurant for the walk to her apartment.

"Go on," Joe said. "Let it out."

For a moment, she thought he was referring to her feelings of passion. "Let what out?" she asked.

"Everything you want to say about Mother and Mary Louise. Go on. I can take it."

"Oh." She laughed. "I can't. It wouldn't be right."

"Better than letting it fester inside you."

"Well, first of all, you egged them on by taking them to Seville's."

"*You* certainly seemed to like it, though," he said.

"The food was good," she agreed.

"I wasn't talking about the food."

She laughed again. Every line of that painting was etched in her mind. Her body felt hot when she thought about it.

"So," he said, bringing her back to the moment. "Mother and M.L."

They turned the corner, the street lined with row houses. "Well, they are hypocritical, bigoted, prissy and rather superficial to boot," she said.

Joe laughed. "You left out 'bitchy.'"

Although she was surprised to hear Joe use that word, especially in reference to his own mother and sister, she had to agree. "That, too," she said.

"You handled them wonderfully," he said, stopping suddenly on the sidewalk as he turned to face her. His hands on her shoulders, he kissed her. "This was your big test," he said.

"And I failed miserably."

"With Mom and Mary Louise, maybe, but you're a victor in my eyes." Holding her hand high in the air, he walked her over to the steps of the nearest row house. With a flourish, he took off his jacket and set it on the top step, then motioned her to sit down on it.

Sarah glanced at the windows in the row house and took her seat, giggling like a young girl. "What are we doing? What if someone comes out of—"

"Sh." Lowering himself to one knee, he kissed her hand. "Now that I know you can hold your own with mother and Mary Louise," he said, "I feel confident asking you to marry me. Will you?" he asked. "Marry me?"

She was stunned, not that he would one day ask her this question, but that it would come now, after his mother and sister had made their disdain for her and her religion and her profession so very clear.

"You might lose them," she said. "Your family."

"I love them," he said. "Despite the fact that they are...all those things you said they are. But it's you I want to spend the rest of my life with, not them. So will you?" In the porch light of the row house, his eyes were bright and hopeful.

"Of course I will," she said.

Her roommate was away for the weekend, and she and Joe had the apartment to themselves. Sarah made Joe a cup of tea, then disappeared into her bedroom. Her heart beating fast, she undressed and slipped into her robe. Then she called him in.

He stood in the doorway, clearly surprised at finding her in her robe. He said nothing, but leaned against the door-jamb, a smile on his face.

Untying the robe, she let it slip to the floor. The air in the apartment was cool against her skin, and she watched his eyes drift over her body as she walked toward him.

He didn't touch her when she neared him. He seemed to be letting her take the lead, and that was what she wanted.

She unbuttoned his shirt, slipping it from his shoulders. She unbuckled his belt, then lowered the zipper on his trousers, and she heard his sharp intake of breath as her hand accidentally brushed over the rigid mass beneath his shorts. Then it seemed he could stand it no longer. He tore off the rest of his clothes and began covering her face and throat and shoulders with kisses, at once tender and feverish. As he pulled her tightly against him, she felt the steely heat of his erection.

He drew down the covers on her bed and lowered her gently into it. Then he lay next to her, caressing her, loving her, and she thought there was nothing more she would ever need to make her world complete.

Joe's mother and sister refused to come to the wedding, which was held in the small Methodist church Sarah had attended over the years. Joe didn't complain about their absence. The joy he felt in Sarah's company seemed to make up for whatever loss he might endure.

They went to Florida for their honeymoon, to the wilds of the Everglades, as close to the atmosphere of Africa they could afford. They left by plane immediately after the small reception. It was Sarah's first time in a plane, and she clung to Joe's hand nervously, feeling the solid strength in him. For the first time in her adult life, she had someone to lean on. That realization brought tears of joy to her eyes, and she stared out the window so Joe wouldn't see them and misinterpret them.

The morning after their wedding night, Joe turned to her in bed.

"I have a wedding gift for you," he said, touching her cheek. He rose from the bed, and she watched his long, beautiful body as he walked toward the dresser. From the top drawer, he removed a small, wrapped box and carried it back to the bed. Sarah waited for him to get under the covers again before opening the package.

Inside was a stunning gold brooch. She turned it around in her fingers.

"It goes this way," Joe said, taking it from her hands. "It's our initials, see?" He ran the tip of his finger over the smooth gold. "Here's a *J* for me, and an *S* for you. Do you see it?"

"Oh, it's beautiful!" she said. "Oh, thank you, Joe. I'll always wear it."

Drawing her to him gently, Joe buried his lips in her hair. "We're going to have a phenomenal marriage, Sarah," he said. "We'll travel and see plays and laugh together. You'll wear your pin every day. And at least once a week, we'll go to Seville's for inspiration."

Sarah laughed as she reached behind him to set the brooch on the nightstand. Then she pulled her husband into her arms, hoping she could stay in bed with him for hours and hours, on this, the very first day of their phenomenal marriage.

They had reached the entrance of the retirement home when Sarah came to the end of her story. Laura pushed open the front door for her, and Sarah looked surprised.

"Is this it?" she asked. "Is this where I live?"

"Yes," Laura said. "We walked a long way today."

"Oh my, yes, we did." Sarah walked across the threshold into the building, raising her hands over her head in a show of victory that reminded Laura of Sylvester Stallone in the Rocky movies. She couldn't help but laugh.

Inside the foyer, Sarah pointed in the direction of her apartment. "That way?" she asked.

"That's right." Laura walked with her down the hall to be certain Sarah found the right apartment. She was feeling a sadness she could not quite label. Hearing the intimate details of Sarah's relationship with her husband had made her a bit uncomfortable, although Sarah seemed to have no qualms about sharing them. More than discomfort, she knew she felt some envy. Yes, she'd been married to a fine man, but she had never experienced the sort of intense love, passion and tenderness that Sarah had described so well.

"Come in for a while," Sarah said when they reached her apartment door.

"I can't," Laura said. "I have to get back to Emma. My little girl."

"Oh." Sarah pushed her door open. "I'll see you tomorrow, then?"

"No," Laura said gently. "Remember I said I'd come on Wednesday? I'll see you next Wednesday."

"Oh."

Laura wasn't sure if she saw disappointment or confusion in Sarah's face. Perhaps both. "I enjoyed hearing about your life with Joe," she said. "You were very lucky to have had him."

"Yes," Sarah said. "I was very lucky. But luck has a way of changing."

17

Laura didn't sleep at all the night before her appointment with Dylan Geer and Heather Davison. In the morning, she nearly forgot to give Emma her breakfast, and Emma, of course, said nothing to correct her mistake. She finally made her an English muffin with jelly and a glass of orange juice.

"You'll have to eat it quickly," she told her. "I have to take you over to Cory's so I can go out for a while."

Emma stopped chewing her muffin, alarm in her eyes.

"Her father's not there," Laura said. "He won't be back till the weekend."

Emma relaxed and resumed her chewing.

"Though he's really a very nice man," Laura added, not wanting Emma to think her fear of Jim Becker was well-founded.

Emma dawdled over her food as she usually did, and Laura finally had to take the muffin away. "Go wash your hands and then we'll go," she said.

The phone rang as soon as Emma left the room, and Laura stared at it. She didn't have time for a call. But what if it was Heather canceling the appointment? She picked up the receiver.

The editor from Ray's new publishing house was on the line. He introduced himself quickly, his name instantly flying from Laura's memory, then got to the point of his call.

"Listen," he said, "we need you to send us a picture of Ray for the book jacket and for us to use in any promo we do. Do you have one?"

"Well, yes. I'm sure I can find one." She ran her fingers through her hair as she tried to recall the pictures that had been taken of Ray in recent years. Most of them were casual family shots. There would be few of him alone. "I could use his university picture," she said.

"Good. We need it as soon as possible. And I wanted to let you know that the marketing people will be in touch with you soon, and I know they'll have a lot of questions for you. We're all thrilled about this book," the nameless editor continued. "I know it's really ironic, and this probably sounds terrible to you, but the truth is, your husband's book is more valuable because of his death. It makes him a martyr for his cause. Would you say that Ray killed himself over his frustration at not being able to do more for the homeless? Would that be an accurate statement?"

Laura was taken aback by the question. She had not yet absorbed the idea that Ray was a martyr for his cause.

"Um, I think there were many factors leading to his taking his life." *Primarily me,* she thought.

"What exactly did he do for the homeless?"

"What didn't he do would be an easier question to answer," she said. "He organized a tent city. He set up tutoring programs for homeless kids. He—" She saw Emma reappear in the doorway of the kitchen and glanced at her watch. "He did too much to summarize right now," she said. "I'm afraid I don't have the time. I'm on my way out."

"Well, all right then. I'll have the marketing people give you a call. And you'll get that picture to us, okay? Can you express mail it?"

"Yes. I'll take care of it."

"Oh, and one more thing," he said. "We need to change the title. *No Room at the Inn* doesn't have the punch we need."

She thought of all the nights Ray had lain awake trying to come up with the title for his book. "But I like it," she said.

"We were thinking of *For Shame*."

She frowned. "I don't get it."

"Well, as Ray points out in his book, the current social policy is cruel. It perpetuates the problem of homelessness. We should be ashamed of it."

"Oh," she said. "I'm not sure Ray would have liked it."

"We think it works," the editor said. "Listen, you get me that picture, okay?"

Laura shuddered as she got off the phone. It had been like conversing with a vulture. Forcing a smile, she turned to Emma.

"Come on, sweetie," she said. "Let's go see Cory."

Dylan sat in Heather Davison's waiting room, leafing through an old *People* magazine without really seeing the pages. The receptionist, a motherly looking woman whose name plate read "Mrs. Quinn," occasionally caught his eye and smiled at him. He wondered if she knew why he was there. Did she know how crazy this whole thing was? Could she tell that part of him wanted to bolt out the door?

This was the right thing to do, he kept telling himself. Not the easy thing, certainly, but the right thing. The child was his; he had stared at her picture long enough to know that without any doubt. And as long as she was his, he had to do whatever he could to help her. No way around it.

He hadn't seen or spoken to Bethany in a week, not since the night she delivered the picture to him from his mailbox.

She'd left a few messages for him, and he'd left a few in return, carefully timing his calls to when he knew she'd be out. He was afraid she'd ask him more questions about Emma. It wasn't that he was hiding anything from her. He just didn't want to get into it. He missed her, but he wouldn't see her until he had this situation clear in his own mind. So, instead of seeing Bethany, he'd gone out with a different woman, a woman he knew simply wanted to have a good time, someone who avoided heavy questions as much as he did.

He had never been to a therapist before. Not of his own volition, at any rate. After the crash, it had been required, but one session had been enough for him, and he'd quit therapy and the airlines the same afternoon. It had seemed ludicrous to him then that talking could do anything to help him. Talking wouldn't have brought Katy back.

The front door to the office opened and Laura Brandon walked into the waiting room. He saw the relief on her face when she spotted him, as if she hadn't actually expected him to show up.

"Hi," he said, getting to his feet. Her face was flushed and she looked pretty. He could understand why he might have been drawn to her at that party years ago. Her long, thick brown hair was laced with gold, and her brown eyes were large and dark-lashed. Emma looked far more like him than she did her mother.

"Thanks for agreeing to come," Laura said.

"You're welcome." He was about to take his seat again when another woman walked into the room.

"Hi, Laura," the woman said. She held her hand out to Dylan. "I'm Heather Davison," she said. "And you must be Dylan?"

"Yes. Hi." He shook her hand, surprised. She looked

like a kid. Her hair was pulled back in a ponytail and she wore burgundy overalls over a pink T-shirt.

The three of them walked into Heather's office. The therapist plunked herself down in the large leather chair, while he and Laura took the two upholstered chairs, neatly angled side by side. He felt odd sitting next to Laura, as though they were supposed to be a couple.

"Well, Dylan," Heather began, "I have to compliment you. I have a lot of respect for you, coming in here like this. It takes guts."

He shifted in his seat with discomfort. "I'm not feeling particularly gutsy at the moment," he said.

"What's this like for you?" Heather asked.

"Uh…terrifying," he said, and the two women smiled at his honesty.

"Well, I'm very glad you're here, but I want to be certain you understand the gravity of the situation before you make any decisions that could affect the rest of your life. And Emma's."

Dylan swallowed. He couldn't believe how nervous he felt.

Heather leaned forward. "It's critical that you don't agree to come into Emma's life unless two things exist. One, that Laura feels completely comfortable with you doing so, and two, that you feel absolutely certain you can commit to Emma. She's already lost one father, and it's left her shell-shocked. The trauma of losing a second father could be too much for her."

She sounded like a genuine therapist now in spite of the overalls, and Dylan nodded.

"I understand that," he said. "But what I *don't* understand is what's really going on with Emma. Laura said she hasn't talked since her father died."

"That's right," Heather said. "Not only doesn't she

speak, but she's regressed in a number of other ways, as well. She's become very clingy, hasn't she, Laura?''

Laura nodded solemnly.

"She's uncomfortable around men, and that's the main reason I wanted to see what sort of guy you are and if you might want to help her out. She thinks of men as angry, hostile beings. You'll have to be careful how you handle your anger around her."

He nodded again. Why was this kid so screwed up?

"She also suffers from nightmares," Heather continued, "or at least we assume that's what's happening. It's difficult to know exactly, since she can't talk to us about them. And she wets the bed. She'd been completely dry for nearly two years."

"But why?" Dylan asked. "Other kids lose their fathers and it doesn't cause them to...regress that much."

Heather turned to Laura. "Doesn't Dylan know how Ray died?" she asked.

Laura shook her head. "I haven't really had a chance to tell him," she said. Dylan braced himself. This wasn't going to be good.

Laura looked at him squarely. "My husband committed suicide," she said. "I was out of the house. Ray was supposed to be watching Emma. He shot himself in our bedroom. When I got home, Emma was standing at the bottom of the stairs, screaming. She was inconsolable. I don't know if she saw him do it, or if she only saw him after it happened, but one way or another, it left her...the way she is now."

Dylan saw the sheen of tears in Laura's dark eyes. Emma was not the only person scarred by her father's suicide.

"God," he said. "That was cruel of him to do it when she was home."

"He was really depressed, and I think depressed people don't think too clearly," Laura said.

She sounded only mildly defensive, yet Dylan wished he could take back his words.

"It's true that Ray suffered from clinical depression for most of his life," Heather said, her eyes on Dylan, "but Laura has a strong need to defend him. Yes, Ray did some very good things during his life, but from what I've gathered, he wasn't a very loving or attentive parent for Emma." She looked apologetically at Laura for exposing that fact.

"He was also trying unsuccessfully to get a book published," Laura said, continuing her defense. "And he was upset with me because he thought I was more dedicated to my career than I was to him."

"What kind of work do you do?" Dylan asked. He realized he knew almost nothing about this woman.

"I'm an astronomer," she said. "I work at the Air and Space Museum and teach at Hopkins, and I do research that requires me to travel a lot. At least I did all of that until recently. I'm taking time off for Emma."

Dylan saw the guilt in her face and felt a weird desire to reach out and squeeze her hand in an effort to erase it. He kept his hands to himself, though. "I used to fly for the airlines," he said. "I know how hard travel can be on a relationship."

"If you were to get involved in Emma's life," Heather interrupted their conversation, "it wouldn't be as a substitute for Ray, but as a completely separate, unique individual. Her birth father."

"Can Emma have picked up her problem from her father somehow? From her adoptive father?" Dylan asked. "I mean, if he was mentally ill, could she have—"

"No." Heather sat forward, legs apart, elbows on knees,

the picture of sincerity. "And this is important for you to understand, Dylan. Emma is simply a healthy, normal child who suffered a trauma. She has what we call posttraumatic stress disorder."

The words *healthy, normal child* reassured him. Not that it would make a difference in what he had to do.

"Well," he said, "I'd be lying if I said this doesn't make me more than a little anxious. I mean, I have zero experience with children. I was the youngest in my family. My sister has two children, but I rarely see them." Even when he did see his sister's kids, he was never sure what to say to them. "And taking on the responsibility of a child, especially one like Emma, wasn't exactly part of my plan for my life." He smiled. "But nothing I've heard changes the fact that she's my daughter. I have an obligation to her, maybe even more so now that I know all she's gone through. I want to meet her."

Heather did not look so sure. "I'm worried you might have a romanticized notion about her," she said. "What if she drives you crazy? What if you just plain don't like her?"

He drew in a long breath and let it out. "You know, I didn't want this," he said. "I didn't want any of it. I tried not to look at her picture, but I couldn't bring myself to throw it out. And then I looked at it and…that was that. She's mine. And maybe she *will* drive me crazy sometimes. But don't all kids do that? Isn't that part of the parenting package? I'm not expecting perfection, in her or in myself. But I want to help her. I can't know that she—that my flesh and blood—is out there, struggling, and do nothing to help her."

He looked at Laura. She had turned away from him, and he saw that she was fighting back tears.

"I want Emma to meet him," Laura said suddenly. "I want her to know who her father is."

Heather looked less certain of the decision but nodded nonetheless. "Is there anyone," she asked Dylan, "a woman, maybe, who would be upset by the sudden appearance of your daughter in your life?"

"No." He shook his head, thinking only briefly of Bethany. "I'm unattached and have no plans to change that."

"Well, then," she said. "Let's figure out the best way to handle your meeting Emma."

The three of them talked awhile longer. Heather suggested a book Laura could read to Emma to help the little girl understand the difference between her adoptive father and her biological father. She suggested a couple of books for Dylan to read as well, and he wrote down the titles.

"Sometimes," Heather said to him, "a new person stands a better chance of getting a voluntarily mute child, like Emma, to talk. If the stranger simply acts as though he *expects* the child to talk, she may sometimes comply. I tried to do this when I first met Emma, but it didn't work. Maybe you'll have better luck."

Driving home, Dylan thought of how both women had described Emma. He hated the idea that her adoptive father had not treated her well. Aside from that, what had her childhood been like? Had she needed anything he might have been able to provide for her if he'd known of her existence? She had a wacko mother, that much he knew already. A mother who would sleep with a guy the first night she met him. *Watch the double standard, Geer.* A mother who would trick him into taking her up in the balloon to tell him about his daughter. Furious though he'd been at the time, the memory of her misguided ruse made him laugh out loud.

This was nuts. He had friends, mostly men, who had

children they never saw and they viewed their noninvolvement as a blessing. Well, maybe they didn't know what it was like to grow up without a father. If anyone had asked him a year ago how he would feel if he found out he had a child, he, too, might have expressed indifference.

But that would have been before he saw her picture.

18

Laura was short of breath. She'd noticed it first in the grocery store as she tried to decide what to serve Dylan for dinner that night. Deciding Emma's needs were far more important than Dylan's, she bought hamburger meat along with corn on the cob and Emma's favorite red-skin potato salad. She'd watched the young woman dishing the potato salad into a plastic container and wondered if something was wrong with her heart that she couldn't seem to take in a deep breath.

She was still short of breath late that afternoon while shaping the hamburger patties and husking the corn, but by this time she was certain it was nerves. The same anxiety was evident in Emma, who raced around the house, a naked Barbie in her hand, stopping to stare out the front window every few minutes.

"He'll be here at 5:30," Laura said the fourth time she caught Emma looking toward the driveway. "See?" She pointed to the clock. "He'll be here when the big hand is on the six, and the little hand is between the five and six."

Emma listened to Laura's explanation, studying the clock, then ran into the living room and turned on the television. A few minutes later, though, she was back at the kitchen window, and Laura wished she knew whether her daughter was dreading or looking forward to meeting the stranger.

A few days earlier, she'd had a long, one-sided talk with her.

"Do you remember Marti, Emma?" she'd asked as she was tucking her into bed. "The little girl you used to play with in our old neighborhood?"

Emma had nodded.

"Do you remember that Marti had two daddies?"

The nod again. Emma hugged her bunny close to her cheek.

"Well, the daddy she lived with was her *adoptive* daddy, and the daddy she went to visit was her *birth* daddy."

Staring at the ceiling, Emma frowned.

"You know how a mother and father have a baby together?"

Emma nodded. She knew about sperm and eggs, although she'd never asked exactly how the two got together.

"Well it's the birth father whose sperm helps make the baby. He's responsible for that baby ever being born. But sometimes the birth father isn't the one who raises the baby. That's the *adoptive* father. So Mr. Linder was Marti's adoptive father."

Mr. Linder was no such thing, in reality. He was simply Marti's stepfather, and not a very good one at that. But for the purpose of illustration, he would have to do.

"Not everyone has both an adoptive daddy and a birth daddy," Laura continued. "Most people, like Cory, just have a birth daddy. But you happen to have both."

Emma looked surprised at that, and Laura knew she was following her.

"Ray—Daddy—was your adoptive father. He loved you just as much as if he was your birth father, though. You were very special to him."

Emma picked at the bunny's ear with her thin, delicate

fingers, her eyes turned away from Laura's. *She doesn't believe that for an instant,* Laura thought.

"You also have a birth daddy," she said, "although you've never met him. I talked to him the other day. He'd like to meet you."

Emma's eyes widened in either surprise or terror. Laura couldn't tell which.

"Not yet, though," she said quickly. "Not till you're ready to meet him. I have a book that will help you understand about birth fathers and adoptive fathers. We can read it tomorrow, okay?"

Emma didn't react. Laura bent over to kiss her, turned on the fairy night-light and left the room, realizing as she did so that laying this on Emma right at bedtime had been a stupid thing to do. Emma had enough trouble sleeping without having something this enormous rolling around in her head. Sure enough, she was up and down for most of the night.

They read the book Heather had recommended together three times, and Dylan sent Emma pictures of himself so that he would not be a complete stranger when she met him. Still, Laura had no idea how much of the situation Emma understood, much less how she felt about it.

At five o'clock, she and Emma walked down the lane to the string of mailboxes lining the road. Laura got their mail, sorting through it on the way back to the house. There was another long white envelope bearing no return address, and she fingered it for a moment before tearing it open. She stopped walking to read.

Memory loss can be a blessing. Sarah is nothing to you. Don't go again.

The message sucked the remaining air from her lungs. Was this some sort of warning? She looked at the front of the envelope. This one had been mailed from Trenton rather than Philadelphia.

Emma tugged at the hem of Laura's T-shirt.

"All right, honey," she said, walking again. She folded the letter and put it in the pocket of her shorts. *Don't go again.* Was there an "or else" implied in that demand? Should she call the police? They would think she was making something out of nothing, and she probably was. Once she was back inside the house, though, the isolation of living on the lake suddenly overwhelmed her, and she locked the doors.

At exactly 5:30, Dylan arrived. Emma was at the window, and when she saw him coming up the walk, she ran upstairs to her bedroom. Laura let her go.

In the living room, she pushed open the screen door. "Hi," she said.

"You're out in the middle of nowhere." Dylan stepped into the living room carrying a foil-covered plate and a rectangular-shaped gift box. He was wearing a blue short-sleeved shirt and khaki shorts.

"You should talk," Laura said.

"True." He followed her into the kitchen. "Is there really a lake out there?" He looked through the back window at the thick screen of trees.

"Uh-huh. Through there." She pointed to the patch of blue-gray beyond the trees.

"I brought some dessert." He stepped away from the window and held out the covered plate. "Chocolate cake. Does Emma like chocolate cake?"

"Loves it, thanks." Laura took the plate from him and set it on the counter. The wrapped package was still in his hands, and she knew what it contained. Doctor Barbie. He'd asked her what gift Emma might like. *"Doctor Bar-*

bie?'' he'd said. "I didn't know there was such a thing. Barbie's come a long way, huh?"

"How about some lemonade or iced tea?" Laura asked. "Then I'll go see if I can convince her to come downstairs."

"Iced tea, please." If he was nervous about this meeting, it didn't show.

She poured a glass of tea for him. "By the way," she said, "when I was at the library to get the book Heather recommended for Emma, I picked up those books she'd suggested for you, as well. Save you a trip." She hoped he wouldn't think she was being pushy, but her daughter's well being was at stake.

"I've already read them," he said.

She looked at him in surprise. "You *have?*"

"I want this to work, Laura," he said. "I don't want to screw it up." Then he laughed. "I've read so much, I could probably get a job in a child care center by now."

She felt like hugging him. Instead, she put the pitcher back in the refrigerator and went upstairs.

Emma was sitting on her bed, leaning against the wall, surrounded by her stuffed animals. Her thumb was deep in her mouth. She looked like a three-year-old.

"Come on downstairs, honey," Laura said, cheer in her voice. "Dylan would like to meet you."

She'd expected a struggle, but to her surprise, Emma slipped off the bed and reached for her hand. They walked together down the stairs to the kitchen.

Dylan faced Emma with a smile. "You must be Emma," he said.

Emma slipped behind Laura, who put her hand on her daughter's head. "Emma, this is Dylan. Your birth father. Remember?" She couldn't see her, but she knew that Emma was peering out at Dylan, suspicion in her eyes.

"I brought a little present for you," Dylan said, holding the gift out in front of him. "It's to celebrate our meeting."

Emma shifted position ever so slightly behind Laura's back.

"Go ahead, honey," Laura said. "Take the present."

Emma moved slowly toward him, took the box from his hand, then stepped back to Laura's side to open it. She tore off the pink paper and was unable to hide her delight when she saw what was inside. Her eyes lit up, and she wore one of those rare, genuine smiles Laura saw so infrequently these days.

"Do you like it?" Dylan asked, and Emma, clutching her new treasure to her chest, slunk once again behind her mother.

"Well," Laura said to Dylan, "I hope you don't mind a casual dinner. We're having burgers. They're Emma's favorite, and I thought—"

"Good idea," Dylan said. "What can I do to help?"

"I thought you and Emma could make the salad," Laura said, hoping to ease the tension by putting them to work together. "Emma, let's wash your hands, honey."

Emma set the box containing Doctor Barbie on the counter and obediently climbed onto the footstool by the sink to wash her hands. Then Laura handed her a bowl of clean lettuce leaves. "You can tear these up and put them in the salad bowl, okay? Dylan, maybe you could chop the tomatoes and cucumbers."

Dylan asked Emma a few questions as they worked on the salad. What had she done that day? What was her favorite toy? Did she like to swim in the lake? Emma responded with her stony silence, concentrating on tearing the lettuce into various shapes, and Laura felt sorry for Dylan. He was trying, and she knew how frustrating it could be. Catching his eye above Emma's head, she gave him a sympathetic smile. At least Emma was helping him with the salad. Laura had been afraid she'd hide out in her room all night. But when Laura stepped out to the deck to light the grill, Emma jumped off her stool and ran after her, obviously not wanting to be left alone with the stranger. Laura didn't make an issue out of it, and once they were back in the kitchen, Emma climbed onto the stool again.

Pulling a ceramic bowl from one of the cabinets, Laura asked Emma, "Do you know what kind of work Dylan does?"

Emma concentrated on her task.

"He flies hot air balloons," Laura said.

Emma raised her head at that, a blank look in her eyes.

"Do you know what a hot air balloon is, Emma?" Dylan asked.

She stared at him without answering.

"Maybe I could draw a picture of one," Dylan said.

Laura was about to walk into the family room for some paper when Emma beat her to it. She returned with a box of crayons and a sheet of paper and set them on the counter next to the salad bowl.

It took Dylan less than a minute to draw his balloon, complete with its swirly striped design and a couple of people in the basket. "See?" he said. "I light a fire right here and that heats the air inside the balloon. When air is hot, it rises, so the balloon goes up in the air. People stand in this big basket and get to float through the air, above the treetops." He added some trees to the picture.

Emma was nearly smiling, and it warmed Laura's heart. Watching the two of them, father and daughter, talking about the balloon, she wondered if Dylan saw what she did—his own face reflected in Emma's.

Still, Emma did not want to be alone with him. She followed Laura outside each time she went onto the deck to check the grill.

"Take your new Barbie upstairs," Laura said, "and when you come back down we can eat."

She and Dylan walked out to the deck, and Dylan watched while she checked the hamburgers.

"I was hoping I could get her to talk," he said. "You know, like Heather said. If a stranger acted as though they expected her to talk, maybe she would." Dylan looked as though he'd failed.

"I'm her own mother," Laura said as she transferred the hamburgers to a plate. "The person she should be most comfortable with in the world, and I haven't been able to get her to talk. So don't feel bad. She's relating to you, at least. That's far more than I'd hoped for."

"I was overly optimistic, I guess." He took the plate from her and carried it to the picnic table. "She looks so much like my sister's kids," he said.

"She looks like *you*."

He smiled. "I knew from her picture that she was mine, but seeing her in person, I just... It's hard to believe. I actually have a child."

Emma returned from upstairs and the three of them sat at the picnic table, Laura and Dylan making one hundred percent of the conversation as they ate. Dylan talked a bit more about the hot air balloon, then changed the subject. "Your mom told me she's an astronomer," he said to Emma. "That must be a very interesting job."

Emma suddenly left her seat and ran into the house. Dylan and Laura looked at each other.

"Was it something I said?" Dylan asked.

"Your guess is as good as mine," Laura said, perplexed.

In a moment, Emma returned to the table. Standing next

to Laura, she handed Dylan the framed photograph of Laura's fifth comet.

"She's trying to tell you I've discovered some comets," she said, touched by her daughter's gesture.

"You did?" Dylan held the picture in front of him. Then it seemed to dawn on him. "Laura Brandon," he said. "You're not...this isn't one of the Brandon comets, is it?" he asked.

Emma and Laura nodded at the same time. "That's Brandon Comet Five," she said.

Dylan was clearly stunned. "I had no idea." He looked at Emma. "Your mom is very famous, did you know that?"

Emma slid behind her mother, the direct question making her shy once again.

"I used to pilot big planes," he said. "Jets. And I remember how much I loved to fly on a clear night back then when this comet was in the sky. It was a beauty."

"I saw it from a plane once, too," Laura said. "You feel like you're right next to it."

"You've found another one since then, haven't you?"

"Actually, five since then," she said.

"Five! You mean ten all together? That must be a record."

"No." She laughed. "Not even very close. But the last one I found is going to be bigger than this one." She pointed to the photograph. "You'll be able to see it without a telescope next summer."

"So, this is your area of research? Comets?"

"Actually, no. Professionally, I study planetary atmosphere. Finding comets is my hobby. I do it on my own time, with my backyard telescope."

"No kidding?"

Laura could tell that Emma was growing bored with the

conversation, and she'd barely touched her burger. Ordinarily, she'd try to get her to eat a little more, but not tonight.

"How about we play some games?" she suggested. "Then we can have some of the cake Dylan brought."

In the family room, they played Fish and Candyland. Emma was still clingy, still eying Dylan with distrust, but Laura felt optimistic. He was a nice guy. This might work out.

She put Emma to bed at eight, and the little girl literally gripped Laura's hand in her own, obviously not wanting to be left alone. Or, not wanting Laura to go back to the family room where Dylan was waiting for her.

"Did you have a good time tonight?" Laura asked her.

Emma gave a shrug and hugged her bunny closer to her chest.

"Maybe some day we can watch Dylan go up in the hot air balloon. Would you like that?"

Emma nodded.

"You sleep tight, now, honey." Gently extracting her hand from Emma's, she leaned over to kiss her.

Emma pointed to the night-light.

"I'll turn it on," Laura said. She did so, then walked downstairs to the family room.

Dylan stood near the bookcase, studying a photograph of Laura, Ray and Emma. Emma was only two in that picture, a dark-haired little waif.

"Is this your father?" Dylan asked. "Emma's grandfather?"

Laura laughed. It was not the first time she'd heard that question. "That's Ray," she said.

"Your husband?" His eyes were wide.

"Uh-huh."

"Oh, I'm sorry. I thought..." Two coins of color sprang to Dylan's cheeks, and Laura laughed again.

"It's a common mistake," she said. "Ray was twenty-one years older than me."

Dylan returned his gaze to the picture. "Emma was a cute kid," he said. "Still is. It's got to be so hard on you, though, trying to figure out what she's thinking all the time."

"It is, but I figure it must be a thousand times harder on her, trying to communicate without being able to speak."

"What was she like before...it all happened?"

"Would you like to see a video?" Laura asked.

Dylan's eyes lit up. "Yes."

She culled through the videos in the drawer under the TV and put one into the VCR. "Emma's four in this one," she said, sitting in the chair closest to the TV, the remote in her hand. Dylan sat on the sofa. "This was in Brazil, where I was working at an observatory. She and her baby-sitter's little girl were playing dress-up and putting on a skit for us."

Emma and little Carlita came into camera range, giggling and tripping over the fabric they had tied around their waists. Scarves covered their hair and big earrings drooped from their ears. They proceeded to perform a skit that had no rhyme nor reason to it, as far as Laura had been able to tell, but it obviously had some meaning to the two little girls. Emma did most of the talking, some of it in the Portuguese she'd picked up from the sitter and Carlita. She was garrulous, actually, interrupting Carlita loudly when the smaller girl would try to speak. Dylan sat on the edge of the sofa, transfixed. Laura hadn't looked at this tape in a long time. It was painful to watch. Emma had completely lost that vitality and self-confidence.

Once the tape had finished, Laura clicked off the video, and she and Dylan sat in silence.

"My God," he said finally. "She didn't shut up once."

"That's the real Emma," Laura said.

"She was so feisty."

"She was born feisty," Laura said, "and started talking early. She talked constantly, even if it was gibberish. She'd talk to anyone who was around, and if no one was around, she'd talk to herself." It saddened her to remember the child Emma used to be. "She was the great communicator. I wonder what it's like for her now. What's it like for someone who was always sharing her thoughts to suddenly lose her voice? How can she tolerate it? Her gabbiness could drive Ray and me crazy sometimes, but now I'd give anything to hear it again."

Dylan stared at the blank TV. He swallowed hard, and for a moment she thought he might cry. She felt like crying herself.

"I feel powerless," he said.

The tone of his voice held such defeat that she was afraid he might give up on Emma. "Can you hang in there?" she asked.

"Oh, definitely," he said. "I promise you that, Laura. I'm in for the duration." His face was very serious and she knew he was telling her the truth. He looked back at the television. "I missed out on a lot by not knowing her all this time."

"Are you angry with me for not letting you know about her?"

"Angry? No way. I would never have been ready to be a father to her before now. Believe me. I was in no shape for it."

Laura sighed and leaned back in her chair. "I feel like a detective these days," she said. "The people I care about are mysteries to me. I don't know what's going on in Emma's mind. And there's this woman…'' She waved the thought away. Why get into that?

"What woman?" Dylan asked.

"Oh, it's a long story," she said.

"I'm not going anywhere." He settled deeper into the sofa, as if readying himself for a long story.

She told him about her father's death and the promise she'd made him. She told him about her visits to Sarah Tolley and her inability to discover the attachment between the old woman and her father. And she told him about the notes, pulling the second one from the pocket of her shorts to read to him.

"'Memory loss can be a blessing,'" she read. "'Sarah is nothing to you. Don't go again.'" Reading the note aloud sent a fresh chill up her spine.

Dylan sat forward, arms on his knees. "Weird," he said. "She has no family?"

"My father said she doesn't. And the attendant at the retirement home says no one's ever visited her till now."

"And you haven't been able to figure out any connection between her and your father?"

She shook her head.

"Lovers?" he suggested.

"Well, it's possible, I guess. My mother died when I was seven, and as far as I knew, he never had a girlfriend, although he did have some women friends. But if he had been seeing Sarah, I knew nothing about it. And unfortunately, Sarah doesn't seem to, either."

"Oh, he was seeing someone." Dylan nodded with certainty. "Man doesn't live by bread alone."

She smiled. "I suppose not. But I sure haven't found any indication of it."

"Could she—Sarah—remember and just not want to let you know for some reason?"

That hadn't occurred to her. "I guess it's possible," she said.

"So let's say your father was her lover at some time. Maybe someone doesn't want you to know that and that's why they've sent you the notes."

"Doesn't make a whole lot of sense," she said.

"I suppose not." He looked as perplexed as she felt. Then his gaze shifted to the window. "Hey, it's a clear night," he said "Do you have a telescope?"

She laughed. "Do you have a balloon? Of course." She looked at her watch. "Want to see my latest comet?"

They walked upstairs and down the hall. Dylan stopped short at the entrance to the skylight room. "Wow!" he said, looking up through the Plexiglas ceiling. "Incredible!"

She pulled open the sliding glass door that led onto the deck. "We'll take the telescope out here since it's so gorgeous tonight." She carefully wheeled the telescope onto the deck and around to the north side of the house.

"This is a phenomenal setup," Dylan said.

"We have to give our eyes a chance to adapt to the dark," she said.

She adjusted the settings on the telescope, knowing exactly where her comet would be at this time of night. After a few minutes, she peered through the lens, spotting the small, fuzzy object that promised to grow into something spectacular as it neared the earth.

"Take a look," she said.

He lowered his head to the eyepiece.

"See that globular cluster in the right side of the field?" she asked.

He laughed. "Oh, sure. What's a globular cluster? Oh, that white mass there?"

"Right. Well, just to its left, smack in the middle of the field, is a tiny fuzzy ball. See it?"

"Uh-huh. That's the comet?"

"Right."

"It doesn't have a tail."

"You can't see one yet, but I think it's going to have a terrific tail next year."

"Will it be as big as Hale-Bopp?"

"Bigger, I think. It's hard to predict that for sure yet."

He was quiet as he continued observing the sky, and Laura braved asking him the question that had been on her mind for a while.

"Have you ever been married?" she asked. It seemed peculiar for a forty-one-year-old man never to have married. "You were adamant about being unattached at Heather's office."

"No, never married," he said, without lifting his head. "I lived with a woman for many years, but that's a long and miserable story. So now I'm sort of…leery of commitment."

"Because of the long and miserable story?"

"Mostly."

"Well, you said you would commit to Emma."

"Different." He stepped back from the telescope and looked at her. "She's my daughter."

The words touched her in a way she couldn't describe. She no longer felt so alone.

They spent half the night staring through the telescope. She hadn't done that since before Ray's death. Spending the night with the stars had lost its magic for her; her time with the telescope had contributed to Ray's unhappiness. But tonight, she recaptured the sense of wonder and joy instilled in her by her father. And each time she explained some phenomenon to Dylan, she heard the life in her voice, the confidence. The sky was the one thing she understood and could count on when everything else in her life was a mystery.

19

"Is it a clock?" Sarah asked, a puzzled expression on her face.

"It's both a clock and a calendar," Laura said, still pleased with her purchase. She was hanging the white plastic device on Sarah's kitchenette wall, while the older woman watched her, perplexed. It was quite large. On its right side was a clock with large black numbers. On the left side, the month, the date and the day of the week were displayed.

"All you have to do every morning is push this button and it will change the date," Laura said as she began pushing the button. "See? Now I've got it up to today's date. And it says Wednesday. So, if you push the button every day, you'll know when Wednesday comes and that I'll be here to take you for a walk. Or if it's raining, like last week, I'll bring a movie."

The previous Wednesday had been stormy, so Laura had picked up *African Queen* at the video store, remembering that Sarah had mentioned the movie when she spoke of her courtship with Joe Tolley. Sarah seemed to thoroughly enjoy the movie, though Laura missed hearing her talk about her life.

"You ready?" Laura asked now, but the question was unnecessary. Sarah already had the door open and was walking into the hall.

Outside the retirement home, Laura tried to steer Sarah in the other direction for a change, but the older woman stood glued to the sidewalk. She wanted to take the familiar route, it seemed, so Laura gave in and joined her.

"Remember I told you that Dylan wanted to meet Emma?" Laura said as they walked.

"Dylan?" Sarah asked.

Of course she didn't remember. Laura wasn't sure why she tried talking to Sarah about her own life. It seemed pointless, but it was a way to start the conversation.

"Yes. My little girl, Emma's, father. Biological father. They met for the first time the other night."

"My," said Sarah. "How old is...the little girl?" Emma's name was lost in the tangle of Sarah's memory already.

"Five. She was pretty shy with him, but I think it went well for a first meeting."

"Does she like him?"

"Well, Emma doesn't speak, so I'm not sure how she feels about him. She had a terrible scare a few months ago and it left her mute." Laura was about to explain the meaning of *mute,* but Sarah seemed to understand.

"Ah," she said. "Who is...the girl, again? Your daughter?"

"Yes," Laura said.

"How old is she?"

"Five," Laura repeated patiently.

"And she's mute. Must be very frustrating for you at times."

"Yes. It sure is."

Sarah looked into the distance, toward the clock tower several blocks away. "I had a patient who was mute once."

"Did you?" Laura asked, sincerely curious.

"She about drove me to become a patient myself," Sarah said.

Laura laughed. "Tell me about her," she said.

Sarah, 1956

"That's Saint Margaret's?" Sarah asked Joe as he turned the car into the long drive. Ahead of them, at the crest of a broad, grassy hill, stood a huge building constructed of stone, which had grown dark and dirty with age.

"That's it," Joe said, pointing. "See the sign?"

Sarah's eyes followed his finger to the small white sign wedged into the side of the hill. *Saint Margaret's Psychiatric Hospital.* Hard to believe.

"It looks more like a house of horrors," she said.

She was there for an interview as a nurse. She and Joe had moved to the Maryland suburbs shortly after getting married and were now living in a darling little house next to a park. Saint Margaret's would be much more convenient to their new home than Mercy had been, and Sarah was thrilled to have this interview. Saint Margaret's was a top-class facility. From the outside, though, one would never guess.

The driveway curved around in front of the main entrance, and Joe stopped the car. "Are you sure you'll be all right taking a taxi home?" he asked.

"Of course. I'll be fine." She leaned toward him for a kiss.

"Good luck, then," he said. "Call me at the office to let me know how it went."

She stepped out of the car and waved after him as he headed down the driveway. Then, smoothing the skirt of her uniform, she took a deep breath and pushed open the huge, intimidating wooden door of the house of horrors.

She was in a large square foyer, three stories high, rich with dark wood trim. Light poured through glass panels in the ceiling high above her, forming golden columns in the air. Voices echoed softly around her. The floor was formed of large, black-and-white, diamond-shaped tiles. There was a sense of aged elegance, and she could not detect the pervasive hospital smell she was so accustomed to at Mercy.

The reception desk was at one side of the foyer.

"I have an appointment with the nursing supervisor," Sarah said to the clerk seated behind the desk. "Mrs. Love, I believe her name is."

She was told to take a seat, and she waited for nearly ten minutes on a lovely floral-patterned couch before Mrs. Love arrived. The supervisor was a young, attractive woman in a nurse's uniform. Her smile was engaging, and there was a bounce in her step as she ushered Sarah down a long, dim corridor and into her office.

Sarah took a seat across the broad desk from the supervisor.

"What a beautiful pin!" Mrs. Love said.

Sarah touched the collar of her uniform. Joe had suggested she remove the pin for the interview, but she couldn't bear to take it off. As she had promised, she wore it every day.

"My husband gave it to me as a wedding gift," she told Mrs. Love. "My supervisor at Mercy didn't mind me wearing it. But if you—"

"Oh, it's not a problem. We all have special little things we do here to individualize our uniforms. This is mine." She touched the delicate gold chain at her throat.

"It's stunning," Sarah said.

"Well." Mrs. Love glanced at the papers on her desk. "I've looked your résumé over," she said, "and I'm very impressed. The work you did at Mercy should prepare you well for what you'll do here.''

What you'll do here. She made it sound as though Sarah already had the job. And indeed, the interview that followed was more a friendly chat than any sort of interrogation. Mrs. Love did most of the talking, telling Sarah about the innovative programs at Saint Margaret's, about the state-of-the-art equipment in the hospital, and about the hospital's director, Dr. Peter Palmiento. Mrs. Love's cheeks glowed a vibrant rose color when she spoke about the director. ''Surely you've heard of him,'' she said.

Of course Sarah had heard of him. Everyone wanted to work with Peter Palmiento. He was changing the face of psychiatry. ''Yes, I have.'' She smiled.

''He's put Saint Margaret's on the map,'' Mrs. Love said. ''He's a man of incredible power, yet a lovely human being, and he's the reason we have all the equipment you could ever hope for. There's a great deal of very exciting research going on here, and Dr. P. is a wizard at getting funding to keep it alive. Everyone adores him.'' It was difficult to tell if Mrs. Love was talking about a man or a god. ''This is an extraordinary place to work,'' she added.

''It sounds like it,'' Sarah said, a little overcome.

Mrs. Love took in a long breath, composing herself. ''So,'' she said. ''Let me tell you about your salary and the hours you'll be working.''

''Are you saying I have the job?'' Sarah asked.

Mrs. Love laughed. ''Yes, of course. That is, if you want it.''

''Oh, I do!'' She couldn't wait to tell Joe.

After discussing the work schedule and salary, Mrs. Love took Sarah on a tour of the hospital. The huge, glowing foyer was only the beginning of the surprises. Mrs. Love showed her an empty patient room, and Sarah thought it looked more like a room one would see in a charming old hotel than in a psychiatric hospital. There was even a private bath. Not all the rooms had them, Mrs. Love hastened to say, but there were many rooms just like that one.

Down the hall, there was a sunny patient lounge with game tables and a television set in the corner. Some of the patients glanced up when Sarah and Mrs. Love peered into the room, but they quickly resumed their activities. Next to the lounge was a small theater, and next to that, a beauty parlor. "The better the patients look, the better they seem to feel," said Mrs. Love. "It does wonders for those suffering from depression."

"This is an extraordinary facility," Sarah said, nearly breathless with wonder. Mercy was woefully behind the times compared to Saint Margaret's.

They took the curved staircase to the third story—ward three, Mrs. Love called it—and there was an almost palpable difference in the air as soon as they opened the door to the hallway. There was a leaden silence, broken occasionally by some mumbled sounds and, at one point, a piercing scream.

"The isolation room." Mrs. Love pointed to the door from behind which the scream had emanated.

Sarah nodded. She'd heard those piercing screams of sheer loneliness coming from the isolation room at Mercy. That was nothing new. What *was* new to her was the EEG lab, the room where they could painlessly assess a patient's brain waves. They hadn't even had an EEG machine at Mercy, much less a whole lab. Sarah was truly impressed.

"May I learn how to operate these machines?" she asked.

"Absolutely, dear," Mrs. Love said. "That's one thing you'll discover about Saint Margaret's. You're encouraged to expand your skills and to learn just as much as you desire.''

Across the hall, Mrs. Love allowed her to peer through a small window cut into a door. In the room beyond, several beds were lined up against the walls, and in the beds lay sleeping men and women. ''We call this the slumber room,'' Mrs. Love said.

''Are they drugged?'' Sarah asked, voicing her suspicion.

''Yes. We're using experimental drugs in here to see what medication works best on which type of patient. This is part of Dr. Palmiento's research.''

Sarah felt a twinge of discomfort. Human guinea pigs. Yet, what else had she expected in a research facility?

They walked past the electroshock treatment room. It, too, was larger and had far more elaborate equipment than Sarah was used to. She had detested the idea of treating patients with electroshock therapy back when she was a nursing student, but after she'd seen the dramatic difference it could make in some of her most depressed patients, she'd changed her mind. It would often leave the patients with partial memory loss, but that was temporary—usually—and as their melancholia lessened, they became functional human beings again. In most cases. Not all. And it was impossible to know who would respond and who would simply get worse. Maybe that was something worthy of researching. Maybe she could talk to Dr. Palmiento about it. She smiled to herself, caught up in the excitement of working in such a dynamic institution.

''Here's our surgery,'' Mrs. Love said when they'd reached the end of the hall.

''Surgery?''

''Lobotomies, mainly,'' Mrs. Love said, and Sarah hoped the supervisor didn't see her cringe. Although lobotomies were being performed at many hospitals around the country, they had not been done at Mercy, and Sarah could not shake her feeling that they were barbaric. She knew she was out of step with the times. The procedure had won the Nobel Prize, for heaven's sake.

"This is Dr. Palmiento's office." Mrs. Love pointed across the hall. "Oh, look! He's in. Would you like to say hello to him?"

"Uh...I don't want to disturb him." Sarah felt intimidated by the man after all she'd heard about him.

Mrs. Love knocked on the door and poked her head inside. "Good morning, Dr. P. Would you like to meet our new nurse?"

Through the glass window in the door, Sarah saw a man in his late fifties look up from his desk. "Of course," he said. "Bring her in."

She stepped into the office behind her new supervisor.

"This is Sarah Tolley," Mrs. Love said. "Mrs. Tolley, this is Dr. Palmiento. Or Dr. P., as we call him around here."

He stood up and walked around the side of his desk, a warm smile on his face.

"Hello, Doctor." Sarah reached her hand toward him, and he pumped it with enthusiasm. He was unabashedly handsome. No wonder Mrs. Love had a crush on him.

"Good to have you on board, Mrs. Tolley." His hair was light brown and only beginning to gray, and his face was softly lined. There was a gentleness in his features—except for his eyes, which were green, riveting and disconcerting. They did not fit the rest of his demeanor. Sarah had experienced that sort of impaling eye contact before—from several of her psychiatric patients. Patients who looked perfectly healthy otherwise, but whose eyes gave away the psychosis within. She withdrew her hand from his as quickly as she could without seeming discourteous, disturbed by her own reaction. Here was a brilliant doctor, by all accounts a caring human being, who simply happened to have piercing eyes. She was being silly to think it was anything else.

"And where will Mrs. Tolley be working?" He spoke to Mrs. Love, but his gaze was still locked on Sarah, and she had to look away.

"Ward three." Mrs. Love said.

"Aha!" He sounded overjoyed, a man who clearly loved his work. "You must be a highly skilled nurse, Mrs. Tolley. Joyce wouldn't put just anyone on ward three."

Sarah smiled at the supervisor. "Thank you for the vote of confidence," she said.

"I put her there because she's excited about research and she has some surgical experience."

"Not really," Sarah said quickly. "Not since nursing school, anyhow." She didn't want to find herself assisting at lobotomies.

They ignored her weak protest. "I do most of my work in ward three," Dr. Palmiento said. "That's where our more seriously disturbed patients are housed."

"I've heard wonderful things about you and the work you're doing." Sarah hoped she didn't sound quite as reverential as Joyce Love.

Palmiento nodded with a smile and rested his hand on Sarah's shoulder. "You're going to be a fine addition to our team," he said.

Once back in the corridor, Mrs. Love turned to Sarah.

"Isn't he something?" she asked.

"He seems very excited by his work," Sarah said, still unnerved by her mixed reaction to the director. He was a doctor, not a patient, she reminded herself. A nationally recognized psychiatrist. And she should know better than to think she could diagnose anyone from the quality of their eye contact.

Her first week at Saint Margaret's went smoothly enough. She was assigned to just two patients, women, both of whom suffered from depression, and she found them likable. She was drawn to her patients, and she firmly believed that a positive relationship between patient and caregiver was the catalyst for healing whatever was wrong with the mind. She often talked lovingly with her patients or even held them when they needed comforting.

Toward the end of Sarah's first week, a new patient, Karen, arrived on ward three and was assigned to her. Forty years old, mother of three children and the wife of a politician, Karen had been completely mute for the past six years. It was the first time Sarah had encountered such severe, pervasive mutism. Karen's husband denied remembering any triggering event. One spring day, Karen had simply stopped talking, he said. To him, to their children, to the neighbors. She even stopped singing, and she had sung in the church choir for ten years.

Sarah was determined to get to the root of Karen's problem. She spent hours with the woman, day after day, talking to her, trying gently to unearth the trauma that had led her to lose her voice. She was patient and very, very kind, hoping that Karen would one day realize she could trust her and open up to her.

Dr. P. had an entirely different approach. On the third day of Karen's hospitalization, Sarah was talking to the mute woman when Dr. P. suddenly burst into the room.

"You hideous wench!" he shouted.

Sarah's jaw dropped. Which of them was he talking to? Karen looked at him with her big, sad eyes.

"Your husband told me you neglected your children," Dr. P. said, his green eyes flashing wildly. "You're the sort of woman who should be fixed. Shouldn't ever have been allowed to have children at all!'' With that he was gone, leaving Sarah trembling and Karen's face as blank as before.

Sarah touched Karen's arm and stood up. "I'll be right back," she said, walking toward the door.

She found Dr. Palmiento outside the slumber room. It was the first time she'd spoken to him since their initial meeting in his office, and she rued that their first real contact was to be a conflict. But she was angry.

"Excuse me, Dr. Palmiento," she said. "I don't understand why you broke into Karen's room that way. She's very fragile."

A warm smile came to his lips, and he touched her shoulder. "Are you questioning my methods?" The words were combative, but it almost sounded as if he were teasing her.

"No...I mean, yes. I think she needs support, not—"

"You handle her your way, and I'll handle her mine," he said, as though engaging her in friendly competition. "We'll see which of us wins."

For several weeks, Sarah continued to sit for an hour each day with Karen, talking to her, sometimes holding her hand. And during those same weeks, Dr. P. yelled at and berated the patient. If he spotted Karen walking down the hall, he would flood her with insults.

On one occasion, Sarah was walking toward the lounge with Karen when Dr. P. passed them in the hall. Once he was a few steps behind them, he called to them, loud enough for those in the foyer to hear. "I hope you're taking her down to the beauty parlor, Mrs. Tolley," he shouted. "Though I'm not sure what they'll be able to do for her there. Better try a plastic surgeon first."

Karen swung around, and for the first time Sarah saw

life in the woman's eyes. "Leave me alone, you god-damned son of a bitch!" she said.

Sarah stood frozen, stunned at hearing Karen's voice. Down the hall, Dr. Palmiento laughed as he walked away.

"I believe I win that round, Mrs. Tolley," he called over his shoulder.

Everyone loved him, and Sarah grew increasingly confused by her feelings about him. He was mercurial—warm, fatherly and immensely human one minute, clinically detached, even cruel, the next. Everyone thought he'd been very clever in getting Karen to talk. Once her silence had been broken, Karen continued to make progress, although much of her language was peppered with blasphemy and evidence of delusions. Yes, Sarah had to admit, Palmiento's approach had worked. But at what cost? What did it do to someone's spirit to be insulted and treated like a project instead of a human being?

The rest of the staff thought it was exciting that Dr. P. was experimenting with new drugs on his patients. "If my mother needed to be in a psychiatric hospital," Sarah heard one of the nurses say, "I'd want her to be here so she could get the latest treatment." But Palmiento's experimentation made Sarah nervous. He'd inject depressed patients with something called LSD, day after day, in an attempt to "break down their walls." The LSD scared Sarah. Patients reacted to it in unpredictable ways. They'd scream, or try to climb the walls of their rooms, literally, or they'd attempt to throw themselves through their windows. Others slept for days at a time, tossing from wild, unimaginable dreams. And Dr. P. observed it all from his clinical perspective, writing copious notes on the patients' reactions and applying for yet another grant to fund more research into the next drug possibility.

There were other patients, some of them Sarah's, on

whom he performed electroshock treatments. Sarah, herself, had suggested it for one patient who was so depressed she tried to hang herself from a doorknob with her underpants. But at the time, Sarah had not known about Dr. P.'s experimental approach to ECT. He used 150 volts several times a day instead of the usual 110 volts every few days. Instead of one shock, he would fire off eight or more of them, right through the patient's convulsions. The patients no longer knew where they were or even who they were. Then Dr. P. would combine that treatment with his unique brand of drug therapy. He was after "extreme confusion," he explained. His approach would wipe clean the slate of the patients' old maladaptive ways of thinking and behaving. Then he and the staff could teach them healthier ways to live. The theory was sound enough, yet it seemed to Sarah that few patients were actually getting well.

She finally went to Mrs. Love with her concerns.

Mrs. Love smiled at her, condescension in her expression. "Dr. P. is way ahead of his time," she said. "You're a smart woman, Sarah. You know people tend to laugh at geniuses. Or berate them. Look at Einstein. People thought he was retarded. And Copernicus. They thought he was crazy."

"I'm concerned that his methods might be making some of the patients worse rather than better," Sarah said.

"You haven't been here long enough to see the real progress yet," Mrs. Love said. "You must keep the big picture in mind. The things we'll learn from Dr. P.'s treatments here at Saint Margaret's will one day be applied to other patients in other hospitals in the future. You'll see."

"I've just…it's so different from what I was used to at Mercy," Sarah said.

The condescending smile again. "I don't want to say anything negative about Mercy," Mrs. Love said. "It's a fine hospital. But the truth is, their approach to mental illness is rather antiquated. Don't stand in the path of progress, Sarah.''

She wondered if Joyce Love might be right. Everyone seemed so enamored of Dr. P., so respectful of the "important work" he was doing. Was she the type of person who would have laughed at Copernicus? She would have to keep a more open mind.

20

The dark, early morning air had a chill to it, despite the fact that it was the middle of August, and Laura opened the car windows as she drove toward the wine country.

"Doesn't it feel wonderful to be up this early?" she asked Emma, who was strapped into the back seat behind her.

Emma had frowned when Laura told her they were going to visit Dylan, and it must have seemed odd to her that they were getting up in the dark to do so. But she nearly leapt out of her bed when Laura told her they would watch him fly his balloon. "He flies it very early in the morning so he and his passengers can watch the sunrise," she'd added, suddenly realizing that the hot air balloon might be the key to Emma's heart.

The day before, she and Emma had taken an early morning drive in the opposite direction, into Maryland. Laura needed to see Saint Margaret's, the spooky, old mental hospital Sarah had described so vividly. Saint Margaret's, she discovered, no longer existed. At least not as a hospital. It was now a boarding school, but viewing it from the street, she had to admit it still had that house-of-horrors appearance, and she could imagine the jokes the students who lived there made about it.

She'd wanted to see the inside. The high-ceilinged foyer, at least. Parking the car in the circular driveway, she and

Emma walked up to the foreboding double doors. Inside, she found the foyer much as Sarah had described it, except that the light from the skylights was milky and indistinct. And rather than nurses and doctors, girls in navy blue uniforms roamed the diamond-patterned floor.

"Can I help you?" a young woman asked as she approached her and Emma.

Laura smiled at her. "I just wanted to see the foyer," she said, even though she would have loved to see the rest of the building, as well. Did students now live in the slumber room? But the expression on the young woman's face told her she didn't have a snowball's chance in hell of getting past the foyer unless she could come up with a better reason for being there.

Holding Emma's hand, Laura walked back outside and into the hazy sunlight. She'd been a little crazy to drive all the way out here just to see this building. Ray had been right. She was becoming obsessed with Sarah Tolley, just as she had with every other project in her life.

Two deer stood in the darkness at the edge of Dylan's driveway.

"Look, Emma!" She stopped the car on the side of the road and pointed toward the deer. "A mother and a baby."

Emma pressed her face against the car window, but it was too dark for Laura to see her expression. Emma used to know that a baby deer was called a fawn. Was that word going through her mind right now? Laura felt a sudden, near-tears sort of exasperation. *Talk to me, Emma,* she wanted to say. *Tell me what you're thinking.*

She drove down the long driveway, the woods surrounding them in darkness. There were two vans in front of the garage this morning, and she parked to the side, trying not to block anyone in. Getting out of the car, she spotted several dark figures standing in the center of the field.

Taking Emma's hand, they walked toward the activity. Laura felt her daughter's mounting resistance in her lagging step and the tight grip of her fingers. She was probably a bit spooked by the darkness.

"Those people are working on the balloon." Laura pointed toward the center of the field. The crew was bustling around the huge balloon, which still lay on the ground as it filled with cold air from the fan. The sky was lightening quickly, and by the time she and Emma reached the balloon, Laura could see that Dylan was working on the burner. She thought of pointing him out to Emma, but decided against it, remembering Emma's frown from earlier that morning.

Dylan glanced up from his task, and Laura waved. He said something to Alex, who was working next to him, and walked toward her and Emma.

"Hey," he said as he neared them. "Two of my favorite ladies." He gave Laura that smile that made her remember exactly why and how her daughter had been conceived, then knelt down in front of Emma. He was wearing his blue jumpsuit again and heavy work gloves. "Did you come to watch the balloon go up?" he asked.

Emma sidled halfway behind Laura.

"Can you explain a little of what you're doing?" Laura asked him.

"Sure." He stood up again. "First we're filling the envelope—the balloon—with cold air, and after it's partway filled, we'll heat the air. Remember I told you about hot air making the balloon rise, Emma?"

Laura wasn't certain if Emma nodded or not.

"The way I do that is with a very big flame. So when you see the flame, you don't need to be afraid. It's supposed to be there."

Dylan's gaze was drawn to something behind them, and

Laura turned to see a man and woman walking across the field from the driveway.

"Excuse me," Dylan said, and he started toward the couple.

He spoke to them for a few minutes, then returned to the balloon, and the man and woman came to stand near her and Emma. They looked as though they might be close to seventy, and they wore anticipatory smiles.

"You must be the passengers for this morning," Laura said to them.

"Yes," said the man.

"I don't know how I let him talk me into this," said the woman, laughing.

"It's our fiftieth anniversary," the man said. "And this is something I've always wanted to do, so she gave it to me as a present."

"Congratulations," Laura said, thinking of her sham birthday flight. "What a wonderful way this will be to celebrate."

"Have you ever been up in one of those things?" the woman asked, clearly hunting for reassurance.

"Yes," Laura said, and Emma looked up at her in sharp surprise. "I have, honey," she said to Emma. "I went up with Dylan a few weeks ago." To the woman she said, "It's breathtaking. You're going to love it."

"You must be friends of the pilot, then," the man said. "Of Dylan Geer's."

"That's right. I'm Laura, and this is Emma."

The man turned his attention to Emma. "What a pretty name," he said to her. "How old are you, Emma?"

Emma pressed her face against Laura's hip.

"She's shy," Laura said. She hated calling Emma "shy" but didn't know what else to say. Coping with a mute child wasn't in the parenting books. Still, she was afraid that by labeling her shy, Emma would begin to think of herself that way. Well, it was becoming the truth, wasn't it? But it was the last word Laura would have used to describe her in the past.

Emma suddenly gasped, and Laura looked at the balloon. Dylan was standing in front of its large, round opening and had lit the flame.

"Watch now," she said to Emma. "He's heating the air and the balloon will slowly rise up."

Dylan was silhouetted in the circle of light from the balloon opening. The muscles in his arms were cut by the light from the fire behind him, and Laura wondered if she could possibly be feeling the heat from the flame from where she stood. She was reminded for a moment of Sarah, staring at the paintings of nudes in the restaurant, growing hotter by the minute, and she stifled a laugh.

He's Emma's father, she told herself, unnerved by the sudden visceral attraction. *That's all you need him to be.*

As the colorful fabric began to rise above the basket, Emma slowly moved apart from Laura and closer to the balloon. Laura thought of calling her back but didn't dare squelch this small act of independence as long as Emma was not in the way. Emma stopped a safe distance from the balloon, and there she stood, small hands knotted behind her back, and although Laura could not see her face, she was certain the little girl's eyes were wide with wonder. She was so tiny. Her hair was in a ponytail, and her neck looked thin and fragile. Laura finally stole her gaze from her daughter to watch the balloon herself, trying to imagine how magical it would look through Emma's eyes.

She and Emma watched as the man and woman climbed into the basket. The woman giggled like a schoolgirl, making Laura smile. She reminded Laura of Sarah. Why, though, had fate allowed this woman a husband, a fiftieth anniversary and the means to climb into a balloon and sail into the air, while Sarah was left alone with her fading mind in the retirement home? Laura was surprised by the quick rise of tears, and she blinked them back. Maybe she could visit Sarah more than once a week.

"See you in about an hour," Dylan called to them from the basket. "I'll make you and Emma breakfast. Bye, Emma." He waved.

He was good about this, she thought. For a guy who knew nothing about children, he remembered that Emma was there, and he spoke to her even though she would not speak back.

They watched the balloon rise into the air. Alex got into his truck, which was parked in the field, and Brian walked with Laura and Emma back toward the driveway.

"Dylan said for you two to follow me in your car while we chase the balloon," Brian said to Laura. "Keep a close eye on me, though. You never know when we're going to have to turn and go in another direction. You know, like if someone gets sick or something." He grinned at her, and she guessed that he knew the true nature of her birthday ride deceit.

"Okay," she said with a smile.

She buckled Emma into the back seat of her car, then followed Brian's van down the driveway to begin the chase.

Alex and Brian were waiting for him. Dylan saw them as he guided the balloon toward one of his favorite landing sites—an empty pasture belonging to a balloon-friendly farmer—but it wasn't his crew he was looking for.

"Is it going to bounce when we land?" his female passenger asked him.

"Nope," Dylan said. "This is going to be one smooth landing."

The woman had relaxed once they were in the air, enjoying the ride with her husband, but she'd become unnerved again as he began the descent and they swept over the tops of the trees.

Searching the pasture, he finally spotted Laura and Emma walking toward his crew, and he felt relief at seeing them there. Relief and trepidation. He wanted to help that little girl, and he didn't know how. There'd been wonder in her eyes earlier when he was readying the balloon, and he wished he could tap into that wonder somehow. Free her up enough to talk. Usually, children who were around when he was inflating the balloon were filled with questions and curiosity. They'd try to get too close, the questions spilling from them as they inched nearer. Why doesn't the balloon catch fire? How do you steer? He'd seen those questions burning inside Emma. It had to be the worst thing in the world to be filled with questions and unable to get them out.

He was in over his head with this child, but he was in for good.

Once Dylan had helped his passengers out of the basket, he worked with the crew to dismantle the balloon. Then he sent the elderly couple back to his house in Brian's van to pick up their car, while he rode with Laura and Emma.

The moment Emma stepped inside his cabin, she ran over to the aquarium in the wall of the living room, instantly attracted to the colorful, exotic fish. Dylan stood next to her, as close as she would allow, and told her about each type. Emma's hands were linked behind her back, her head raised to see the fish, and her eyes reflected the colors in the tank. She had her mother's long, smoky eyelashes and a small, perfect nose. One strand of dark hair had come loose from her ponytail, and he longed to slip it behind her ear, but of course, he didn't dare. He settled for standing there, engaged in a monologue, a tightness in his chest that had something to do with his feelings for this little girl.

They ate fruit salad and toasted bagels for breakfast. Laura asked the sort of questions about the balloon that a child might ask, and he knew she was asking them for her daughter. Answering them in basic terms, Dylan shifted his gaze between his two guests, and although Emma appeared intent on her food, he knew she was listening.

Laura helped him with the dishes after breakfast, not uttering a word about the fact that he had no dishwasher, while Emma wandered back into the living room.

"She loves those fish," Laura said as she dried a plate.

"Has she ever had one?" Dylan asked. "A fish for a pet?"

"No. Just a guinea pig named Michael, who is no longer with us."

"What do you think about me getting her an aquarium?" He rinsed a soapy glass under the tap, already thinking about the types of fish he could put in it.

"It's a great idea," Laura said.

Dylan looked out the window as Alex pulled in the driveway, the balloon neatly folded in the back of his truck. He watched as Alex turned onto the dirt road leading to the barn.

Laura followed his gaze through the window. "He and Brian really seem to know what they're doing," she said.

"Oh, yeah." Dylan handed her another glass. "They're great. Alex is working on getting his license, though, so I'll lose him eventually. He's going on a cruise next week with his girlfriend to get me used to him being gone, or so he says."

Laura suddenly stopped drying the glass. She looked at him with a surprised expression on her face. "That's it!" she said.

"What's it?"

"You know Sarah? The woman I visit in the retirement home?"

"Your father's friend." Dylan nodded.

"She used to be a nurse on a cruise ship. My father took a few cruises over the years. Maybe that's where he knows Sarah from. Maybe they met on a cruise."

"I bet you're right." Dylan turned off the water and picked up the sponge to wipe the counters. Laura seemed a bit consumed with trying to figure out the relationship between her father and the old woman, but he had to admit he'd wondered about it himself.

He heard a sound from the living room, a vaguely familiar squeaking sound, and it took him a few seconds to place it. When he did, his heart leapt into his throat.

"The guns!" he said, dropping the sponge. He ran into the living room and spotted Emma balancing on the armchair below the glass cabinet that contained his father's old gun collection. She had the cabinet door open and was reaching for one of the guns.

"Get down!" Dylan yelled as he raced toward her. "Get away from there!"

Emma turned toward him, cowering, terror in her eyes at the angry sound of his voice. Losing her balance, she fell onto the arm of the chair and toppled over backward, landing on the floor. Dylan tried to reach for her, but she got quickly to her feet. Crying loudly, she ran to Laura, who was standing in the doorway between the living room and the kitchen, a stunned look in her own eyes. Emma grabbed hold of her mother, burying her head against Laura's stomach and sobbing.

Dylan turned back to the gun cabinet, his hands shaking as he closed the door. He didn't even know if those damned guns were loaded. Probably not. He'd probably blown it with Emma over a bunch of harmless guns.

Laura leaned over her trembling daughter. "You know better than that, Emma," she scolded, her voice firm but soft. "You mustn't play with guns."

Dylan looked at Laura helplessly. "I'm sorry," he said, shaking his head. "I was afraid she'd—"

"It's all right," Laura said. "You had to stop her." She bent over her daughter again. "Did you hurt yourself when you fell?" she asked. "Are you okay?"

Emma pressed her face more firmly against her mother's stomach.

Laura glanced toward the TV in the corner of his living room. "Can she watch cartoons while we finish cleaning up?"

"Of course."

He went into the kitchen while Laura settled Emma on the sofa in front of the TV. When she returned to the kitchen, she leaned against the counter, arms folded across her chest.

"They're loaded?" she asked.

"I don't know." He'd picked up the sponge, but now set it down again. "They were my father's. I'm not a...gun guy." He smiled weakly. "I just stuck the cabinet up there with the guns in it and never bothered checking to see if they were loaded or not. I never had to worry about it before." He sounded like an idiot. Who would have guns in his house and not even know if they were loaded?

"She's had a fascination with guns ever since Ray killed himself," Laura said. "She plays with them—with the toy guns—in her therapy sessions. She probably thought they were toys."

He ran his hand through his hair. "I shouldn't have blown up at her like that," he said.

"You had to," Laura said again. "It was an emergency."

"I'm supposed to watch my anger around her. That's what Heather said."

"This wasn't anger," Laura said. "This was fear. True?"

"Yeah, but I'm sure it all sounds the same to her."

"She'll get over it," Laura said, but he heard the lack of certainty in her voice.

Looking through the doorway toward the living room, he could just see the top of Emma's head above the back of the couch. He imagined how she would look from the front—eyes puffy and red from crying, thumb in her mouth. If she could speak, she'd be telling her mother she wanted to go home, to get away from that mean man who was pretending to be her father.

"Thanks for helping me clean up." He looked around his kitchen. It was in pretty good shape.

"You're welcome. And thanks for breakfast and for letting us watch the balloon go up."

She walked into the living room, and he followed her.

"Come on, honey," she said to Emma. "Time to go home."

Emma flicked off the TV and ran to the front door, not even glancing at her mother or Dylan. She was out the door quickly, and when he and Laura walked onto the porch, she was standing on the steps with her back to them.

"Whoa, she's mad," Dylan said quietly to Laura, his sense of powerlessness mounting. He would never be able to turn this around.

"Tell her why you did it," Laura said to him, just as quietly.

He took a step closer to Emma and spoke to her back. "I'm sorry I yelled at you, Emma," he said. "I got scared.

I was afraid you might hurt yourself if you tried to play with the guns. They're real guns. Some of them might... have bullets in them. I was trying to protect you."

Emma scrunched her shoulders up to her ears as if she could block out his voice.

Laura touched his arm and offered him a smile as she passed him. "We'll be in touch," she said. "Thanks again. And don't beat yourself up over this."

21

"Do you think my father might have met you on a cruise?" Laura asked as she and Sarah set out for their walk. "I remembered the other day that he'd taken several cruises over the years."

"What cruise line?" Sarah asked.

Laura tried vainly to remember. "I don't know."

"Where did he go?" Sarah asked. "I was mostly in the Caribbean. Though Alaska was my favorite."

"I know he'd been to the Caribbean at least once."

"What was his name again?"

"Carl Brandon."

"He flies dirigibles, right? I saw the *Akron* once. I think I was about ten."

"Dirigibles? No, he—"

"Hot air balloons!" Sarah said. "He flies hot air balloons?"

"No, that's Dylan. My daughter's father. I was talking about *my* father. Carl."

Sarah shook her head, a helpless expression on her face. "I'm lost," she said, and the words sounded so small and pathetic that Laura put her arm around her shoulders and gave them a squeeze.

"Don't worry about it," she said. "It's not important. Let's just enjoy our walk. And you can tell me more about your job at Saint Margaret's."

Sarah, 1956-1957

"They're poisoning me," the new patient, Julia, said as she pushed away her breakfast tray.

"No, they're not," Sarah said. "Which food do you think is poisoned?"

"The potatoes."

Sarah picked up the teaspoon from the tray and swallowed a mouthful of the mashed potatoes. "See?" she said. "I certainly wouldn't eat them if they were poisoned. They're delicious, actually." She pushed the plate toward the patient again.

Julia slowly picked up her fork and began to eat, and Sarah smiled to herself. She was making progress with this patient everyone had described as impossible to deal with.

Julia was twenty-eight years old and very beautiful. Her thick auburn hair fell to her waist, and it was the one thing about herself that she bothered to take care of. She brushed her hair many times a day and kept it very clean. It was a lovely sight to behold.

Julia was diagnosed as a paranoid schizophrenic, and she had been on ward three since breaking the nose of an orderly on ward two. Already, since she'd been moved, she had injured one of the aides and cracked her own head against the wall of her room. And she'd spent one entire night singing at the top of her lungs. That was after Dr. Palmiento gave her the injection of LSD.

"Julia Nichols is one of the most deeply disturbed patients we've had here in a while," Dr. P. had said at a staff meeting. "She broke a neighbor's boy's arm when she thought he was stealing from her. She claims to hear voices telling her to harm others and herself. The LSD will open her up. It will break down the walls of her resistance to treatment. It may be the only way to get to the root cause of her illness.''

Sarah was not so sure. Dr. P. was bolder than ever with his syringe of LSD, using it on his patients with, it seemed to Sarah, little concern for their diagnoses. She'd seen the drug work well on a couple of patients, freeing them up so they could finally talk about their deepest troubles. But in most cases, she thought the drug made patients lose touch with reality altogether. It made Julia sing, and Dr. P. was itching to inject her again.

Sarah was beginning to feel old-fashioned in her approach. All she had to offer was herself. She used to believe a relationship with a concerned and empathetic person could be enough to help her patients. Such an approach was beginning to seem ludicrous in light of Dr. P.'s advanced techniques.

In the staff cafeteria one afternoon, a young woman took the seat across the table from Sarah.

"Hi." The woman smiled. "I'm Colleen Price." She was petite with an adorable, blond pixie haircut, and Sarah recognized her as a nurse from ward two.

Sarah lowered her sandwich to her plate. "Sarah Tolley," she said.

"I was the nurse assigned to Julia Nichols when she was on ward two," Colleen said. "I hear she's yours now."

They talked a bit about Julia's history. "Dr. Palmiento's trying LSD with her," Sarah said.

Colleen lifted the top slice of bread on her sandwich, removed the lettuce leaf and set it on the edge of her plate. "And is it helping her?" she asked.

"Too soon to tell," Sarah said.

"Do you think that's the right approach for her?"

Sarah hesitated. It was blasphemy to disagree with Dr. P., but when she looked at Colleen, she knew she was looking into the eyes of a comrade. "No," she said. "I'm not one hundred percent sure it's the right approach for anyone."

Colleen smiled. "Neither am I. Nor am I sure about half the things Dr. P. comes up with." Her voice was barely more than a whisper.

"How long have you been here?" Sarah asked.

"Nearly a year."

"I've only been here a couple of months," Sarah said. "I'm shocked by some of the things he does. The high voltage of the ECT, for example."

"And doing ECT every day on some patients."

"And the slumber room."

Colleen rolled her eyes. "What are you giving the patients in there? When I was up on ward three the other day, I saw a couple of them walking around like zombies, bumping into the walls. One of them peed right there on the floor."

"They get a mixture," Sarah said. "A little bit of everything." She rattled off the names of the drugs. "Have you seen the isolation room?"

"I did," Colleen said softly. "It just about made me cry."

The isolation room had been a terrible shock to Sarah. It was not a room at all, but rather a long, rectangular box, barely larger than a coffin. The patients wore goggles designed to keep them in total darkness and earphones that emitted a constant, monotonous hum. Their arms and legs were padded to reduce their sense of touch. Except for bathroom and meal breaks, they remained in the box as long as a month. It was another way to achieve the extreme confusion Dr. P. valued so much.

"I feel old-fashioned," Sarah said, "but I simply can't

understand how such treatment can help more than it can harm.''

Colleen nodded her agreement. ''The word *torture* comes to mind,'' she said.

Sarah sat back in her chair, both relieved and disconcerted by this conversation. ''I thought I was going crazy,'' she said. ''Everyone seems to think what Dr. P. is doing is so great. So innovative. I figured I must be the one out of step.''

''Well, you may be. But if you are, then I'm out of step with you.''

''I'm beginning to think this is the wrong place for me,'' Sarah admitted. ''I'm upset every night when I go home.''

Colleen surprised her by reaching across the table and grabbing her hand. ''You mustn't leave!'' she said, leaning closer. ''Listen to me. I've thought of leaving a million times. But if those of us who really care about the patients leave, who's left to speak up for them?''

''Don't you think the rest of the staff cares?'' Sarah asked. ''Don't you think Dr. P. truly wants his patients to get well?''

Colleen looked thoughtful. ''I *do* think Dr. Palmiento believes he's doing the right thing,'' she said after a minute. ''He has tremendous optimism and self-confidence in his ability to cure people, and I like that about him. He tries hard, and his ultimate goal is the same as ours. And the staff cares, too. I think they believe they're doing the right thing in following Dr. P.'s treatment protocols. But I don't agree with them, and neither do you. And I think we have to stay here to provide some balance.''

''Are there others who disagree with Dr. P.'s methods?''

''There are a few. And there were more. But as soon as they spoke up, they were fired. So I don't speak up.'' Colleen swallowed a bite of her sandwich. "What do you think Julia Nichols needs?" she asked.

Sarah set her plate and its unfinished sandwich to the side of the table. "I think she needs antipsychotic medication," she said, "and then I think she needs to be treated with respect and understanding. She needs to be listened to by someone who cares. Who empathizes. Dr. P. listens, but if she doesn't tell him what he wants to hear, he berates her." She looked across the table at her new friend. "How can we expect her to get well...to become a mentally healthy woman...when we treat her like she's less than human?"

"We can't," Colleen said. "That's why she needs you. You and I have the same approach. Some day we'll open up our own little clinic, but for now, we'll stay here and do all we can to help these patients."

Colleen was right. They would have to stay at Saint Margaret's, quietly doing their best despite the uphill battle.

"Are you married?" Colleen suddenly changed the subject.

"Yes. My husband is a reporter for the *Washington Post*." She felt the tension ease out of her body at the thought of Joe. "How about you?"

"I'm divorced," Colleen said quietly, as if the fact shamed her. "But I have a little boy, Sammy, who's two. He's my sunshine." She grinned. "Do you have any kids?"

"Not yet." She and Joe were trying their best. "What do you do about a baby-sitter for Sammy while you're at work?"

"My ex-mother-in-law takes care of him. She's a gem, even if her son is a jerk."

Sarah began eating lunch with Colleen every day. Talking with her friend, whether about work or their private lives, gave her the strength to go back upstairs and face the suffering on ward three.

She thought she was making some progress with Julia. For as long as an hour, Julia would talk rationally with her about her childhood, and citing this, Sarah was able to discourage Dr. P. from giving her any more LSD. He'd spoken of putting Julia in the slumber room, but Sarah had been able to thwart that, as well. Then it all blew up in her face.

She walked into Julia's room after lunch one day while the patient was brushing her glorious hair. At first, Julia smiled at her, but the smile quickly disappeared. Pulling open her top dresser drawer, she began flinging the clothes from it into the air, as if hunting for something buried among the garments.

"You stole it!" she shouted at Sarah, who took a step back, disturbed by the anger in Julia's voice.

"Stole what?" she asked.

"My pin!" She pointed to the pin attached to the collar of Sarah's uniform. "It was right here in my drawer, and you took it!"

"This?" Sarah touched the pin. "This was a wedding gift from my husband," she said. "You've seen me wear it many times before, Julia."

Julia ripped the drawer from the dresser and turned it upside down, shaking it. "It was here and now it's there!" she screamed, staring at Sarah's collar.

"No, see?" Sarah dared to step a bit closer. "See the way the pin is formed? It's an *S* and a *J* together. It stands for Sarah and Joe. My husband and me."

Julia did not seem to hear her explanation. With impressive physical power, she swung the drawer forward and let it go, sending it flying through the air in Sarah's direction. Sarah ducked, but the corner of the drawer caught her right temple.

The pain was instant and searing. Pressing her hand to her head, Sarah opened the door and ran into the hall.

"Security!" she called.

The bulky men dressed in white were already racing toward the room. Someone must have overheard the altercation and called them. Sarah leaned against the wall, the blood dripping through her fingers and down her wrist, as she listened to the men try to subdue the shrieking, furious woman who thought she'd been robbed.

Another of the nurses ran up to Sarah and pressed a piece of gauze against her wounded temple. "You'll need a couple of stitches," she said. "And Julia Nichols needs a month or so in the slumber room."

"No," Sarah said weakly. And then she fainted.

The following morning, Dr. Palmiento called her into his office.

"How are you?" He stood up and put one of his big hands on her shoulder, genuine concern in his face. He led her to a chair.

Her temple was bandaged. The cut had required only three stitches, but her head still ached from the blow.

"I'm all right." She smiled. "I shouldn't have argued with her. I should have found some other way to—"

"Hush," he said softly. He leaned against his desk, half sitting on its edge. "I've made a decision about Julia Nichols that I want you to know about," he said.

The slumber room, she figured. She was not sure she had the strength to argue with him about it. "She was doing well with me," she said. "I think she was—"

He stopped her with a hand in the air. "I let you try your way with her," he said. "The talking approach. It's been tried for many years with these patients, but it simply isn't enough when they're so disturbed. Still, I wanted to give you free rein with her, and I thought perhaps it was helping.

But the reality is, there is only one way to rid Mrs. Nichols of her violent behavior." He hesitated, his green eyes impaling her. "I've scheduled her for a lobotomy on Wednesday."

"A *lobotomy?*" Sarah stared at him.

"Yes. She'll be in far better control of herself—"

"That's because she'll be in a stupor!" Sarah nearly shouted. "For the rest of her life!" She knew she was being either courageous or extraordinarily stupid to speak to him that way. "Please, Dr. P., let me do some research into other methods that have been effective with patients like Julia." Perhaps the word *research* would have an impact on him. "Please. Let me try before you do something as permanent as a lobotomy."

"There are no other methods that are effective with someone like her," he said. He leaned toward Sarah, looking at her as though she were slow-witted. "Deep in your heart, you know that, don't you?"

"But a lobotomy is not a cure," she said. "It's simply a way to make her easier to take care of. To turn her into a docile, dim-witted, childlike—"

Palmiento stood up straight. "You need to read up on lobotomies, Sarah," he said. "We can't have you working here if you don't understand the valuable place that procedure has in the treatment of the mentally ill."

Sarah looked down at her hands where they lay folded in her lap. Her head throbbed.

"I've been in this business thirty years to your…ten, is it?"

"Thirteen." Sarah straightened her spine with pride.

"And as you know," Dr. Palmiento continued, "I'm considered one of the top psychiatrists in the country."

"Yes, I know that."

"So, it would behoove you to acknowledge the fact that

I just may be better qualified than you are to decide what should be done in the case of Julia Nichols. She will have a lobotomy at three o'clock Wednesday afternoon. And I want you to be there, since she's your patient.''

"You want me to...?" The thought horrified her.

"You've had some surgical training, isn't that right?"

"As a student, yes, but—"

"And I haven't failed to notice that, although you are still unrealistic about what works and what doesn't in the treatment of mental illness, you are one of our most skillful nurses. I want you to be able to assist me in the future with surgical procedures. We'll start training you with Mrs. Nichols."

She didn't know what to say. This was her job. She had to do as she was told.

That night, she snuggled with Joe in bed. She'd told him what had happened and her horror at the thought of her patient being lobotomized.

"Maybe he's right," Joe said, stroking her hair. "Maybe there are people whose lives are so tortured and unbearable that destroying the hurtful part of their brain is the only way to help them. There must be some good reason the procedure won a Nobel Prize."

"I refuse to believe it's the only solution," Sarah said. "Julia is so...she's beautiful, Joe. She's young. She has such spirit."

Joe lightly touched the bandage on her temple. "She has spirit, all right." He laughed.

"It's going to be horrid," Sarah said. "At least Dr. P. agreed not to shave her head, after I pleaded with him. Her hair is extraordinary, and it's the one thing she truly cares about."

"She's lucky she has you," Joe said, leaning over to kiss her. "And so am I."

* * *

The orderly wheeled Julia into the operating room on a
gurney. She was wearing a hospital gown and had been
given only mild sedation, just enough to take the fight out
of her. Her eyes were open, and she smiled at Sarah when
she spotted her in the room, recognizing her in spite of
Sarah's surgical cap and mask.

"Hello, Julia," Sarah said through the mask. She helped
the orderly transfer Julia from the gurney to the operating
table. Joyce Love was also in the room, ready to assist in
the surgery.

Julia reached for Sarah's hand. Surprised by the gesture,
Sarah held the young woman's hand tightly, knowing she
must sense that something dreadful was about to happen to
her. Sarah was now glad to be there. It would be an ordeal
for her, but Julia needed someone she knew cared about
her in that room.

Dr. Palmiento entered the OR dressed in a surgical gown,
his mask in place. "How are you feeling, Julia?" he asked
in that fatherly tone he was so good at employing. He
squeezed Julia's shoulder.

"Fine," she replied.

"Now, I'm just going to slip this eye mask over your
eyes," he said. "Then this bright light won't bother you.
It's annoying, isn't it? The light?"

He put the mask in place, then reached for the razor. He
couldn't be preparing to shave her head, Sarah thought, but
sure enough, he began to do exactly that.

Sarah looked at him across the operating table. "You
promised," she said.

"This—" he held up a long, loose tress of auburn hair
"—won't mean a thing to her in half an hour." He sounded
annoyed, and Sarah said no more, although inside she was
seething.

"Syringe," he said, and Joyce Love handed him the syringe she had filled with a local anesthetic. He injected the anesthetic around the area of Julia's scalp to be incised.

Sarah hated that patients undergoing lobotomies only received local anesthetic, but Dr. P. said it was necessary for him to be able to know when he had "destroyed the offending portion of her brain."

Although she was not usually squeamish, the sound of the drill and the spray of bone shavings into the air turned Sarah's stomach. She stared at the wall instead of watching the surgery, hoping no one would notice.

Dr. P. requested one instrument after another. From the corner of her eye, Sarah saw Joyce hand them to him, but she kept her gaze steady on the wall. Finally Joyce handed Palmiento the steel spatula, and Sarah knew the moment for destruction had arrived.

"Julia, how old are you?" Dr. P. asked as he worked.

"Tenny-eight," Julia slurred.

"Good." Dr. Palmiento said. Sarah imagined him digging deeper into the burr hole with his spatula.

"Can you count to ten for me, Julia?" he asked.

Julia grunted something unintelligible, and Dr. P. continued his destruction.

"Sing me a nursery rhyme, Julia," he said after a few minutes. "How about the one about Mary and her lamb?"

"Blah. Gibble," Julia said.

"Count to ten, Julia," Palmiento asked.

Nothing.

The wall blurred in front of Sarah's eyes. Julia's fight and fire were gone.

The moment she could escape, Sarah excused herself from the operating room and went into the staff rest room. Shutting herself inside one of the stalls, she cried, knowing that the scars from Julia's surgery would forever be etched across her own heart.

22

Laura had finally gotten Emma to sleep after a couple of hours of nightmares and tears. Now she lay in her own bed, surrounded by the books on Alzheimer's she'd borrowed from the library. She was searching through indexes and chapter headings, trying to determine if someone with Alzheimer's could make up stories rich in detail and told with clarity and enthusiasm. Laura was beginning to wonder if Sarah's description of the goings-on at Saint Margaret's might be a figment of her imagination. The events were beginning to border on the unbelievable. Who would put a psychiatric patient in a "coffinlike box" for a month? Probably, Laura reasoned, Sarah had simply confused the facts in her memory.

One of her books stated that "the Alzheimer's patient's vivid recollections from the past may lead the caretaker to think the patient is more lucid than he or she actually is." That fit Sarah, certainly. It was almost eerie. On their walks, Sarah would slip into the past, losing her infirmity as she described an incident in what seemed like perfect detail. A moment later, she would look down the street and have no idea where she was, or even if she was on land or water. Sarah didn't even remember Laura's name from one visit to the next. She did know, however, that Laura's appearance meant she could go for a walk.

The phone rang a moment after Laura had turned out the

light and settled under the covers. She picked up the receiver from her night table.

"I hope I didn't wake you." The voice was Ray's, and Laura stopped breathing for a second before realizing it was Stuart on the line.

"Stuart!" she said. "You sounded so much like Ray, for a minute I thought…"

"Oh, sorry," he said.

"It's hardly your fault." She laughed.

"Well, listen. I know it's late, but I just came across an article in the latest *Publishers Weekly* and I wanted to read it to you."

"Go ahead."

He began reading about Ray Darrow's upcoming book, *For Shame.* The title still made Laura cringe, but the author of the article had nothing but words of praise for the book, and Laura listened with a lump in her throat. The piece described Ray as a great humanitarian.

"'If every politician reads this powerful book,'" Stuart read aloud, "'much needed social change is sure to follow.'" He paused. "Pretty nice, huh?"

Laura closed her eyes. "I only wish Ray could hear that."

"It's his legacy," Stuart said. "It's exactly what he would have wanted."

For a long time after hanging up the phone, Laura lay on her side, eyes wide open, sleep evasive. Reaching out to touch the empty mattress where Ray should have been, the pain of losing him washed over her. He'd been a good husband.

Except for his anger over her father's last request.

Except for his impatience with Emma.

She shook her head, annoyed at how Heather Davison kept picking away at Ray's image, and at herself, for beginning to think that Heather might be right.

23

Alison Becker called while Laura and Emma were eating breakfast.

"We have to postpone Cory's party," Alison said. "She was up all night with some stomach bug."

"Oh, how miserable," Laura said, but she wasn't thinking of Cory as much as she was of Sarah. She'd told Sarah she'd visit today while Emma was at the birthday party. Now, though, Emma was left with no place to go. Most likely Sarah didn't remember Laura saying she'd come today, but what if she did? The thought of her waiting for her with her walking shoes on was more than Laura could bear.

"Anything I can do to help?" Laura asked Alison.

"No, thanks. Jim went out for ginger ale and saltines, so I think we're all set."

Hanging up the phone, Laura took her seat again across from Emma.

"Well, honey, that was Cory's mom. Cory's sick today, so she won't be able to have her birthday party."

Emma looked out the window in the direction of the Beckers' house.

"I know you're disappointed." How did she know that? How did she know anything her daughter was thinking or feeling? She was in the middle of a colossal guessing game, dividing her time between a small child who refused to communicate and an old woman who couldn't.

One of the library books she'd been reading suggested linking the Alzheimer's patient with a child. In many ways, they were at the same level of ability.

"Since you can't go to Cory's party," she said, making a split-second decision, "you can go with me to visit a friend."

When Sarah opened her apartment door, her eyes fell immediately on Emma.

"You brought Janie with you," she said, a broad smile on her face.

"Janie?" Laura asked. "No, this is Emma, my daughter. Emma, this is Mrs. Tolley."

Emma leaned into Laura's leg, though not with her usual shyness, and she didn't hesitate to go into the apartment with Laura. She eyed Sarah with curiosity. There had been few elderly women in her life.

Sarah was so focused on Emma as she led her guests into the living room that she walked right into one of the end tables, knocking her late husband's picture to the floor. Laura picked up the framed photograph and placed it on the table again.

"Will Janie go on our walk with us?" Sarah asked.

"If that's all right with you," Laura said. "But her name is Emma. Do you remember me telling you about my daughter, Emma?"

Sarah sat on the edge of the sofa, making herself Emma's height. "What a beautiful doll!" she said. "What's her name?"

Emma held the Barbie out to Sarah, who took it on her lap.

"What's her name, Janie?" she asked again.

"Do you remember that I told you Emma doesn't speak?" Laura said.

"You stopped talking, Janie?" Sarah seemed almost obstinate in her refusal to call Emma by her name. "Why did you do that, dearest?"

Emma wrinkled her nose and shrugged, leaning restlessly against the arm of the sofa.

"Good," Laura said to Sarah. "You have your walking shoes on already." She looked at Emma. "Do you need to use the bathroom before we go for a walk, honey?"

Emma shook her head.

"Well, I do," Laura said. "I'll be out in a minute."

Walking toward the bathroom, she noticed the big plastic calendar-clock on the kitchenette wall. The date was set three days ahead, and she took a moment to set it back. Sarah must be pushing the button more often than once a day.

She was washing her hands at the bathroom sink when, through the paper-thin door, she heard Sarah ask, "Are you in school yet, Janie?" Where the heck was this "Janie" stuff coming from? she wondered.

"I'm *not* Janie!" Emma's voice rang out clearly. "I'm *Emma*."

Laura caught her breath. It had been so long since she'd heard that voice that she'd almost forgotten how it sounded. Low-pitched for such a tiny girl, and loud. And right now, a bit indignant.

She wanted to run out of the bathroom and pull her daughter into her arms, but she didn't dare break the spell. Pressing her head against the door, she listened as Emma answered Sarah's questions, even though they were directed to a child with a different name.

"My doll's name is Barbie," she said.

"I'm five."

"I'll go to kindergarten soon."

Laura glanced in the bathroom mirror. There were tears in her eyes and her nose was red. She dried her tears with toilet paper and left the bathroom, deciding it would be best if she didn't treat Emma's talking as if it were anything out of the ordinary, but rather something she'd expected her to do one of these days.

"Are you ready to go for our walk, Emma?" she asked, waiting for the answer.

But Emma merely took her Barbie back from Sarah and trotted over to the door to wait for them.

On their walk, Sarah was far too preoccupied with Emma to slip into her memories of the past, but no matter what she asked the little girl, Emma was done talking. It hurt Laura to know that her presence was the cause of Emma's return to silence. She answered most of Sarah's questions about Emma, and eventually gave up trying to get her to call her by her right name.

"You must know a little girl named Janie," Laura said.

A faraway look fell over Sarah's face. "Yes, I knew a Janie," she said, "but I'm not allowed to talk about her." She stepped out ahead of her walking companions, and Laura knew that the conversation had come to an end.

She called Dylan that night from the phone in the sky-light room, where she lay stretched out on the floor pillows. The night was thick with clouds, but the moon appeared from time to time, peeking through the smoky veil.

"Emma spoke today," she said.

"You're kidding!" Dylan said. "Tell me all about it."

"Well, I had to take her to Sarah's apartment with me this morning, and while I was in the bathroom, I overheard Sarah asking her—"

She suddenly heard a woman's voice in the background, calling "Dylan?"

"You have someone there," she said, chagrined. "I'm interrupting."

"No, don't worry about it. Hold on."

She heard muffled voices and knew he had cupped his hand over the receiver and was talking to the woman who was...his date? His lover?

"Hi," he said, coming back on the line. "So, you had Emma over at Sarah's and Sarah was asking her something?"

"Yes. I was in the bathroom and Sarah kept calling Emma 'Janie' for some reason, and all of a sudden, Emma said, very indignantly, 'I'm not Janie!'"

Dylan laughed. "All right, Emma! Then what? Oh, hold on another second."

She heard the woman's voice in the background again, her words indistinct, and this time Dylan didn't bother covering the phone when he answered her. "They're in the closet," he said. "Top shelf. The stool's right inside the door there." Then to Laura, "Okay. I'm back."

"I am seriously interrupting you," Laura said.

"No, you're not. So, did she keep talking? Is she talking now?"

"No. She stopped when I came out of the bathroom."

He was quiet for a moment. "I'm sorry," he said. "That must not feel too good."

The compassion in his voice surprised her, brought her to the brink of tears yet again. "At least she spoke," she said. "At least I know she can still do it."

"Could Sarah have called her by another name in an attempt to get her to speak, do you think? Maybe she knew perfectly well what she was doing, and was just trying to provoke Emma."

She hadn't thought of that. "You know, she told me about a mute patient she had when she was a psychiatric nurse. The psychiatrist got her to talk by taunting her."

"So maybe Sarah was doing the same thing."

It seemed unlikely. "I don't know. Sarah's not that clear-headed."

"Maybe she's more clearheaded than you think." He paused. "I'm going out in a few minutes," he said, "but when can I see Emma again? If she'll see me at all after I screamed at her about the guns. Wish I had *that* morning to do over."

"How about coming over Monday evening?" she suggested. "Emma and I have a therapy session with Heather in the morning. I'll be painting the living room in the afternoon, and I'll probably be a paint-speckled mess by the time you get here, but we could order pizza or—"

"I'll come over in the afternoon and help you paint," he said.

"Oh, no! I don't want you to do that."

"It's my day off," he said. "I'll be there around one-thirty, okay? You have an extra roller or should I bring one?"

"I have one."

"See you then."

After getting off the phone, she poured herself a glass of iced tea and carried it out to the screened porch. She sat down in one of the rockers. The night was very still except for the rhythmic croaking of the frogs that lived along the bank of the lake. She ordinarily found comfort in a quiet evening on the porch, yet tonight it did not calm her.

Dylan was a genuinely kind person, and she was convinced of his sincere interest in Emma. That was all she'd wanted him to be: a kind and attentive man who would take an interest in her daughter. So, why was she so disturbed by the fact that he had a woman at his house? It was absurd. Dylan owed her nothing. He didn't even remember the night they'd slept together, and he had been clear about his desire to remain unattached. Why couldn't she simply shrug off the sound of that woman's voice? What were they doing tonight? She pictured Dylan laughing with the anonymous woman in his living room, or maybe lying in the hammock in his backyard. She pictured them in bed together. Pictured him touching her, making love to her, consciously, not the way he'd made love to Laura so long ago.

So what? She didn't own him.

She turned her mind to other things, managing to think about Emma's talking, and Sarah's fixation on calling her Janie, and what color she would paint the living room. Yet she knew that when she climbed into bed that night, her dreams would be filled with Dylan Geer.

24

"**Y**our mind is still back on that phone call," Bethany said on the drive to the theater.

He couldn't deny it. Emma had spoken! He would have liked to talk with Laura longer, but that would have made them late for the movie.

"Sorry," he said. "Tell me about work. You said your agent had a big job for you?" Wasn't that what she'd told him when she arrived at his house? Something about needing to make a decision because the job would interfere with her photography business? He couldn't remember for certain.

Bethany was quiet. "I don't want to talk about work, Dylan," she said. "I want to talk about what's going on with us. Or maybe the correct statement should be what *isn't* going on."

"I'm not following you." He kept his eyes on the road, unaccustomed to the accusatory tone in Bethany's voice.

"Look, I know the rules," she said. "I know we have no ties to each other. But I'd still like to be treated with some respect."

"What are you talking about?" He'd always treated her with respect.

"I haven't heard from you in weeks," she said. "What am I supposed to think?"

"We've been playing telephone tag." The argument was

weak. He could have found the time to call her when he knew she'd be home.

They'd arrived at the theater parking lot, and he pulled into a space and started opening his door.

"No," she said. "Let's sit here till we've talked this out. Please."

Letting go of the door handle, he turned to face her. "All right." Her hair was so black he could barely see it in the darkness, but her eyes were clearly visible and they were filled with questions.

"Be honest with me, Dylan. We've both been up-front with each other from the start. We both see other people, and we know it. But we've also been special to each other, haven't we?"

"Yes." He reached for her hand. "That's true."

"So I need to know if someone's taken my place. I won't get crazy about it. But I need to know."

He hesitated for a minute, looking through the windshield toward the marquee of the theater. "Yes," he said finally, tightening his fingers around her hand. "Someone's taken your place. And she's five years old."

Bethany tilted her head, frowning. "I don't understand," she said. "Oh! You mean the little girl in the picture?"

"That's right."

"I knew she was your daughter."

"How did you know?"

"You just needed to take one look at her," Bethany said. "She has your eyes, your hair, your smile."

He was smiling now himself. "Yeah, she does, doesn't she?"

"So, I assume that wasn't her on the phone. It was her mother, right?"

"Right."

"And...what is her mother to you?" There was fear in

the question. Another person might not pick up on it, but he knew Bethany too well.

"Just her mother." He tried to sound reassuring. "That's all. Emma...the little girl...lost her father recently and she hasn't spoken since then, so her mother called to tell me that Emma spoke today. That's it."

"Are you...involved with Emma? I mean, do you see her?"

"Yes." He let out a sigh. "This is hard to explain, Beth," he said. "I haven't been in touch with you, or with anyone really, because I just want to focus on the girl right now. I have five years to make up for. Can you understand that?"

There was a small smile on her perfectly shaped red lips. "Yes," she said. "And I love you for not being able to turn your back on her. Still..."

"Still?"

"I wish you'd never found out about her."

The movie was boring to him, although obviously not to Bethany. She couldn't stop jabbering about it in the van on the way home. He barely knew what she was talking about when she referred to scenes or characters, because he'd let his mind wander to Emma again. He imagined seeing her Monday afternoon, winning her over, somehow erasing that incident with the gun cabinet from her mind. He'd buy a paintbrush her size and let her help him and Laura paint.

By the time they pulled into his driveway, Bethany was snuggled close to him in the van, her silky hair against his chin and her hand stroking the inside of his thigh with an insistent pressure. He was not interested. Not at all. And he was not sure what he was going to do about it.

Stopping the van in front of his garage, he took her hand

from his thigh and held it firmly on his knee. "I think we still have some talking to do," he said.

"Well, I don't want to talk." She extracted her hand from his and slipped her fingers inside his shirt, between the buttons. "I want to make love."

"I know you do, Beth, but…"

"But what?" She pulled away to study him from a distance. "You're not yourself tonight, Dylan," she said. "That was your kind of movie. I picked it especially because I could see you needed to get your mind off things. But it backfired. You seem even more distant from me than before."

"I know. And I'm sorry. But I'm…going through something. I don't know how to explain it, even to myself. I never wanted kids, and now I suddenly have one, and I feel an obligation to her. More than that. I think she's…adorable." The word sounded bizarre coming from his mouth. "I was sitting there in the movie trying to think of what I could bring her next time I see her, or where I might take her for fun, or how I can make her feel safe enough to talk again. I can't stop thinking about her. Maybe that's crazy, I don't know. But it's what's happening to me."

"I don't think it's crazy," Bethany said. "But frankly, I wish it was another woman you were hooked on. I'd know how to fight that. I don't know how to compete with a five-year-old."

"You don't need to compete with her. You just need to be patient with me."

She sighed, her mouth pursed tightly. "You don't want me to stay overnight, do you?"

She was beautiful. He could see the swell of her breasts in the moonlight. All week he'd been thinking about sleeping with her tonight, waking up together in the morning the way they used to, laughing and talking and making love again, but right now the memory of her hand on his thigh was more of an irritant. He really was losing it.

"Not tonight, Beth," he said. "I'm sorry."

She tried to smile but failed. Leaning over, she kissed him on the cheek. "Call me, okay?" she said.

He watched her get out of his van and into her car. After she'd driven down his driveway, her car's taillights disappearing in the woods, he walked into the house. He was sorry he'd hurt her, yet he felt nothing but relief at being alone with no one to interrupt his thoughts about his daughter.

25

Laura could still hear Emma speaking to Sarah. Even as she spread the drop cloths around the living room, the irritated little voice ran through her head. "I'm not Janie!" Remembering it made her grin.

At the therapy appointment that morning, Heather had suggested Sarah join Emma for her next session. Laura recoiled from the thought: it would confuse Sarah. Even Laura's proposal that they start their walk in a different direction threw her into a tizzy. Sarah needed the familiar. Yet, maybe it would work. And maybe it would help Emma.

Emma was sitting smack in the middle of the living room floor with her finger paints spread out around her, and she was already engrossed in her work. Laura hadn't yet told her that Dylan was coming over to help her paint, but she had to tell her now; he was due in a few minutes.

"Emma?" she said as she pried the lid off one of the cans of cream-colored paint.

Emma looked up from her own painting. Her fingers were blue, and the smell of finger paint filled the air.

"Dylan is coming over soon. He's going to help with the painting."

Emma instantly returned her attention to her painting. She was not pleased.

"I know you think he was mean to you when we were

at his house," Laura said. "But I hope you understand that he was just concerned you might hurt yourself with the guns. He cares about you."

Emma smeared blue paint across the top of her paper, as if she hadn't heard, and Laura began painting the wall nearest the kitchen.

The crunch of gravel in the driveway announced Dylan's arrival. Wiping her hands on the rag tucked into the pocket of her shorts, Laura met him at the front door. Emma didn't budge from her seat on the floor.

"You've already started," he said, eying the wall near the kitchen. "Nice color. And I see Emma's doing some painting of her own."

Emma didn't even bother to raise her head at the sound of her name.

"I was hoping Emma could help us," Dylan said, pulling a brush from his back pocket and crouching down next to her. "Do you think you can help us paint the walls?" he asked.

"She's really too young, I think." Laura didn't want to step on Dylan's toes, but she knew Emma could not do what he was asking. To her surprise, though, Emma took the brush from his hand and stood up.

"How about over here?" Dylan guided her to the far wall with a light hand on her shoulder. "You can be the first-coat girl. Your mom and I will paint the second coat on top of what you do."

Laura bit her lip as she watched her daughter slowly spread paint on the wall. Although Emma painted with great attention and care, it would have to be done again, but that hardly mattered. She watched as Dylan helped Emma remove excess paint from the brush by pulling it across the rim of the roller tray, and she was filled with warmth for both of them.

The three of them worked the entire afternoon, although Emma ended early to play with Cory in her bedroom.

"Exactly how many Barbies do they have?" Dylan asked, after seeing Cory arrive with her boxful of dolls.

Laura laughed. "You don't want to know," she said. She felt awkward keeping him there when Emma had gone off to play. He was supposed to be there for Emma, not simply to help her paint. "Please feel free to take off whenever you like," she said. "This goes beyond the call of parental duty."

"We don't have much more to do," he said, standing back to examine their work. "And then, if you and Emma don't have any plans for tonight, I thought we could go ice-skating."

"*Ice*-skating! In August?"

"At the rink in Upperville. You haven't been there?"

"I didn't even know it existed."

"It's a bit off the beaten track. The serious skaters from all over the area go there to practice," he said. "But the best part is the pizza. We can do dinner there. That is, if you think Emma would like to go."

Laura hesitated, unsure what Emma's reaction would be. "She's never been skating." There was a chicken thawing in the refrigerator, and her back ached. Still, she loved the spontaneity of the idea—and the fact that Dylan would be around all evening. He would not be with the woman at his house. The relief she felt at that realization was irrational.

"Let's do it," she said.

"She loves this." Laura watched her daughter glide across the ice ahead of them. She'd expected Emma to be wobbly her first time on skates, but the little girl took off as though she'd been skating all her short life. She came back to take Laura's hand from time to time, whenever she needed a taste of security, but she seemed quite happy to be off on her own, and it overjoyed Laura to see that independence in her.

"She hasn't had the opportunity to do this sort of thing very much," she said. "Ray would read to her, maybe take her to a museum." *Or the streets of D.C.* "But he wasn't a very...physical person."

"Did he teach her to ride a bike?" Dylan asked. "Or swim? Or hit a softball?"

"None of the above." Laura remembered the softness of Ray's body and the sharpness of his mind, and she felt a twinge of guilt for belittling him in front of Dylan. "It wasn't his fault," she said. "He was already fifty-six when she was born, and he was more of an intellectual than an athlete. He couldn't do things with her like this. Take her skating. I taught her to ride her bike with the training wheels. And last summer I taught her how to swim. Although she seems to have forgotten how. She's afraid of the water now."

"Maybe I could help with that," Dylan offered. "We could all go swimming sometime. Is there a beach at the lake?"

"A small one, yes."

"I get antsy when I'm holding still," Dylan said. "I have to be doing something physical or I'll go out of my mind." He did a spin on the ice as if to back up his words, and she laughed.

They skated in silence for a moment, Laura's gaze fixed on Emma as the little girl tried to emulate an older child who was skating backward. Emma did a fair job of it, pursing her lips with the effort. Laura thought of what Dylan had said about teaching her to swim.

"I hope you don't feel as though I'm using you," she said to him.

"Using me?" he asked. "You mean, helping out with Emma?"

She nodded.

"Impossible," he said. "I don't do things I don't want to do."

"I have this sense of you as a very committed bachelor who has his life just the way he wants it and who's going to keep it that way, no matter what."

"That's me," he said.

"Except that you've taken on my daughter, for some reason."

He slowed his skating to a near standstill and looked at her soberly. "Because she's *my* daughter, too," he said.

"But still. You didn't have to. And she definitely has the ability to interfere with this life-style you've carved out for yourself."

He started skating again, motioning her to fall in beside him. They skated side by side for a moment before he spoke again.

"My father left when I was seven," he said.

"Oh," she said. "He left? You mean…"

"He deserted the family. My mother, myself and my nine-year-old sister. He'd actually been a fairly good father, which made it worse. He was very involved with us, my sister and me. I worshiped him. And then one morning, he was gone. Just like that." Dylan snapped his fingers. "My mother was stunned."

He suddenly grinned, interrupting himself. "Look at her," he said, pointing toward Emma, who was now trying to do a pirouette on the ice. She fell down with a splat, but a young boy helped her up again, and she doggedly skated on.

"I think she's a natural," Dylan said. "We're gonna turn this girl into an athlete yet." He looked at Laura, taming his enthusiasm. "With your permission, of course."

Laura laughed. "If you can get *her* permission, you've certainly got mine." She let a moment of silence pass between them. "So," she said, "why did your father leave?"

"Well, it took a while for the pieces to fall into place," Dylan said. "Turns out he had a woman and a couple of kids in another state. He traveled a lot for his work, and he'd been living a double life. The other woman knew about us, and she finally got sick of the situation and told him he had to make a choice. So he did. We lost."

Laura flinched, imagining that pain. "Didn't he keep in touch at all?" she asked. "Didn't you see him on holidays or—"

"He quit us cold turkey," Dylan said. "We never saw him again. We found out the truth from his cousin. He's dead now, my father. Had a heart attack when he was fifty, and I hope I haven't inherited his genes for heart disease or for dishonesty and duplicity and deceit." His voice was bitter. "Anyhow, do you see now why I can't let a child of mine go without a father? Not if I can help it?"

"Yes, I do," she said.

"I hate the guy, yet I keep his stupid gun collection because it's all I have of him. I hate guns, too." He laughed, but she heard the pain behind the sound.

"It must have been very hard for you, growing up."

"Oh, you know." He shrugged away her sympathy. "It made me strong, and all that. But I would have preferred getting strong some other way. Not having a father left an...emptiness in me."

She thought about her own life. She'd lost her mother at the same age Dylan had lost his father, yet that loss had been no one's fault. Her father had poured his love of science into her, and she'd never for a moment felt empty. Challenged, pushed, inspired and, at times, controlled, but never empty.

"Does Emma understand what happened to Ray?" Dylan asked suddenly. "I mean, does she know what death is?"

"Heather says kids don't really understand the concept of death—the irreversibility of it—until they're about seven. So I don't..." She felt the weight of her frustration. "Frankly, I have no idea what she understands and what she doesn't, Dylan, or what scares her, or what she's thinking, because she won't *talk* to me."

Dylan rested his hand under her elbow as they skated. "She will," he said with an assurance she didn't feel. "She's spoken to Sarah. It's just a matter of time now."

They skated in silence for a moment, Laura relishing the warmth of his hand on her arm.

"I'm going to bring Sarah to Emma's next session with Heather," she said finally. "Though I worry it's not fair to Sarah. I'm afraid it will confuse her. Upset her somehow."

"You worry a lot about other people, you know?" he said softly. "You worry about sullying Ray's memory. You're worried you might be using me. You're worried you might be using Sarah. Sarah and I can take responsibility for what we do or don't do."

She was struck by his words, having never thought of herself as someone who worried excessively about others. But he didn't understand. "You, okay," she said. "But Sarah is like a child in many ways. She doesn't have the ability to say 'No, I don't want to go with you.' She won't even understand what I'm talking about when I ask her to go." Her voice threatened to break.

Dylan squeezed her elbow. "You are a very sweet person," he said.

No one had ever used the word *sweet* to describe her before. She thought about the articles that had been written about her, describing her as a "brilliant astronomer," a "dedicated scientist," a "mulishly devoted surveyor of the skies." No one had ever said she was sweet. Dylan did not know her very well.

"I was thinking about your father and Sarah," Dylan said. "Maybe they *did* meet on a cruise, but maybe they weren't lovers. Maybe they were nurse and patient."

Laura stopped skating. "That's it! Maybe Sarah treated my father for something. Maybe she saved his life. It didn't have to be on a cruise, necessarily, but maybe that's the connection."

"So he felt he owed her."

"I'll never know for sure, though," Laura said with resignation as she started skating again. "Sarah won't remember."

She glanced at Emma, who seemed to be slowing down. Soon they would have to leave.

"I'm sorry if I interrupted you with my phone call the other night," she said, after another minute of silence.

"You didn't."

"I thought you said there was no woman in your life."

"I didn't say that. I said I wasn't attached. No serious relationship. No one particular woman."

"Oh. So, you go out with a lot of different women?"

"'A lot' might be pushing it." He laughed. "But a few."

"Don't they mind that you're seeing other people?" she asked. "Or don't they know?"

"Oh, they know," he said with certainty. "Remember what I said about not wanting to inherit my father's genes for deceit? That's one thing I can't handle, and won't indulge in, no matter what the cost to me."

Honesty was his driving value. She could trust him.

"And yes," he continued, "it's bothered some women I've gone out with, so they just say no the next time I ask them out."

"I can't imagine any woman tolerating that sort of arrangement."

"You'd be surprised," he said. "There are plenty of women who don't want a serious attachment any more than I do."

He perplexed her. She supposed his own experience with his parents' marriage had discouraged him from ever attempting marriage himself. And then there was that "long and miserable story" he'd alluded to a couple of weeks ago.

"She's getting tired." Dylan pointed to Emma.

"I know."

"Think we should pack it in?"

"It's time," she said, hoping she had not annoyed him by probing into his love life. She watched as he skated toward Emma. Reaching the little girl, he crouched down on his skates and spoke to her for a moment, then stood up straight and skated back to Laura.

"She's ready to go," he said. "At least I think she is. She didn't nod yes, but she didn't shake her head no, either." He laughed.

Emma turned to wave to them as she skated toward the side of the rink.

"You're good with children," Laura said, wondering if that comment sounded as alien to him as when he'd told her she was sweet.

Indeed, he laughed. "No one's ever said that to me before," he said.

"Well, maybe you never really cared before." It seemed

a bold thing to say, but he gave a small smile and a nod as he glided over the ice.

"Maybe that's it," he said, and he followed Emma toward the side of the rink.

26

26

"Come in, dear," Sarah said, holding the door open for Laura. She looked a bit flustered and surprised. "I'll just put my walking shoes on and then I'll be ready." She disappeared into the bedroom. It was apparent that, even with the fancy new calendar, Sarah had no concept of what day it was.

Laura waited for her in the living room. From where she stood, she could see that the clock-calendar on the kitchenette wall was once again ahead of the date, this time by two days. She reset it, then returned to the living room.

Sarah walked into the room in her stocking feet. "I can't find them," she said.

"Shall I come help you?" Laura asked. She followed Sarah back into the small, tidy bedroom. The bed was covered with a pink floral bedspread, which matched the curtains hanging at the window. Someone had attached labels to the dresser drawers to help Sarah know where to store each article of clothing. The room was immaculate.

In the closet, Sarah's walking shoes were clearly visible among several other pairs of shoes lined up on the floor.

"Here they are," Laura said, picking them up. She handed them to Sarah, who looked at them as if she'd never seen them before.

"Are these the ones for walking?" she asked uncertainly.

Laura nodded.

"All right," Sarah said with a shrug. Sitting on the edge of the bed, she began to put on the shoes. Her confusion was worrisome. What happened on those days Laura wasn't around? How many times a day did Sarah forget where she was, or put her skirt on inside out? From all Laura had read, she knew it would only get worse.

A soft, cool breeze enveloped them when they walked out the front door of the retirement home.

"Is it spring?" Sarah asked.

"No, although it does *feel* like spring." She didn't want Sarah to think she could get nothing right. "But it's actually August 26, nearly the end of summer. Doesn't the cooler air feel good?"

"Oh, yes." Sarah picked up her pace, and Laura took a double step to catch up to her.

"I wanted to ask you something," Laura said when they'd walked half a block. "Last time I was here I had my little girl, Emma, with me. Do you remember that?"

Sarah frowned. "No," she admitted, her expression pained. She was still coherent enough to be bothered by her loss of memory.

"That's all right," Laura said. "But Emma was with me, and she was mute. Or at least, she was mute most of the time. And I remembered you telling me about a mute patient you had long ago named Karen. Do you remember Karen?"

"Dr. P. was a bastard to her."

"That's right. And he finally got her to talk by badgering her. And that's what you did with Emma. You badgered her, right? You did it on purpose to make her talk?"

"I wouldn't badger someone."

"Well, maybe that's the wrong word. But you called her

'Janie,' over and over again until she finally spoke up and told you her name was Emma.''

Sarah raised her hand to her mouth, a thoughtful look in her eyes. ''Was Janie here?'' she asked. ''I thought I dreamt that.''

''No, Janie wasn't here. At least not when I was here.'' She studied Sarah's profile. ''Is there really a Janie?'' she asked. ''I thought maybe—''

''Janie's real,'' Sarah said. ''But I'm not supposed to talk about her.'' She glanced over her shoulder as if she expected to see someone following them.

''Who says you can't talk about her?'' Might Alzheimer's patients, in their childlike condition, create imaginary friends? Did Janie fit that category? Maybe someone had told Sarah she'd be thought crazy if she talked about her.

''Dr. P.,'' Sarah answered. ''And Mr. D.''

Mr. D.? Laura was saddened by how out of touch with reality Sarah seemed to be today. She put her arm around her shoulders. ''I'm your friend, sweetheart,'' she said. ''You can tell me about Janie, if you like.''

Sarah looked at her as if assessing the truth in her words. And then she began to talk.

Sarah, 1958

Finally, after nearly three years of marriage, Sarah became pregnant. Joe was every bit as excited as she was, buying more things than they could afford for the baby, wallpapering the little room they planned to use as the nursery and running out in the middle of the night to assuage Sarah's cravings for olives or chocolate bars.

Sarah worked at Saint Margaret's until her sixth month, when she was showing too much for it to be considered proper for her to continue in her job. She and Joe had frequent talks about whether or not she would go back to work after the baby was born. She knew Joe was ashamed of the fact that he didn't make enough money to support all three of them without her income as well. It would be possible, but they would have to stretch every dollar. It saddened her, though, to think of leaving her child with a sitter while she went to work.

Yet, she knew she wanted to go back. She was good with the patients, and as Colleen had said, Dr. P.'s treatment methods needed to be balanced by her own empathetic approach. She sometimes lay awake at night, worrying about what the patients might be enduring without her to advocate for them.

Colleen was a good role model. She had a young son, yet still worked full-time. Of course, Colleen *had* to, having no husband on whom she could rely for support. And she had a mother-in-law to leave Sammy with during the day. Joe's mother had cut all ties with them, but Sarah and Joe's neighbor, an older woman who lived next door, was begging to take care of the baby when it came. Sarah finally suggested to Joe that she take six months off after the baby was born. They would budget very carefully during that time and see how they fared. Then she would decide.

One April night, while she and Joe were watching "Gunsmoke" on television, Sarah's contractions started. She was barely eight months pregnant. It was too soon, and she was frightened.

Joe rushed her to the hospital, where they told her she was having "false labor." They kept her overnight, more to calm Joe's anxiety than her own, then sent her home.

The following night, she went to bed with a backache that wouldn't let her sleep. Joe rubbed her back as she lay on her side, but the pain was so intense that she barely felt his attempts to soothe her.

Just before dawn, the contractions started again.

"We should go to the hospital," Joe said.

"They'll only send me home again," Sarah said. But then she realized that the bed was wet, and she remembered from nursing school that some women had back labor. A new contraction followed close on the heels of the last one. "I think you're right," she said, gasping, trying to rise from the bed. "We'd better go."

Joe was up in an instant, grabbing some of Sarah's clothes from the closet and racing over to her side of the bed.

She was already standing, and she knew there was no way she was going to make it to the hospital.

"Joe." She kept her voice as calm as she could. "The baby's coming too quickly for you to drive me to the hospital," she said. "I'm going to lie down again while you call the rescue squad."

"What?" Joe, usually so calm, looked frantic. "You're going to have the baby *here?"* He tried to help her back into bed, but she shooed him away.

"I'm all right," she said. "Go make the call."

She was not all right, though. By the time she lay down again, she knew the baby was going to beat the rescue squad. And it was too soon. The baby would be too small. Pain and fear forced tears from her eyes.

Joe ran back into the room. "They're on their way," he said, hurrying to her side.

"The baby's coming now, Joe," she said.

"What do you mean?"

"Just what I said." She felt suddenly irritated with him, then immediately contrite. She shouldn't take it out on Joe; he was all she had right now. "I mean, you'll need to help," she said.

There was a flash of panic in her husband's eyes, but it

was instantly replaced by the calm strength she'd seen in him many times before.

"All right," he said. "I'm here. Can you tell me what to do?"

She was moaning now, barely able to answer, and Joe took her hand helplessly in his own. She had seen only a few births during her training, and none, of course, under these circumstances.

"Get clean towels from the linen closet," she said, breathless from the sensations low in her belly. Throwing off the covers, she hiked her nightgown up to her hips as Joe left the room.

"It's coming too fast," she said when he returned, his arms full of yellow terry cloth.

"What should I do?" Joe asked.

"Towel...under me," she said, suddenly lost in a swirl of pain and the need to push. Was it too soon to push? She had no idea, and she no longer cared. She was only vaguely aware of her husband sitting on the edge of the bed, his entire being focused on the world between her legs.

"Use another towel to catch the baby," she panted. "He'll be slippery, and—"

"I can see the baby!" Joe cried. "What should I do? Should I try to get it out?"

"No," she managed to say. "Is it his head, or...?" Her teeth were chattering so hard she felt the vibration in her temples.

"Yes, his head. Lots of hair."

"Don't let me tear," she said. "Hold your hand against his head. Don't push. Just put your hand there so he doesn't come..." She let out a scream, and knew it was too late to prevent herself from tearing, but within an instant, she didn't care. The baby was in Joe's towel-covered hands.

"Is he all right?" she gasped, raising her head, trying to see.

"*She,*" Joe said. He was smiling.

"Is she all right?" Sarah raised herself to her elbows, but could see nothing more than a blur of red in the yellow towel.

"I...I don't think she's breathing." Joe's voice was calm, but there was terror in his eyes.

"Use the towel, the corner of the towel, to clean out her mouth," she said, panicked. She remembered one of her co-workers who had lost a baby at birth the year before. *Dear God, let my baby be all right.*

Joe did as he was told, and in a moment, the baby let out a squeal, then a hearty cry. Sarah lay back in relief, shutting her eyes, and the world outside their little house filled with the wail of a siren.

Sarah and the baby spent nearly a week in the hospital, although both of them were truly well. Joe visited constantly, leaving his office during the day, staying until they kicked him out at night. Sarah thought the nurses let him stay a little longer than they did most fathers because he was so involved with his daughter. He had delivered her, after all, while the other fathers hadn't been allowed within shouting distance of the hallowed delivery room.

They named the baby Jane, after Sarah's beloved aunt, and Sarah was relieved to see that her daughter seemed to resemble Joe and not herself. The bond between Joe and Janie went far beyond the bond shared by most fathers and daughters, and Sarah could only attribute it to the fact that Joe had been first to hold her, to admire her, to weep over her. He was as capable and enthusiastic in caring for Janie as Sarah was. Janie was going to grow up to be his little princess.

It was obvious, though, that in order to continue living

in their house by the park, Sarah would have to go back to work. She felt torn. The thought of leaving Janie with their neighbor, Mrs. Gale, and being apart from her five days a week, made her body ache. Yet, she knew deep down that she was not a woman meant to stay at home. She wouldn't admit that to anyone except Joe, because that feeling seemed so wrong to her. So selfish and unmotherly. But she needed the stimulation of her job, and the patients at Saint Margaret's needed her, too.

Her feelings had nothing to do with being a woman, Joe told her. He felt the same way and doubted he would feel any differently if he were a woman. He would shift his work schedule so he could be home with Janie for a few hours each morning. Then she would only have to be with Mrs. Gale for the afternoon.

One evening, shortly before her return to work, Sarah was feeding Janie in the living room when Dr. Palmiento appeared on the TV news. Quickly turning up the volume, Sarah stared in shock as she watched Palmiento shake hands with President Eisenhower. The newscaster reported that Palmiento was receiving an award for his research at Saint Margaret's. Sarah sank back in her chair, torn between pride that she worked with the man and dismay that his questionable methods should be rewarded.

"I am so glad you decided to come back to work," Colleen told Sarah in the cafeteria line on her first day back. They'd moved Colleen to ward three during Sarah's absence, and she seemed disturbed by the experience. "Things have gotten worse here," she said as they sat down with their sandwiches. "I need one other sane person working on ward three to let me know I'm not going completely out of my mind."

"What do you mean by 'worse'?" Sarah asked.

Colleen rolled her eyes. She'd let her hair grow out from its pixie cut, and now it framed her face with short blond waves. "This man…this *kid*, actually, was hired while you were gone," she said, "and he's suddenly Dr. P.'s right-hand man. Mr. D., they call him."

Sarah laughed. "Mr. D.?" she repeated. "And he goes along with Dr. Palmiento's methods?"

"Goes along with them?" Colleen asked. "He's even inventing new ones. He's the head of the Psychic Driving Program."

"Psychic driving? What's that?" In the eight months she'd been gone, things seemed to have changed a great deal.

"No one except Palmiento and Mr. D. seem to know for sure, but it involves—" Colleen leaned forward as if what she was about to say was a secret "—these helmets."

"Helmets?" Sarah laughed again, still lighthearted from her time off with her husband and new daughter but knowing that feeling could not last long at Saint Margaret's.

"They look something like the helmets football players wear," Colleen said. "But inside each helmet is a headset that's attached to a big tape player they put on the patient's bedside table. The tape plays constantly, and when it stops, they start it over again, and the patient listens to it for fifteen hours a day!"

"You are making this up," Sarah said, suddenly suspicious. It was too ludicrous.

"You'll see for yourself soon enough."

"What's on the tapes?"

"Messages Dr. P.'s recorded for them. Each tape is specific to that patient. Things like, 'You're an imbecile. You destroyed your marriage. You're worthless.'"

"*What?*" Sarah asked.

"That plays over and over on the tape, and they listen

to it for about a month. Then they get a positive tape. 'You love your family. You are an excellent wife and mother. You worship your husband.'"

Sarah's jaw had dropped nearly to the table. "Tell me you're joking," she said.

"The patients who aren't drugged or shocked into oblivion sometimes cry or even scream when they're listening to the tapes," Colleen said.

Sarah let out a sound of exasperation. "When are they going to come up with something that will actually help people get better?"

"They say this will," Colleen said. "It's one of those 'get worse before you get better' sort of treatments."

"Just like everything else they do here," Sarah muttered. "Palmiento will probably win an award for this, too." She looked down at her sandwich, then pushed it away. Her appetite was gone. She was back at Saint Margaret's.

Dr. Palmiento seemed pleased to have her back and had her assist him in two lobotomies that first week. It worried her that she no longer fell apart as she observed someone's spirit being destroyed. She feared she had grown hardened to the experience.

One of her new patients was a woman called Cinderella by everyone on the staff, because she thought she had cinders in her hair and on her clothes and was constantly trying to brush them off. A middle-aged woman, she was unkempt and overweight, but her face and demeanor were very sweet, and Sarah was drawn to her. It was through Cinderella that she finally met Mr. D., although she'd been hearing about him since her return.

Mr. D. called her into his office to discuss Cinderella. His office was next to Dr. Palmiento's, and nearly as large. Sarah knew immediately what Colleen had meant about him being a "kid." He looked nineteen, at best, although everyone said he had to be older than that, since he was in a doctoral program studying psychology. Hard to believe, though. His cheeks were still dotted with acne.

"Please sit down." Mr. D. remained standing as he waited for Sarah to take her seat on the other side of his desk. He wore an engaging smile, and she felt herself soften toward him. "I'm pleased to finally meet you, Mrs. Tolley," he said. "I've heard fine things about your nursing skills."

"Thank you."

"I wanted to explain to you our treatment plan for your patient, Mrs. Lucas. Cinderella, I guess she's known as." He spoke like someone much older, his words a bit stilted. She'd expected him to be cocky; what young man in his position wouldn't be? *Cocky* was not a word that fit him, though.

"Cinderella, yes," she said.

"We plan to enter her into a program that is probably unfamiliar to you, since you've been gone a while. It's called psychic driving."

"The tapes," Sarah said.

"That's right. It's quite exciting." His cheeks flushed with color. "We will give her whatever combination of medications Dr. P. decides is appropriate in her case and put her in the slumber room. Then we'll fit a helmet to her head with earphones fixed inside it. The earphones will be connected to a tape recorder, and she will listen to the tape for most of the day. She can have occasional bathroom breaks, and she can take the helmet off for her meals and sleep. But the rest of the time she'll be listening to the tape. You, of course, will be providing the usual slumber room care—turning her to prevent bedsores, bathing her and such."

Sarah squirmed in her seat. "What will be on her tape?" she asked.

"Something from her sessions with Dr. P. We'll pick whatever she revealed that's most emotionally charged for her. We'll also attach a wire to her lower leg, and each time she hears the negative message, she'll receive a small electrical shock."

"Oh, Mr. D.," Sarah protested. "That's too much."

"Not at all." He leaned toward her, smiling, his black hair catching the light from above, his dark eyes gleaming. Even with the acne, he was a handsome young man. "This is a way to wipe those negative thoughts from her mind and replace them with positive ones," he said. "It's a way to change her behavior without thousands of hours of therapy."

And without human contact, Sarah thought, but she kept the words to herself. He was a kid, yes, but he was already in a position of power, and she had the distinct feeling she should not challenge him.

"Have you seen this treatment help anyone?" she dared to ask, keeping her voice as even and pleasant as possible.

"We're still in the early stage of our research," he said, averting his eyes and shuffling a few of the papers on his desk. "But we're beginning to see some improvement." Piling a few of the papers together, he stood up, and she knew she was being dismissed.

He was a not a good liar, she thought as she left his office. He believed everything he'd said up to his last comment about patient improvement, when his eyes shifted and his anxiety betrayed him. Good. At least she would know when he was trying to pull the wool over her eyes.

In three weeks, Cinderella no longer brushed imaginary cinders from her clothing. As a matter of fact, she did nothing except lie in the slumber room, eyes closed or staring at the ceiling, listening numbly to the tape playing in her helmet. Her features were flat. She ate her meals in silence. Was this improvement? Sarah didn't think so.

"They kill the unique personality in each of their patients and call it progress," she said to Colleen in the cafeteria one day.

"I know." Colleen raised a spoonful of soup to her mouth.

"I think we need to do something," Sarah said.

"What can we possibly do?"

"We need to tell someone what's going on here."

Colleen laughed. "Saint Margaret's is considered one of the top psychiatric hospitals in the nation, and Dr. P. won the coveted whatever-it-was award," she said. "Who's going to think a couple of nurses know better than someone like Palmiento what's best for the patients? And maybe we don't, Sarah. Maybe we are old-fashioned. Maybe this sort of treatment is going on at all the best hospitals."

"I certainly hope not." She leaned toward Colleen. "Even if it ultimately worked, the cost is too high. I don't think we've succeeded if we've taken away a patient's dignity in the process of treating them."

"Well," Colleen said, "if we make waves, you can bet we'll lose our jobs. I don't know about you, but I need this income. We'd probably never be able to get a job anywhere else, either. Palmiento's hardly going to give us sterling references after he fires us."

Colleen was right, on all counts. And yet, Sarah could not shake her discomfort over what was happening at Saint Margaret's. Even when she was home with Joe and Janie, her mind was often filled with concerns about work. Occasionally, she'd awaken in the middle of the night, having dreamt that she was in the isolation room, and she'd have to reach out to reassure herself that Joe was lying next to her. She'd get up to bring Janie into bed with them. Only when the three of them were cuddled together, safe and warm, did she feel truly at peace.

"Quit the job," Joe said to her one night. "We'll get by somehow. It's taking too much out of you."

They were sitting in the living room. Janie had just eaten and was asleep on Sarah's shoulder.

"I can't just quit," she said. "I think something is terribly wrong there. I can't turn my back on those patients."

"If you truly think something's wrong, then you need to do something about it," Joe said.

She shrugged. "But what if I've simply built this up in my mind into something it's not?"

Joe picked up his ever-present pad and pencil. "Let's make a list of all the things that bother you there," he said. "Then we'll take an objective look at it."

She rattled off the things that disturbed her, and it was a relief to say them out loud. "The lobotomies," she said, watching as Joe wrote down her words. "I know they're still being done elsewhere, but I doubt it's with such frequency. The electroshock treatments. He—Palmiento—uses a very high voltage, and gives them far more frequently, jolting the patients over and over again, even while they're having convulsions. The isolation room. The isolation *box*, really. And this crazy Psychic Driving Program of Mr. D.'s. And the drugs. They use far too many drugs, with little concern for what's wrong with the patient. There's not much human contact with the patients, either, except from some of the nurses. It's as though they're trying to automate psychiatric care." She kissed Janie's temple, then stood up and lowered her into the bassinet next to her chair.

Joe studied the list while she sat down again. "Are you

sure these methods aren't becoming common all over? After all, Palmiento—"

"I've looked through recent journals," she said. "There's no mention of anything like it. If anything, lobotomies have fallen into disfavor. There are some experiments being done with the new medications, but nothing like what's happening at Saint Margaret's."

Joe leaned back in his chair, the list balanced on his thigh. "I think you *do* need to take some action," he said. "How about a call to the American Board of Psychiatry? You wouldn't have to identify yourself."

She hadn't thought about making the call anonymously, and the realization that she could do so relieved her. Now that she'd verbalized her concerns to Joe, she knew she had no other choice but to tell someone in authority what she knew.

The following morning, she sat at the kitchen table and called work to say she would be in late. Then she contacted the board of psychiatry, asking to speak to the person in charge of investigating unethical practices. After a short wait, a man came on the line. Sarah had Joe's list on the table next to the phone, and she slowly enumerated the procedures that distressed her at Saint Margaret's. She pictured the man at the board writing down her concerns as she spoke, but he gave her little feedback. His flat voice reminded her of the voices of the patients in the slumber room.

"I appreciate the information," he said finally, "but I didn't get your name."

"I'd rather not give it," she said.

"We need it for our records," said the man. "And to give your report here some credibility."

"I work there. That should be credibility enough."

"How do I know you're not just a patient there?"

"I'm not. I've worked there…" She nearly told him how long she'd been there before realizing that information might make her identifiable. "You'll have to take my word for it," she said.

"Well," the man said, giving up, "I'll pass this information on to the proper authorities."

Sarah got off the phone, feeling lighter than she had in a long time. She had done all she could.

Laura held the retirement home door open for Sarah, and the older woman stepped inside, her gait far slower than when they'd started out. They had walked a good distance today, and even Laura felt exhausted, more from hearing about the odd goings-on at Saint Margaret's than from the exercise. She'd been startled to learn that Sarah had a daughter. Laura's father had said there was no other family. Joe could easily be dead by now, but Janie?

"Where is Janie now?" Laura asked when they reached the door bearing the movie projector silhouette. She was afraid of the answer, afraid of opening up a sad memory for Sarah.

"She's gone," Sarah said.

"Do you mean…" She couldn't bring herself to ask if Janie had died.

"Janie's hiding," Sarah replied. She said goodbye to Laura, went into her apartment and closed the door behind her.

27

Emma's grip tightened on Laura's hand. They were walking back from the lakeside playground, and Laura followed her daughter's gaze to their house, barely visible through the trees. Behind the screen of maple leaves and kudzu vines, she spotted Dylan sitting on the front porch, holding a large box in his arms.

"Dylan's here!" Laura said cheerfully, ignoring the anxiety behind Emma's lock on her hand. Laura had been expecting Dylan to stop by sometime today, and she knew what was in the box. "I think he has something for you," she added.

Emma's fingers loosened their grip then, and Laura shook her head. How had she and Ray managed to raise such a materialistic child when they had lived so modestly?

Laura had spoken with Dylan the night before, giving him the okay to bring over the gift and telling him about Sarah's daughter, Janie. They'd spent a futile half hour trying to decipher what Sarah might have meant when she said that Janie was in hiding.

Dylan walked down the porch steps when he saw them approaching.

"I have something here for you, Emma," he said.

"That was nice of you, Dylan." Laura looked down at her daughter, whose eyes were on the wrapped box. "Do you want her to open it out here or in the house?"

"It's heavy," he said. "Let's take it inside."

Emma ran into the house and waited for them in the middle of the living room, eyes huge with anticipation.

Dylan laughed. "Greedy kid you've got there," he said under his breath to Laura.

"She's your kid, too," she whispered back.

He set the package on the floor. "Have at it, Em," he said.

Sitting on the floor, Emma ripped off the wrapping paper, exposing an empty aquarium. She stared at it, her face expressionless.

"Do you know what it is, Emma?" Laura asked.

Emma nodded, a hint of a smile crossing her lips, and Dylan joined her on the floor, the aquarium between them.

"We need to find a place to set it up," he said. "Would you like it in your room, or somewhere else in the house?"

Whoops, Laura thought. He hadn't asked a yes or no question, and Emma simply stared at him.

"In your room?" Dylan repeated.

Emma nodded.

"Okay. We have to filter the water we put in it and let it heat up a bit. And while we're doing that, we can drive to the fish store in Middleburg and get some pretty fish for it."

Emma looked quickly at Laura.

"I'll go, too," Laura said, interpreting the fear in her daughter's eyes.

"Okay," Dylan said, rising to his feet. "First thing we have to do is find a good spot for it. You want to show me your room?"

Emma stood up and grabbed Laura's hand, then marched with the two of them upstairs.

They found the perfect spot by turning a short, broad bookshelf perpendicular to the wall and setting the aquar-

ium on the top shelf, so that it could be seen from both
sides. Dylan filtered water, poured it into the tank and in
stalled the heat pump, while Emma and Laura watched.

"I'll take care of cleaning the tank every couple o
weeks," Dylan said to Emma. It was part of the promise
he'd made to Laura when getting her permission to brin
the aquarium into the house. "Your mom said she'd tes
the water and check the filters and heaters every week. Bu
you'll have to feed the fish, Emma, twice a day. Mom car
watch you do it, at least at first. Do you think you car
handle it?"

Emma nodded, and Laura smiled at Dylan calling he
Mom. Even Ray had never referred to her with such casua
intimacy. "Your mother will watch you," Ray would have
said. She liked "Mom" much better.

Dylan and Laura talked about fish during the twenty
minute drive to Middleburg, Laura learning more than
she'd ever wanted to know about algae and live bearers and
the pH of water. Once in the fish store, she took a back
seat to the action as Dylan and Emma picked out fish and
accessories. Standing next to the aquariums, her nose prac
tically pressed to the glass, Emma wanted every beautifu
fish she saw. Dylan was patient as he explained to her why
certain fish would not thrive in her small, sure-to-get
minimal-care aquarium, and that she needed to start with
just a few fish in order to keep them healthy. She accepted
his explanations, and by the time Dylan carried the carto
of fish-filled plastic bags to the car, Emma seemed quit
content.

Laura was sitting on the corner of Emma's bed, watchin
as her daughter and Dylan transferred the fish into the
aquarium, when the phone rang. She stood up to take the
call in her bedroom, and Emma left the aquarium to follow

her. Laura looked apologetically at Dylan. Emma still was not ready to be alone with him.

Dylan shrugged. "I'll just stay here with the fish," he said. "Just me and the neon tetras."

Emma flung herself onto her mother's bed as Laura picked up the phone from her night table.

"Hello, Mrs. Darrow?" It was a woman's voice. No one ever called her Mrs. Darrow, and Laura assumed the woman was a solicitor.

"I'm sorry, there is no Mrs. Darrow," she said, and was about to hang up when the caller rushed ahead.

"Ray Darrow's wife?"

She hesitated. "Yes," she said. "Who is this?"

"Oh, you go by Brandon, don't you?" the woman said. "I forgot. Sorry. I'm Becky Reed, the publicity person at Lukens Press who'll be handling your late husband's book."

"Oh," Laura sat on the edge of the bed, and Emma shifted so that her head rested on her mother's lap. "Sorry," Laura said. "I didn't mean to be rude. My name is Laura Brandon."

"No problem," Becky said. "I just wanted to talk to you about the promotional punch we're planning to give *For Shame*. We've sent out press releases, and we're already getting requests from talk shows."

"Talk shows? But Ray's...dead."

"Yes, but *you're* alive, right? Talk shows are an incredible avenue for promoting a book, so we certainly want to make use of all the offers we can get. We're hoping you'll be willing to speak for him. Surely nobody knew Mr. Darrow better than you."

Speak for Ray? "But I don't—"

"I know you've had experience handling interviewers because of the comet discoveries," Becky Reed continued.

"I remember reading an interview with you last year in...*Time,* was it?"

"Yes, probably." Laura's mind felt foggy. "What would I talk about?" she asked. "The book was based on Ray's work, not mine."

"But you certainly know about his work with the homeless and his other humanitarian endeavors. The information would have so much meaning coming from you. It would be very poignant."

"I'm not sure I'd have time to do it," she said, although that argument seemed weak. She wasn't even working, yet it was true that she felt overburdened these days. "I'm trying to devote my energy to my daughter," she said, stroking Emma's hair. "She's had a difficult time of it since Ray died. And—"

"We'd try to accommodate your schedule," Becky said. She paused briefly, and when she spoke again, her tone was more than a bit didactic. "I'm not sure you understand the significance of *For Shame,*" she said. "There have been lots of books on the homeless, but this one's going to hit the mark by pushing everyone's guilt buttons. That chapter about the mentally ill being out on the streets will do it, if nothing else. It's going to be the most talked-about book on Capitol Hill. We expect that even the president will read it. And getting it on the talk shows is absolutely critical to its success. Please consider doing this for us."

"All right," she said with a sigh. "I'll think about it." She said goodbye and hung up the phone, then looked down at Emma. The little girl's thumb was in her mouth again, but her eyes were wide open, staring at her mother.

"Come on, sweetie," Laura said, gently moving Emma's head from her lap to the bed. "Let's go see how Dylan's making out with your new fish."

Dylan had all the fish in the aquarium by the time sh

and Emma returned to the room. Emma walked slowly toward the tank, thumb still in her mouth, and she was far more subdued than she'd been a few minutes earlier.

"The fish look beautiful," Laura said, and they truly did. Gold and blue and spotted brown. The light from the window shone through the water, splashing color through the room. Still, Dylan seemed to sense the preoccupation behind her enthusiasm.

"You look kinda green," he said, cocking his head at her. He was standing on the opposite side of the aquarium, wiping his hands on a rag. "Bad phone call?" he asked.

"Not bad, exactly." She sat down on Emma's bed again. "Just...troubling."

Dylan set the rag down on the bookshelf. "Well?" he said. "Spill it."

"It was Ray's publisher. They want me to go on talk shows to promote his book."

"Hey, that's good news, isn't it?" Dylan asked. "Not too many books get touted on those shows."

"Yes, it's good. So, why don't I feel good about it?"

"I don't know," he said. "Why don't you?"

Laura rubbed her temples with her fingers. "Ray's gone," she said. "I want to close that chapter, not reopen it and relive all the pain. And it just feels like one more thing for me to worry about in a string of things. Yet, that's ridiculous. I'm turning into a wimp who can't handle more than one situation at a time without decompensating."

Emma had been staring at the fish, but now she walked slowly toward her bed. With a sudden movement, she dropped to the floor, rolling beneath the bed, and Laura felt the sting of alarm. Emma had spent hours burrowed under furniture in the few weeks after Ray's death. The first therapist they'd seen had said it was a normal reaction to what had happened, that Emma was simply seeking a sense of security, and not to make an issue out of it. But for Emma to suddenly begin doing it again was unnerving.

Dylan gave Laura a puzzled look, and she shrugged, wondering if her face gave away the fear she felt over Emma's strange behavior.

"Well," Dylan said as though nothing were unusual, "the so-called things you have to handle are pretty taxing, Laura. The other day you said your life's turned into a guessing game. You don't know what's really going on inside...the people you're trying to help." He glanced toward the bed, as if uncertain whether to speak this way in front of Emma. "You're already carrying a burden," he said. "Don't do the talk shows if it feels like too much for you."

The solace he offered felt alien to her. "I should do them for Ray, though," she said.

Dylan glanced at the bed again, then nodded for Laura to walk with him outside the room.

Laura followed him into the hallway, her eyes hot with tears. "She hasn't done that in months," she said, once they were out of hearing distance of the bedroom.

"I think it's because we're talking about Ray."

"She must still be confused or upset about his death," she said.

"And she can't tell you what's confusing or upsetting her. And you wonder why you feel overwhelmed. Laura, you're dealing with too much. You have my support, for what it's worth, to tell the talk shows to take a hike."

She smiled weakly. She wanted to touch him, to wrap her arms around him, but she settled for offering him a simple "Thank you."

"Hey, no problem," he said. "Any time you need some sense talked into your head, you know who to call." He looked at his watch. "And now I've got to run."

He walked into Emma's room on his way down the hall. Laura listened from outside the room as he spoke to his invisible daughter. "I'm leaving now, Emma," he said. "But I wanted to tell you something first. You know my big fish tank? Whenever I'm feeling upset or angry or scared or sad or any of those bad feelings, I just sit and look at my fish. They make me feel very calm. Just wanted to tell you that."

He stepped back into the hall, waved to Laura, then headed for the stairs.

She leaned against the wall, watching him go, and for the first time in her life, knew she was falling in love.

28

"It's raining," Laura said when Sarah opened her apartment door.

Sarah turned to peer out the window, disappointment etched on her face. "Not that much," she said.

"It's been heavy off and on," Laura said, walking inside the apartment. She held up the video of an old movie she'd rented. "I brought a movie we could watch," she said. "Except I'd really rather talk." The fact that Sarah had a daughter had been troubling her. She wanted to know what had become of Janie.

"Yes, I'd rather talk, too," Sarah said. "I'll tell you what happened to Joe. I didn't already tell you that, did I?"

"To Joe?" Laura combed her fingers through her damp hair. "I was wondering what happened to Janie, actually."

"But Joe is before Janie." Sarah looked around her as if hunting for something. "I think that's right. Actually, they both hurt to remember."

"You don't have to talk about them if you don't—"

"Today would have been Joe's birthday," Sarah said with a smile. "May 3."

Laura peered into the kitchenette. The large plastic calendar read August 31; the actual date was August 29. But she didn't have the heart to burst Sarah's bubble.

"Then today's the perfect day for you to be thinking about him," she said.

"Right." Sarah walked toward the sofa. "So, I'll tell you what happened to Joe. To the love of my life."

Sarah, 1959

Sarah waited for changes to occur at Saint Margaret's as a result of her call to the board of psychiatry, but as far as she could tell, her concerns had been ignored. Things continued as they had, with patients slipping into the shocked and drugged stupors that resulted from so much of Dr. Palmiento's treatment. All of his approaches had one thing in common: they were attempts to wipe the patient's mental slate clean. Whether he used drugs or shock treatment or isolation or the tapes, Palmiento was trying to rid people of their pasts. In the process, he was ridding them of their souls.

Sarah grew increasingly distressed by what she perceived as the deterioration of her patients. At times, she doubted her own sanity. At staff meetings, Dr. P. presented cases illustrating supposed progress in a patient, and Sarah would wonder what was wrong with her that his definition of progress and her own seemed so diametrically opposed.

One night, Sarah had another frightening nightmare. She was not in the isolation room this time, but rather had been drugged and was and lying, paralyzed, in the slumber room. She was wearing a helmet, and Mr. D. was pushing the portable electroshock treatment machine toward her. She awakened with a scream.

Joe pulled her into his arms, and she felt like a fool. Here she was, an adult woman with a year-old child, waking up like a baby herself more nights than not.

"I have a plan," Joe said, once she had calmed down.

"What do you mean, 'a plan'?" She leaned back to look at his face, but it was too dark to see his expression.

"I'm going to get myself admitted to Saint Margaret's," he said. "I'll find out first hand what's going on there. Then I'll report it in the Post."

Sarah sat up with a gasp. "You will do no such thing!" she said.

"I think it's a great idea," Joe said. "I'll check in under an assumed name. No one will know I'm your husband. They'll think I'm just another patient. I'll get to see exactly how they treat someone."

"Joe, this will never work," Sarah said sternly. "They'll medicate you, for heaven's sake. Within a day you won't remember your own name."

"They'll give me the medication, and I'll spit it out after they leave the room, all right?"

"And what will you do if they take you for shock treatments?"

"You'll be around to make sure nothing terrible happens to me."

"Joe, this is crazy!" She tried to laugh, hoping he was joking, but she knew her husband entirely too well. He'd never met a challenge he didn't like. "You don't understand," she said. "I wouldn't be able to be with you every minute. You might not even be assigned to me. And I don't have as much power there as you seem to think."

"What's happened to your spirit of adventure, Sarah?" He sounded serious.

Was she being stodgy about this? Was she turning into a cautious old lady?

"Look." He sat up and held both her hands on his knee. "I'll keep my wits about me," he said. "I can take care of myself, and someone has to find out and expose what's really going on there, don't you think?"

"Maybe, but not you."

"I'm going to do it."

"I'll quit working there, Joe. If that's what you want."

"Too late. My mind's made up." Always the risk-taker and ever the journalist. Sarah knew there would be no fighting him.

"Mrs. Gale will have to watch Janie in the mornings while I'm there." He'd apparently been planning this for a while. "I'll miss that time with her. The dad-and-daughter time."

"Joe, I can't believe you would—"

"So tell me what symptoms I should have," he said. "How do I stand the best chance of getting to wear one of those nifty helmets?"

The idea was frightening, and yet it might work. The benefits of uncovering what was going on at Saint Margaret's might be worth the risk. But she would have to keep a very careful eye on him.

Feigning the severe depressive symptoms Sarah coached him to adopt, Joe signed himself into the hospital under a fictitious name, Frederick Hamilton. Sarah was afraid to tell even Colleen about Joe's plan, not wanting to put her friend in a difficult position, so no one at the hospital knew that Joe was not a genuine patient. That was the way he wanted it.

Sarah was a wreck the day he checked in. She knew he was down the hall, being evaluated in Dr. Palmiento's office, and she had no idea which ward he'd be assigned to. He would only come to her ward if he were deemed sick enough, and she couldn't imagine Joe being able to pull off that convincing a charade. But he must have managed to do so, because at two o'clock, he arrived on ward three. He walked past her in the corridor, his slender frame flanked by two bulky orderlies. He winked at her as he walked by, and one of the orderlies whispered to her, "Watch out for him, Mrs. Tolley. Fancies himself a ladies' man." Sarah nearly laughed with relief at knowing her husband would be nearby.

Once alone with him in his room, she found Joe animated, delighted to be in the midst of an adventure. "I fabricated a terrible life for myself," he said. "That Dr. Palmiento ate it up. I'm a better actor than I ever imagined."

"Sh," Sarah said, fluffing his pillow for him. "Don't get smug. You have a few rough days ahead of you."

"Told you this would work, though. I've got you for my nurse." He gripped her wrist and tried to pull her toward him for a kiss.

"We can't," she said, although she was laughing. "We've got to keep up the ruse. I don't know what would happen if they figured out who you are." The thought made her shudder.

For two days, Sarah slipped the medication prescribed for Frederick Hamilton into the pocket of her uniform. On a few occasions, when another nurse or Dr. P. was around, Joe would simply pretend to take the pills, turning them over to Sarah when the coast was clear. Sarah instructed him to act sleepy and unaware of what was going on around him, and he did so, although he was actually quite alert. He was a good actor, though. Good enough to fool Dr. Palmiento and Mr. D. when they came to examine him one morning. Joe feigned a deep sleep, and that afternoon, he excitedly told Sarah that he'd overheard a conversation between the two men that definitely had not been meant for his ears.

"What did they say?" she asked.

"I don't remember verbatim. I'm afraid to keep notes

here, so I have to store it in my head. But the gist of their conversation was that they're involved in some sort of experimentation with personality restructuring.''

"I know that," Sarah said. "They're trying to rid people of their maladaptive—"

"No, it's more than that," Joe said. "Bigger than that. They're trying to develop mind control techniques. You know, like the Russians use."

"Mind control! You *are* crazy."

"I know it sounds crazy, but that's what they were talking about. Making someone do what they want him to do, against his will. They were discussing a man in the slumber room and how they were *brainwashing* him. That's the word they used. Brainwashing. They were excited about it. 'It's working.' That's what they said. And then one of them, Dr. P., I'm quite sure, though my eyes were closed, said something about it being a first step toward mind control."

Stunned, Sarah sat on the edge of Joe's bed and risked taking his hand. "I just thought they were trying out new, and not very beneficial, techniques to help psychiatric patients," she said. "But I always did have a sense that the patients here were simply being used as guinea pigs."

"They are," Joe said. "Doesn't everything you've witnessed here fit the definition of experimentation? Treatment methods you've never seen anywhere else?"

"But...they're doing research," she said lamely.

"This goes beyond any sort of research I've ever heard of," Joe said. "This is completely unethical."

"Okay, now you've figured it out," Sarah said. "Now check yourself out of here, while you still can."

"I've only just begun, Sarah," he said. "I don't have anywhere near enough to go on."

She looked down at their interlocked hands. "I'm tired of sleeping without you," she said.

"Me, too," he acknowledged. "And I miss Janie more than I can say. It must be awful for the genuine patients to be in here so long without seeing their families."

"Well." She stood up, afraid that if she sat there with him any longer she would start crying. "Get what you need and get out of here, before you turn into a genuine patient yourself," she said.

The following day, Dr. P. held a therapy session with Joe, and he was obviously unhappy with the results.

"I was hoping the oral medication would be enough to get him to open up," he told Sarah. "But he's more repressed than I anticipated. We'll use LSD injections for a few days. Give him the first tonight."

Sarah didn't dare protest. Why should she bother? There was no way she was giving Joe an injection of LSD.

Joe eyed the syringe when she brought it to his room that evening. "Does that go in my vein or my hip or where?" he asked.

"Neither," Sarah said. "Ordinarily I'd inject it into your upper arm, but in your case, my dear, it's going into your mattress." Removing the cap from the syringe, she planted the needle in the side of his mattress and pressed the plunger.

Joe watched in fascination. "So how am I supposed to react to this stuff?" he asked.

"Any way you like," she said, capping the syringe again. "I've seen it all. You can climb the walls or cry like a baby or hallucinate. Take your pick." She heard the irritation in her voice and hoped he knew it was her fear speaking. "Please give this up, Joe," she pleaded. "It's getting too dangerous. Every time I see Dr. P. in here with you, I panic. He gives LSD injections himself sometimes.

It was just luck that he asked me to do it today. And a few of the nurses are out sick with a stomach virus and I have a triple load of patients. I may not be able to—''

"Maybe I should take it for real, once." Joe wasn't even listening to her. "Otherwise, how do I know what the patients are actually feeling?"

"Don't even talk that way, Joseph Tolley."

"How long does it last? I mean how long do I keep up the act?"

"It varies," she said. "Four or five hours, usually. Sometimes longer. Some people never really seem to come back from the experience." She tossed in that last detail as a warning as she left his room.

The distant sound of retching greeted her in the corridor, and she knew one more of the patients had contracted the virus that was sweeping the unit. She prayed Joe wouldn't get it. That was all she needed.

In the morning, she found her husband in the throes of his act, and it appeared he had elected to take the hallucination route. He was on his bed, huddled in the corner, and there was a frighteningly real look of paranoia in his eyes.

"You make a good psychiatric patient, Joe," she said.

Joe closed his eyes. He was trembling, and she knew that something wasn't right. Checking his chart, she scanned the notes quickly, and found exactly what she feared: Dr. Palmiento had been in to see Joe the night before. Pleased with the effects of the LSD, he'd given him yet another injection.

"Oh, Joe, you let him do it!" She sat on his bed, reaching out to touch her frightened husband's cheek. "You mustn't let him do it again," she said. "Do you hear me?"

Joe nodded, squeezing his eyes shut again. His hands were wrapped tightly across his chest, and he shivered against the wall. Sarah pulled the blanket out from the foot of his bed and wrapped it around his shoulders.

Had Joe fought the injection, she wondered, or had he accepted it in the name of his investigation? It didn't matter now. What did matter was that he was suffering, and it was time for her to get him out of there. She would wait until the drug had done its worst, since he would be impossible to move while he was like this, and then she would sneak him out. She had the keys to the locked doors. Frederick Hamilton would disappear, and because his name and identity were pure fiction, no one would be able to track him down.

Once she had Joe's escape mapped out in her mind, Sarah relaxed a bit. Dr. P. ordered her to give Joe another injection that evening, an order she had no intention of following. She kept a careful eye on Joe the entire day, and when he seemed to be growing rational once again, told him her plan.

"I've called Mrs. Gale," she said, putting the syringe filled with LSD on his bedside table. "She'll watch Janie until seven. So once the day shift has left, you and I can go down the back stairs and get you out of here."

"I'm not leaving," Joe said. "Now I know what that drug—what was it?"

"LSD." That he had already forgotten the name of the drug worried her.

"Now I know what it does to people. And it ain't fun. I was…" He shuddered. "Everything was purple. *Everything.* Purple and soft. I was truly afraid I was stuck there, in that purple, soft world. But now I'm back and I'm all right, and it's time to try out the tape room. Or the slumber room. Or whatever it's—"

"No, Joe." Sarah tried to keep her voice low, but was unable to control her fear and mounting anger. "You can't stay here. Look what happened when I was away last night? It's too dangerous.''

"I survived, didn't I?''

"Joe, please. No story is this important.''

"I think this one is,'' he said. "You were right, Sarah. Something's going on here and someone's got to find out what it is.''

One of the other nurses called to Sarah from the hallway outside Joe's door. Standing up, she looked at her husband.

"I'll be back around six,'' she said. "And you're going with me, Joe. This has gone far enough.''

Joe grabbed the syringe from the bedside table, yanked off the cap, and rammed the needle into his thigh, straight through the hospital-issued pajamas. "I'm staying,'' he said, and she knew she was not dealing with her ordinarily rational husband. She was dealing with a man on LSD.

At six, he was far too loud and wild for her to take him down the back stairs without attracting attention. She would have to wait one more day. As she left Joe's room, she nearly collided with Mr. D., who looked at her with what she could only label suspicion. Had he heard her trying to talk to her husband? She forced a smile.

"Do you think he's ready for the tapes?'' Mr. D. asked her.

"Yes!'' she said, with far too much enthusiasm. She never wanted anyone to be subjected to those helmets and their repetitive messages. But maybe the tapes would finally satisfy Joe's investigative hunger and he would get out of there. And at least in the slumber room, she would know where he was at all times.

"I'm not so sure,'' Mr. D. said, and she knew by the tone of his voice that he'd been testing her with his question.

The next morning, Sarah awakened with the stomach virus that was devastating ward three. She dressed for work and had managed to take Janie next door to Mrs. Gale's when the nausea struck with full force. She just made it back to her own home before the vomiting began.

She had to get to Joe, she thought, filled with terror. The LSD would have worn off by this morning, and she had to prevent him from receiving any more drugs.

But it was ten in the morning before she was able to drag herself out of the bathroom and into the living room to call the hospital. She reached Colleen on ward three.

"Listen, Colleen," she said. "Listen carefully. I'm sorry to put you in this position, but—"

"What's wrong?" There was immediate concern in Colleen's voice.

"Joe is there," Sarah said. "He checked himself in as a patient because he wants to do a story on what's going on at the hospital."

"Are you kidding?" Colleen's voice was soft, and Sarah knew she was not alone.

"He's the patient in room eleven. He's under a fictitious name, Frederick Hamilton. I've been pretending to medicate him, but Dr. P. got some LSD into him. And I caught that stomach bug and can't get over there." The bile rose in her throat again and she swallowed hard. "Maybe I can get in by this afternoon, but I need you to check on him. Make sure he's all right."

Colleen was quiet.

"Colleen? Do you understand?"

"Um…" Colleen was probably watching her words, not wanting to give anything away to whomever was listening to her part of the conversation. "Uh, I helped Dr. P. with that patient this morning," she said. "In the electroshock room."

It took Sarah a moment to understand. "What are you saying? Colleen, you can't mean—did Joe get ECT?"

"Mr. Hamilton did, yes."

"Oh, my God." Sarah leaned back against the wall, battling nausea. "Why couldn't they just put him in the slumber room?" Remembering the suspicion in Mr. D.'s face when she'd bumped into him in the hall the day before, she feared she knew the answer. ECT would be the quickest, surest way to scramble Joe's memory of anything he'd learned as a patient in ward three. "I have to get off," she said, hanging up the phone without waiting for a response from Colleen.

She was sick three more times, impatiently retching in the bathroom when she needed to be back on the phone. She called the hospital and asked to be put through to Dr. Palmiento's office, her mind racing as she tried to formulate what she would say. She was desperate enough to resort to the truth. At least, some of the truth.

"Yes, Mrs. Tolley?" Palmiento's voice was expectant.

"Dr. Palmiento, a terrible mistake has happened," she said. "The patient on ward three, Frederick Hamilton, is actually my husband, Joseph Tolley. He's a reporter and he wanted to do a story on...what it's like to be a psychiatric patient. I tried to talk him out of it, but I wasn't able to. I'm sorry I deceived you. But he's really a very sane man, and I want to check him out of there. Right away."

There was no response on Dr. P.'s end of the line, and she had the feeling he was trying to prolong her suffering.

"I know this means the end of my job," she said. "I understand that. But right now, I just want to get my husband home." Her voice cracked on the last word, and she drew in a long breath.

"Do you really think a 'very sane man' would check himself into a mental institution?" Dr. P. asked her.

"A reporter would. Someone who really wanted to find out—"

"And what exactly did your husband find out?"

"Well, just a little of what it's like to be a patient. I mean, he experienced LSD. And now I guess ECT." She pinched the phone wire with her fingers, fighting her tears. "So I think that's enough. I'd like to come get him now."

Palmiento made her endure another moment of silence. "I know this is hard to hear, Mrs. Tolley," he said finally, in that fatherly tone that now grated on her, "but I believe your husband, out of his love for you, has been trying to protect you. He didn't want you to know how unhappy he was in his current life. He suffers from a true, clinical and quite severe depression, dear. His signing into the hospital was indeed a ruse, but you were the victim, not us. He didn't know how to tell you that he really wanted to be here. That he really needed treatment."

"That just isn't true!" Sarah said. "I know my husband. He's one of the happiest, most contented people I've ever—"

"He kept it all inside, Sarah," Dr. P. said kindly. "You've known patients like that, haven't you? It takes the medication and other treatment to help them open up."

"I'm coming to get him."

"He doesn't want to go," Palmiento said. "He signed himself in, and he signed the form allowing us to provide whatever treatment we deem best in his case. You know those forms, don't you, Sarah?"

She did. The form gave blanket approval for any and all treatment deemed appropriate by the staff. "But he...but this was...he's not really a *patient!*"

"Perhaps you could use a few sessions with a therapist yourself, Sarah. You need to accept—"

"You're mad!" she said.

There was another pause on his end of the line. Then he spoke in a clipped tone. "And you, of course, are fired." He hung up, and Sarah clutched the phone in her hand, shivering from nausea and fear. As she tried to stand, dizziness washed over her and she leaned against the arm of the sofa. She had to get to Joe. They knew who he was. They would want to know if he'd learned anything more momentous than what it felt like to be on LSD. They might torture him to get him to talk. She thought of the isolation box. She would not put anything past them.

Her stomach would not let her leave the house until late that afternoon. She drove to the hospital, feeling as though she'd been hollowed out, left with barely enough strength to sit upright. She took the stairs up to ward three and walked as quickly as she was able to Joe's room. There was another patient in Joe's bed, and she turned from the doorway in a panic.

"Where's Mr. Hamilton?" she asked the nearest nurse.

"He left this morning," the woman said.

"Left to go where?"

"I don't know."

"The slumber room?" Sarah asked. "The isolation room?"

"No," the woman said. "He left the hospital."

They discharged him! Her call to Palmiento had some impact after all. But if he'd gotten out that morning, why hadn't he come home? He could be at his office, she thought. It would be just like him to rush immediately into work. Although...Colleen said he'd had shock treatment. He wouldn't have been able to go anywhere on his own after that. Her heart began to race again; her head felt light. Would they have put him out on the street in that condition? She walked down the hall to Dr. Palmiento's office, running her hands against the wall for support.

"Come in," Palmiento said after she knocked. He stood up and reached for her shoulder, but she shrugged his hand away. "Please sit, Mrs. Tolley. We need to have a talk."

"Where is my husband?" She made no move to sit.

Dr. P. remained standing but leaned back against his desk, his arms folded across his chest. "I reevaluated him after our talk this morning," he said. "His depression was so deep and intractable. I knew there was only one thing we could do."

Sarah froze. "Where is he?" she asked, praying that her suspicion was not correct.

"The lobotomy went well," Dr. P. said.

Sarah laughed, the sound tinny and unnatural. "Is this some sort of joke?"

He pursed his lips and looked at her with his false sympathy. "I know this must be very hard to understand," he said. "Why, just a few days ago you thought you had a hale and hearty husband. He'd kept his distress so very well hidden. But believe me, he's much better off now. No more of that terrible psychic pain."

"I don't believe you at all," she stood up. "Where is my *husband?*"

He handed her Frederick Hamilton's chart, and she opened it slowly, studying Dr. Palmiento's notes. *Severe and intractable depression. Suicidal ideation.* And the final note. *Lobotomy performed 1:00 p.m., May 7, '59. Patient tolerated procedure well.*

Closing the folder slowly, she lowered herself into the chair. "Where is he?" she asked, her voice quieter now, less insistent.

"We transferred him for custodial care. Surely you know you can't care for him at home now."

"Where to? To an asylum? A home?"

"Right now, it's best for you not to know," Dr. P. said. "You're far too distraught. You—"

She was up from the chair and across the room in an instant, her arms raised for battle, and Dr. P. held up his hands to thwart her attack. Speaking to her in the gentle, patronizing voice she loathed, he grasped her wrists. Wrenching free, she spit at him, then turned on her heel and ran out of his office as fast as her weakened legs could carry her.

Once in her car, she sat behind the wheel, struggling to catch her breath. She would find Joe. She had to. Yet she knew she had lost her husband to his foolhardy scheme. Even if she found him, Joe probably would not know who she was.

"Where was he?" Laura asked. She had moved next to Sarah on the sofa, taking the older woman's hand when she began to cry near the end of her story.

"I don't know." Sarah blotted her eyes with the tissue Laura had handed her. "I never found him, although I looked and looked. And I never saw him again."

"My God." It seemed impossible, and once again, Laura wondered if the story might be an elaborate figment of Sarah's imagination. It had been too rich with detail, though. The events hung together too well to be so easily discounted.

"What did you do?" Laura asked. "Did you call the police or—"

Sarah suddenly stood up, putting an end to Laura's questions with a wave of her hand.

"No more." She shook her hands as if trying to rid them of a sticky substance. "Don't you have a movie? Let's watch it now."

Laura looked at her watch. "I'm sorry, Sarah, but I have

to get home. I can leave the movie with you,'' she said, even though leaving the movie would make it woefully overdue. But Sarah seemed in desperate need of something to take her mind off the past.

Sarah looked uncertain for a moment. "All right," she said finally. "Will you put it in the...thing for me?"

"The VCR? Sure." Laura readied the movie in the VCR, then gave Sarah a hug. "I'll see you next week," she said.

On the drive back to Lake Ashton, Laura could think only of Sarah's torturous memories about Joe and the evil aura surrounding Saint Margaret's. It wasn't until she was halfway home that she remembered the cryptic notes of warning she'd received in the mail. Maybe the writer of those notes was not trying to keep Sarah isolated and lonely. Maybe they were simply trying to protect her from a past too painful to remember.

29

He was going to sleep with Bethany tonight. It had been a long time, and he'd been thinking about it all day.

Except...Bethany was not in a great mood. She'd been quiet at the restaurant, and even quieter since they'd returned to his cabin. Sitting next to him on the sofa, she sipped the decaf he'd made her and stared blankly at his aquarium, not saying a word.

He put his arm around her. "I feel like I'm with Emma tonight," he said, "having to guess what you're thinking." He touched her temple lightly with his fingers. "What's going on in that head of yours?"

"Nothing," she said.

A loaded response. Whatever was bothering her, he had to deal with it before they went to bed. Sleeping with Bethany when she was annoyed was never a good idea. Whatever was disturbing her would come out immediately after they'd made love, and he'd be up all night trying to make amends.

He tried to think back to when her sullen mood had started, and the answer came to him quickly: she'd been upset from the moment she'd arrived at his cabin, her overnight bag slung over her shoulder, and found him on the phone with Laura.

Emma and her friend, Cory, were pretending their Barbies worked at an aquarium, Laura had told him, and the entire bookshelf had been converted into doll-size offices in the aquarium building.

Then she told him about her disturbing visit to Sarah that afternoon, something unbelievable about Sarah's husband pretending to be a psychiatric patient and getting himself lobotomized in the process.

That's when Bethany showed up, loudly announcing her arrival, and Dylan had cringed at her timing. Laura must think he had a constant string of women parading through his house.

"I'm interrupting again," Laura had said. He hadn't bothered denying it this time. He told her they could talk again tomorrow and thanked her for calling.

"Who's that?" Bethany had asked when he got off the phone.

"Laura." He told her about the Barbies and the aquarium and the bookshelf, while Bethany stared at him as if he'd gone mad.

"I can't believe you're talking about Barbie dolls," she said. Then she kissed him and poured him a glass of wine, but there was a stiffness in her movements that let him know she was not pleased. Was that what was still bugging her now, hours later?

He gave her shoulders a squeeze. "I know something's bothering you," he said. "It's not 'nothing.' Tell me what's going on."

Bethany leaned forward to set her mug on the coffee table, then turned toward him, escaping his arm in the process. "Do you know how many times you said the name 'Emma' tonight?" she asked.

He shrugged. "A few, I guess."

"Thirty-four," Bethany said. "And I only started counting at the restaurant."

"You *counted?* What was the point in—"

"And how about 'Laura'?" Bethany didn't wait for him to answer. "Twenty-three."

Twenty-three? "Come on, Beth—"

"You say you're not interested in Emma's mother, but you sure talked about her enough," she said. "And guess how many times you said the name 'Bethany'?"

He knew he was not going to win this game, no matter what he answered. "I don't know," he said, giving up.

"Twice, Dylan. *Twice.*" There was anger in her eyes. "And now you expect me to stay overnight, don't you?"

"I thought you wanted to," he said. "You brought your—"

She stood up. "Forget it! I'm not staying." She marched toward the kitchen where she'd left her overnight bag.

"If it bothered you so much when I talked about Emma, why didn't you just say so?" he asked, angry now himself as he followed her into the kitchen. "Were you too busy counting? Too busy trying to trip me up somehow?"

Pulling the strap of the bag over her shoulder, she headed for the door. "Good old Bethany," she said. "She's always there whenever you need her. You can dump all your problems on her, and she listens with sympathy. And she'll sleep with you, too! What a pal! Well, I'm sick of being your pal, Dylan." She let the screen door slam behind her as she left the house.

Dazed, Dylan stared after her. What the hell had just happened? One minute they were sipping coffee and cuddling on the sofa, the next minute she'd blown sky-high. It had been building in her all night, obviously. Building in her while he'd blathered on about Emma.

He called her half an hour later, when he knew she'd be home, but she refused to talk to him.

"Don't call me, okay?" she said. "Don't call until you've figured out what you want." There was a pause, and he knew she was crying. "I love you, Dylan," she said. "I know you don't feel the same way, and I can't wait any longer for you. And…I guess I'd better tell you that I'm going to sleep with…someone else. For all I know, you're never going to get over this fixation."

Hanging up the phone, he lay back on the sofa. The aquarium was the only light in the room, and he watched one of the fish glide smoothly from one end of the tank to the other. He remembered telling Emma that he watched the fish when he was upset or sad. Well, he was both those things now.

He wanted to see the aquarium building Emma had created in the bookshelf. He wanted to watch her play with it. Had she named her fish? How would he ever know? Those names would stay locked in her head forever. No, not forever. Just until she was ready to start talking again.

Bethany was right: he was consumed with his thoughts about his daughter.

But what was this bit about Laura? he wondered. Had he really said her name twenty-three times?

30

Laura returned to the retirement home the next day. She'd slept poorly the night before, worried that she'd left Sarah alone with memories of her husband's tragedy. One good thing about her preoccupation with Sarah: it prevented her from stewing over the fact that Dylan had a woman at his house again the night before.

"Can we go for a walk?" Sarah asked as soon as she saw it was Laura at her door. "I have my shoes on."

"Of course." Laura walked into the apartment, her gaze falling instantly to the photograph of young Joe Tolley on the end table. He looked different to her this morning. He wore a cockeyed grin and there was a sparkle in his eye. She could imagine him plotting that dangerous charade at Saint Margaret's.

"Did you enjoy the movie?" Laura asked.

"Movie?" Sarah looked at her blankly.

"The movie I left in your VCR yesterday."

"Oh." Sarah glanced at the VCR. "I don't think I watched it. I was thinking about Joe all day."

Laura extracted the movie from the machine and left it next to her purse on the kitchenette counter. She opened the apartment door for Sarah, and they walked into the hall.

"You told me some disturbing things about Joe," she said, wondering if it was cruel to probe Sarah's memory further.

Sarah only nodded.

"And you said you never saw him again. Was that right?"

Sarah let out a sigh. "Joseph Tolley was a kind, lovable, smart and adventurous man," she said. "But in the end, he was a fool."

Sarah, 1959

Minutes after learning about Joe's fate from Dr. Palmiento, Sarah picked up Janie at Mrs. Gale's. Her mind was reeling, and her stomach was still in turmoil from her bout of sickness that morning. She did not know what to do. She went through the motions of feeding Janie, playing with her a bit, tucking her into bed. Then she sat in her living room, staring out the window at the streetlight.

Joe was gone—the Joe she had known, at any rate. The thought of that sharp mind and easygoing manner being quelled forever by such barbaric surgery was simply incomprehensible to her. Yet she had seen Dr. Palmiento perform surgery on other patients who did not seem to merit it. And he had probably figured out what Joe was up to. What better way to prevent Joe's report from ever seeing the light of day than to destroy his mind?

Yet *her* mind was still clear, and she knew what Joe had learned. Palmiento was experimenting on his patients, he'd said. Something about mind control. Brainwashing. She would go to the authorities with what she knew. The police or the FBI. First thing in the morning, though, she would call the board of psychiatry again and tell them what had happened to Joe. Palmiento needed to be punished for what he'd done.

She cried in bed the entire night, as if trying to get the

tears out of the way. Once she started her fight, there would be no room for them.

In the morning, she reached the president of the board. This time she identified herself. As she began reciting what had happened, he interrupted her.

"I can't understand a word you're saying," he said.

In spite of all the weeping she'd done overnight, she was still crying as she spoke. Crying and raising her voice. She knew she must sound like a madwoman.

"I was a nurse at Saint Margaret's Psychiatric Hospital," she said, getting her emotions under control. "I thought some strange things were going on there, so I reported them to you...to the board."

"What sort of 'strange things'?" he asked.

"Cruel and inhumane experiments," she said. "Then my husband, who is a reporter for the *Washington Post,* checked himself in as a patient so that he could find out what was really going on there. When they—Dr. Palmiento and Mr....D., I don't even know his real last name—when they found out what my husband was up to, they lobotomized him. And they won't tell me where he is."

The president of the board did not respond right away. "This sounds rather far-fetched," he said finally.

"Please believe me! Send someone to look at his chart. Only it's not under his real name. It's under the name Frederick Hamilton."

"Peter Palmiento is one of the top psychiatrists in the country," the man said.

"I'm aware of his reputation, but maybe he doesn't deserve it," Sarah countered. "Do you have a record of the last report I made?"

"I'll check on it. If you called, I'm sure we have it."

"I made it anonymously. And you never *did* anything

about it. My husband's not the only one who's suffered there.''

"All right, Mrs. Tolley. I'm having a hard time accepting what you're telling me, but I'll look into it personally. Okay?"

"When? They won't let me see him. I want to see him."

"I'll call Pete today," he said.

Pete. As though he and Palmiento were old buddies.

She got off the phone and sat curled up in one corner of the sofa, staring into space. It seemed impossible that they would have moved Joe so quickly after surgery. Maybe they'd only told her they'd moved him and he was still there. She called Colleen at the hospital and began telling her what had happened, but Colleen interrupted her.

"I know," she said. "They found out he was snooping into their experiments and they lobotomized him. I'm so, so sorry, Sarah."

Hearing the words from Colleen's mouth made them horribly real.

"Do you know where they took him?" she asked.

"I looked at his chart," Colleen said. "It doesn't say."

"I can't believe they moved him that quickly. Do you think he might still be there? Would you check, Colleen? Could you check any room where they might have put him for postsurgical care?"

Colleen hesitated. "Mr. D. called me into his office this morning," she said. "He told me about you being fired and said I should...that I shouldn't have any contact with you."

"Why?"

"He said if I wanted to keep my job, I should avoid you."

"Colleen, *please.* Please look for Joe. No one needs to know what you're doing." That Colleen would put Mr. D.'s demand ahead of their friendship stung her.

"All right." Colleen sounded reluctant. "I'll check the other wards on my break."

The day was very long. Sarah took Janie for two walks in her stroller, and in between the walks, she held the little girl on her lap until Janie whimpered to be set free. She nearly forgot to feed her. Food was the last thing on her mind.

Colleen called that evening to tell Sarah that she'd checked the hospital from top to bottom. Joe was not there.

"I remembered that an ambulance was at the hospital yesterday afternoon," Colleen said. "I didn't make the connection at the time, but they were probably transporting him."

Or maybe Joe had died during the surgery, Sarah thought with horror. It happened. She'd never seen a patient die during a lobotomy, but she'd heard plenty of stories. Perhaps they had made certain that Joe died. That's why they wouldn't tell her where he had been taken.

She was already up and sitting in the living room, planning her next move, when the phone rang early the following morning. It was Dr. Palmiento's secretary, asking her to come to the hospital immediately for a meeting with him.

She dressed quickly, dropped Janie off with Mrs. Gale and drove to Saint Margaret's.

Both Palmiento and Mr. D. were in the director's office. They stood as she entered, but she had no time for such niceties.

"I demand to know where Joe is," she said. "Or did you kill him during surgery?"

"Sit down, please," said Dr. P.

"Just tell me—"

"Sit down, dear," he said, more firmly this time, and she took a seat. Why did she allow this man to have such power over her?

Palmiento sat down again, hands folded on top of his desk. "I had a meeting with the president of the psychiatric board yesterday," he said pleasantly, though his sharp eyes clashed with the tone of his voice. "We met on the golf course, so I had a good long time to explain the entire situation to him. I told him all about your husband's psychiatric illness. And about your need to deny it."

"He did not have a psychiatric illness." The words came out in a growl. She felt like a wild animal, ferocious and ready to defend her family.

Mr. D. sat in the chair next to hers. "This must be very difficult for you," he said.

His voice was so kind that, despite her fury, she was tempted to rest her head on his shoulder. But he was a wolf in sheep's clothing.

"You must feel terribly betrayed by Mr. Tolley," he said.

"By *Joe?*"

"Yes. To your face, he pretended everything was all right. To us, when you weren't around, he told us how miserable he was in his life. He'd even considered suicide. The thought tormented him."

"That wasn't Joe speaking. That was Frederick Hamilton. Complete fiction!"

Mr. D. gave her a rueful smile. "It wasn't fiction," he said. "They were Joe's true feelings. His checking himself into the hospital as a supposed scheme was actually his cry for help, can you see that?"

"No!" She started to stand, but Mr. D. stopped her with a hand on her shoulder. "Joe loved me," she said. "He loved Janie, our little girl. He wouldn't want to—"

"We have documentation in his record of his deteriorating condition," Dr. P. interrupted her. "I offered to show that material to Cliff, but he said it wasn't necessary."

Sarah could imagine that conversation. *She's in denial, she's crazy, she's angry about being fired.*

"All right," she said, raising her hands in surrender. "I give up. Just tell me where Joe is, and I'll—"

"Cliff agreed with me that, at this point in time, it would be better for you not to see him," Dr. P. said. "You are far too fragile and—"

"God damn it!" She stood up, too quickly for Mr. D. to stop her this time. "I am not *fragile*. I am not crazy."

Mr. D. reached a hand toward her. "Sit down again, Mrs. Tolley." He looked at Dr. Palmiento and received a nod. "We have something very, very important to discuss with you."

The somber tone of his voice quieted her instantly, and she lowered herself back into her chair. The nausea from the day before toyed with her again, and she steeled herself against it. She would not get sick here.

Mr. D. rolled his chair in front of hers until he and Sarah sat face-to-face. "Dr. Palmiento and I have discussed this matter at great length, and we've decided it's necessary to take you into our confidence. We are fully aware that you've been communicating with the board of psychiatry. We knew that even before yesterday."

"How did you—"

"It doesn't matter," he said. "What matters is that you tell no one—*no one*—anything you know about the techniques being used here at Saint Margaret's. It's a matter of national security, Mrs. Tolley."

"I don't understand."

Mr. D. leaned forward in his seat, and she knew the concern in his eyes was genuine. "The Soviets and the Chinese are far ahead of the United States in the development of mind control techniques," he said. "Some disturbing things have happened that you may not know about.

For example, during the war in Korea, over seventy percent of the American prisoners of war being held in China signed petitions calling for an end to the American war effort, and some of them made false confessions. The frightening thing is, they stuck to those confessions even when they were finally safe at home. They were brainwashed, Sarah. Don't you think that's alarming? That other countries, that our *enemies,* can brainwash our men and we don't have a clue how they're doing it? It's up to Dr. Palmiento and a handful of other...*pioneers*...to perfect mind control methods for our use. Our enemies have the upper hand. We have to get it back.''

Sarah was overwhelmed, by both his words and his zeal. ''But...what do you mean by mind control techniques, exactly?'' she asked. ''Psychic driving? The shock treatments? The isolation room?''

''All of that is being researched,'' Mr. D. said. ''Along with the use of certain drugs.''

''LSD.''

''Yes, among others.'' Mr. D. sat back in his chair with a sigh. ''I'm telling you a great deal, Sarah. Perhaps too much for your own good. But Dr. Palmiento and I felt you deserved to know.''

''Who has authorized these...experiments?'' she asked.

''The United States government,'' Mr. D. said. ''As a matter of fact, if you were to go to the FBI or the CIA with what you've witnessed here, you'd only be telling them something they already know—in fact, something they're financing.''

''Financing!''

''Yes, but that fact *must* stay in this room, Sarah,'' Mr. D. said. ''Only Dr. P. and myself, and now you, are aware of the source of our funding.''

"It's unconscionable, though," Sarah said. "You're experimenting on unwitting patients."

"Only those patients who are deemed expendable by virtue of their psychiatric condition are being taken to the highest levels of experimentation," Mr. D. said.

"I still think it's wrong," Sarah said. "I think someone should blow the whistle on what's going on here."

"And harm a carefully engineered program?" Dr. Palmiento finally spoke up. "A program sanctioned by the government and designed to develop methods to counter the Communist threat?"

"Joe was just a casualty in all of this, wasn't he," she asked. "He knew too much. You needed to shut him up."

"Not true at all," Dr. Palmiento said. "Joe was unwell."

She knew she would never get him to admit to anything else, and he was the well-respected, award-winning genius of the psychiatric community. She was the fragile, unstable, deluded wife.

"Here's the main reason we wanted you to know and understand what we're doing here," Mr. D. said. "We need you, Sarah. We want to keep you on as a member of our team. We know you'll need some time to cope with what happened to your husband, but you're a skilled nurse, truly the finest nurse on ward three, and you'd be a valuable asset to us. Surely you can see the importance of the research we're doing."

Sarah stood up. "I don't want anything to do with your so-called research or with either of you or Saint Margaret's," she said. "You've destroyed my husband, you've harmed my patients, and now you want me to join forces with you? Never!"

"You're not thinking clearly," Mr. D. said, with real sympathy in his voice. "That's certainly understandable.

Please consider what we've said. About this being a matter of national—''

"I don't believe you!" she said. "This is a free country. We don't destroy our own people in the name of national security. I don't believe for an instant that the government sanctions what you two are doing. And you can bet that when I leave here, I'm going straight to...to someone in authority with what you've told me." She started toward the door.

"Just one minute, Mrs. Tolley." Dr. Palmiento stopped her with the threat in his voice. He rose slowly to his feet, his eyes pinning her to the wall.

Sarah closed her own eyes to shut out his impaling glare. She'd been right about him in their first meeting. He was crazy as a loon. "What?" she asked.

"You have a young daughter, don't you?" His voice was merely inquisitive, but the menace was clear. "Do you want her to suffer the same fate as your husband? Or worse, perhaps?"

Sarah gasped. "That's an empty threat," she said, but her voice was shaking.

"I don't make empty threats," Palmiento said. "I see a problem and I solve it. Your husband Joseph Tolley was a problem, and I took care of it. Rather quickly, too, wouldn't you say?"

Mr. D. moved to stand between them. "I don't think we need to resort to threats," he said, obviously trying to placate them both, and for the first time Sarah realized that the young psychology student might not be completely supportive of his mentor's methods.

"I think we do," Dr. P. said. "If Mrs. Tolley understood how grave the consequences would be if she revealed anything about our work, that would be fine. We could let her go. But she doesn't seem to comprehend the gravity of the situation. So, I say to you, Mrs. Tolley—keep your mouth shut about what you know and no harm will come to you or your child. Speak up, and there are people far more powerful and zealous about this cause than I am who will be sure you never speak again. Understand?''

Sarah said nothing. Her knees were about to give out.

Dr. Palmiento walked toward her. ''Do you understand?'' He repeated. ''Swear to us that nothing you know about Saint Margaret's will ever leave this room.''

She turned her head from his gaze. ''I swear it,'' she said, backing away from him. Then she fled from the office, fled from Saint Margaret's, hoping she would never have to set foot in that house of horrors again.

31

There was a long message from Becky Reed, the publicist for Ray's book, on Laura's answering machine when she arrived home from Sarah's. Laura leaned against the kitchen counter, listening.

"Sorry to call on the weekend," Becky said on the tape, "but this can't wait. We have tentative dates scheduled for two local talk shows, as well as—hold on to your hat— *Oprah*. That's a major coup, I'm sure you know. That particular show won't air until November, when *For Shame* is released, but it will be taped the end of next month. So we need to know right away if you're willing to do it—and we certainly hope you are." Becky left her home number with a request to call her "right away."

Still preoccupied by what she'd learned from Sarah that afternoon, Laura could barely concentrate on the message. The walls of the kitchen were closing in on her. The last thing she felt like doing was boning up on Ray's work with the homeless.

She called Stuart in Connecticut and told him about the message.

"*Oprah!*" Stuart said. "That's fantastic."

"The taping date is in late September," she said. "It's too soon. I—"

"It's more than a month away." Stuart paused. "How

come you don't sound more excited about this, Laura? This is everything that Ray wanted.''

''I'd rather not do it,'' she said bluntly. ''Maybe you could do it.''

Stuart was quiet. ''It wouldn't have nearly the same impact coming from me as from his wife,'' he said finally. ''And you're already a household name, practically, with your comets and all. What the hell's the problem?'' He didn't usually swear, and she knew he was not pleased with her.

''I don't know, Stu. I'm just wiped out by my life right now.'' She looked out the window toward the lake. Some of the leaves were already beginning to color, and it was only the end of August. ''Emma still won't talk, and she's crawling under furniture again.'' It had only happened that once, and she felt guilty taking advantage of the behavior to support her own need. ''I'm trying to coordinate a relationship between her and her birth father, and—''

''You are?'' Stuart asked. ''So soon?''

''It's been eight months, Stu.'' She explained how Dylan came to be involved in their lives.

''Still seems awfully soon,'' Stuart said. ''Are you sure that's the best thing for Emma?''

No, she wasn't sure, but that was the choice she'd made and she was too tired to defend it. ''He's a nice guy,'' she said, ''and her therapist seems to think it's the right thing to do.''

''You sound really upset, Laurie.''

''I just came from visiting Sarah. You know, the woman my father asked me to look after? And she told me some things that are…disturbing.''

''What sort of things?''

She sighed. ''I really don't want to go into it now.''

''Maybe it would help to talk about them with some—''

"I'm too tired, Stuart."

He was quiet for a moment. "Laurie, why are you doing this to yourself? Why do you still visit her when it upsets you? What's the point? It sounds like it's not doing you any good, and with everything else you have going on—"

"But it does *her* good. At least, I think it does," she said. "She loves to get out for a walk. And besides, I *like* her, Stu. I would miss her if I didn't—"

"You're too wiped out to promote your husband's book, but you have time to—"

"I didn't say I wouldn't do it," she said quickly.

"Don't you at least think you owe him that much?"

Her guilt over Ray's death hit once again with full force.

"All right, I'll do it," she said. "I'm just nervous about it. I'm nervous about knowing what to say. How to explain his death. How to—"

"Look," Stuart said, "how about I come down to Virginia sometime soon? I have a sales trip down that way the second week of September. You and I can sit down and plan what you should say."

"That would help," she said. "Thanks."

She got off the phone feeling weak, badgered and ashamed. What was wrong with her that she had no interest in being her husband's champion?

The following afternoon, Dylan came over to go swimming with her and Emma. Emma had loved swimming the year before, but the one time Laura had taken her to the lakeside beach this summer, she wouldn't even set foot in the water. She would only agree to go now if Cory could come along.

Laura herself had a moment of anxiety that morning as she pulled her two bathing suits from the bottom drawer of her dresser. One was at least ten years old, and the elastic in the legs was nearly nonexistent. The other suit was new—well, three years old at the very most—but it was a one-piece, black, old-lady sort of suit. She wore clothes for service, not for style, but that morning she wished she'd remembered these two flabby old suits and gotten a new one with a little more flair.

She threw the oldest suit in the trash and put on the black suit, studying her reflection in the mirror. She'd lost a lot of weight since Ray's death. Her legs were thin, and her breasts looked as though they'd shrunk. She had a vague tan, but it stopped at the middle of her thighs and a few inches below her shoulders. A year ago she wouldn't have noticed, and it irritated her that now, simply because Dylan would be with them, she felt self-conscious about her looks. She pulled a pair of shorts over the suit for the walk to the beach.

Dylan arrived in baggy trunks, a Hawaiian shirt and his own farmer's tan. He stood in the living room, holding his arm out next to hers. "I can see that both of us need to get to the beach more often," he said.

Emma ran into the room at that moment, stopping short when she saw Dylan, falling once again into shyness.

"Just think, Emma," Dylan said. "Every time you look around this room, you know that you helped make it look so pretty."

Emma looked at the walls.

"She helped me pick out the curtains, too," Laura said.

"A regular Martha Stewart," Dylan said.

Laura laughed. "Go get your flip-flops, honey," she said to Emma.

They stopped by Cory's house on their way to the beach, and the two little girls skipped ahead of her and Dylan along the paved path surrounding the lake. It was a hot day, and Laura was perspiring by the time they'd walked a short distance.

"That water's going to feel good," Dylan said when the beach came into view.

The beach consisted of a small crescent of sandy soil. Only the families living around the lake were permitted to swim there, so the beach was never crowded. A teenage boy sat on the lifeguard stand, his hair nearly white from the sun and his skin the color of caramels. Two teenage couples baked on their blankets. The only people in the water were a young woman and her little boy, standing in the shallow section roped off for children.

Laura and Dylan laid a blanket on the sand while Cory slipped into her green, dragon-shaped tube.

"C'mon, Emma!" Cory said, running toward the water.

Emma didn't budge.

"Do you want your raft?" Laura asked her.

Emma shook her head. Her thumb slipped into her mouth.

"Come *in*, Emma," Cory called. She was already up to her calves in the water, and Laura, the raft in her arms, followed her in to keep an eye on her. Once in the water, she turned to see Dylan crouch down on the beach next to Emma, talking to her. Emma didn't move away from him, but she didn't look at him, either, and Laura wished she could hear what he was saying to her.

"*Push* me, please," Cory begged, and Laura bounced Cory and her tube around in the water.

After a while, Dylan stood up and walked into the lake himself, and Laura saw the look of resignation on his face.

"Thanks for trying," she said when he'd come close to her and Cory.

"Couldn't get her to budge," he said.

The little boy paddling around with his mother called to

Cory to come play with him. "Can I go over there?" Cory asked Laura.

"Yes," Laura said, waving to the boy's mother. "Stay right there, though, so I can see you."

She watched Cory paddle off, then boosted herself onto the raft. Lying on her stomach, she watched Emma, the little blue-and-beige statue whose toes barely touched the water.

"I feel so sorry for her," Dylan said, his hands on his hips as he looked toward the beach. "She wants to come in. You can see it in her face."

"I know."

"And watching Cory play with you and now with this little boy has to make it doubly hard on her." He looked at Laura. "You deal with this day and night," he said. "How do you cope with it? With how terrible this feels?"

"Not too well," she admitted. "I'm a little more hardened to it than you are, though."

Dylan lowered himself into the water, leaning back against the ropes. "So," he said. "How's Laura?"

"Laura's a wimp." She ran her fingers through the water. "I agreed to do the talk shows."

"How'd that happen?"

"Ray's brother pushed my guilt buttons last night."

"You are so *weak,*" he said, with mock disdain.

"I know. But what kind of a wife would I be if I didn't do it?"

Dylan ignored the question. "So, what did that decision do to your stress level?" he asked.

"It's sky-high." She didn't tell him that trying to find a bathing suit to wear in front of him had only added to her anxiety. The water glistened on the dusting of dark hair on his chest. His arms were stretched out along the rope, and he was more muscular than she'd imagined him to be. Probably from working on the balloon. What was he thinking about her body? About her pale legs? The cellulite on the back of her thighs?

"What was this you were telling me on the phone the other night?" he asked. "About Sarah's husband getting lobotomized? That sounded unbelievable."

"You haven't heard the half of it," she said. "After the lobotomy, they took Sarah into their confidence." She described Dr. Palmiento's allusions to government-sanctioned mind control experiments.

"That actually happened," Dylan said. "But not here. At least, I didn't think it was here." He looked up at the sky as if trying to remember. "It was in Canada, I think. In the fifties. The CIA was involved."

"I vaguely remember something about it, too." Laura said. "It sounded familiar when Sarah started talking about it. Did they actually experiment on psychiatric patients?"

"I think so. Along with some other unsuspecting victims."

"I've been wondering if the person who sent me those letters might actually be trying to protect Sarah from her memories."

"Could they be from her daughter?" Dylan suggested. "The elusive Janie?"

Laura pondered the possibility. It would certainly make sense that Sarah's daughter would want to protect her from any distress. "But if Janie cared enough to protect her mother from me, then wouldn't she also be involved in Sarah's care? Wouldn't she at least visit her?"

"Maybe she can't. If she's actually in hiding, for whatever reason, maybe she'd be afraid to see her mother."

Laura watched Cory and the little boy splash each other. "I would really like to find out what happened to Joe," she said. "Sarah never found out where he was institutionalized, or if they killed him, or what actually happened to him. I think it would give her some comfort to know. He might even still be alive.''

''Can people live that long after a lobotomy?'' The sun was beginning to sink in the sky, but it still gave his eyes that translucent look that mesmerized her.

''I don't know,'' she said. ''He was younger than Sarah. Seven years younger, I think, so maybe it's possible, though I'm sure he'd be in horrendous shape. But I'd like to see if I can find him.''

''Is this for Sarah's sake or for yours?'' he asked.

''Not sure anymore.'' She smiled. ''And while I'm at it, I think I'll try to track down Janie, too.''

''Hey, why not?'' he teased. ''You don't have anything else to do.''

She sobered instantly. ''My obsession is showing.''

''No, your *interest* is showing. Your *excitement* is showing. Ray was cruel to try to squelch that in you.''

She started to defend Ray but managed to bite her tongue before the words left her mouth.

Dylan suddenly groaned. ''I can't take this,'' he said, his gaze on the beach. ''I can't take watching Emma stand there like a lost, lonely little waif. Let's go in.''

''All right.'' She slipped off the raft and began walking toward the shore.

The sun had fallen behind the trees when they reached the beach, and Emma and Cory were sitting side by side on the blanket, Cory shivering in her beach towel.

''Would you like to stay for dinner?'' Laura asked Dylan as she dried off.

He shook his head. ''Got a date, but thanks for the invitation.''

''Some other time,'' she said, paying more-than-reasonable attention to the task of drying her shoulders.

Well, at least he hadn't lied to her. She may have been admiring his chest out there in the water, but to him, she was Emma's mother, a woman in an old-lady bathing suit, nothing more. He dated numerous women who were probably glamorous and carefree. *Child*-free. Okay, so that meant that she and Dylan were friends. And if they were friends, she could ask him about his date that night. Who was the woman? Where were they going? How did he feel about her?

But she didn't ask him. She didn't want to know.

32

It was a blind date, one of those exercises in futility to which he hadn't subjected himself in years. But this woman was a friend of a friend of Alex's, and with Bethany on hold, he'd allowed himself to be talked into it. Driving to her house to pick her up, he swore to himself he would not talk—would not even *think*—about Emma and Laura. He still remembered Bethany's tallies of how often he said their names.

He found the Middleburg town house easily. Her front door was marked by a wreath of dried flowers, and he rang the bell.

"Hi, I'm Sherry," she said as she let him in. She was a very attractive woman, with long dark hair and a body that was impossible to ignore. He watched her as she moved around her living room, hunting for her purse, her keys, her glasses for the movie. Then she disappeared into another room, and he heard her speaking to someone. She came out, smiling at him. "Just had to give the sitter her final orders," she said.

A sitter. She had kids. Ordinarily that would have meant nothing to him, but tonight, it elated him. He tried to keep the pleasure from showing in his face.

He was able to refrain from talking about Emma throughout dinner, asking Sherry questions about her work and her hobby of horseback riding, and he tried to listen attentively to her answers, with some success.

The movie was one of those overly long, slow-moving British types, and his mind was back on the beach, wondering if there had been something else he might have said to Emma to encourage her into the water.

On the drive back to Sherry's town house, he finally allowed himself to ask about her children.

"I have three," she said. "All girls. Nine, seven and five. I hope that doesn't blow you away." There was an apology in her voice. Probably the disclosure that she had three kids sent many of her suitors running for cover.

"Not at all," he said. "I've been spending a lot of time with a five-year-old girl myself recently." He felt himself slipping like an alcoholic at a bar, knowing he would not be able to shut up once he started.

"Really?" she asked. "What do you mean?"

He could lie. Say Emma was his niece. But lies did not come easily to him. "She's my daughter," he said, enjoying the unfamiliar sound of the words.

"You have a daughter?" Sherry asked. "I thought you'd never been married."

"That's true," he said. "And I didn't know she existed until a month or so ago."

"Oh," Sherry said, obviously aware there was a long story behind that revelation and wise enough not to push for it.

"Tell me about your five-year-old," he asked. "What is she like? What sorts of things does she like to do? Emma...my daughter is having some problems. I'm not sure what's normal for her age."

"Well, Jenny loves to swim. She's in a tumbling class. And she collects Beanie Babies and Barbie dolls."

"So does Emma," Dylan said. "The Barbie dolls, anyway.'' He told Sherry about the aquarium he'd given Emma and how she turned the bookshelf into an office building for her dolls.

"Yes," Sherry said. "They can be pretty creative."

Was that boredom in her voice? He didn't care. "Emma used to love to swim," he said, "but she's suddenly afraid of the water. Do you have any idea how I can get her excited about it again?"

"No, I don't, really," she said. "All three of mine are regular fish." She tried to steer the conversation back to adult topics. The balloon business. The movie they'd just seen. It bothered him that she had three daughters and didn't seem to want to talk about them.

He pulled into the parking lot and stopped in front of her town house.

"I'd ask you in," she said, lifting her purse from the floor of the van, "but it's late and I have to get the sitter home."

"I'll walk you up," he said, opening his door. She didn't like him. It was obvious. And that was okay. He walked her to her door and left her without a kiss, which he figured was fine with both of them.

Driving home, he realized she had asked him nothing about Laura.

"Tell me," she might have said. "What exactly is your relationship with your daughter's mother?"

"It's, uh, we're friends," he would have stammered.

He glanced out the van window at the diamond-lit sky, remembering the night he and Laura had watched the stars through her telescope. He wished he were doing that right now.

33

Laura sat across the waiting room from Sarah, watching the older woman stare at the nameplate on the receptionist's desk. She was mouthing the name "Mrs. Quinn" to herself, over and over. Finally, she looked at Laura.

"Are we still at Meadow Wood Village?" she asked.

"No," Laura said. "We're at Emma's psychotherapist's office, and you and Emma will spend some time together here in a playroom. Since Emma has spoken to you, when she hasn't spoken to anyone else, her therapist thought it might be helpful to have you here with her."

Sarah looked at Emma, who sat in the corner of the room trying to balance a plastic horse on top of a pile of blocks. "I'll play with Janie?" Sarah asked.

"Yes. But not out here," Laura said. "There's a special room to play in. You'll be helping Janie...I mean, helping Emma, by playing with her. I'll be very grateful."

Sarah nodded, but Laura was still not certain she knew what was being asked of her. Sarah wore that resigned look of confusion that made Laura want to hold her.

Heather came out of her office and introduced herself to Sarah. She ushered Sarah and Emma into the playroom, seating them at a broad table topped with a box of small dolls and a dollhouse, and Laura was relieved to see that Sarah had no problem lowering herself into one of the child-size chairs. Then Heather and Laura walked into the next room, hiding behind the two-way mirror.

Instantly, Emma began to talk. "Pick out the dolls you want," she directed Sarah, holding the box of plastic figures in front of her.

Laura glanced at Heather, who grinned at hearing Emma's voice for the first time.

Sarah reached for one of the male dolls.

"No, not that one!" Emma said. Then more gently, "Can I have that one, please?" She took the male doll from the box without waiting for Sarah's response.

"This one is pretty." Sarah plucked a young girl doll from the box. "Did you want this one, Janie?"

Emma rolled her eyes in exasperation, and the gesture made Laura laugh. "My name is Emma Brandon Darrow," she said sternly. "Now, put that doll in one of the rooms. Please," she added.

"At least she hasn't forgotten her manners," Heather whispered to Laura.

For half an hour, they watched Emma and Sarah play. Emma was bossy, frequently telling Sarah what to do.

"This is too cool," Heather said as she watched them interact. "This is a side to Emma she's never let me see."

"That's the way she used to be," Laura said. "Self-confident and a bit overly assertive." Not the quiet little shadowy figure living at the lake house. Not the child who feared the dark, and wet her bed, and stood alone on the beach while her friend played in the water.

"This is very encouraging," Heather said. "She has so much going for her. I know it's hard to believe right now, Laura, but I think she's going to be fine."

"If she knew I could see her, though, she'd clam up," Laura said. "That hurts."

"For now," Heather said reassuringly. "Can you bring Sarah again? She seems to be enjoying herself."

"Maybe," Laura said as she watched Sarah play with her daughter. Sarah seemed caught between the roles of child and woman, occasionally playing with the dolls as intently as Emma, occasionally guiding Emma in a more parental manner, and always, no matter how vociferously Emma objected, calling her Janie.

When the session was over, Laura buckled both old woman and child into her car for the return trip to the retirement home.

"Did you have a good time?" Laura asked them as she pulled out of the parking lot.

"Where were we?" Sarah asked.

There was silence from the back seat, where Emma sat.

"You were at a therapist's office," Laura said. "Playing with Emma in a playroom."

"Do we go for a walk now?"

"Not today," Laura said. "I'll drop you off at your apartment, and then I have to take Emma home. But I'll come visit you again tomorrow and we can go for a walk then, all right? It's supposed to be a beautiful day."

"I'll put my walking shoes on first thing in the morning," Sarah said.

"That's a great idea." Laura glanced at Sarah and saw that she was smiling broadly at the thought of taking a walk. "And maybe while we're walking," she said, "you can tell me what you did after you left your job at Saint Margaret's."

Sarah, 1959

Sarah was afraid of Dr. Palmiento and Mr. D. She knew the damage they had been able to do within the confines of a legitimate institution. The lengths they might go to outside that institution was a frightening unknown. Obviously, they would protect their so-called research at all costs. Dr. P.'s veiled threats toward Janie still rang in Sarah's ears.

She decided to move to a different town. After selling the home she'd owned with Joe, she moved to an apartment thirty miles away. The move was painful. She felt as if she were wiping Joe and her memories of him from her life. But she still had Janie, the greatest connection she could possibly have with her husband. And every day, she wore the pin he'd given her.

She took a job in a blessedly conventional psychiatric hospital, Emery Springs, near her new home, and was relieved to find that the "progressive" techniques used at Saint Margaret's were not being employed there. In her spare time, she tried to find either a Joseph Tolley or a Frederick Hamilton in the institutions in or near the metropolitan area. Driving from place to place, Janie in tow, she searched for him. None of the institutions had a record of either man ever being there, and she wondered if they might have checked him in under yet another fictitious name. That was, if he'd survived the lobotomy at all.

The only person from Saint Margaret's she dared stay in touch with was Colleen. Colleen had been fired from the hospital immediately after Sarah left, and she'd been given the same threats regarding her own child, Sammy. Colleen was desperately searching for another job. She couldn't afford to move, and Sarah felt guilty for her predicament, knowing it was Joe's foiled scheme that had led to her unemployment.

Despite her relentless sorrow over Joe, Sarah tried to be cheerful and optimistic for Janie's sake. Gradually, she began to relax and feel safe in her new home and job, although in the back of her mind, she was constantly trying to think of a way to tell someone in authority what was going on at Saint Margaret's. She did not believe for an instant that the experimentation was sanctioned by the government. She should call someone at the FBI. If the government *was* behind Dr. Palmiento's work, she wouldn't be telling them anything they didn't already know. If not, she could finally put an end to the suffering the patients were being forced to endure. Still, she was afraid to call, knowing that Dr. P. had managed to learn it was she who originally contacted the board of psychiatry. Yes, she was worried about the patients, but she had to put Janie's safety— and her own—first. She had the FBI's number on the wall next to her kitchen phone, though, in case she one day got the courage.

Early one Saturday morning in November, Sarah was cleaning her apartment when her doorbell rang. She was expecting one of her neighbors to stop by for a cup of coffee, but the woman was a little early.

She leaned the mop against the kitchen wall and walked past Janie, who was contentedly playing by herself in her playpen. Pulling the apartment door open, Sarah gasped and took an involuntary step back into the living room.

Mr. D. smiled from the hallway. "I didn't mean to alarm you," he said.

"Why are you here?" she asked. "How did you find out where I live?" She thought she'd left no trail behind her.

"May I come in for a moment?" Mr. D. asked. "It's important."

Sarah hesitated. "All right." She would leave the door open and scream if anything happened. Her neighbors would hear her.

"This is your little girl," Mr. D. walked over to the

playpen, and Janie reached her arms up toward him. Janie was too hungry for a man's touch these days.

"Sit down on the couch," she commanded Mr. D., stepping between him and the playpen.

He sat down, but she remained standing.

"What do you want?" she asked.

"Just a few things." He seemed unperturbed by her rudeness. "First, I wanted to let you know how much you're missed at the hospital. You really were one of the very best nurses we had. I wanted to make sure you know that you're welcome to return any time. Bygones will be bygones."

"Never in a million years would I go back to that hellhole," she said.

He nodded his understanding. "I know that Dr. Palmiento can be...difficult," he said, "but his work is truly brilliant, and—although I know you are not yet convinced of this—critical to the security of the country."

"Look—" Sarah walked toward the door "—there's no point in talking about this any further. I know you think Dr. P. is God and doing God's work. I don't happen to agree. So let's just—"

"You've been talking to people," he said, not budging from the couch.

"I...what do you mean?"

"Your co-workers at Emery Springs."

"How do you know where I work?" The hair on the back of her neck stood on end.

He chuckled. "You are a very easy target, Sarah. I know a great deal about you. You leave for work at eight each morning. You drop little Jane there off with your neighbor, Mrs. Sucher, on the first floor of this building. You arrive at Emery Springs about 8:30. You come home at five each day, like clockwork. Your closest friends in this building are Paula Rose and Susan Taylor. You visit with them occasionally in the evenings. You shop at the A & P on Terrace Street. You go to bed at ten-thirty each night. You are quite regimented.''

"How do you know all this?" She folded her arms across her chest, suddenly very cold.

"We told you there are people in the government willing to go to any length to protect our research," he said. "But how we get information truly doesn't matter, Sarah. What matters is that you said—you *swore*—you would tell no one about Saint Margaret's, and you haven't kept your word.''

"I haven't told anyone who has the power to do anything about it," she said.

He laughed. "True, because that person doesn't exist." He leaned forward. "Maybe Dr. P. and I should have made it clearer to you. When we told you not to tell anyone, we meant *anyone*.''

"All right. Fine. I understand. Now, please leave."

To her relief, he stood up and moved toward the door. "Listen to me," he said. "I don't mean to be so harsh, but you have to understand how important it is for you to keep all of this to yourself. Peter Palmiento is driven. And he's a genius. And sometimes geniuses border on the maniacal. Do you understand?''

She nodded.

"Good," he said. "And good luck to you, Sarah.''

She closed the door after him and locked it. Trembling, she pulled Janie from the playpen and sat on the couch, holding her little girl in her arms. She'd thought she was safe in sharing some of her experiences at Saint Margaret's with her co-workers. Who had told? She shouldn't have trusted them, nor should she trust her neighbors. She would move again. Change jobs. Should she change her name?

No, she couldn't lose that much of Joe. But she would have to stop searching for him. Maybe her inquiries were being reported. An easy target, Mr. D. had called her. She would have to change that.

This time, she moved across the state line to Virginia, taking a less-satisfying job in a smaller hospital. She hired a woman to sit with Janie in the safety of their own apartment during the day. And she threw away the number she had for the FBI. She didn't dare think about making that call.

Still, her dreams were haunted by images of the patients at Saint Margaret's, those wounded people who put their trust in their caretakers, only to be slowly and methodically destroyed.

34

Laura was reading a book to Emma in the living room when the phone rang.

"I've had a late cancellation for the sunset ride tonight," Dylan said, instead of hello. "Would you and Emma like to go up with me? I'd have to talk to Emma first, to be sure she could handle it. Plus, you'd need to be here in an hour."

"I thought you didn't take up children under eight." Laura distinctly remembered him telling her that on the day of her own flight.

"That's true. That's why I want to talk to her. Do you think she'd be afraid? Can you put her on?"

She looked down at her daughter, sitting next to her on the couch. "It's Dylan, Emma," she said. "He wants to know if we'd like to go up in his balloon tonight."

Emma gasped. She flew off the couch and began jumping up and down with excitement, making Laura laugh in surprise. "No," she said into the phone. "She's not afraid."

"Let me talk to her, then," Dylan said.

"He needs to talk to you." She held the receiver out to her daughter, who simply stared at it. "There are important rules you need to know."

Emma reached for the receiver and held it to her ear.

"She's on, Dylan." Laura spoke loudly.

She heard the hum of Dylan's voice on the other end of

the line, and Emma listened with concentration. Once she actually smiled, and she nodded a few times, as if Dylan could see her. Then she handed the phone back to Laura.

"Hi," Laura said.

"I told her I've never taken a five-year-old up before and that I can only take her if she can act very grown-up and do exactly what I tell her to do," Dylan said.

Laura looked at Emma. "Do you really want to go?" she asked.

Emma nodded.

"And did you understand what Dylan said about doing what he tells you to do?"

Again, the nod.

Laura spoke into the phone again. "We're on our way," she said.

It was the first time Laura had seen the balloon being readied in daylight, and the sight was not quite as dramatic as it had been before dawn, when the flame filled the opening of the balloon and turned the crew into silhouettes. Still, Emma was thrilled, her step bouncy as they walked across the field.

Amazing, Laura thought. Emma was afraid of the water and the dark, but she seemed completely fearless about floating a thousand feet above the ground.

When they reached the balloon, Dylan stopped what he was doing and walked over to them to give them the pre-flight instructions, and Emma solemnly nodded her understanding. She was taking this acting grown-up business very seriously.

Dylan climbed into the basket first. Emma hesitated for just a minute as Laura helped her up the stepladder, probably realizing that she would have to be alone in the basket with Dylan until Laura got in.

"Go ahead, honey," Laura said. "I'm right behind you."

She watched as Dylan helped Emma onto the propane tank and then down to the floor of the basket. Emma's little body went rigid when Dylan touched her, but she was smiling broadly by the time Laura got into the basket herself.

"Okay, Emma," Dylan said. "Once we get going, you can stand on the propane tank and then you'll be able to see." Emma could barely see over the leather rim of the basket. "But for now, I need you to stand right there in that corner and hold on tight to those ropes handles." He glanced at Laura. "You, too, Mom," he said.

Emma and Laura did as they were told, and Alex and Brian untethered the balloon from the truck. Emma jumped when Dylan fed the flame, the pillar of gold stretching high into the balloon, but she didn't budge from her corner. Still holding on to the rope handles, she tried to stand on her tiptoes to see over the side of the basket. She was so precious. Laura's heart ached with love for her.

The balloon rose slowly from the ground until it was above the treetops.

"Okay, Emma," Dylan said. "Careful now. Step on this tank." He helped her, and she didn't balk at his touch. "Still hold tight to the handles. That's it."

Emma's eyes were wide with wonder as the lush sea of green flowed beneath them. When the trees fell away, she let out a gasp and pointed to the ground. Laura looked at the pasture where she was pointing, but saw nothing in particular. Dylan was first to spot what had drawn Emma's attention.

"That's right, Emma!" he said. "It's an Appaloosa. That's a type of horse. And there are more of them. Usually five. Can you find them?"

She found the rest of the horses and a few cows as well.

The sky turned peach and pink and purple, and Dylan told Emma what made those colors appear at sunset. He pointed out shapes in the clouds. He showed her the mountains in the distance, and he and Emma waved to children swimming in a pool far below them. Dylan even spotted what he said was a fox. Laura thought it looked more like a small, mangy dog from that height, but Emma was so enthralled that Laura said nothing to correct him.

She was surprised that, even after an hour, Emma did not seem the slightest bit bored.

"We need to start going down now," Dylan said. "Our landing site is just over those trees."

Emma whimpered, not wanting the ride to end, and Laura saw the smile spread across Dylan's face.

"You can stand up there a bit longer," he said to Emma. "Then you'll have to go back to the corner and hold on for the landing. Okay?"

Emma nodded, not budging from her stance on the propane tank as they skimmed over the treetops.

"Get in the corners, now, both of you," Dylan said after a minute.

Laura held Emma's arm as the little girl stepped off the propane tank and into the corner of the basket. There she stood facing Dylan and holding tight to the rope handles.

Laura tried to catch her eye, wanting to let her daughter know how proud she was of her for doing everything Dylan had told her to do and for being so good and patient during the ride.

But Emma's eyes were on Dylan. On her father. And the expression on her face was something close to adoration.

Dylan left Alex and Brian in charge of dismantling the balloon, then walked over to the fence where Laura and Emma were standing. Emma had amazed him. Hard to believe she was the same child who'd been afraid of the water at the beach.

"The crew will take care of the balloon," he said to Laura. "They brought my van along with the truck, so how about we go back to my place? Brian gave me a couple of lobsters. They're in my bathtub, swimming in blissful ignorance."

"That sounds great," Laura said as they began walking toward his van.

"Have you ever eaten lobster, Emma?" Dylan asked.

Emma took Laura's hand and skipped along next to her without answering.

"I don't think she has," Laura said.

"And she might not want to, once she sees them in my tub," he said under his breath. "I always have peanut butter and jelly."

"We'll see." Laura smiled.

He was afraid that Emma might still equate his house with the gun cabinet incident, but she marched in the front door and over to his aquarium. She was a different child tonight. She'd loved the balloon ride, and he was glad he'd set aside his misgivings about taking up a five-year-old. She'd let him hoist her over the side of the basket to Laura once they'd reached the ground, even raising her arms up to him to let him lift her. He'd reacted as though that gesture was nothing special, but inside, he felt lighter and fuller than he had in years.

Although Emma cried a little when he dropped the live lobsters into the pot of boiling water, she ate all the meat from one of the claws, along with an ear of corn and a few slices of the fresh tomato he'd plucked from his small garden.

He'd bought her the video of *Beauty and the Beast* on the recommendation of the salesclerk in the video store, and he popped it into the VCR to keep her occupied while he and Laura cleaned up.

Laura was standing with her back to him, her hands in dishwater, when he walked into the kitchen.

"There's a new lock on the gun cabinet," he said, in case she was worried.

Laura turned to look at him, and her face was as unworried as he'd ever seen it. Her cheeks were rosy, her smile soft. She looked younger and more relaxed than she had even a few hours earlier, and he felt a quick and confusing flicker of desire.

"You were terrific with her tonight," she said.

He reached for the dish towel, anxious to look away from Laura's face. "I can't believe she let me pick her up," he said.

"Neither could I." Laura handed him a bowl from the rinse water. "But I think something happened up there."

"Like what?"

"I think you sort of became her hero." Laura grinned.

He felt himself blush. "Always wanted to be somebody's hero," he said.

She leaned forward to peer through the window. "When we're done here, can we use your telescope?" she asked.

He glanced through the window himself. A crescent moon hung above the trees. "Let's go now," he said, laying the towel on the countertop. "I can do these later."

They walked through the living room. Emma was curled up on his sofa, eyes glued to the TV, thumb deep in her mouth, and Dylan dared to tousle her hair. "How're Beauty and the Beast doing?" he asked, not expecting an answer and not getting one.

He lifted the embarrassingly amateur telescope from the corner of the living room and carried it onto the deck. "It's all yours, for what it's worth," he said to Laura.

Laura's hair spilled over her shoulders as she focused the telescope on the moon. "There," she said, stepping back. "Take a look."

He looked into the eyepiece. Centered in the circle of stars was the sharp, white crescent moon, but the rest of the orb was clearly visible as well. He could even make out the craters. "Wow," he said.

"That's known as 'the old moon in the new moon's arms,'" Laura said.

He turned his head from the eyepiece to smile at her. "A little bit like Sarah and Laura, huh?" he asked.

Laura's own smile disappeared, and she bit her lip.

"Uh-oh." Dylan stood up straight. "What did I say?"

She leaned against the deck railing. "You know," she said, "I may never figure out how Sarah knew my father, but I hope he was a very good friend to her. I hope he gave her some happiness, even if she can't remember it. 'Cause she sure had more than her share of misery in her life."

He moved next to her, leaning against the railing himself. "Have you seen her since the last time we talked?" he asked.

Laura nodded. "Yesterday, she told me she moved to get away from Saint Margaret's, but they were able to track her down. That weird psychology student, Mr. D.—"

"The psychic driving guy?"

"Right. He showed up at her door, and he knew everything about her. He got the information with help from the government, it sounds like. He even knew what time she went to bed. It was eerie, listening to her talk about it. So, she had to stop trying to find Joe then. She figured they'd tracked her down because she'd contacted various institutions trying to find him. I feel more strongly than ever that I want to find out what happened to him and Janie."

"How, though?" Dylan asked. She *was* obsessive about this, but he didn't blame her.

"I'm not sure. Maybe I can somehow look at old institution records. Or maybe the library has some resources I can use. Next week, I have to go up to Johns Hopkins to fill out some paperwork extending my leave, and I can use the university library up there. I'll have to take Emma with me, though, and keep her occupied somehow while I do the research."

"I have an idea," Dylan said. "I'll go with you, and you can drop Emma and me off at the Baltimore aquarium on your way to Hopkins." He wondered if Emma would go into the aquarium alone with him.

Laura looked dubious. "We can try it," she said. "But if she resists going with you, I don't want to force her."

"No, neither do I. But now that I'm her hero..." He shrugged with false modesty, and Laura laughed. She reached out and rested her hand on his forearm.

"You really are a nice guy, Dylan," she said.

He could see the crescent moon's reflection in her eyes and had a sudden desire to kiss her. But Emma was right inside. Besides, it was a very bad idea.

He moved toward the telescope again. "So," he said, "what day do you want to go to Hopkins?"

In bed that night, he felt annoyed with himself. What was this sudden attraction to Laura all about? Maybe he'd been without a woman for too long.

Or maybe he'd focused his attention on Emma so much that his feelings for her mother had simply crept up on him, unnoticed.

Well, it was good that he liked his daughter's mother. Nothing wrong with that. But when he closed his eyes, he remembered the ride in the balloon, and the way the tinted light from the sunset formed a halo around her hair. He remembered the way she'd touched his arm on the deck and the sliver of moon in her eyes.

It would only confuse things for him to get involved with Laura. If their relationship hit a rocky patch or fell apart, Emma would suffer the fallout. And if he were seeing Laura, he'd feel guilty about dating anyone else. And wouldn't *that* confuse the hell out of Emma. It was a bad idea. Very bad.

He reached for the phone.

Bethany answered almost instantly.

"Want to go out Saturday night?" he asked. "I promise not to say the *E* word or the *L* word. And I'll use lots of *B* words."

Bethany laughed, and he felt momentarily back in control.

"Not this weekend," Bethany said. "I'm going to be out of town."

Alone, he wondered, or with the guy she was sleeping with?

"How about next Saturday?" he asked.

There was a pause. "Are you getting yourself straightened out, Dylan?" she asked.

"Uh-huh." He didn't think he sounded too convincing, but she bought it.

"That's good," she said. "Well, okay then. I'll see you next Saturday."

He got off the phone, worried that he'd lied to her. It was true that, right this minute, he felt straightened out. Five minutes ago, no. And ten minutes from now was anyone's guess.

35

They drove to Baltimore in Laura's car. Dylan listened as Laura described the afternoon's arrangements to Emma: she would drop them off at the aquarium, go to the library for a few hours and come back to pick them up. Emma, as usual, kept her reaction to herself, and Dylan was not certain she understood the plan. He wondered if there would be a scene when they reached the aquarium.

Apparently, Laura was concerned, too. She pulled up to the entrance of the Baltimore Aquarium and stopped the car. "Don't know if this is going to work," she said to Dylan under her breath.

Dylan turned to look at Emma in the back seat. "Okay, Emma," he said. "Mom is going to the library and you and I will stay here and visit the fish. How's that sound?"

Emma looked at Laura, who nodded. "You're gonna love it," Laura said as she stepped out of the car.

Emma unbuckled her seat belt and got out of the car herself. Dylan met Laura's look of surprise.

"How long do you need?" he asked Laura.

"I'll meet you back here at three, if that's all right," she said.

Emma had already started walking toward the entrance to the aquarium.

"Do you think she understands that you're not coming with us?"

"Hey." Laura grinned. "She's mute, not stupid."

"Well, take your time, then," Dylan said, his confidence about this outing growing. "And good luck."

He caught up to Emma, making his hand available to her without demand, but she kept her own hands at her sides. After he paid their admission, they walked inside the beautiful, triangular-shaped building.

"What shall we look at first?" he asked as they stood in front of the map of the aquarium.

She pointed to the picture of a dolphin.

"Okay, but the dolphin show isn't for a half hour," he said. "Want to see a really amazing fish tank while we're waiting?"

She nodded, and they spent the next half hour on the ramp inside the enormous cylindrical aquarium with its abundance of sea creatures.

The afternoon went without a hitch. Emma was crazy about fish, the way her mom was crazy about stars. She might be a mute child, he thought, but he would never describe her as an unhappy child. The dolphin show made her clap her hands. The puffins made her giggle. And at each fish tank they passed, she stopped to press her face against the glass to study the inhabitants more closely.

The only snag in the entire afternoon came halfway through the dolphin show, when Emma began squirming in her seat. It took him a while to realize that she had to go to the bathroom. He had not discussed that potential problem with Laura. He couldn't go into the ladies' room with her, and he didn't want to take her into the men's room. Finally, he collared a woman who was taking her own daughter into the ladies' room and asked if she would keep an eye on Emma while she was there. Emma returned to him unscathed, skipping, heading for the sharks.

They were about to visit the hands-on learning center

when Dylan heard someone call his name. He turned to see a woman sitting on a bench across from the learning center entrance. Her dark hair was very short and she wore oval-shaped glasses. He recognized her as someone he'd dated years ago but could not remember her name.

"Hi," he said. "Are you here with your kids?" He hoped he was right in guessing she had more than one.

"Yes. They're in there." The woman pointed to the learning center. "And who's this?" She smiled at Emma.

"This is my daughter, Emma." He rested his hand lightly on Emma's back, wondering how she felt about being referred to so casually as his daughter. "Emma, this is…"

"Lynn." The woman quickly filled in the blank. "It's definitely been a while," she acknowledged. "I didn't know you had a daughter." She leaned forward. "Hi, there, Emma. You sure do look like your daddy, don't you?"

Emma sidled close to him, the way she would with Laura when she felt insecure, and his heart nearly burst at that simple display of trust. He shifted his hand to her shoulder and gave it a squeeze.

"Have you been in the hands-on center yet?" Lynn tried again. "They have a very cool hermit crab in there."

Emma only stared at her.

"Shy?" Lynn asked him.

He thought of simply nodding, but what good would it do Emma to know he was lying about her? "No, she's not shy at all, actually," he said. "But she's stopped talking for a while. When she's ready, she'll start again."

Lynn looked puzzled. "I see," she said.

"Well." Dylan looked toward the enclosure. "I think we'll see what's inside. Nice seeing you, Lynn."

"You, too, Dylan. Have fun. And," she added, "you have a truly adorable daughter."

* * *

The librarian guided Laura to the microfilm collection and showed her the drawers containing ancient copies of the *Washington Post.*

"Is there an index?" Laura asked, pulling out one of the huge drawers, filled end to end with microfilm reels.

"Not for newspapers before 1972, I'm afraid," the woman said.

"Whew." This would take longer than she'd expected. She pulled out a few reels from the late fifties and sat down in front of one of the large microfilm readers.

During the past few days, Laura had spent her spare time trying to track down Joe and Jane Tolley. She'd called the state libraries in Maryland, Virginia and the District, attempting to learn what long-term care institutions had been in existence at the time of Joe's hospitalization. She got the names of several, but a few more phone calls quickly told her that those old medical records were no longer in existence. She would have to find another avenue for her search.

In the local public library, she found a book describing ways to track down people, which told of a computer database containing death records. She checked the database for both Joseph and Jane Tolley, and found one of each name on the list, but their birth dates were far off the mark. It looked like both Joe and Janie were still alive.

She found a person on the Internet who claimed to be able to locate anyone. He immediately berated her, via E-mail, for not having Joe or Jane's social security numbers, but Laura could think of no way to obtain them. Joe's birthday might be May 3, she said. Around 1930. She remembered Sarah mentioning that Janie had been born in April 1958. The people-finder did not sound hopeful, but he said he would get back to her shortly.

Within a few hours, he contacted her again. Joseph James Tolley had been born May 3, 1930, in Washington, D.C., he told her in his E-mail message. Jane Elizabeth Tolley had been born on April 8, 1958, in Maryland.

Laura was excited at first but quickly sobered. How would that help her find them now?

Did she have any other information on them? the researcher asked. An occupation, perhaps?

That's when Laura remembered that Joe had written for the *Washington Post*. Maybe the *Post* would offer some clues as to what had happened to him. But this search through the old *Post*s, page by tiresome page, was making her eyes glaze over, and her mind drifted back to the aquarium.

How strange it had been, watching Dylan and Emma walk away together. She remembered all the times she'd seen Emma and Ray walking together, Emma holding Ray's hand. She hadn't seemed interested in holding Dylan's, but neither had she looked back at Laura for reassurance as she walked off with him. Dylan had a brisker, lighter step than Ray, and he chatted with Emma as he walked. His mind was on her, instead of on the next chapter of his book.

Maybe Emma had to hold Ray's hand to remind him she was there.

A few days ago, Laura had sat behind the two-way mirror, watching Heather Davison attempt to talk with Emma, who was too absorbed in her drawing to bother with the therapist. She pressed hard with the crayons on a sheet of paper, her tongue held between her lips in total concentration.

"I know you've been talking to Sarah," Heather said.

Emma slipped the crayon she was using into the box and took another one.

"Would you talk to me, too?" Heather asked.

Shaking her head, Emma continued drawing.

"I guess Sarah must be an easy person to talk to," Heather said.

Emma lowered her head very close to the paper, pressing hard with her crayon. Suddenly she sat back in her chair, holding the paper in the air, and Laura smiled when she saw the picture of a hot air balloon. The enchantment of the sunset balloon ride was still lingering in Emma's mind.

Emma jumped from her chair and rooted through the box of dolls in the corner of the room. Pulling one of the male dolls from the box, she held it against the basket of the balloon and pranced around the room, taking both drawing and doll on a graceful, fanciful flight.

Joseph Tolley.

It was a byline, the first of his she'd come across, and she shifted her attention back to the microfilm. She devoured the article, hungry to feel in touch with him, even from this distance of many years. Suddenly, the papers were filled with articles by him, many of them on the editorial pages. One eye on her watch, Laura raced through them. Joe did indeed have a sensitive and creative approach to his subjects. Reading his words, knowing how alive, how bright and sharp-witted he had been when he wrote them, Laura was saddened by the thought of his destruction.

There was one article about Joe himself, written in November 1959. Journalist Suffers Breakdown, the headline read. Laura scanned it quickly.

According to Dr. Peter Palmiento, director of Saint Margaret's Psychiatric Hospital, the article read, *Washington Post* reporter Joseph Tolley was treated at the hospital for severe depression, then transferred to another institution for an indefinite period. Palmiento would not release the name of the institution for the privacy of the patient. Mr. Tolley's wife, Sarah, could not be reached for comment.

Laura made a copy of the article, then turned off the machine. She stared at the blank screen for several minutes, trying to pull herself back to the present. Yet as she left the library for the drive to the aquarium, her thoughts and her sympathy were still with Joe Tolley.

320   Breaking the Silence

36

Although she'd been expecting Stuart, Laura still felt a jolt when she opened the door to find him standing in the front porch light. There was so much of Ray in his face. He even stood with the same slight slouch.

"Hi, Stu," she said as he walked into the living room carrying his overnight bag. She kissed him on the cheek. "Thank you for coming."

Stuart looked at his watch. "Is Emma in bed already? I was hoping I'd get here in time to see her."

"I tucked her in about half an hour ago, and for once she seems to have zonked out immediately," she said. "You can see her tomorrow."

Stuart looked tired from the drive. He was getting too old to traipse all over the East Coast selling textbooks, she thought.

"The guest room's made up for you," she said. "Have you had something to eat? Do you want to go right to bed?" That would disappoint her. He was here to help her think through what she could say on those talk shows, and the sooner she had that under control, the sooner she could relax about it.

"I ate on the road," he said, "and I'm not really tired. Let me just put my bag in the guest room and wash up a bit, and then I'll be ready to go to work. I'll have to leave tomorrow afternoon, so the more we get done tonight, the better.''

She made a pot of decaf and set it and a plate of brownies on the coffee table while Stuart was in the bathroom. He came into the room with a notepad, and she picked up one of her own from the desk in the corner.

''Okay,'' Stuart said as he sat on the sofa. ''Let's talk about Ray.''

They began listing the questions she might be asked, brainstorming ways to address Ray's suicide so that he could not be easily discounted as a mentally ill fanatic. It was great having Stuart there. Although Laura certainly knew about Ray's altruistic pursuits during the past ten years, Stuart knew those dating back to his childhood.

After they'd been talking for nearly an hour, Laura heard the crunch of gravel in the driveway. Peering out the window, she saw Dylan's van. She had not been expecting him, especially not at nine-thirty at night, and his timing was terrible. Yet, her heart made a small leap at the sight of the van.

She excused herself from Stuart and opened the front door.

''Hope you don't mind my stopping by,'' Dylan said as he walked up the porch steps. ''I was in the neighborhood...well, sort of...and—'' He spotted Stuart sitting on the couch. ''Oh, I'm sorry. I'm interrupting.''

''Come in and meet Stuart.'' Laura stepped back to let him in. ''He's Ray's brother. Emma's uncle.''

Stuart stood up, and the two men shook hands.

''Stuart, this is Dylan Geer,'' Laura said. ''Emma's birth father. Remember I told you about him?''

''Ah, yes.'' Stuart smiled.

''Listen,'' Dylan said, holding a thick cardboard folder in front of her. ''I don't want to intrude, but I was visiting a friend a few miles from here, and he gave me this. He works at the D.C. office of the *New York Times* and he owed me a favor. So I asked him to see what he could find out about the mind control experiments, and he copied a bunch of articles from a variety of sources for you. I haven't had a chance to go through them yet. I thought you might like first crack at them.''

"Wow.'' Laura took the heavy folder from him. ''Thanks so much,'' she said. ''And thank your friend.'' Glancing at Stuart, she wondered how to handle the social situation. ''Stuart and I are discussing what I should say on the talk shows, but we can take a break, can't we, Stu? Would you like a cup of coffee and a brownie, Dylan?''

''No, thanks,'' Dylan said. ''It sounds like you guys are into something that shouldn't be interrupted.''

''I think he should stay,'' Stuart said quickly. ''He can be our audience, if he's willing. Maybe he can be more objective than we are. Tell us what to include and what to leave out.''

Laura looked at Dylan. ''It might bore you,'' she said.

''I don't think so,'' Dylan said. ''I'd like to hear about Ray.''

''Have a seat, then. I'll get another cup.''

From the kitchen, she heard Stuart ask, ''So what's this about mind control experiments?''

''Oh,'' Dylan said, ''Laura's been visiting an elderly woman who worked in a psychiatric hospital where they might have been doing research on mind control.''

Laura walked into the room with the third cup.

''You're still seeing that Sarah woman?'' Stuart asked, disapproval evident in his voice.

''I have to, Stuart,'' she said. ''I think she really counts on my visits now.'' She looked at Dylan. ''It upsets Stuart that I'm involved with Sarah because Ray had asked me not to see her. He was afraid it would take my time away from him and Emma."

"Whose wishes do you think a woman should put first, Dylan, her husband's or her dead father's?" Stuart asked.

"Uh…" Dylan laughed uncomfortably. "I think I'd better stay out of this one."

"It wasn't that simple," Laura said to Stuart as she took her seat again. "I wish you understood that."

"I think Ray was right, though," Stuart said. "You have a habit of getting obsessed with your projects, and it looks like you've gotten yourself obsessed with this Sarah woman, just as he'd been afraid you would. That's why he killed himself."

"Oh, Stuart, there were many reasons why he killed himself." She felt torn between anger and guilt.

"You can't deny that your father's request precipitated it," Stuart said.

"I don't know *what* precipitated it."

Dylan leaned forward and rested his hand on her arm, the gesture at once comforting and electrifying. "Don't do that to her," he said to Stuart. "Even if Laura's visit to Sarah was the trigger, Ray's suicide was not her fault. Don't pin that on her."

Tears welled up in Laura's eyes, more at Dylan's defense than Stuart's accusation.

"I don't mean to say it's Laura's fault," Stuart back-pedaled.

"That's what it sounded like," Dylan said.

"Enough, you two." She tried to smile. "It's in the past. And in a few weeks I've got to sit next to Oprah and tell her all about Ray. So can we get back to work, please?"

Dylan let go of her arm and sat back in his chair, un-smiling. He was so damned good-looking, even wearing that sober, ready-to-fight expression on his face. Laura felt sorry for Stuart. He was coming to his brother's home to see his brother's wife and daughter, and here this good-looking and considerably younger interloper was criticizing him. Yet, he'd certainly asked for it.

Stuart pretended to interview her, and although she felt awkward having Dylan present as she sang Ray's praises, she soon found herself caught up in the nobility of her late husband's life and the sadness that his death came too soon, before the publication of the book that had been his passion for so many years. She talked about the employment programs he'd created to find jobs for the homeless, the one-on-one work he'd done with mentally ill street people, teaching them how to get food and groom themselves. She described the food and clothing drives and the training of volunteers to work in the shelters. And she talked about the programs Ray would set up for the homeless each Christmas, leaving out the fact that, two Christmases ago, he'd collected truckloads of gifts for homeless children and forgotten to get a single thing for Emma.

She sank back into her chair when Stuart announced he had no more questions. "You'll knock 'em dead on *Oprah*," he said.

Dylan set his empty coffee cup on the end table. "Sounds like Ray was some kind of guy," he said.

"He was," Laura agreed.

"Are you feeling more confident?" Stuart asked her.

"Definitely." She truly did.

"Well." Dylan stood up. "I need to hit the road."

"Take a brownie for the trip." Laura pointed to the few remaining brownies on the plate, and Dylan picked up one of them and wrapped it in a napkin.

"Nice meeting you, Stuart," he said.

"And you." Stuart got to his feet.

Laura walked Dylan onto the front porch, where he turned to her, the polite facade gone from his features.

"Don't listen to him, okay?" he said. "He obviously worshiped his brother and needs to make some sense of his death. But it doesn't do any good to assign blame."

"Thank you," she said. "I'm glad you were here."

He smiled and ran his hand down her arm. "Why don't you say good-night to ol' Stu there and tuck yourself into bed with that folder of goodies."

"I will. Thanks." She stood on the porch and watched him drive away, and she was still standing there long after the sound of the van was replaced by the buzz of cicadas.

She did as Dylan had suggested and took the folder to bed with her. It was filled with newspaper and magazine articles from the seventies, when the magnitude of the mind control experiments finally came to light. There had been a congressional hearing in 1977 to uncover the depth of the abuses on unwitting subjects. The hearing led to legislation designed to protect patients through drug regulation and the requirement of informed consent.

But back in the fifties, few safeguards had existed. Although mind control research involving psychiatric patients had been illegal in the United States, there had been no such restrictions in Canada, and the United States government had funded research on patients at the Allan Memorial Institute in Montreal. Dr. Peter Palmiento desperately wanted to be involved in this research, but since he practiced in the United States, he could not get official sanction from the government to do so. Nevertheless, some government officials were so obsessed with discovering the secrets of mind control that Palmiento was able to get their covert support for his research. He considered himself a groundbreaking pioneer in the field, but the articles described him as a "rogue physician" who eventually wound up a psychiatric patient himself. That outcome made Laura chuckle. Sarah had diagnosed him correctly in her first meeting with him. Palmiento died in 1968, the articles said. Laura could find no mention of Mr. D.

She was tired by the time she reached the last article in the folder. It had been written in 1977 and appeared in a Lake Tahoe paper, and she read through it, quickly at first, then again, more slowly. The style of writing was strangely familiar. She looked at the byline. John Solomon. Solomon obviously had an ongoing column in the paper, complete with his picture. Laura held the picture closer to her night table light. It couldn't be, she thought. Her mind was playing tricks on her. John Solomon bore a striking resemblance to the man in the framed photograph of Joe Tolley in Sarah's apartment. But that was impossible, and Laura's memory of that photograph was sketchy at best. Also, Solomon's report on the mind control experiments was completely objective, with no indication of any personal involvement.

Still, Laura set the article on her night table, and when she finally fell asleep, the picture of the author haunted her dreams.

37

"You put this girl on the stairs," Emma commanded Sarah, handing her the girl doll. Sarah obeyed, starting to make the small plastic figure walk up the steps inside the dollhouse.

"No, not yet, Sarah!" Emma said quickly. Then a bit more gently, "Not quite yet. I have to get the man doll." Rising to her knees, she reached past the dollhouse for the box of figures.

"She's a pip," Heather whispered to Laura. They were watching from behind the two-way mirror.

"Don't I know it," Laura said. "I don't care what she says. I just love hearing her voice."

It was a little after one o'clock. It had been a long morning. She and Stuart had taken Emma fishing from the pier on the far side of the lake. Emma had been nervous about getting too close to the edge of the pier, but she seemed to enjoy herself despite the fact that none of them caught a fish large enough to keep.

As they were walking back to the house from the pier, with Emma running ahead and out of earshot, Stuart asked Laura if she'd been seeing Dylan before Ray's death.

Laura looked at him in openmouthed shock, her anger quickly rising. "What? What the hell are you implying?"

"Well, it just seems like the two of you are pretty close for having just reconnected a month or so ago."

"You are so out of line, Stuart." Laura's cheeks burned. "I got in touch with him when Emma's therapist suggested it, not before. That was in July. He didn't even know who I was, for heaven's sake."

Stuart kicked a stone off the path. "So he fell in love with you that quickly, huh?"

"Fell in love?" She laughed. "He's Emma's dad, Stu. That's it."

"Maybe. But the way he looked at you and was so quick to defend you against me...I'd say there's something more there."

"If there is, I certainly don't know about it," she said.

Stuart left after lunch, and although he'd been an immense help in planning her presentation for the talk shows, she was happy to see him go. His unfounded accusations and his idolatry of Ray were more than she could take.

She'd changed Emma into clean clothes and then driven with her to Sarah's apartment, where she'd spotted the old photograph of Joe Tolley on the end table.

"Sarah, is there a chance I could borrow this picture?" she asked. "Just overnight?" How could she explain why she wanted it without confusing her or giving her false hope? "I saw a picture in an old newspaper, and I wanted to compare—"

"Of course, dear," Sarah said absently as she walked past her into the kitchenette. She opened the door to her refrigerator and stood in front of it, studying the pitcher of iced tea, the orange on the top shelf. Laura saw a puzzled expression come over her face.

"What am I looking for?" Sarah asked. Shaking her head, she shut the refrigerator door.

Although Laura was not at all certain Sarah had understood her request to borrow Joe's picture, she slipped the framed photograph into her purse. She would compare it to the picture of John Solomon as soon as she got home.

"She's going for the gun again," Heather said, nudging Laura back to the present. "She hasn't done that for a while."

Emma had indeed picked up the child-size silver gun from the box on the other side of the room and returned to her seat at the table. She tried to hand the gun to Sarah.

"Now, you take this gun, Sarah," she said, "and you shoot the man in the head."

The muscles stiffened in Laura's shoulders.

"I don't want that gun." Sarah refused to take it.

"You've *got* to," Emma said.

"No. I don't like guns."

Emma tightened her lips in irritation. "I'll do it then," she said. Lifting the male doll in her left hand, she held the gun against his body. Laura leaned close to the mirror to try to make out what she was doing. Although the gun was nearly as large as the plastic figure, Emma seemed to be pretending the doll was holding it in his hand. She forced the doll's arm to bend at an unnatural angle so that the gun was aimed at his head.

"Bang!" Emma shouted. She threw the doll across the room, then sat still for a moment, staring at it.

"You shot him," Sarah said.

"He shot himself," Emma said in a somber voice. Then she turned to Sarah, speaking almost too quietly for Laura to hear. "If you talk too much, he'll kill himself," she said.

A chill ran up Laura's spine. She turned to Heather. "Does that mean…?" she whispered. "Do you think—"

"Sh." Heather touched Laura's knee. "Let's watch awhile longer."

After a few more minutes of observation, Laura moved into Heather's office, while the therapist settled Sarah and

Emma in the play area of the waiting room under Mrs. Quinn's supervision. Laura couldn't sit still. She paced around the small room, looking at Heather's framed diplomas and certificates without really seeing them. When Heather finally came into the room, Laura nearly pounced on her.

"She was always talking," she said. "And Ray was always asking her to be quiet. He couldn't concentrate with her around, he'd say. She could drive him crazy. He'd *pay* her to be quiet. 'I'll give you a quarter if you can be quiet for an hour.' But he was never mean about it. Emma just thought it was a game."

Heather nodded. "Have a seat, Laura," she said.

Laura forced herself to sit down and drew in a deep breath. She was trembling.

"If you knew that Emma's chattering could get to Ray," Heather said, "you can bet that Emma knew it, too."

"But...what does that have to do with him killing himself?"

"Is it possible that Ray asked Emma to be quiet the day you went to see Sarah? And is it possible that she didn't obey him?"

"Very possible," Laura said. "Very likely. But he wouldn't kill himself over that."

"No, but Emma doesn't know that. All she would know is that she disobeyed him and then he killed himself."

Laura pressed her hand to her mouth. "I never should have left her with him when he was so depressed." How horrible that Emma was carrying that guilt around inside her. Laura knew firsthand how painful those feelings could be.

"You couldn't have known what he was going to do," Heather said.

"No, but still…" Laura's voice trailed off. "So now what do we do?" she asked. "How do we help her?"

"We let her play it out, over and over again if need be. I'll be there with her, to correct her thinking. It will work, Laura."

"Can I just talk to her directly about it?"

"She needs to work this through at her own speed," Heather said. "She'll set the pace for her recovery."

Laura could barely speak on the drive back to Sarah's apartment, so it was very quiet inside the car. She walked Sarah into the retirement home and down the hall to her apartment, promising to take her for a walk the following day. Then she drove home with a child who was afraid to speak, afraid of the power in her words.

She and Emma made dinner together and ate it while watching *Beauty and the Beast,* which had rapidly become Emma's favorite video. But Laura could not concentrate on the story. Her tears were close to the surface. She kept her eyes on her daughter, trying to absorb the enormity of the guilt and shame she'd been suffering all these months.

She managed to help Emma with her bath and put her to bed before finally allowing herself to cry. Only after she had some control over the tears did she call Dylan.

"Something important happened at Emma's therapy session today," she said.

"What's wrong?" Dylan asked. "You sound upset."

She thought her voice had sounded neutral, but he'd picked up the anxiety behind her words. "I'm all right," she said, fresh tears contradicting her words. It took her a minute to find her voice again. "It just shook me up."

"Would you like me to come over?"

Yes. "It's a long way—"

"I'll be there in thirty minutes. Do you need anything? Anything I can pick up for you?"

"No. Just...I'm glad you're coming," she said.

She hung up and waited for him in the darkened living room, relief mingling with her pain. She was not alone in this.

He arrived in less than the promised thirty minutes, and she had the door open for him by the time he was on her front porch.

"What's going on?" he asked as he stepped inside.

"I think we figured out why Emma stopped talking," she said.

"Really? What do you mean?"

She sat down, and he joined her on the sofa, where she explained about Emma's session with Sarah and how she'd made the doll shoot himself. "She said, 'If you talk too much, he'll kill himself.'"

Dylan flinched as if he himself had been shot. "Is that why she thinks Ray killed himself?" he asked. "Because she talked too much?"

Laura nodded. "I think so. He was always telling her to be quiet. He probably told her to be quiet that day, and she is, or at least she used to be, incapable of being quiet for more than a minute or two. He probably got frustrated with her and let her know it, and then, the next thing she knew, he'd shot himself."

"Did you explain to her that her talking had nothing to do with it?" he asked.

"Heather thinks it's better to let her act it out in play again, while she's there to steer Emma straight in her thinking. She says we need to let her go through this at her own pace." She began to cry again. "Can you imagine what this has been like for her? How afraid she must be that if she talks she might cause someone to die?"

Dylan moved closer to her on the sofa, putting his arms around her, and she let herself sink into his embrace. "I know," he said, his breath warm on her neck. "But she's strong, Laura. She's tough. She's got your intelligence and my orneriness." He was rubbing her back, and Laura did not want to let go of him.

"I know she's strong," she said. "I'm just sad that she ever had to go through this. That I didn't protect her somehow."

"Sh, that's hogwash," he said. He continued to hold her although her tears had stopped. She was the one to finally pull away.

"It helps having you care about her," she said. "I'd feel so alone otherwise."

"I care about *both* of you, Laura," he said. Abruptly, he moved to the end of the sofa, as though he'd stung himself with those words. "So," he said, in an awkward change of topic, "did you get a chance to look through that folder of articles?"

She struggled to shift gears. "Yes," she said. "Oh! I nearly forgot. Stay right here."

She went upstairs to her bedroom to get the article written by John Solomon, but her mind remained back on the sofa with Dylan. He had not meant to say he cared about her. Was that because it was a lie, or because he didn't want to share those feelings with her? She remembered Stuart's assertion that Dylan was in love with her. A big leap, she chastised herself, from caring to loving.

Downstairs, she handed the article to Dylan, then pulled the framed photograph of Joe Tolley from her purse.

"When I saw this article last night, I thought this guy resembled the picture of Joe Tolley I'd seen in Sarah's apartment. Even before I saw the picture, though, I thought I recognized the writing style. I'd read about twenty of his—Tolley's—articles in the library the other day. So, today I borrowed the picture from Sarah to compare them. I want to see how they look side by side.'' She switched on the light and sat next to Dylan, holding the framed picture close to the article.

''That's the same guy,'' Dylan said.

''Do you think so?''

''Definitely. Look at the eyebrows. And the way his mouth slants to one side.''

He was right. Although John Solomon had less hair, much of it gray, his eyebrows were identical to Joe Tolley's.

''He has the same earlobes,'' she said.

''Uh-huh.''

''But how can they possibly be the same man?''

''Well, it looks to me like Joe, here, never did get himself lobotomized. Or else it was a pretty poor job.''

''But why would he have changed his name? And why wouldn't he have contacted Sarah? That makes no sense.''

''Got me,'' Dylan said with a shrug.

''I wonder if this John Solomon is still alive,'' she said, studying the newspaper clipping.

''You said Sarah's husband would only be in his sixties, so if that's who he is, I'd say there's a decent chance of it.''

''Let's see what we can find on the Internet,'' Laura said, getting to her feet.

They spent the next half hour on her computer in the skylight room, using the Internet to search for John Solomon's address. They found only two men by that name in Nevada—one in Reno, the other in Serene Lake.

''Okay,'' Laura said, jotting down the addresses and phone numbers. ''I'll write these guys a letter. Want to help me compose it?''

''Why write?'' Dylan moved from his seat by the computer to the pillowed floor. He stretched out on his back, arms beneath his head. "Let's call them," he said. "It's ten here, so it's only eight there."

She looked at her watch. In a few minutes' time, she could be speaking to Sarah's long-lost husband—who probably did not want to be found. "It seems so...forward," she said.

"What do you have to lose?" he asked. "Want me to do it?"

She shook her head. "All right." She studied the addresses. "Reno or Serene Lake?"

"Serene Lake," Dylan said. "Sounds more interesting."

Logging off the computer, Laura picked up the phone and dialed. A man answered almost instantly.

"Is this John Solomon?" she asked.

"Yes." He had a deep, friendly voice. "Who's calling?"

"You don't know me, Mr. Solomon. My name is Laura Brandon, and I—"

"*The* Laura Brandon?"

It took her a minute to understand. "Oh," she said, smiling. "Actually, yes. That's me."

"Well, why is a famous astronomer giving me a call?" He sounded nice. Really nice.

"It's hard to explain, Mr. Solomon, and I'm not even certain I have the right person. Are you a journalist?" she asked. "Can you tell me if you ever worked for the *Washington Post?*"

He was quiet a long time, and Laura felt Dylan's eyes on her.

"I have a feeling this is not something we should discuss over the phone," John Solomon said.

Laura let out her breath. *It's him.* She mouthed the words to Dylan. "I live on the other side of the country, Mr. Solomon, and so I don't know how we can... Could I just ask you a few questions?"

"No," he said firmly. "I'd certainly like to hear what you have to say, but there's no way we can discuss this by phone."

"May I write to you, then?" Laura asked.

"It'd be worse in a letter."

"Maybe I could come out there," she said, feeling impulsive. "I...let me think about it and get back to you. Would that be all right?" She saw Dylan raise himself up on one elbow to get a better look at her. He must have thought she'd gone mad.

"Uh...you really have me mystified," Solomon said. "What would an astronomer care about my work at the *Post?* Are you really Laura Brandon? Tell me something only Laura Brandon would know."

"I wear a size seven-and-a-half shoe," she said, grinning. She liked this guy, whoever he was.

Solomon laughed. "Who manufactured the telescope you used to find your first comet?" he asked.

"I did," she said. "I built it myself. And I used it to find the first three, actually."

"All right, then," he said. "You're legit. Can you tell me what... No, never mind. Not on the phone." He sighed. "I hope you do decide to come out here," he said. "Give me a call when you know your plans."

She told him she would, then hung up and looked at Dylan. "I want to go," she said. Resting her head on the back of her chair, she looked at the dark sky through the Plexiglas ceiling and thought through the ramifications of making such a trip. "I'd have to take Emma with me."

"And me, too." Dylan lay back on the pillows.

"What? You have a balloon business to run."

"I know someone who can cover for me for a few days," he said. "You'll need me. I could watch Emma while you talk with John Solomon."

If she went, she wanted him to come with her, and not only because she could use a baby-sitter.

"I'd want to go very soon," she said. "And it would be hugely expensive to get tickets so close to the flight."

"Just one more reason why you need me," Dylan said. "I'm an old airline pilot, remember? I can pull strings. When would you like to go?"

"Yesterday."

He sat up from the pillows. "Let's call the airlines now," he said.

"No," she said. "This is insane. And what kind of friend are you, trying to talk me into this wild-goose chase?"

"A friend who wants to know if this guy's Joe Tolley just as much as you do," he said.

Dylan opened his windows on the drive home to let the cool September night air fill his car.

He had not had this feeling since before Katy died. This exhilaration. This odd mix of satisfaction and longing. But with Katy, he'd been sure of himself and his feelings for her. His affection for Laura was not that cut-and-dried, and it was colored by the love he felt for Emma.

He'd meant it when he said he cared about her, but he hadn't expected those words to slip out of his mouth just when they did. Had they surprised her as much as they had him?

If Laura were willing, maybe they could chance having something more than friendship. He wanted to give it a try, although it would mean losing his freedom to date anyone he wanted, whenever he wanted. He remembered Laura's disbelief that he could find women willing to put up with that arrangement and knew she would never tolerate it herself. Right now, though, the thought of seeing anyone else was unappealing. No one but Laura would ever feel the way he did about Emma.

What if it didn't work out between them, though? What if she wanted more than he was willing to give? They would have to go into this with their eyes open, putting Emma's needs first. If he and Laura screwed up their relationship, he didn't want Emma to get screwed up along with it.

Maybe Laura wasn't even interested. Always a possibility. Whether she was or not, though, didn't matter right now. He still had a phone call to make once he got home.

It was after eleven when he reached his house, but Bethany was a night person. Sure enough, she sounded wide-awake when she answered the phone.

"Hi, Beth," he said.

"Hey, Dylan. Are you calling to firm up plans for tomorrow night?" she asked.

"Actually…I have to cancel." He was sitting on his bed, gazing at the aquarium. "I'm sorry."

"Is everything okay?"

"Yeah, everything's fine," he said, "but I wanted to let you know that you were right. I was more hung up on Emma and Laura than I knew. It took me a while to admit it to myself, I guess."

"Laura, too?" she asked.

"Yes. I don't know if she and I will actually…get together, but my mind is on her. I'm not fit company for anyone else right now, as you've noticed."

Bethany let out a long sigh. "Well, shit," she said.

"I'm sorry if I misled you."

"Oh, you never misled me, Dylan," she said. "I knew you didn't know what you were doing and what you were feeling. Even though you were clueless. It was pretty obvious."

"I'm not going to be seeing anyone else for a while," he said.

"You mean, like me."

"Like anyone."

"For a while?"

"Well, at least."

That sigh again. "Can't say I didn't see this coming."

"Thanks for being so understanding."

She laughed. "I only wish you'd been a lying, cheating bastard," she said. "It would have been so much easier to write you off."

He hung up the phone, lay back on his bed and forgot about Bethany more quickly than was charitable. His mind was already on the possibility of a trip to Nevada, traveling with his two favorite women.

38

There would be no walk today. The rain sheeted over Laura's windshield as she drove to the video store, and for the first time since spring, she turned on the car's heater.

By the time she'd run from her car into the store, she was soaked. Shivering, she picked out an old movie she hoped Sarah would enjoy and ran back to the car, where she sat and stared at the jewelry shop next to the video store. The jeweler had been leaving messages for her for months, asking when she was coming in to pick up her repaired necklace. She'd put it off. Her beloved old pendant had become linked to unpleasant memories: her father's final moments, when he'd accidentally torn it from her throat, and the day of Ray's suicide, the day she'd taken the necklace in to be repaired.

Grow up.

She got out of the car again and went into the jewelry store.

There was no answer when she knocked on Sarah's apartment door. Possibly she was in the lounge or one of the activity rooms. Laura knocked again, and was about to try to find Carolyn, the attendant, when Sarah slowly drew the door open. She was smoothing her half-buttoned blouse with her hand, looking as if she'd dressed in a hurry. Her eyes were rimmed with red, her gray hair tousled. Laura was alarmed by the sight of her.

"Sarah," she said, pushing past her into the living room, "what's wrong?"

Sarah fumbled in the pocket of her skirt for a tissue and wiped her eyes. She seemed too distraught to speak.

"Is it the rain?" Laura asked, although surely this was an extreme reaction to not being able to take a walk. "I brought a movie we can watch instead."

"It's Joe," Sarah managed to say.

"Joe?"

"I can't find him!" A look of despair came into her face.

"Oh, Sarah, I know, dear." Laura slipped her arm around the older woman's shoulders. "I know you looked everywhere for him and couldn't find him. That must have been terrible."

"No, no!" Sarah protested. "I can't *find* him." She pointed to the end table, and Laura suddenly understood. Joe's picture. That's what Sarah was talking about. The framed picture that was in Laura's purse.

"You mean Joe's picture?" she asked. "It's right here. Remember, I borrowed it yesterday? You don't need to be upset." She reached into her purse and withdrew the photograph, hoping Sarah didn't ask her why she'd wanted it. She would not tell her about John Solomon until she had all the facts.

"Oh!" A smile spread across Sarah's face. She took the picture from Laura and held it to her chest.

Laura waited for her to ask her why she had it, but Sarah did not seem at all interested. All she cared about was that she had Joe back.

She settled Sarah into her favorite chair, then inserted the video into the VCR. Sarah watched the movie halfheartedly, still sniffling, and occasionally running her fingers over the picture in her lap.

And Laura knew for sure that she would make the trip to Nevada.

39

Laura leaned over to check Emma's seat belt. Emma was a seasoned traveler, and as had been her habit since she was a baby, she'd fallen asleep as soon as the jet was in the air. Dylan, though, was another matter. At first Laura thought she was imagining his anxiety. His hand had a small but noticeable tremor when he handed his boarding pass to the attendant, and his face had been ashen as they looked for their seats. Laura had said nothing. It had to be her imagination. He'd been a pilot for many years. Maybe it was making this trip with her and Emma that had him uptight.

Now that he'd ordered his second drink, though, she had to know what was bothering him.

"Are you all right?" she asked.

He offered her a weak smile. "I will be, as soon as we land in Reno."

"You're...afraid of flying?"

"I don't like the word *afraid*," he said. "Makes me sound like a wimp."

"What word would you prefer?"

"I...simply don't care for it," he said.

"Oh. Well. Is that why you quit the airlines?"

The flight attendant delivered his drink, and he took a swallow, staring at the seat in front of him. "Six years ago," he said, "I was scheduled to fly a 747 from New

York to San Francisco, but I had an ear infection and decided not to fly. Usually the doctor grounds you with that sort of infection, but the company doc said it was my choice. Well, I didn't see the point in risking my eardrum, so I canceled." He took another sip of his drink. "That plane crashed," he said.

"Oh, my God."

"Everyone on board was killed. The investigation was short and swift. It was pilot error. He'd been up late the night before, had some drugs and too much to drink." He looked at her squarely. "If I'd been flying that plane, it wouldn't have gone down."

"But you were sick."

"True. But I could have flown. It was my call."

"It was the pilot's fault," she said, "not yours."

"I know that, in my rational moments, at least." He set his drink on his tray table and rubbed his palms together, slowly. "Some of the crew on that plane were my friends," he said. "Including one of the flight attendants. Her name was Katy. We'd lived together for years. We'd finally decided to get married. The wedding had been planned for a few months after the crash."

The enormity of what he was saying took a minute to sink in. Laura wrapped her hand around his arm. "I'm so sorry," she said. No wonder he was the way he was. No wonder he dated women helter-skelter, committed to his life of no commitment.

"The crash changed everything," he said. "I quit the airlines. I started drinking. That's when I met you. Or at least, so you say. I still don't remember it."

"That's okay." She squeezed his arm.

"I sort of…lost my direction," he said. "The accident made me realize that my life—that *anyone's* life—is nothing more than a fleeting blip on the screen of eternity."

She nodded. "You can't be an astronomer and not be aware of that fact," she said. "Studying the stars makes you come to grips with your insignificance pretty quickly."

Dylan eyed his drink but didn't touch the glass. "Well," he said, "when I figured that out, I decided I would live for the day. I wouldn't think about the future. There was no assurance I'd have one, so what was the point? And that's how I've been existing ever since. It's actually not a bad way to live, one day at a time. But then I met Emma." He wrinkled his nose. "Hard to have a child and not think about the future," he said.

"I know," she agreed.

He handed his unfinished drink to the attendant as she passed by his seat. "I really don't want to get drunk," he said, leaning his head against his seat. He looked at her. "Although once when I got drunk, a wonderful thing happened."

"It did?"

He nodded toward Emma, and she understood.

"We are a guilty little threesome," she said. "You for the crash, Emma and me for Ray's death."

"Not doing us a hell of a lot of good, is it?" He closed his eyes, a small smile on his lips. "Wake me when we get to Reno."

Truckee was a quaint little town just across the border in California, not far from Serene Lake. The woman at the car rental company had suggested they stay there, and they were able to find adjoining rooms in a small hotel near the main street.

With a few hours to kill before going to John Solomon's house, they drove to Lake Tahoe and rented a sea kayak. It took them a while to persuade Emma to get into the boat. The young man in the rental booth told her that the kayak could not possibly tip over, and although Laura thought he was twisting the truth a bit, she didn't mind. He also fitted Emma with their "very best, highest quality" life jacket. Still, Laura was surprised when Emma actually agreed to climb into the boat. She sat in the center, while Dylan took the stern and Laura, the bow.

The air was chilly but not uncomfortable, and the lake was beautiful, surrounded by mountains and filled with deep green, translucent water. Although Laura was anxious to meet John Solomon, this time with Dylan and Emma felt precious to her. There was a lightness inside her she had not experienced in a very long time.

The drive to Serene Lake took about forty-five minutes. From the road, the lake looked small and calm, the water a luminous blue. The houses circling it were of the mountain chalet variety, and each of them had a long covered walkway extending from the front door to the street, to cut down on snow shoveling, Laura supposed. There were already a few inches of snow on the ground, but the roads were clear.

They found John Solomon's address. He lived in an A-frame cabin close to the lake's edge. In the side yard, Laura spotted a huge woodpile and an ax jutting from a tree stump. In the backyard, a red canoe rested upside down on a couple of sawhorses. It suddenly seemed doubtful that they had the right man. This was the house and the life-style of someone young and active.

She didn't voice her concern to Dylan as they walked up the covered path to the front door. Emma clung to her hand, as if uncertain about this new situation, but she laughed when Laura pulled the leather strap hanging from a bell on the door, producing a resonant *clang*.

In a moment, a man stood in the doorway, and Laura couldn't help but smile. She *did* have the right man. She remembered Sarah's description of Joe Tolley when she'd first spotted him on the train so long ago. He'd looked like Jimmy Stewart, she'd said. And he still did.

"Mr. Solomon?" She held out her hand. "I'm Laura Brandon."

"Come in, Laura," he said.

They stepped into a slate-floored foyer. The living room was directly beyond the foyer, and the triangular glass wall gave them a magnificent view of the lake.

"This is my friend, Dylan Geer," Laura said. "And my daughter, Emma." Emma leaned against her leg.

A female voice came from behind them. "Let me take your coats."

Laura turned to see a woman walking toward them. She was no older than sixty, with short salt-and-pepper hair, a warm smile and a vibrancy that radiated from her. A woman hard to dislike, Laura thought, and yet she instantly wished her gone from this scene. She had not pictured another woman in John Solomon's life.

"This is my wife, Elaine," John said.

They walked into the living room, and Laura felt Dylan's hand squeeze the back of her neck in a gesture of comfort.

"What a beautiful setting you have," Laura said as she sat down on the long, contemporary sofa. All the furniture had straight, trim lines. The flow of the room was open and clean, spilling out into the treed yard and the lake, and she found herself blinking back tears at the comparison between this life, this space, and Sarah's tiny apartment and fading mind.

The conversation was at first superficial. They talked about the weather and the Lake Tahoe area.

"How much snow do you get?" Dylan asked. He was leaning forward, elbows on his knees, looking as though the answer to that question truly mattered to him.

"About seven hundred inches a year," John said, some pride in his voice. "And would you believe our son and daughter both moved to Alaska in the last few years? Seven hundred inches wasn't enough for them, I guess."

"You have children?" Laura could not keep the surprise from her voice. Could that daughter be Janie, perhaps?

"Uh-huh," Elaine said. "Just the two. And a grandson about Emma's age. As a matter of fact, Emma, I have one of those neat coloring books from the last time he was here. You know, the kind where you paint water on the pages and the colors appear?"

Emma nodded, suddenly interested.

"Would you like to color in it?" Elaine waited for an answer.

"She's not talking too much these days," Laura said. "But I think she'd love it."

Elaine walked into another part of the house, returning a moment later with a glass of water, a paintbrush and the coloring book. She settled Emma at the coffee table, then took a seat on the arm of John's chair.

"So," John said to Laura. "How did you know I used to work for the *Post?*"

Laura took in a deep breath. "This feels very awkward now that I'm here." She smiled an apology at her hosts. "Do you know Sarah Tolley?" she asked.

The hearty color drained from John Solomon's face, and from his wife's, as well. Elaine put her hand on her husband's shoulder.

"Go on," John said to Laura.

"It's a bit complicated," she said. "For some reason I still haven't figured out, my father, just before his death, asked me to check up on Sarah. I'd never heard him mention her before. I had no idea who she was."

"What was your father's name?" John asked.

"Carl Brandon." She looked at him with hope. "Does that mean anything to you?"

He shook his head.

"So, I went to see Sarah. She lives in a retirement home, where she has her own little apartment. She's in the early stages of Alzheimer's, so she can't—"

"Alzheimer's," John said.

"Yes. And she isn't allowed out on her own. She doesn't have any family, at least none that they know of. She's told me a lot, though. We go for walks. She loves to get out. Her memory of the past is very, very clear. She told me about Joe Tolley."

She looked at John's face. There were tears in his eyes, or perhaps it was only the blur of her own tears that made her think so. John nodded for her to go on.

"She told me about meeting Joe on a train. Falling in love with him and marrying him. She told me about her work at a psychiatric hospital—"

"Saint Margaret's," John interrupted her.

"Right. Where they were doing mind control experiments. And Joe—*you*—"

John nodded.

"Checked yourself in to do some investigative reporting, but you disappeared and they told her they lobotomized you and—"

"That's what they told her?" He leaned forward in his chair, and Laura could see that there were indeed tears in his eyes.

"Yes. And they wouldn't tell her where they'd taken you. She tried to find you in the institutions around there, but she couldn't. They threatened her. And they threatened your daughter."

"Janie." He was leaning forward so far, he was almost

out of his seat. "You said Sarah has no family. Where is Janie?"

Obviously Janie was not the daughter he'd mentioned. "I don't know," she said. "Sarah once told me that Janie was hiding. But Sarah doesn't think clearly. I know that the doctors at Saint Margaret's made some veiled threats about harming her. Harming Janie."

John's nostrils flared. "Those doctors were capable of anything," he said. He looked up at his wife and took her hand, then leaned back in his seat again, eyes on Laura. "This is very hard for me to hear," he said slowly, then hastened to add, "but I'm glad you've come. Very glad. I've needed answers. And you need them, too, don't you?"

"Please," Laura said.

"First let me assure you that Elaine knows everything about Sarah and the past," John said. "You don't need to mince words with her."

Laura nodded.

John continued. "Obviously, or at least I hope it seems obvious to you, I've never been lobotomized. And I had not known that Sarah was told that lie. I figured they told her I was dead."

"What did they do with you, then?"

"Well, my memory is sketchy on this. I was pretty thoroughly drugged. I'd had shock treatment. I was physically very weak. But I am assuming, piecing things together, that someone—or several someones—from the government whisked me away from Saint Margaret's. At least they told me they were from the government. I've never known for sure. They flew me here, to Nevada. To Reno. They gave me a complete new identity. New social security number, Nevada driver's license, everything in my new name, John Solomon. They told me never to try to contact Sarah or Janie, or their lives would be in jeopardy. Frankly, I was so out of it, I wasn't sure who Sarah and Janie were. I wasn't sure some days if I was really Joe Tolley or John Solomon. They set me up in some ratty hotel in Reno, and I stayed there for over two years, just trying to survive. The drugs they gave me had a lasting effect. To be honest, I don't remember much about those years even now. But very slowly...*very* slowly...the fog began to lift. I remembered my life back in Maryland. I remembered the threats made against Sarah and Janie if I tried to find them, but I tried, anyway. They were my family. All I had.'' John shut his eyes momentarily, and his Adam's apple bobbed in his throat. Elaine rubbed his shoulder as he continued. ''I even hired a private investigator,'' he said, ''but I couldn't find them. Sarah seemed to have disappeared. Old neighbors wouldn't talk to the P.I., and I think, in retrospect, that they—Palmiento and his government gang—got to them. Threats were cheap in those days, and soon, even the P.I. wouldn't return my calls.''

''You think they'd threatened him, too?'' Dylan asked.

John shrugged. ''Anything was possible. I thought maybe the people who'd gotten rid of me had gotten rid of Sarah the same way. Spirited her away and given her a new identity. I've always hoped she was able to make a new life for herself and Janie. That was the only thing that got me through that time. Now I realize she was trying to avoid being found, not by me but by the good doctors of Saint Margaret's.''

''That's right,'' Laura said. ''They were able to track her down very easily, so she moved several times, always trying to cover her tracks.''

''I met Elaine in 1969,'' John said. ''Ten years after I'd become John Solomon. We moved in together in 1970. We're not legally married, although we've always referred to each other as husband and wife to make it easier for the kids. I didn't know if Sarah was dead or alive, and as long as there was that uncertainty, I didn't feel it was right to remarry, no matter what my identity.''

Relieved by his integrity, Laura nodded.

''We've had a good quasi-marriage,'' Elaine said with a smile as she rubbed her husband's shoulder again. ''It's been truly wonderful. But I know that John has never forgotten Sarah and his daughter.''

''I told my son and daughter just last year what happened to me,'' John said. ''I also told them they have a half sister somewhere. My son tried to find Janie, without any luck. I figured that they'd changed her name, too, and she'd be impossible to find. But now that you tell me that they never did change Sarah's identity, I don't know what to think.''

''I received a couple of unsigned letters warning me to leave Sarah alone,'' Laura said. ''Dylan and I wondered if they could possibly be from Janie. I don't understand what her motive would be, but she's our best guess.''

''Maybe they are.'' John looked excited. ''Where were they sent from?''

''One was from Philadelphia and the other from Trenton. Of course, there were no return addresses on them. And they were typed.''

''Not much help, huh?'' John said, sinking back in his chair. He suddenly looked exhausted, and Laura wondered if she was wearing out her welcome.

''Well, I think I've dumped enough on you two for one day,'' she said, standing up. She leaned over the coffee table. ''You need to finish up, honey. We're going back to the hotel now.''

John looked at Elaine, communicating something with a glance. Then he turned to Laura again. ''Can you to come back tomorrow?'' he asked. ''Elaine and I could use some time to talk, but I want to speak with you further about this. Will you still be in town tomorrow?''

''Yes,'' Laura said. ''We'll see you then.''

40

"This has been one of the longest days of my life."
Laura dropped into the love seat in Dylan's hotel room.
The room was cozy, decorated in a Western motif that included a lampshade made out of a cowboy hat and a branding iron hanging on the wall. The coffee table, covered with empty cardboard boxes and paper plates from their dinner, was nothing more than a plank of wood set on top of two small wagon wheels.

They'd come back to the hotel in Truckee after leaving Serene Lake, and while Laura gave her exhausted daughter a bath, Dylan went out in search of dinner. He returned with a huge grocery bag filled with Mexican food. Emma only managed to eat a bit of a taco before her eyes closed, and Laura steered her into the room they were sharing and tucked her into one of the double beds. Then she'd returned to Dylan's room to finish eating and perform a postmortem on the day.

"So, I found Joe Tolley," she said. "But what's the point? He's essentially married to someone else."

Dylan stood next to the window. He took a final swig of his soda and tossed the empty cup on the pile of litter on the table. "At least you solved a long-standing mystery for him," he said. "And a short-standing one for yourself."

"I *am* obsessive, you know that?" Laura said. "I ge

caught up in something and I can't quit it until I've examined every angle.''

"I think that's an admirable quality, actually." Dylan walked over to the wall switch. He surprised her by flicking off the overhead light and coming to sit next to her.

"There's something I want to tell you," he said.

The room was dimly lit from the lights outside, but she could still see the blue of his eyes.

"What's that?" she asked.

"I've decided I want to give up my 'living day to day' existence," Dylan said. "I'd rather focus my time and energy on you and Emma. If that's all right with you, of course."

She was not certain what he was telling her. "Are you saying—''

"I'm saying I'd like to quit being a multiple dater and be a one woman man, instead."

"One woman?"

"One woman. Yes. You. If you're interested, that is."

She couldn't stop her smile. "You think you can survive without all your girlfriends?" she teased.

"I'm sure of it. Except…" He took her hand in his. "I have to be honest. I'm worried about this. If we go into this, we have to be very…*adult* in the way we handle it. If it turns out we've made a mistake getting together, I don't want Emma to be hurt when we split up. Though, of course, you still haven't told me if you're interested."

"Oh, Dylan, of *course* I'm interested, but I don't know if it's a good idea, either," she said, although she desperately wanted it to be. "I've never been very good relationship material," she admitted. "You've only known me during a break in my career. You don't know how dedicated I can be to my work. When I start working again, you'll see a different side of me. It hurt Ray terribly. It hurt

Emma. I plan to never be that selfishly driven again, but you have to know, that's my nature.''

"I'm aware of that," Dylan said. "You were just saying how obsessed you got with Sarah. I've witnessed that, remember? And I imagine you have that same sort of fixation when you're working. I can handle that, Laura." He looked out the window at the scattered lights of Truckee. "What I'm *not* sure I can handle are comparisons to Ray," he said.

"Comparisons to Ray? What on earth do you mean?"

"Ray sounds like a real mixed bag to me. A great and altruistic man on the one hand, and a lousy husband and father on the other, and—"

"He wasn't a lou—"

"That's what I mean." Dylan cut off her defense. "You have him on a pedestal, whether he belongs there or not. How can I ever compare to that?"

Laura tucked her feet under her and turned toward him, holding his hand on her knee. "Ray was a special person, that's true," she said. "He did a lot of good in his life. He made some real changes for the homeless, and his book will probably make more. But you said he had no right criticizing me for my obsessions, and you were right. He was more obsessed with the homeless than I ever was with my career. There were many times that I felt Ray's charities were more important to him than Emma and I were. He was good to me. He didn't have to marry me, but he did. He wanted to take care of me. But he…he didn't really know how to do it. He wasn't cut out for it. That's where you're different, Dylan. When I watch you with Emma—" she smiled at the thought "—I'm so amazed at how you give her all your attention. You have *energy* for her. Please don't worry about not filling Ray's shoes. You two are apples and oranges. Impossible to compare."

He stared at her a moment, then leaned forward to kiss her, and Laura felt a moan escape from her throat.

"Do you remember anything at all from the night we made love?" Dylan asked in a whisper.

"Everything," she admitted.

"You're kidding."

"No, I'm not. I remember it all."

He pulled her close to him. "Tell me," he said.

She leaned her head against his shoulder. "There was one light on in the bedroom," she said. "It was a small Tiffany lamp on the dresser in the corner, and it gave the whole room a sort of pale blue cast. There was a huge bay window, and you could see the snow falling outside. Blowing sideways."

"You have some memory," he said.

Of that night, yes, she did. "The bedspread was green," she said. "Hunter green. And we lay down on top of it."

Dylan's hand was on her throat, and she let her head fall back against the sofa and closed her eyes. She felt his lips on the line of her jaw, then his tongue circling her ear.

"It was a...four-poster bed," she said, the words slow in leaving her mouth.

"Let's do that now," he said. "Let's move over to the bed."

She raised her head again, feeling a little woozy. "That bedspread's blue," she said.

"Good." He stood up and held his hand out to her. "I don't want to re-create that night in every detail. This one, I want to remember."

Laura stopped to quietly shut the door between Dylan's room and the room she shared with Emma, then joined him on the bed. He rolled on top of her, gently spreading her legs with his own, and although they were both fully clothed, she felt the seductive pressure of his erection.

He kissed her deeply, then drew away to look at her. "I'm glad you're Emma's mom," he said.

The words were a gift, and she wanted to reciprocate. "When Ray and I made love…" She bit her lip, knowing that making this confession would be more intimate than anything else she might do in this bed. "I used to pretend he was you," she said.

He stared at her solemnly for a moment, then rolled onto his side, raising his hand to stroke her cheek.

"I love you, Laura," he said.

"I love you, too."

His gaze still on her face, he began unbuttoning her blouse, reaching the last button just as a wail came from the room next door.

Laura grabbed his hand and listened. The cry came again.

"It's her nightmare sound," she said, extracting herself from beneath him. She was off the bed, smoothing her hair down, making the transition from lover to mother in a few steps across the room.

"I'm here, Emma," she said as she walked into the other room. She flicked on the light.

Emma was ashen-faced, tears streaming down her cheeks. She held out her arms to Laura.

Laura sat on the edge of the bed, drawing her daughter into her lap. "It's all right, honey. We're in a hotel in Truckee, remember? That town with the funny name? And I was just talking with Dylan in his room next door."

Emma slipped her thumb into her mouth and leaned against Laura's chest, sniffling, her body quaking with the residue of fear. Rocking her, Laura looked up to see Dylan standing in the doorway of the room.

"You sure you want to give up life in the fast lane for this?" she whispered to him.

She knew by his smile that he was ready and willing to do exactly that.

41

The following morning, Laura, Dylan and Emma drove back to the Solomons' house on Serene Lake. Things had changed overnight. They were more of a threesome than they had been the night before. Emma might not have been aware of it, but Laura knew that both she and Dylan felt the difference. Although she'd spent the rest of the night with Emma while Dylan had slept alone in his room, there was a connection between them that had not existed the day before.

The weather was quite warm, the snow along the side of the road receding.

Elaine opened the cabin door and ushered them into the living room. She'd set out coffee and juice on the coffee table, along with muffins warm from the oven. John slid open one of the doors along the back of the A-frame to let in the mild air.

"Well," he said, sitting next to Elaine on the love seat. "I need you folks to help me make a decision." He took Elaine's hand. "I know I have some legal things to take care of," he said, "but more important, should I go to Virginia to see Sarah or should I not?"

Everyone looked at Laura. Having thought about this much of the night, she had her own answer. She set her coffee cup down on the table. "Two things could happen," she said. "Sarah might not recognize you. That's very likely. She still loves you—she has your picture displayed in her apartment. But she loves the man in that picture. I'm not sure she'd connect you to him. So, then there would be little point to the visit.''

"And the second thing?" John asked.

"If she *does* recognize you, you would have to tell her you're...with another woman." She felt her lower lip start to tremble. "I don't want her to have that sort of pain and confusion."

Elaine nodded. "That would be terrible," she said.

Dylan put his arm around Laura, and Emma looked worriedly at her mother at the sound of that catch in her voice.

Laura studied John's face for his reaction, but he said nothing. His gaze was fastened on her throat.

"Where did you get that pendant?" he asked.

Laura touched the necklace. "It belonged to my grandmother," she said.

Frowning, he suddenly stood up. "It's warm enough for the canoe," he said. "Let's take a little ride, Laura. Elaine, will you entertain Dylan and Emma for a bit?"

Elaine looked surprised by the abrupt change of plans but quickly turned to Dylan. "Maybe you and Emma would like to go for a walk with me?" she asked.

"Sounds good," Dylan agreed.

John was already out the back door. Offering Dylan a confused shrug, Laura followed her host into the yard.

With the strength of a much younger man, John lifted the canoe off the sawhorses and carried it to the water's edge.

"You go ahead and sit in the bow," he said as he steadied the craft.

She did as she was told. John handed her an oar, then climbed into the stern.

They paddled silently and at a leisurely pace for a while,

Laura wondering if John was less rational than she'd originally thought. What was the purpose of this unscheduled outing?

"Let's stop for a while," John said finally. "Turn around and face me, Laura, please."

She obeyed him again, lifting her feet over the seat to turn around but feeling a bit anxious now. They were a good distance from shore.

John again had his gaze fixed on her pendant. Then he raised his eyes to Laura's face.

"When Sarah and I got married," he said, "I had a pin made for her. I believe that pendant you have on was made from her pin."

Laura touched the necklace again. "That's impossible. I told you it had been my grandmother's."

"Have you ever seen another like it?"

"No. That's one reason why I treasure it. It's so unusual."

"If you look closely at it, you'll see that it is actually a combination of an *S* for Sarah and a *J* for Joe."

Laura could easily picture the pendant. It had always reminded her of a woman in an old-fashioned, wide-brimmed hat. Resting her oar across the sides of the canoe, she unfastened the necklace and placed it on her knee. There was the woman in the hat, as usual. "I don't see it," she said.

John carefully made his way toward her. "See?" he traced the design with his fingertip. "Here's the *S*. Here's the *J*."

"My God," Laura said. "How can this be?"

"Turn it over. Can you see where it had once been a pin?"

Indeed, there were tiny raised bumps of gold on either side of the pendant where the clasp of a pin might have been fixed. Those minuscule protrusions had always been there, but she'd never thought anything of them.

John returned to his seat. "Tell me again how you got it," he said.

"It belonged to my father's mother," Laura said. "I never knew her, but I was named after her. My father gave the necklace to me when I was about eight, shortly after my own mother died. He told me I should always wear it. The pendant was really too big for me then, but I loved it. I've worn it nearly every day of my life since he gave it to me."

"Somehow," John said, "your father got it from Sarah."

Laura thought hard, feeling like she'd gone around in a circle, once again trying to determine her father's connection to Sarah.

"Look at me, Laura," John said.

She raised her face to his.

"The moment I opened the door yesterday and saw you standing there, you reminded me of my daughter who lives in Alaska. The resemblance is very strong. Elaine even mentioned it."

"What are you saying?" she asked.

"I believe you're Janie."

Laura laughed. "John, I'm sorry, but that's totally ridiculous. I know who my mother and father were."

"How old are you?" he asked, then caught himself and smiled. "Forgive the rudeness," he said.

"It's true I'm about Janie's age," Laura said, "but I was born in July of '58. She was born in April." Her hands shook as she fastened the pendant around her neck again. She recalled with a sudden lurch of her heart that there were no baby pictures of her in her family albums. *We lost them when our basement flooded,* her father had told her.

"I'd like you to go back to Virginia and learn the truth," John said. "Show Sarah the pendant. Then call me to tell me what you've discovered."

42

Their flight arrived late in Washington after a few long delays, and Laura was distressed. It was already five. It would be at least an hour before they got to the lake house, where Dylan promised to watch Emma for her, and another half hour for her to drive to the retirement home.

She had spoken little to Dylan on the plane, consumed with her own thoughts, and he seemed to understand. He held her hand and let her doze against his shoulder without pushing her to tell him what was going through her mind. She wouldn't have been able to describe her thoughts in a coherent fashion, anyway.

The sky was darkening by the time Laura arrived at the retirement home, and Sarah looked surprised to find her at her door.

"Hi, Sarah," Laura said. "I know it's late. But I really need to see you."

"Isn't it too dark for a walk?" Sarah asked, looking behind her to check the window.

"Yes, it is. We'll have to just sit and talk, all right?" She could hear the television blaring. "Am I interrupting a TV program?"

"No," Sarah said. "That's all right. You come in and find a seat."

She watched Sarah sit down on the sofa and fumble with

the buttons of the remote control until she found the correct one to turn off the TV.

"Sarah," Laura sat next to her. "I need you to tell me about Janie. About what happened to her."

"No." Sarah shook her head.

"Yes," Laura said firmly. "I know it's hard to talk about. I know that. But it's very important that you tell me." For an instant, she thought she saw something of herself in Sarah's face. She looked down at her own fingers, then at Sarah's where they ran nervously over the buttons of the remote. She and Sarah both had slender hands and white-tipped nails. "Sarah, please tell me."

Sarah's lips turned down at the corners. "It's sad," she said.

"I know it is," Laura said, more gently. "But I need to know what happened to her."

Sarah stared at the blank television screen, then suddenly sighed and sat up taller on the sofa. "All right," she said. "I'll tell you."

Sarah, 1960

It was late March, and the month was going out like a lion. There was a nip in the air and the wind blew around Sarah's legs as she walked home from the hospital where she'd been working for the past few months. She was looking forward to getting inside her apartment and heating up the stew she'd made the night before for dinner. Janie was nearly two now, and she loved picking the vegetables out of the stew and popping them into her mouth.

Turning the corner onto her block, Sarah saw a woman walk from the entrance of her apartment building to a car parked in the street. It looked like Mrs. Berenworth, the sitter she'd hired to take care of Janie, but that was impossible. Yet, wasn't that the kerchief she wore? And wasn't that her car?

She started to run. "Mrs. Berenworth!" she called. "Wait!"

The woman had the driver's side door open and was about to get in, but she looked up at the sound of Sarah's voice.

"Hello, Mrs. Tolley." She smiled, tucking a strand of her gray, windblown hair into her kerchief.

Sarah slowed, out of breath. "Why are you out here?" she asked. "Where's Janie?"

"Oh, there's a surprise for you inside," Mrs. Berenworth teased.

"What do you mean?"

"You'll see."

"No, please tell me." Sarah wanted to wring her neck. "You're upsetting me."

"All right, all right," Mrs. Berenworth conceded. "No need to trouble yourself. Your brother's inside with her."

"My *brother?*"

"Yes. He showed up to visit you as a surprise. He told me I could leave and he'd watch Janie until you got home." Mrs. Berenworth looked a tad worried herself now. "That's not a problem, I hope?"

"I don't have a brother!" Sarah shouted over her shoulder as she ran toward the building. She took the steps to the third floor two at a time and breathlessly flung her apartment door open.

Mr. D. sat on Sarah's sofa, Janie on his lap, and Janie did not look the least bit disturbed at finding herself there.

"There's your mommy," Mr. D. said.

Sarah ran toward him and grabbed Janie from his arms. "How dare you!" she snapped. "Get out of my home." Tears burned her eyes. He'd found her again.

"I'm so sorry to have frightened you," he said, standing up. "But I thought it was very important for you to see how easily you and Janie can be located. And therefore, how critical it still is for you to remain silent about what you know."

"I *have* been silent!" she said. "What more do you want from me?"

Janie began crying at the sound of anger in her mother's voice, and Sarah lowered her into the playpen at the side of the room.

"Hush, dear," she said. "Everything's all right."

"Please sit down and let me talk with you a bit," Mr. D. said.

"I want you to leave." She tried to speak calmly now, not wanting to upset Janie any more than she already was.

"I'm here to help you, Sarah," he said. "I know you don't believe that, but it's true. Peter—Dr. Palmiento—is growing increasingly...paranoid. He doesn't trust anyone anymore, and he keeps bringing up you and Colleen Price as people who turned against him."

"How do you expect me to trust you?" she asked. "To believe anything that comes out of your mouth? You're Palmiento's right-hand man."

"I was." Mr. D. nodded. "And I think that he still assumes I am. But I've grown very concerned about his tactics, and I'm walking a fine line these days. Doing a real balancing act. I still believe in the importance of the research he's doing at the hospital, but I'm worried that his paranoia is getting out of hand, and so now I feel a need to warn people. To warn you, for example. Peter's even bought a gun. I'm telling you, he's thrown himself off the deep end, headfirst."

She simply didn't know if she should believe him or not.

Yet, what if he *was* telling her the truth? What if she was in danger from a crazed doctor with a gun?

She felt helpless. She'd left no forwarding address with this last move. She had three locks on both doors of her apartment. Her phone number was unlisted. She spoke to no one at work about her past.

Unwinding the scarf from her neck, she sat down. "I've already moved twice," she said. "I don't know what more I can do."

"I think you should move again," Mr. D. said. "Far away this time. Change your name. Go into hiding." He seemed completely serious.

"That's too much," she said. "For all I know, *you're* the crazy one. Why should I uproot myself and my daughter again? Then you'll show up on *that* doorstep and tell me to do something else."

"Whether you believe it's me or Peter doesn't really matter at this point." Mr. D. looked down at his hands, and it was a moment before he spoke again. "I didn't want to tell you this," he said, "but I don't know how else to impress upon you that this is serious business." His dark eyes were somber. "Your friend Colleen's son is dead."

Sarah's heart gave a great thud against her ribs. "Sammy?" She remembered pictures Colleen had shown her of her darling little boy. "Sammy's dead?"

"He was in an accident."

"What happened?"

"He was playing in the tree house in his backyard and it collapsed," Mr. D. said. "He broke his neck."

Colleen had told her about that tree house. Her father-in-law had built it, and surely he'd made it sturdy enough to withstand any mischief a five-year-old boy might dish out. Suddenly, she understood what Mr. D. was trying to tell her.

"Are you saying Palmiento had something to do with it?" she asked, horrified.

"No, I didn't say that," Mr. D. said. "But I am saying that it's an interesting coincidence that he threatened her through her child, and now that child is dead."

She had to call Colleen. She stood up, and Mr. D. instantly got to his feet and came toward her. Letting out a small scream, Sarah stepped away from him.

He held his hands in the air. "I'm sorry," he said. "I didn't mean to scare you. I—"

Sarah raced across the room to the door and pulled it open. "Go," she said. "Just get out. Get out of my life."

"All right." He spoke quietly. "Please think about what I said, though. For your daughter's sake."

Slamming the door after him, she quickly secured all three locks. Moving from room to room, she pulled all the shades. That wouldn't be enough, though. They knew where she was. They would always know.

She went into her kitchen, still wearing her coat, and called Colleen. Maybe Mr. D. had made the whole thing up. She prayed that was the case as she listened to the ringing of Colleen's phone.

"Hello?" Colleen barely sounded like herself, her voice was so flat and distant.

"Colleen," Sarah said. "Are you all right?"

"You heard?"

"Heard..." Sarah shut her eyes and sank into one of the kitchen chairs. "You mean, about Sammy?"

There was sudden sobbing on Colleen's end of the line.

"Colleen, what happened?" Sarah asked.

"He was playing in the tree house, and it just...*fell*."

"Oh, God, Colleen. I'm so sorry."

"Palmiento's behind it."

"How do you know that?" She desperately wanted Colleen's reasoning to be fallacious.

"Oh, I know it," Colleen said. "He'd threatened to do something to me or Sammy often enough."

"Have the police questioned him?"

"They have. Once. Palmiento claims he doesn't know a thing about it, and the cops believe him. After all, he's God, you know." There was bitterness in her voice. "They said one of the boards on the house wasn't nailed right, or something. My poor father-in-law's beside himself with guilt. I told him I'm sure someone tampered with those boards, but he thinks I'm just trying to spare him."

"Can you try the police again?" Sarah suggested weakly. She couldn't seem to breathe. In the next room, Janie howled for dinner.

"I've even talked to the FBI," Colleen said. "They look at me like *I'm* the crazy one. Soon they're going to lock me up and cut out my brain like they did to Joe."

Sarah winced. Janie's howling grew more insistent.

"I'm sorry, Sarah," Colleen said. "I shouldn't have said that."

"I don't know what to do," Sarah said. "Mr. D. was just here. He told me about Sammy, although he wouldn't say there was a definite link between his death and Dr. Palmiento. But he warned me to leave. To move again. I just don't know if I have the strength, Colleen."

Colleen was quiet for a long time. "It's pointless," she said. "Moving is pointless. They have some way of finding us. It's like a giant conspiracy and we're completely powerless against it. They are going to get Janie, Sarah. I would strap her to me. I'd quit my job and just strap her to my body and never let her out of my sight. It's the only way. I should have done that with Sammy. Kept him with me every second of the day and night."

They are going to get Janie. The words echoed in Sarah's ears.

"I can hear Janie crying," Colleen said, her voice flat. "You're lucky to still have her, Sarah. You'd better go to her."

Sarah fed her daughter, unable to eat anything herself. She bathed Janie and put her to bed. She pushed an upholstered chair against the front door and the kitchen table against the fire escape door. She took her sharpest knife from the kitchen drawer and held it in her hand as she sat up all night long next to Janie's crib, afraid to close her eyes. The wind blew branches and twigs against the windows, and she jumped at every sound.

Janie slept like an angel in the crib, her long, golden brown eyelashes resting against her cheeks. She was a beautiful child, and she was in terrible danger simply by being Sarah's daughter.

Had Sammy suffered? A broken neck, Mr. D. had said. He would have died quickly, then. Would it be any consolation, though, if they killed Janie quickly? She moaned with the thought. She could not allow Janie to suffer that sort of fate. But Colleen spoke the truth: no matter where Sarah moved, they could find her.

By morning, exhausted from lack of sleep and still dressed in her uniform from the day before, Sarah had made a decision. She had to give up her daughter. There was no other way to ensure her safety. As long as she was with Sarah, Janie was in danger. Sarah would have to make her absolutely impossible to find. That meant she could not give her to family or friends, nor could she give her to an adoption agency where the records of her adoption might be traceable.

She called in sick to work, unwilling to let her daughter

out of her sight. Keeping the doors locked and the knife close at hand, she came up with a plan by the time she fed Janie lunch.

Thinking about adoption agencies had reminded her of the compassionate social worker, Ann, from the train crash years earlier. If Sarah could find her, maybe Ann could help her go outside the usual channels to place Janie in a safe and loving home.

Sarah riffled through old papers until she found the address Ann had given her after the train crash. Might Ann still be living there? After all, Sarah had moved several times since then. Ann, though, had no one chasing her from one place to another.

She spent an hour packing Janie's clothing and toys, trying to keep her mind on her task rather than the magnitude of what she was doing. But once she was in the car for the three-and-a-half-hour drive to the outskirts of Philadelphia, and once Janie had fallen safely asleep, she let out the racking sobs she'd been holding in all day.

She drove with her eyes focused on the rearview mirror, making certain no one was following her, stopping only once along the way to give Janie her dinner.

She reached Ann's house, a small, well-maintained Cape Cod, in the early evening. The street was narrow and lined with trees. The Cape Cod's windows glowed with yellow light. A gaslight burned on the porch, and a potted azalea rested on the top step.

Please be there, Ann. She lifted Janie out of the car and walked toward the front door. Even if Ann were there, would she believe Sarah's incredible story?

She rang the bell, and it was Ann who answered. Sarah, close to tears with relief that the social worker still lived there, could not even say hello.

"Are you...?" Ann broke into a wide smile. "You're Sarah, aren't you? From the train?"

Sarah nodded, trying to smile, but she started to cry instead.

"Oh, what's wrong?" Ann asked. "Come in, come in."

Sarah stepped into the warmth of Ann's little fire-lit living room, clutching Janie close to her chest.

"Let me take your coat," Ann said. "Is this your little girl? She's so darling. Can I take your coat, too, sweetheart?"

Sarah still could not speak. She let Ann slip Janie's coat from her shoulders, then took off her own.

"You sit by the fire, Sarah, and warm up," Ann said. "I'll get you tea. And I have some soup. Would you like some of that?"

Sarah shook her head. "Tea's fine," she managed to say. She sat in the chair closest to the fire, Janie on her lap, shivering. It was warm, almost too warm in the house, yet her teeth were chattering.

Ann returned with the tea. She poured a cup for Sarah and set it on the end table next to her chair. Then she crouched down in front of her, one hand on Sarah's knee. "Sarah. Dear," she said. "Tell me what's wrong."

Janie reached out sleepily to touch Ann's blond hair.

"Will she come to me?" Ann asked.

Sarah didn't want to let go of her daughter, but she forced herself to do so, and Janie slipped easily into the stranger's arms. Ann sat down on the sofa with her, stroking the little girl's hair.

"Tell me what's wrong," she said again to Sarah.

"You mustn't tell anyone what I tell you," Sarah warned.

"Not a soul," Ann said, and Sarah knew she could trust

this woman completely. She could trust her with her daughter's life.

Through her tears, Sarah explained the entire situation to Ann. She told her of the terrible research being performed at Saint Margaret's, and of Joe's attempt to uncover what was going on there and the price he paid for his recklessness. She told her of Dr. Palmiento's threats and finding Mr. D. on her doorstep no matter where she moved. The color drained from Ann's face when Sarah told her about Sammy's "accident."

"You poor dear," Ann said. "You must feel so trapped."

Sarah cried again at that. "I *am* trapped," she said, the tears rolling down her cheeks. "That's why I'm here. Please, Ann. Please. Is there a way you could get Janie adopted without there being any records? Without her being traceable in any way? She's not safe with me. I'd want her to be—" She swallowed hard and pulled a tissue from her purse to blot her eyes. "I'd want her to be with good parents. *Two* parents. She only has one with me. Two parents who would raise her as their own daughter. They'd have to change her name. And her birthday. She'll be two next month, but they should change that, too, so no one could ever figure out that she was my daughter. So she'd be safe."

Ann was crying herself, silently, as though she didn't want to awaken Janie, who had fallen asleep against her chest. She stared at the ceiling, and Sarah knew she was trying to figure out what she could do to help. She said nothing to disturb her thoughts.

Finally Ann lowered her gaze to Sarah. "I'm no longer a social worker," she said, and Sarah's heart sank. "Remember how terrible I was at it? But, listen to me, dear." She paused, as if collecting her thoughts once again. "I'm engaged to be married," she said quietly. "In two months."

"Oh, that's wonderful," Sarah said politely.

"I learned recently that I'm unable to have children, and my fiancé and I are considered too old to adopt. It's broken our hearts. If you think...if you'd be comfortable with... you don't know our qualifications, or anything about us, really."

"Yes!" Sarah sat forward. "And I *do* know your qualifications. I saw you on the train with that little boy, remember? I knew then that you were meant to be a mother."

Ann laughed through her tears. "I know. I am. But Sarah, you must be sure of what you're doing. I'm thirty-nine. My fiancé is forty-two. We won't be young parents for her."

"You will be far better parents for her than I can be." This was fate, Sarah thought. Fate had put her and Ann together during that train crash. Fate had brought her here tonight. "Tell me about your fiancé," she asked.

"I can assure you he loves children," Ann said. "He's the youngest of eight in his family. He's brilliant." She blushed. "Well, in my opinion, anyway, which, I admit, is a bit biased. He works for a company designing jet engines. He's a good man, Sarah."

Sarah nodded. "All right, then," she said, slowly getting to her feet. Her body felt a hundred years old. "I have her things in the car."

"Oh, Sarah." Ann carefully laid Janie on the couch and stood up, reaching for Sarah's arm. "Don't do this yet. Don't rush—"

"Let me go," Sarah said, brushing past her. "I'll be right back."

She went out to the car without her coat, not even feeling the cold, and returned with Janie's belongings.

Ann took the suitcase from her and set it by the stairs.

"She might be afraid when she wakes up and I'm no here," Sarah said. "But she's very resilient. You saw how easily she went to you. I'm afraid she'd go easily to anyone and that's why..." Her voice trailed off.

"I know, Sarah." Ann touched her arm again. "Listen dear. I think you should have some time alone with Janie I think you need to sit here with her and think through wha you're doing. Maybe there's another way."

Sarah glanced at Janie, sleeping peacefully on the sofa and looked away quickly. "No," she said. "No, I've thought about it enough. I don't want to give myself the chance to change my mind."

"How can I keep in touch with you?" Ann asked. "I' want to let you know how she's—"

"No," Sarah said quickly. "It's too dangerous. We mus never have any contact." She reached for the collar of he blouse and removed the pin Joe had given her. "Give thi to her, please," she said. "When she's older, I mean. Mak sure she knows it came from someone who loved her ver' much."

Ann took the pin from her hand, cupping it in her own "I will," she said.

"Thank you."

Sarah put on her coat, then turned numbly and left th house, knowing Ann's worried eyes were on her as sh walked toward her car. She didn't look back as she drov away, the pain in her heart tempered by the knowledge that with Ann, Janie would be safe.

"Oh, Sarah," Laura leaned forward, resting her hand o Sarah's hand. On her *mother's* hand. "That must have bee so terribly hard."

"It was hard." Sarah nodded. "But it was the righ

thing. I knew she would be taken care of there and no one could find her.''

Laura squeezed Sarah's hand. "I need to tell you something," she said. She lifted the pendant at her throat. "Do you recognize this?"

Sarah squinted at the pendant. "Is it a lady with a hat on?"

Laura smiled. "This was your pin, Sarah. The one Joe gave you."

"No, it's not. Mine was a pin."

"Yes, I know. But it was made into a necklace." She unfastened the necklace and held it out to Sarah.

"Oh, my!" Sarah said. "That looks just like my pin."

"It *is* your pin, dear," Laura said gently.

"Joe gave me one just like it."

"Listen to me, Sarah. I'm Janie. I'm your daughter." Her voice broke, but she continued. "I was the little girl you took to Ann's. Ann raised me as her own daughter. Ann and her husband, Carl. He was her fiancé in the story you just told me. That's how my father knew who you were. He must have tracked you down, somehow. He wanted to be sure you were always taken care of. He was very grateful to you for giving me to him and Ann."

Sarah looked at her blankly.

"You'd asked Ann to give me the pin when I got older, right? She or Carl had it made into a necklace. Into this." She held up the pendant again. "And Carl gave it to me. Do you understand?"

Sarah shook her head, a childlike expression of confusion on her face.

"Sarah, do you know my name?"

Again, Sarah shook her head.

"My name is Laura Brandon. My parents were Ann and

Carl Brandon. I'm the little girl you gave to them. I'm your daughter.''

"No." Sarah looked a bit annoyed. "Janie is my daughter.''

"And I'm Janie." Laura bit her lip in frustration, blinking back tears. "Ann and Carl gave me the name Laura. You'd asked them to change my name, remember?''

"I want to go to bed, now," Sarah said, standing up.

She did not understand. She could tell Laura everything about the past, right down to the potted azalea on the Cape Cod's porch, but she was never going to make the connection between the two-year-old daughter she'd lost long ago and the woman sitting next to her now.

Laura stood up and leaned over to give Sarah a kiss on the cheek. "I love you," she said. "Sleep tight."

43

"They always said they were married in 1957," Laura said. She was sitting next to Dylan on the back porch of the lake house. "But I guess that was to keep me from thinking I was illegitimate."

"And did your father work for a company that built jet engines?"

"He sure did. And they lived in Elkins Park, just outside of Philadelphia. I grew up in that Cape Cod Sarah was talking about. My father built a little deck outside one of the upstairs windows for his telescope."

"You sound so calm." Dylan put his arm around her shoulders. "This has to be overwhelming for you."

"I don't feel overwhelmed," she said. "I feel..." She tried to sort through her emotions. "....Sad that my birth mother has no idea who I am. And terribly sad for how much she suffered in her life. But I was very lucky, and I owe that to Sarah. I don't know if I could make the same choice if Emma were in danger. It must have devastated her, but who knows what would have happened if she'd tried to keep me?"

It was cool on the porch, and she shivered. Dylan tightened his arm around her shoulders.

"She gave me to wonderful parents." Laura thought of Ann. She had not known that her mother was once a social worker. "I wish I'd gotten to know my mother—Ann—

better. And if it hadn't been for my father, I probably wouldn't be an astronomer. He pushed and cajoled me into that career, I have to admit." She laughed. "But I've hardly regretted it."

"And now you have another father."

"I do," she said softly, smiling to herself. "I should call him to tell him what I found out from Sarah."

"Right," said Dylan. "And then you should sleep with me."

She looked at him in surprise, then laughed again. "Yes, I should." She raised her chin to kiss him. "I'll meet you in my bedroom," she said, standing up.

"The skylight room," he countered.

"Okay," she said. "The skylight room." Then she walked into the house to call John Solomon.

She found Dylan in the dark skylight room, lying under the comforter he'd pilfered from her bed. His clothes were piled in the corner of the room, and starlight illuminated his bare chest against the dark fabric of the pillows.

"Do you have anything on under there?" she asked.

"Nope."

Hesitating only a moment, she began to undress, tossing her shirt and jeans on top of his, enjoying the idea that they would have to hunt through that pile later to separate his clothes from hers. She felt the starlight on her own body and closed her eyes against a sudden shyness.

Slipping beneath the comforter, she sank into the pillows. Dylan's hand slid over the curve of her waist as he gently pulled her to him, and she breathed a sigh of relief at the touch of his skin against hers, a feeling she'd never expected to have again outside her fantasies.

This would be new to him, she thought, though not so

to her. He remembered nothing from that night; she remembered all.

Yet her memories were wrong. No matter how intense, how erotic, those memories had been, they'd lacked something that existed now but had not then: Dylan's attentiveness. His consciousness. He was present now, body and soul. His touch was deliberate. His hands glided like a sunwarmed stream over her flesh, stopping to lap gently at her breasts and at the feverish place between her thighs, and she felt a tenderness in him he had not shown her that night long ago.

Afterward, when he tossed the comforter from their hot, damp bodies and they lay exhausted, bathed in starlight, she knew that no matter how familiar Dylan's touch became, it would always arouse in her that same marriage of excitement and safety. She felt sure of his love—for Emma, and for herself.

As sure as she was of the stars above them.

44

Laura turned off the ignition but made no move to get out of the car. An elderly couple walked through the front entrance of the retirement home, and she stared after them blindly.

"Are you all right?" Dylan asked.

"Yes," she said, still not reaching for the door handle. She'd put off seeing Sarah for a few days, afraid she might cry in front of her and confuse her even more than she had on her last visit. But today was perfect for a walk. She'd asked Dylan to join them. He'd been a terrific support to her for the past few days, and she wasn't ready to give that up.

"I just don't know what to say to her now," she said.

"Why don't you ask her what happened to her after she gave you up?" he suggested. "Get her talking, like you usually do."

Sarah, 1960

After leaving Janie with Ann, Sarah sank into a deep depression. She'd quit her job and moved immediately to another town in northern Virginia to get away from friends and neighbors who were sure to ask why Janie had suddenly disappeared. So, she found herself alone in a strange town, working in a small psychiatric clinic where she knew no one.

Dragging herself to work each day took all of her energy, leaving her a mediocre, mistake-prone employee. The only thing on her mind was her child. She could tell no one what she'd done, and the lies and isolation would have been unbearable had she been alive enough to care. Nothing mattered to her anymore. Her new apartment had one flimsy lock on the door, and she didn't even bother turning it at night. Janie and Joe were gone. She didn't care what happened to her now.

Three weeks after leaving Janie with Ann, Sarah received a call from Dr. Palmiento. Apparently, he'd had little problem obtaining her new, unlisted telephone number. That hardly surprised her.

"I'd like you to come to the office I use for my private practice," he said. "It's in my home. I'll give you the address."

"Why?" Sarah asked. "Why on earth should I do anything you tell me to do? I'm finished with you."

"Don't hang up," Dr. P. said quickly. "I have some information I thought might interest you. It's about your husband."

"Tell me on the phone," Sarah said.

"I think it would be better to discuss it with you in person." He sounded remarkably calm and reasonable, and he had information about Joe. The only thing that would be important to tell her in person, though, was that Joe was dead. Still, she felt compelled to go.

A rational woman would not go to the office of a crazy man who owned a gun, she thought as she put on her coat. A rational woman would at least take someone with her, or possibly even ask the police to accompany her. A rational woman would care what happened to herself. Sarah no longer fit that description.

Palmiento's house was set a distance from its neighbors in a wooded section of McLean. The house was dark, except for the windows of a small room attached to the garage. His office, she supposed.

Wrapping her light jacket around her body, she walked up the drive and knocked on the office door. In a moment, Dr. Palmiento let her in.

"Let me take your jacket," he said. He looked different somehow. The craziness in his eyes had spilled over into the rest of his face. The kind, fatherly visage was entirely gone, and she shuddered at the sight of him.

"I'll keep it on." She did not plan to be there long.

They were in a waiting room, tastefully decorated with expensive furnishings.

"Come into my office," he said.

She followed him into the adjacent room, startled to find Mr. D. sitting in a leather wing chair next to a massive desk. He stood when she entered, looking equally surprised at seeing her there.

"What is *she* doing here?" His voice was accusatory, and Sarah wondered what she'd stumbled into.

"I invited Mrs. Tolley here to determine the exact depth of your betrayal," Palmiento said to Mr. D. He sat down behind the desk. "Have a seat, Mrs. Tolley."

"I don't need to sit," she said. "I don't know what's going on here, but you said you had news about Joe. If you do, I'd like to hear it. If you don't, I'm leaving."

"Go, Sarah." Mr. D. moved toward her. "He doesn't have anything to tell you about Joe." He turned to Palmiento, his face blotched with red. "There's no reason to bring her into this," he said. "It's between you and me."

Sarah narrowed her eyes at Palmiento. "Do you have something to tell me about Joe?" she asked.

"Nothing." Palmiento actually smiled.

"God, I loathe you." She turned on her heel to leave.

"And what about Janie?" Dr. P.'s voice was calm, and Sarah stopped walking, her heart tight in her chest. Drawing in a deep breath for courage, she marched boldly over to his chair and leaned close to him.

"What about her?" she asked. *Please God, don't tell me they found her.*

"I am aware that you spirited her away. What I'm not sure about is if Mr. D. suggested you do so. Did he?"

Uncertain what was truly going on in this room, Sarah didn't know how to answer. "I'd...I'd heard about Colleen Price's little boy," she stammered, "and I—"

"Leave her out of this, Peter," Mr. D. said. His hands gripped the back of the chair he'd been sitting in. His knuckles were white. "Yes, I told her she should take measures to keep her daughter safe. And I'm glad she did. You—both of us—have put Sarah through more hell than anyone deserves."

"You son of a bitch." Palmiento slowly stood up from his seat behind the desk, and Sarah, still close enough to touch him, took a step away. "I trusted you," he said to Mr. D. "I let you in on—"

"And that's sacred," Mr. D. hurried to say. "The research is sacred. But you've gone to extremes to protect it, Peter." He moved slowly toward the older man. "Peter, you need help," he said quietly. "I know—"

"Don't come any closer." Palmiento was reaching into one of his desk drawers, and Sarah gasped when she saw him tighten his fingers around the handle of a gun. She should run. Escape. But her feet were frozen to the floor.

"You betrayed me," Palmiento said. He lifted the gun and aimed it at Mr. D., his finger tightening on the trigger.

Instinctively, Sarah hit his arm in an attempt to make the shot go wild. The blast was so loud it hurt her ears, and the bullet caught Mr. D. in the shoulder. He howled in pain as Sarah pushed past him. She ran through the waiting room, out the door and down the driveway to her car. As she pulled out of the driveway, there was one single prayer on her lips: *Dear God, don't let what I just did put Janie in danger again.*

Sarah spent the entire evening sitting in the cramped living room of her apartment, staring at the phone and trembling. She was thinking about calling the police, telling them what had happened. But then she would have to explain about Janie's disappearance. Surely she'd have to say where she'd taken her. And what if Palmiento somehow had the cops in his back pocket, where he seemed to have the board of psychiatry and the FBI and everyone else in authority? She stared at the phone until two in the morning, when her trembling had finally subsided enough for her to go to bed.

Her dreams that night, and for many nights to come, were full of Dr. Palmiento or Mr. D., but she never heard from either of them again. Nor did she hear from Ann. But there was never a day that her thoughts didn't light on her daughter, and she knew she had done the right thing in protecting Janie from the madmen of Saint Margaret's.

"We need to leave," Laura said abruptly. They were sitting in Sarah's living room, the walk having been completed before the end of Sarah's tale, and Laura was anxious to get out of there. Dizziness washed over her, and the room was a blur when she stood up. "Dylan, can we go please?"

Dylan looked surprised by the urgency in her voice. He turned to Sarah. "Is there anything we can do for you before we leave?" he asked.

He was a kind man, but just then Laura wished he were less so. She was relieved when Sarah shook her head and stood up to walk them to the door.

Once outside the retirement home, Dylan put his arm around her. "I know," he said. "It's got to be really upsetting to hear her talk about Janie without realizing that Janie's right in front of her."

"That's not it," Laura said, the vertigo still teasing her. "I can't even explain what it is."

He looked concerned. "Do you want me to drive?" he asked.

She nodded. She didn't trust herself behind the wheel.

They were on the main road before she felt able to voice her fear. "I know this sounds crazy," she said, "but I have a terrible feeling that Ray was Mr. D."

"What?" Dylan laughed. "That's *beyond* crazy, girl. Why would you think that?"

"Ray had a scar from a gunshot wound on his shoulder," she said. She could picture the scar perfectly, the round and ragged protrusion of skin. "He'd always told me he'd been shot in Korea."

"More than one person has been shot in the shoulder," Dylan said.

"There's something else, though," she said. "Ray always used the expression that someone—me, most of the time—was throwing themselves off the deep end, headfirst. He'd say that whenever I was getting involved in a new project."

"So?" There was a crease between Dylan's eyebrows.

"One time Sarah said that Mr. D. used that same expression."

"It's a very common expression, Laura." He sounded overly patient, as if he were explaining something to a child.

"Most people say 'jump' off the deep end. Not throw themselves. And not add that bit about headfirst. It reminded me of Ray when she said it, but I didn't think much about it until now."

"Do you honestly think Sarah is repeating what Mr. D. said verbatim?"

"I don't know." She was frustrated by his attempts to minimize her fear. "All I know is, I'm feeling very uncomfortable about this whole thing."

"What would Mr. D. stand for?" Dylan asked.

"Ray's last name was Darrow."

Dylan reached over to take her hand. "I know this has been hard on you, Laura, but I really think you're looking for trouble where there isn't any. Ray was far too young to have been Mr. D., wasn't he?"

"He was already twenty-one when I was born," she said. "And Mr. D. was very young when he worked at Saint Margaret's. Young enough to have acne, Sarah once said. And Ray had acne when he was in his teens."

"So did lots of teenagers," Dylan said. "So did I, for that matter."

She glanced at his smooth cheek. "Liar," she said.

He shrugged. "One or two zits, anyhow." He smiled at her. "I just don't like to see you getting so worked up over this," he said.

"Sarah said he was a psychology student, though," Laura pondered out loud. "That doesn't fit, I have to admit. Ray's degrees were in sociology."

"Something else that doesn't fit is the book he wrote," Dylan said. "Does Mr. D. sound like the kind of guy who would have that much concern for the homeless and mentally ill?''

''Well, you're right about that,'' she admitted. ''I can't see Ray, of all people, performing torturous experiments on psychiatric patients. But still…'' Her voice trailed off. She could not shake her uneasiness.

''I think you're catastrophizing,'' Dylan said. ''Don't you think it would be a rather major coincidence that Mr. D. wound up married to the daughter he forced Sarah Tolley to give away?''

Laura laughed. He was right. Her thinking was ludicrous.

Yet the disquieting feeling in her gut was still there hours later, after they'd eaten dinner and were playing fish with Emma.

When they'd finished playing, Laura gave Emma a bath and Dylan volunteered to read her a story in bed. Glad for the time to herself, Laura went into the guest room and began digging through the boxes in the closet until she found Ray's old school records. Sitting on the floor of the closet, she studied the records closely. Once again, she was enveloped by the sick feeling that had nearly overcome her in Sarah's apartment.

She met Dylan in the hallway as he was closing the door to Emma's room.

''He was a psychology student,'' she said, holding the records in front of him.

''Who was?'' Dylan glanced down at the papers in her hand. ''Ray?''

''He was a psych major in the late fifties at Catholic University. He eventually dropped out. I didn't know anything about it. He went back to school four years later as a sociology major.''

''Laura.'' Dylan tried to pull her into his arms. ''I still think—''

She drew away from him. "I'm calling Stuart," she said. "I have to know."

She called from the phone in her bedroom while Dylan sat behind her on the bed, rubbing her back. Stuart was on the road, but she managed to reach him in a hotel room in Philadelphia.

"Is something wrong?" Stuart asked. She'd never before called him while he was traveling, and he sounded concerned. "Is Emma all right?"

"I need you to tell me something, Stu," she said. "Did Ray ever work at Saint Margaret's Psychiatric Hospital?"

Stuart was quiet long enough to let her know the answer.

"Oh, Stuart." She pressed her hand to her forehead, and Dylan tightened his fingers on her shoulders. "I want you to tell me I'm wrong," she said.

She heard him expel his breath. "I'll come to Virginia tomorrow," he said. "We'll talk about it then, all right?"

"He was Mr. D."

"Yes."

"But how—"

"Tomorrow, Laura. I'll be there before lunch."

45

"Wait for me, Emma." Dylan quickened his pace on the lakeside path. Emma had darted out ahead of him in her race to get to the playground, and he'd lost sight of her as she turned the bend in the trail.

He caught up to her as she was climbing onto a swing.

"Do you want me to push you, or shall I just swing next to you?" he asked.

She didn't answer, but she pumped hard, rising high into the air, her dark hair flying out behind her. Taking a seat on the swing next to hers, he began pumping himself. He couldn't remember the last time he'd been on a swing. It was dizzying.

He'd come to the lake house half an hour ago, arriving the same time as Stuart, who looked as if he'd aged two years since Dylan last saw him. Pale and subdued, Stuart said he wanted to talk to Laura alone, and Dylan volunteered to take Emma to the playground. Better to spend time with his daughter than to hear whatever ol' Stu had to say. If only Laura didn't have to hear it, either. She'd been so upset the night before. He hadn't been able to stay with her, since he'd had an early balloon flight this morning, and he'd hated leaving her alone in the shape she was in.

He was still swinging, light-headed from the motion, when Emma slid off her own swing and ran over to the merry-go-round. For a few minutes, he watched as she pushed the large wooden disk to start it whirling, then hopped on for the ride. He walked over and began pushing it for her, making it spin so quickly it blurred in front of his eyes. Emma loved it. Standing on the outer edge of the platform, she held on to the rail with one hand, her other arm outstretched as if she were flying. He could hear her making jet engine sounds deep in her throat.

Although Emma seemed happy to fly in a circle forever, Dylan's arms grew tired after a while, and he sat on a nearby tree stump to watch her flight gradually come to an end.

"You like to fly, huh?" he said when the ride was over.

Emma nodded. She flopped down on the platform, looking a bit dizzy herself.

"You okay?" he asked.

She smiled at him. She had the cutest smile in the world.

"Can I tell you something about when I was a pilot?" he asked.

Emma didn't respond, but she was watching him.

"One time I was supposed to fly a plane across the country," he said. "But I got sick and couldn't fly. The pilot who took my place had too much to drink. He was drunk. Do you know what that means?" It was not the exact truth. Alcohol was not all that had been found in the pilot's body, but it would have to do.

Emma didn't nod, but he was certain she understood.

"Anyhow, that pilot flew the plane I was supposed to fly, and it crashed. A lot of people were killed."

There was a frown on Emma's face.

"That's right," Dylan said. "It was terrible. And you know what? For a long time I thought it was my fault. If I hadn't gotten sick, or if I'd flown the plane even though I *was* sick, it never would have crashed and all those people would have been okay. But after a while I realized that the crash wasn't my fault at all. It was the other pilot's fault. I had nothing to do with it. Just like you had nothing to do with your father's death.''

Emma had been watching him intently, but now she lowered her gaze quickly to the floor of the merry-go-round.

''Your father had grown-up problems that caused him to take his life.'' Dylan wondered what Heather would have to say about his direct approach. ''It had nothing to do with you or with Mom. Nothing to do with how much you talked or anything else.''

Emma stood up and hopped off the merry-go-round. She ran over to the cluster of huge, colorful plastic tubes and plowed headfirst into one of them. Dylan sighed at his failure, looking up at the canopy of trees above him. Many of the leaves had already changed to gold and orange. When had that happened?

He glanced toward the plastic tubes. Emma was deep inside them, nowhere to be seen. She'd found the one place on the playground where she could be alone and not have to listen to anything else he might say.

46

"He'd always suffered from bouts of depression," Stuart said, circling the spoon in his glass of lemonade. "But I guess you knew that."

"Of course." In spite of the fact that Laura was angry at Stuart for withholding the truth from her, she was worried about him. In the sunlight coming through the porch screens, Stuart's eyes were rimmed by dark circles, as if he hadn't slept for a week.

"Even when we were kids, he'd talk about wanting to die," Stuart said. "But then he'd pull out of it for a while. As he got older, he became fascinated with the process going on inside his head and decided he wanted to be a psychologist."

"I never knew that."

"No. He never spoke of it, and you'll understand why in a minute." Pulling the spoon from his lemonade, he studied his reflection in its concave surface. "He got a bachelor's degree in psychology from Catholic, and then entered the doctoral program." He lowered the spoon back into his drink. "At the same time, he was very patriotic."

"Ray?" Laura found that hard to believe.

"You have to understand the times, Laura. It was a terribly frightening period. We thought we were under threat, literally waiting for the bomb to drop. The government was convinced that mind control was possible and that our enemies knew how to achieve it. Ray saw a way to help. He'd learned somehow about Peter Palmiento's experimentation, and he'd heard about a type of research taking place in Montreal called psychic driving—"

"The helmets and the tapes," Laura said.

"Exactly," Stuart said. "Ray discussed his plan to use psychic driving in the development of mind control to Palmiento, who was fascinated with the idea and curious to find out what the results would be. So, he hired Ray to develop the Psychic Driving Program at the hospital."

"I can't believe Ray would subject people to that sort of thing. It sounds so cruel."

"It does now, at the turn of the century, but forty or fifty years ago it sounded like a way to alter people's thoughts and behavior, something they were desperate to learn how to do."

"But he was experimenting on human beings," Laura protested.

"Ray came to regret that, Laura, trust me. But it's hard to describe how thrilled he was at being a part of Palmiento's work at the time. He'd found a way to help his country. He couldn't tell anyone, though, except me, and he swore me to secrecy. I don't think he told another soul."

He looked at his sister-in-law and must have seen the revulsion in her face.

"Don't hate him for this, Laura," Stuart pleaded. "Please try to understand. He thought what he was doing was right and necessary. Even the government supported it. His paycheck came from the CIA. It was laundered a bit along the way, but he knew the government was delighted with what he was doing and would do whatever it took to keep word about the research from getting out."

Laura rubbed her arms through her sweater. She felt unclean. The thought of Ray touching her was loathsome.

"After a while, though, Ray began to realize that Peter Palmiento had his own set of psychiatric problems," Stuart continued. "As Palmiento grew more paranoid, he was afraid that Sarah Tolley and a few others who worked at Saint Margaret's might blow his cover, and he felt justified in taking whatever steps he thought were necessary to prevent that from happening. He knew he could get to Sarah through threats to her daughter. Ray felt torn then. He talked to me about it. He was still convinced the experiments were absolutely essential, but he was upset by Palmiento's craziness."

"He warned Sarah to protect Janie," Laura said. "To protect me."

"He probably did. I don't know that for a fact. I do know that the disagreement between Ray and Palmiento grew until it turned into a physical fight, and Ray got shot. After that, Ray was able to get him committed to a different psychiatric institution as a patient. Ray was still dedicated to the research, though, and he was hoping the experiments would continue, but the government would no longer provide support, financial or otherwise, and Ray had to let it go."

"Sarah was there when they fought," Laura said. "She hit Palmiento's arm when he fired the shot. Otherwise, he might have killed Ray."

Stuart looked surprised. "I didn't know that," he said. He took a long drink of his lemonade, draining the glass. Laura didn't bother to offer him more. She wanted him to get on with his story.

"He had no job then, after the research folded," Stuart said. "No way to pay for school, so he had to drop out for a while. He worked in some menswear store for a few years to make money to go back. But while he was out of school, his attitude toward the government changed. Vietnam happened. I watched him lose faith in what we were doing over there. He started to feel like he'd been duped, by the government, by Palmiento and by himself. He really got depressed then. I remember him talking to me, literally crying about all the patients he'd help to torture. That was the word he used. He tried to block the past from his mind and pretend it never happened, and psychology all of a sudden left a bad taste in his mouth. He felt so ashamed of what he'd done at Saint Margaret's. When he went back to school, he majored in sociology. That's when he took up working with the mentally ill who'd been kicked out of institutions and left to fend for themselves on the street.''

Laura stared into the woods. She wanted to feel sympathy for Ray, to understand and forgive what he'd done. The tenor of the times had been radically different in the fifties. The fear of the Communist threat, real or imagined, had been pervasive and oppressive. She remembered Sarah telling her about Donny, the little boy in the train crash who had feared being destroyed by ''the bomb.'' Yet human beings had still been human beings back then. Every person who spent a month in the isolation box suffered as much as she would now if forced to exist in those conditions. The patients who wore those helmets, desperately hoping the treatment would help them feel better, were every bit as trusting, fragile and vulnerable as she would be.

''The one thing he couldn't let go of from those days at Saint Margaret's was Sarah Tolley,'' Stuart said. ''He thought they'd put her through too much. They...I don't remember what they did to her husband, but—''

''They drugged him and shocked him and flew him to Nevada, where they gave him a new identity.'' Laura heard the bitterness in her voice. She was not ready to forgive. ''They—Ray included—told Sarah they'd lobotomized him.''

Stuart winced. ''Well, after that, I guess they threatened to harm her daughter. You. Until Sarah got scared enough to give you away. You know all this, huh?''

Laura nodded. "But what I don't understand is how Ray ended up married to me. It couldn't have been a coincidence."

"No, of course it wasn't." Stuart set his empty glass down on the coffee table. "It tormented him that he didn't know what Sarah had done with you. He didn't know if you were safe or not. So he tried to find you. For years and years, he looked for you with no luck. He gave up, finally. But then, many years later, you discovered the comet. Your fifth, I think. The big one."

Laura frowned. "How did that help him? My picture was all over the place, true, but he couldn't possibly have recognized me. Or my name."

"No, but he did recognize this." He reached out and touched the pendant at Laura's throat. "You had it on in all the pictures and TV interviews. He knew it must have been made from the pin Sarah always wore. It was one of a kind, he said. He did a little detective work and found out your age and was pretty sure you were Janie. Then he finagled a way to meet you and—"

"He came up to me in the cafeteria at Hopkins and asked if he could share my table," Laura remembered.

"Well, he knew after talking to you for a while that you were the one—the little girl he'd hunted down and threatened through her mother so long ago."

"I remember all those questions he asked me," Laura said. "I thought he was simply curious. A rare sort of man to take that much interest in someone."

"He cared about you, Laura. Maybe in the beginning it was because of how he'd changed your life, how he thought he might have hurt you. But I know you two became close friends, and I believe that friendship was completely genuine. When you got pregnant, he didn't think twice before asking you to marry him."

"Out of guilt, it sounds like," Laura said. She felt sick.

"I'd prefer to think it was out of love," Stuart said.

Laura didn't respond. She looked toward the lake, the autumn leaves blurring in her vision.

"Ray panicked when your father asked you to look after Sarah Tolley," Stuart said. "He was afraid you'd learn about his past. He didn't want to face that past himself, can you understand that? That's why he killed himself. It had nothing to do with how hard you worked, or his being rejected by publishers. It was Ray's shame and self-loathing that killed him. He never forgave himself for what he did at Saint Margaret's."

"He should have told me," she said, although she knew her reaction to his past would have been less than charitable.

"I never wanted you to find out, either," Stuart said. "More important, I don't want the rest of the world to know. It would destroy the acclaim and respect Ray's finally going to receive for his book."

"*You* did it," she said, staring at her brother-in-law. "You sent those letters warning me to stay away from Sarah."

"Yes, I did," he admitted. "Coward's way of dealing with the problem, I suppose."

"That was my mother you wanted to keep me from, Stuart," she said angrily. "My *mother*." Both Stuart and Ray had toyed with her, trying to control her actions to serve their own needs.

"I know," Stuart said. "But you didn't have a clue who she was. You could have lived your entire life without knowing, and would that have been such a big deal? I still wish you'd heeded those letters."

Laura thought of Sarah, sitting alone in her apartment with her dwindling memories and her picture of Joe.

"I'm so glad I didn't," she said.

47

"She's ready for a nap," Dylan said.

Laura watched her daughter drag herself into the kitchen, dirt on her knees and elbows and one cheek. "And a bath," she said. "You run upstairs, Emma. I'll be up in a second." She managed to smile at Dylan. "Thanks for taking her," she said. "Stuart's lying down. Can you stay for a while? I can tell you what he said." Her head ached with resentment and rage, and she longed to talk it out. She felt used. Her marriage had not been based on a deep romantic love; that she had always accepted. But it had not even been based on friendship. Marrying her had been a convenient way for Ray to assuage his guilt.

"I can't, Laura." Dylan looked at his watch. "I have to get ready for tonight's flight. I'll come back afterward, though, if that's all right."

"Okay," she said, thinking that Stuart would be around then; it would be hard to talk. The disappointment must have shown on her face.

"You're upset." Dylan walked toward her, checking his watch again. "I can stay for—"

"No," she said, knowing he was already running late. "We'll talk tonight."

He gave her a quick kiss. "What time is Emma's appointment with Heather?"

Laura froze. "I completely forgot about it," she said.

"It's at two-thirty, and I told Heather I'd bring Sarah with us. Maybe I should cancel, with all that's going on."

"I think you should go, if you're at all up to it," Dylan said. "Little pitchers have big ears. Maybe it would help Emma to be able to unload verbally on Sarah."

He had a point, although the thought of getting her daughter and herself organized by two was overwhelming. "I'll try," she said. "Let me get her into the tub."

"I'll go along for the ride, if that's all right with you," Stuart said, when Laura told him about the appointment with Heather. "Her office is over by that strip mall in Leesburg, you said, right? The one with that super bookstore? I'll spend my time in there while you're at your appointment."

Laura didn't feel like having Stuart join them, but she could think of no civil way to discourage him from going. The tension between them was palpable but difficult to address with Emma around.

Stuart tried to talk to Emma in the car, and his nonstop, unanswered questions only served to increase Laura's anxiety. She turned her focus to the meeting with Heather, trying to block out her brother-in-law's voice.

So much had happened since the last therapy appointment. She should probably speak with Heather alone first while Sarah and Emma stayed in the waiting room. The therapist was in dire need of an update.

Laura parked in front of the retirement home and went inside to get Sarah.

"I'll get my walking shoes," Sarah said as soon as she opened her apartment door and found Laura in the hallway.

"You don't need to, Sarah," Laura said. "We're going to Emma's therapist with her today. Is that all right with you?"

A look of confusion erased Sarah's smile. "If you say so." She shrugged and looked around her living room.

"It's right there." Laura pointed to Sarah's purse where it rested on the kitchenette counter.

"Oh, yes." Sarah picked it up. "I'm ready."

"Thanks for doing this," Laura said as she walked with Sarah down the long corridor. "For going to Emma's therapist with her. I know you'd rather be taking a walk. It means a lot to me."

"We had bingo last night," Sarah said.

"Oh. And did you win anything?"

"I don't know. Oh, it wasn't bingo. It was that other game."

Laura didn't ask what game she was talking about, too preoccupied to pursue the conversation.

They stepped outside into the fall sunshine. "My car's right there," Laura said, pointing. She opened the back door for Sarah, since Stuart had taken the front seat. "Sarah, this is my brother-in-law, Stuart," she said, reaching across Sarah to find the other end of the seat belt. She fastened the seat belt and got in behind the wheel.

"So, what was the game you played last night?" she asked Sarah.

There was no answer.

"Sarah?"

Laura looked in her rearview mirror. Sarah's gaze was riveted on Stuart's profile. Glancing at Stuart herself, it suddenly occurred to her that Sarah might see a resemblance to Ray—to Mr. D.—in his features. He and Ray had often been mistaken for twins as they were growing up. Still, Ray had been in his early twenties when he was at Saint Margaret's, and Stuart was now close to sixty. A youthful sixty, though. He had not grown bulky and soft as Ray had. And he still had his hair.

"There's the mall, Stu." Laura pointed toward the strip

of stores as she pulled into the parking lot of the therapy office. "Do you want to take the car?"

"No, I'll walk." Stuart got out of the car and stretched. "It'll feel good."

Sarah didn't budge from the car once Laura had released her seat belt. Her gaze followed Stuart as he walked across the parking lot toward the mall.

"Where's he going?" Sarah asked.

"He's going to those stores over there," Laura said. "And his name is Stuart," she said again, in case Sarah did indeed have him confused with Ray. "He's my brother-in-law."

Sarah slowly got out of the car, then took Emma's hand, something Laura had not seen her do before. Emma accepted the gesture without protest, and the three of them walked toward the office, Sarah turning her head to follow Stuart's progress as he neared the strip of stores.

Emma was already playing with the waiting room's toys by the time Heather appeared. Laura stood up. "I think I should see you first, today," she said.

"All right," Heather said. "Sarah and Emma? You two stay here in the play area and Mrs. Quinn will keep an eye on you."

Sarah made no move toward the play area. She sat on the edge of her chair, and Laura eyed her worriedly as she walked past her on the way to Heather's office. Sarah was not herself today.

In Heather's office, Laura poured out all that had occurred over the last few days, while the therapist's jaw fell lower and lower.

"You must be furious at Ray," Heather said.

"Yes, I am."

"Well, hooray, Laura. It's about time."

"I can forgive what he did at Saint Margaret's, although it's difficult. He was young. The political situation was very different. But I can't forgive what he did to *me*. Keeping me from my mother. From ever learning the truth about myself." Her fists were clenched in her lap. "He was dishonest and deceitful." She suddenly thought of Dylan, of how he valued honesty, and a small current of joy rushed through her in spite of her anger.

There was a knock on Heather's office door and Mrs. Quinn opened it partway. "Are Sarah and Emma in here with you?" she asked.

Laura's heart threw an extra beat against her rib cage.

"No," Heather said.

"They're not in the waiting room, either," the receptionist said. "I looked up from my desk, and they'd disappeared."

Laura was out of her seat in an instant. She darted into the waiting room, which was empty except for a middle-aged man waiting for one of the other therapists. Sarah's purse was on the seat of the chair in which she'd been sitting.

"Did you see where they went?" she asked the man. "A small child and an elderly woman?"

He looked confused by her terror. "There was no one here when I arrived," he said.

"Try the rest rooms," Heather called to her from the hallway. "I'll check the other offices."

The rest rooms were empty, and Laura felt a panic she'd experienced only once before, when she became separated from Emma in an outdoor market in Brazil. That time, she'd found Emma talking up a storm with a merchant who couldn't understand a word of English.

She ran outside, calling for Sarah and Emma, but there was no answer and no sign of them. Standing in the parking lot, she turned helplessly in a circle, wondering which way they might have gone.

Heather came outside and stood next to her. "Let's stay

calm," she said. "They're most likely somewhere in the building. It's four stories. They could have gotten on the elevator. We'll search the building before we panic, all right?"

Laura didn't budge. Her feet were fused to the surface of the parking lot.

"If they were outside," Heather said, "don't you think we could see them from here? An old woman and a small child? How fast could they possibly get away?"

Laura nodded, somewhat comforted by Heather's rationale, although as she headed back into the building, she remembered the times she'd had trouble keeping up with Sarah on their walks.

She and Heather, Mrs. Quinn and the man in the waiting room combed the building, and Laura's panic mounted with each door she opened to find strangers or an empty room. Finally, Heather called the police. And Laura called Dylan, her hand shaking as she dialed his number. He had a balloon flight this evening. He was probably out in his barn. But she was able to reach him, and he did not hesitate before telling her he was on his way.

The police arrived quickly. They were organized, methodical and conscientious, but they were not particularly reassuring. The expressions on their faces were grim.

"A mute five-year-old and an old woman with Alzheimer's?" Laura overheard one of them say to another. "Good luck."

One of the police officers told Laura to stay in the office in case Sarah and Emma returned, and she watched through the window as he and his fellow officers spread out into the neighborhood, the majority of them heading toward the mall.

Within a few minutes, Stuart entered the office and Laura told him that Sarah and Emma were missing.

"I think you reminded Sarah of Mr. D.," she said. "Of Ray." She heard the accusation in her voice.

Stuart looked surprised. "I'm going to look for them," he said, heading for the door.

"No," Laura said firmly. "If it's you who scared Sarah off, she'll just run from you."

With a sigh, Stuart sat down in the waiting room. He had that defeated look Ray had often worn. Laura was sick of seeing it.

For a moment, neither of them spoke.

"I'm sorry, Laura," Stuart said finally. "I'm sorry for everything. For keeping things from you. For trying to keep you from Sarah. I bought into Ray's aspirations. He'd been so miserable when we were kids, and it always hurt me to see that. I wanted things to go well for him, finally. For him to be happy. I tried to protect him, at your expense. I'm sorry."

She supposed she should say she forgave him. Let him off the hook. Maybe some day she would, but she lacked the will to do so now.

"I'm not going on the talk shows," she said.

He glanced at her sharply, as if ready to argue, but simply nodded instead. Then he leaned forward. "Let me at least look through the building again, all right? I have to do something."

She nodded, knowing that Sarah and Emma were not in the building. He could do no harm.

Dylan pulled into the parking lot, scrutinizing the area for his daughter or Sarah. Probably a wasted effort, he thought. It had taken him thirty minutes to drive to Heather's office, and surely they'd been found by now.

In the waiting room of the therapist's office, Laura threw herself into his arms, and he knew the gesture was borne of fear rather than relief.

"They're not back?" he asked.

"No." She pulled away from him. "The police are out looking for them. They told me to stay here in case they showed up, but it's getting so late. It's getting *dark*, Dylan. What if they don't find them before dark?"

"Do they think Sarah just took off with her, or that someone might have—"

"I don't know what *they* think," Laura interrupted him, as though she didn't want to hear him finish that sentence. "But *I* think that Stuart reminded Sarah of Ray, and she's trying to keep Emma safe from him."

Although he wasn't certain what she was talking about, he didn't want to take the time for further explanation.

"I'll look for them myself," he said. There was no way he could stay cooped up in this office and wait. And Laura was right. It was getting dark.

"They're mainly searching right around here," Laura said. "And over at the strip mall. I tried to tell them Sarah can walk fast, but I'm sure they think I'm just raving."

Dylan nodded. "I'll look a little further afield, then," he assured her.

"Go that way, since most of the cops are focusing on the mall." She pointed north.

Once outside, he crossed the parking lot, heading away from the strip of stores.

So, he thought, Sarah is trying to protect Emma from Stuart. She would try to hide, then, right? But where?

He walked slowly, stopping to peer behind Dumpsters and shrubbery. He glanced uneasily at his watch from time to time, wishing the minute hand would slow the hell down. He'd heard a loathsome statistic long ago that now gnawed at his brain: the longer a child was missing, the less hope there was in finding her safe and sound.

After he'd been walking for at least half an hour, he spotted a small, helium-filled hot air balloon flying in the darkening sky. It was illuminated by a spotlight from the ground, and it glowed. He walked toward it. If Emma had been near enough to that balloon to see it, she would have been drawn to it.

As he neared the balloon, he saw that it was an advertisement for a used-car dealership. Red letters on the balloon read *Shaw's Pre-Owned Cars,* and the parking lot beneath it was blanketed with an eclectic mix of used automobiles.

Dylan walked slowly through the lot.

"In the market for a great car?"

Dylan jumped as a salesman appeared out of nowhere. The man was in his fifties and wearing a red baseball cap. "Have some terrific deals tonight," he said.

"Just looking around right now." Dylan turned his back on the salesman and was relieved when the man didn't try to follow him.

He continued to scour the lot, scrutinizing the dark confines of every vehicle until he finally found what he was looking for: Sarah and Emma, huddled together in the back seat of an Oldsmobile, fast asleep.

His tears surprised him, and he took a minute to compose himself before opening the rear door.

Emma opened her eyes a crack. Sleepily, she held her arms toward him.

"Daddy," she said.

It was a voice he had never heard before, but one he hoped to hear for many years to come.

_____ Epilogue _____

Ten months later

"Should I hold on to the ropes, Daddy?" Emma asked.

Dylan turned his attention from Brian, who was standing on the ground outside the basket, to his daughter. "You don't have to hold tight yet, Em," he said. "We won't be going up for another few minutes."

Dylan was wearing a tux that seemed to make his hair darker and his eyes bluer, and Laura could not tear her gaze from him for long. She herself wore a long, pale blue dress that was gauzy and soft and ethereal. The violet-and-lavender dress Emma was wearing was one she'd picked out herself. "That's it, Mom!" she'd shouted a few weeks before as she ran toward the violet-clad mannikin in the store. "We don't have to search any further!"

There were four of them in the basket: Laura, Dylan and Emma, and Dylan's friend, Gregg, who was a minister and who, in a few minutes and several hundred feet above the ground, would make the three of them a family.

Brian and the new crew member, Steve, were wearing tuxedos, as well, and it was comical to see them going over the preflight checklist with Dylan in their formal attire. As they marked off items on the list, Laura turned her attention to the grassy field, which was alive with color and sound and motion. A zydeco band, more friends of Dylan's, pumped out its rhythmic, happy music from a platform set up near the barn, and the guests moved between the lawn chairs and umbrellas and the food-laden tables provided by the caterer. Dylan's family was there—his sister and her family and cousins and aunts and uncles—all of whom had taken Laura and her garrulous daughter into their hearts. There were a few dozen of Laura's colleagues from the Smithsonian and Hopkins among the crowd, and Laura could see John Solomon's son and daughter and their spouses standing by the drinks table. They'd flown in from Alaska a few days earlier for the marriage of their half sister.

Dressed elegantly and sitting in the shade of an oak tree were John and Elaine Solomon and Sarah Tolley. John and Elaine had arrived the week before and were staying at the lake house. Nervous about meeting Sarah, John had tried to prepare himself for any possible reaction she might have. Laura had known there would be no problem; Sarah would not recognize him, nor would she understand when he told her his true identity. Laura had been right. Although John had spent a fair amount of time with Sarah this week, taking walks with her and Laura, picnicking with her at Dylan's cabin, Sarah still had no idea who he was. If she wondered why this man treated her so lovingly, she didn't ask. Memory and mastery were leaving her in small increments, day by day.

"Mommy, what are you looking at?" Emma asked. "You're supposed to be watching Daddy get the balloon ready."

"Look at Grandpa." Laura helped Emma onto the propane tank so she could see more easily over the side of the basket. John had gotten to his feet and was dancing with Elaine, twirling circles around one of the food tables in time with the fast-paced music. Still the risk-taker, Laura thought, chancing a broken ankle on the uneven surface of the field.

"Grandpa's being outlandish again," Emma said with a giggle. Her new word. They were hearing a lot of it these days.

"Back to your corners, ladies," Dylan said as he and Brian finished the checklist.

He helped Emma step off the propane tank, while Laura slipped into her own corner, turning again to face the crowd on the field.

The other night, she and John had sat together on the pier by the lake, watching Comet Brandon and its spectacular tail, while Elaine, Dylan and Emma played a game in the house. Laura and John had talked quietly for a while, and there was an easy camaraderie between them. John said that he felt truly at peace for the first time in his life now that he'd found his daughter.

Looking up at the stars, he commented on their beauty, and Laura was reminded of those nights from her childhood when she'd sit in the darkness with Carl while he quizzed her on the constellations. John didn't care if she knew one constellation from another or if she could pick Jupiter from a sky crowded with stars, she thought. John didn't care if she'd discovered the comet they were observing or had won a dozen awards. All he cared about was that she was his Janie.

Before she climbed into the basket of the balloon, Laura had watched as John leaned forward from his chair to speak to Sarah. She'd heard him ask his former wife if she understood whose wedding they were attending. "Do you know who's going up in that balloon?" he'd asked.

Sarah had nodded. "It's that nice girl who takes me for walks," she'd said.

The facts are public knowledge!

SHARON SALA

Five people have been murdered, and with each victim the killer left a calling card—a single rose. Gabriel Donner knows more about the crimes than any innocent man should. Lately he's heard voices, started sleepwalking and dreamed horrible, vivid dreams... of murder. He can't go to the police, but there is someone who can help him. Can he trust Laura Dane—a psychic who's worked on cases like this before—with his terrible truths?

REUNION

Sharon Sala has a "rare ability to bring powerful and emotionally wrenching stories to life." *—Romantic Times*

On sale mid-January 1999 wherever paperbacks are sold!